The 6th Extinction

ALSO BY JAMES ROLLINS

The Eye of God

Bloodline

The Devil Colony

Altar of Eden

The Doomsday Key

The Last Oracle

The Judas Strain

Black Order

Map of Bones

Sandstorm

Ice Hunt

Amazonia

Deep Fathom

Excavation

Subterranean

BY JAMES ROLLINS AND REBECCA CANTRELL

The Blood Gospel

Innocent Blood

BY JAMES ROLLINS AND GRANT BLACKWOOD

The Kill Switch

The 6th Extinction

A Σ Sigma Force Novel

James Rollins

HARPER **LUXE**

An Imprint of HarperCollins*Publishers*

THE 6TH EXTINCTION. Copyright © 2014 by James Czajkowski. All rights reserved. Printed in the United States of America. No part of this book may be used or reproduced in any manner whatsoever without written permission except in the case of brief quotations embodied in critical articles and reviews. For information address HarperCollins Publishers, 195 Broadway, New York, NY 10007.

HarperCollins books may be purchased for educational, business, or sales promotional use. For information, please e-mail the Special Markets Department at SPsales@harpercollins.com.

FIRST HARPERLUXE EDITION

HarperLuxe™ is a trademark of HarperCollins Publishers

Library of Congress Cataloging-in-Publication Data is available upon request.

ISBN: 978-0-06-232643-0

14 ID/RRD 10 9 8 7 6 5 4 3 2 1

To David,
who keeps me both grounded and
flying high . . . not an easy feat!

Acknowledgments

S o many folks have their fingerprints all over this book. I appreciate all their help, criticism, and encouragement. First, I must thank my first readers, my first editors, and some of my best friends: Sally Anne Barnes, Chris Crowe, Lee Garrett, Jane O'Riva, Denny Grayson, Leonard Little, Scott Smith, Judy Prey, Will Murray, Caroline Williams, John Keese, Christian Riley, Tod Todd, Chris Smith, and Amy Rogers. And as always, a special thanks to Steve Prey for the great map . . . and to Cherei McCarter for all the cool tidbits that pop in my e-mail box! To David Sylvian for accomplishing everything and anything asked of him and for making sure I put my best digital foot forward at all times! To everyone at HarperCollins for always having my back, especially Michael Morrison, Liate Stehlik,

Danielle Bartlett, Kaitlyn Kennedy, Josh Marwell, Lynn Grady, Richard Aquan, Tom Egner, Shawn Nicholls, and Ana Maria Allessi. Last, of course, a special acknowledgment to the people instrumental to all levels of production: my editor, Lyssa Keusch, and her colleague Rebecca Lucash; and my agents, Russ Galen and Danny Baror (and his daughter Heather Baror). And as always, I must stress that any and all errors of fact or detail in this book, of which hopefully there are not too many, fall squarely on my own shoulders.

ANTARCTICA

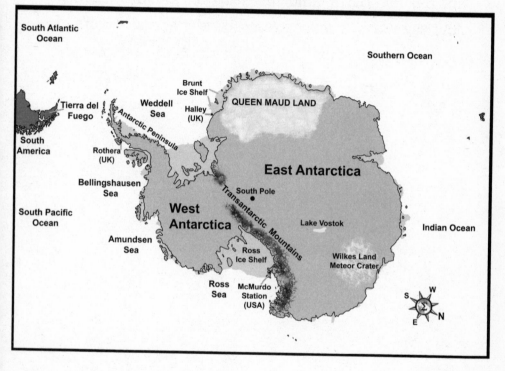

Notes from the Historical Record

Throughout history, knowledge rises and falls, ebbs and flows. What once was known is forgotten again, lost in time, sometimes for centuries, only to be rediscovered ages later.

Millennia ago, the ancient Maya studied the movement of stars and developed a calendar that has not lost a day in 2,500 years. It was an astronomical feat that would take many centuries to be repeated. During the height of the Byzantine Empire, warfare changed dramatically with the invention of *Greek fire*, an incendiary weapon that could not be put out by dousing it with water. The recipe for making this strange flammable concoction was lost by the tenth century and wouldn't be rediscovered until its closest counterpart, *napalm*, was created in the 1940s.

How did such knowledge become lost to antiquity? One example dates to the first or second century, when the legendary Library of Alexandria was burned to ashes. The library, founded in roughly 300 B.C. in Egypt, was said to have held over a million scrolls, a massive repository of knowledge like no other. It drew scholars from around the known world. The cause of its fiery destruction remains a mystery. Some blame Julius Caesar, who set fire to Alexandria's docks; others attribute its ruin to marauding Arab conquerors. Still, what is certain is that those flames incinerated a vast treasure-house of secrets, knowledge from across the ages, lost forever.

But some secrets refuse to be buried. Within these pages is a story of one of those dark mysteries, knowledge so dangerous that it could never be fully lost.

Notes from the
Scientific Record

Life on this planet has always been a balancing act—a complex web of interconnectivity that's surprisingly fragile. Remove or even alter enough key components and that web begins to fray and fall apart.

Such a collapse—or mass extinction—has happened five times in our planet's geological past. The *first* struck four hundred million years ago, when most marine life died off. The *third* event hit both land and sea at the end of the Permian Period, wiping out 90 percent of the world's species, coming within a razor's edge of ending all life on earth. The *fifth* and most recent extinction took out the dinosaurs, ushering in the era of mammals and altering the world forever.

How close are we to seeing such an event happen again? Some scientists believe we're already there, neck-deep in a *sixth* mass extinction. Every hour, three more species go extinct, totaling over thirty thousand a year. Worst of all, the rate of this die-off is continually rising. At this very moment, nearly half of all amphibians, a quarter of all mammals, and a third of all reefs balance at the edge of extinction. Even a third of all conifer trees teeter at that brink.

Why is this happening? In the past, such massive die-offs had been triggered by sudden changes in global climate or shifts in plate tectonics, or in the case of the dinosaurs, possibly even an asteroid strike. Yet most scientists believe this current crisis has a simpler explanation: *humans.* Through our trampling of the environment and rise in pollution, mankind has been the driving force behind the loss of most species. According to a report by Duke University released in May 2014, human activity has driven species into extinction at the rate a *thousandfold* faster than before the arrival of modern man.

But what is less well known concerns a *new* danger to all life on earth, one that has risen out of the ancient past and threatens to accelerate this current die-off, to possibly push us beyond the brink, to take us to the point of apocalypse.

And not only is that threat very real—it's rising right now out of our own backyards.

Extinction is the rule. Survival is the exception.

—CARL SAGAN,
THE VARIETIES OF SCIENTIFIC EXPERIENCE (2007)

The 6th Extinction

December 27, 1832
Aboard the HMS *Beagle*

We should have heeded the blood . . .

Charles Darwin stared down at the words he had scrawled in black ink on the white pages of his journal, but all he saw was crimson. Despite the glow of his small cabin's oven, he shivered against a cold that iced the marrow of his bones—a frigidity that he suspected would never fully melt away. He mouthed a silent prayer, remembering how his father had urged him to study for the clergy after he had dropped out of medical school.

Perhaps I should have listened.

Instead, he had been lured astray by the appeal of foreign shores and new scientific discoveries. A year ago, almost to the day, he had accepted a position aboard the HMS *Beagle* as the ship's naturalist. At the tender age of twenty-two, he had been ready to make a name for himself, to see the world. It was how he had ended up here now, with blood on his hands.

He stared around his cabin. Upon first coming aboard, he had been given private quarters in the ship's chart room, a cramped space dominated by a large table in the middle that was pierced clean through by the trunk of the mizzenmast. He used every remaining free inch—cabinets, bookshelves, even the washbasin—as work space and a temporary museum for his collected specimens and samples. He had bones and fossils, teeth and shells, even stuffed or preserved specimens of unusual snakes, lizards, and birds. Near his elbow rested a board of pinned beetles of monstrous sizes with prominent horns like those of the African rhinoceros. Next to his inkwell stood a row of jars holding dried plants and seeds.

He stared forlornly across his collection—what the unimaginative Captain FitzRoy called useless junk.

Perhaps I should have arranged to have this lot shipped back to England before the Beagle *left Tierra del Fuego . . .*

But regretfully, like the rest of the ship's crew, he had been too caught up in stories told by the savages of that archipelago: the native Fuegians of the Yaghan tribe. The tribesmen shared their legends of monsters, and gods, and wonders beyond imagination. It was such tales that had led the *Beagle* astray, sending the ship and its crew south from the tip of South America, across the ice-choked seas to this frozen world at the bottom of the earth.

"*Terra Australis Incognita,*" he mumbled to himself.

The infamous Unknown Southern Land.

He shifted a map from the clutter atop his desk. Nine days ago, shortly after arriving at Tierra del Fuego, Captain FitzRoy had shown him this French map, dating back to 1583.

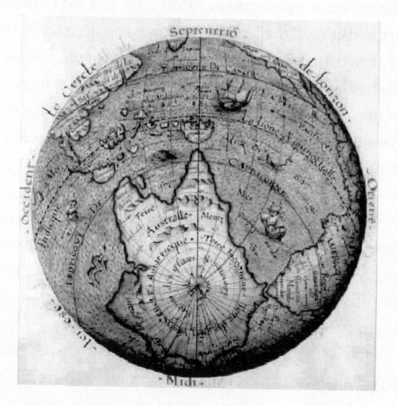

It depicted that unexplored continent at the southern pole of the globe. The chart was plainly inaccurate, failing even to account for the fact that the cartographer's contemporary, Sir Francis Drake, had already discovered the icy seas that separated South America from this unknown land. Yet, despite two centuries passing since this map was first drawn, this inhospitable continent continued to be a mystery. Even its coastline remained shadowy and unmapped.

So was it any wonder that all of their imaginations were lit on fire when one of the Fuegians, a bony-limbed elder, presented an astounding gift to the newly arrived crew of the *Beagle*? The ship had been anchored near Woolya Cove, where the good Reverend Richard Matthews had established a mission, converting many of the savages and teaching them rudimentary English. And though the elder who presented the gift didn't speak the king's tongue, what he offered needed no words.

It was a crude map, drawn on a piece of bleached sealskin, depicting the coastline of that continent to the south. That alone was intriguing enough, but the stories that accompanied the presentation only served to magnify all their interests.

One of the Fuegians—who had been baptized with the anglicized name of Jemmy Button—explained the

Yaghan people's history. He claimed their tribes had lived among the islands of this archipelago for over seven thousand years, an astounding span of time that strained credulity. Furthermore, Jemmy had praised his people's nautical skills, which required less distrust, as Charles had indeed noted several of their larger sailing vessels in the cove. Though crude, they were clearly seaworthy.

Jemmy explained that the map was the culmination of thousands of years of Yaghan people's exploration of the great continent to the south, a map passed from generation to generation, refined and redrawn over the centuries as more knowledge was gleaned of that mysterious land. He also shared tales of that lost continent, of great beasts and strange treasures, of mountains on fire and lands of infinite ice.

The most astounding claim echoed back to Charles now. He recorded those words in his journal, hearing Jemmy's voice in his head: *In times long into shadows, our ancestors say that the ice was gone from the valleys and mountains. Forests grew tall and the hunting was good, but demons also haunted the dark, ready to eat out the hearts of the unwary—*

A sharp scream cut through from the deck above, causing Charles to scrawl ink down the remainder of the page. He bit back a curse, but there was no mistaking the terror and pain in that single piercing note. It drew him to his feet.

The last of the crew must have returned from that dread shore.

Abandoning his journal and pen, he rushed to his cabin's door and down the short hall to the chaos atop the deck.

"Careful with him!" FitzRoy hollered. The captain stood at the starboard rail with his coat unbuttoned, his cheeks red above his dark frosted beard.

Stepping out onto the middeck, Charles blinked away the glare of the southern hemisphere's midsummer sun. Still, the bitter cold bit at his nose and filled his lungs. A freezing fog hugged the black seas around the anchored ship, while rime ice coated the riggings and rails. Puffs of panicked white blew from the faces of the crew as they labored to obey their captain.

Charles rushed starboard to help the others haul a crewman up from a whaleboat tethered amidships. The injured man was wrapped head to toe in sailcloth and drawn up by ropes. Moans accompanied his plight. Charles helped lift the poor fellow over the rail and to the deck.

It was Robert Rensfry, the ship's boatswain.

FitzRoy shouted for the ship's surgeon, but the doctor was belowdecks, ministering to the two men from the first excursion to shore. Neither was likely to see another sunrise, not after sustaining such gruesome wounds.

But what of this fellow?

Charles knelt beside the stricken man. Others clambered up from the boat. The last was Jemmy Button, looking both ashen and angry. The Fuegian had tried to warn them not to come here, but his fears were dismissed as native superstitions.

"Is it done?" FitzRoy asked his second-in-command as he helped Jemmy back aboard.

"Aye, captain. All three barrels of black powder. Left at the entrance."

"Good man. Once the whaleboat's secure, bring the *Beagle* around. Ready the portside guns." FitzRoy turned his worried gaze upon the injured crewman at Charles's knees. "Where's that damned Bynoe?"

As if summoned by this curse, the gaunt form of the ship's surgeon, Benjamin Bynoe, climbed out from below and rushed forward. He was bloody to both elbows, his apron just as fouled.

Charles caught the silent exchange between captain and doctor. The surgeon shook his head twice.

The other two men must have died.

Charles stood and made room.

"Unwrap him!" Bynoe demanded. "Let me see his injuries!"

Charles backed to the rail, joining FitzRoy. The captain stood silently, staring landward, a spyglass at his eye. As the moans of the wounded man grew sharper, FitzRoy passed Charles the glass.

He took it, and after some effort, he focused on the neighboring coast. Walls of blue ice framed the narrow cove where they were anchored. At its thickest point, fog obscured the shore, but it was not the same frozen mist that hugged the seas and wrapped the surrounding bergs of ice. It was a sulfurous steam, a breath from Hades, rising out from a land as wondrous as it was monstrous.

A gust of wind blew the view momentarily clear, revealing a waterfall of blood coursing down that cliff of ice. It flowed along in crimson rivulets and streams, seeming to seep out of the haunted depths beneath the frozen surface.

Charles knew it wasn't in fact blood, but some alchemy of chemicals and minerals exhaled from the tunnels below.

Still, we should have heeded that ominous warning, he thought again. *We should never have trespassed into that tunnel.*

He focused the spyglass on the cave opening, noting the three oil-soaked barrels planted at the entrance.

Despite all the recent horrors that threatened one's sanity, he remained a man of science, a seeker of knowledge, and while he should have perhaps railed against what was to come, he kept silent.

Jemmy joined him at the side, whispering under his breath in his native tongue, plainly resorting to pagan prayers. The reformed savage stood only chest-high to the Englishman at his side, but he exuded a strength of will that belied his small frame. The Fuegian had repeatedly tried to warn the crew, but no one would listen. Still, the stalwart native had accompanied the British to their foolish doom.

Charles found his fingers grasping the darker hand beside his own on the rail. The crew's hubris and greed had cost them not only their own men but one of Jemmy's tribesmen as well.

We should never have come here.

Yet foolishly they had—allowing themselves to be drawn south from their planned route by the wild stories of this lost continent. But what had mostly tempted them was a symbol found on that ancient Fuegian map. It marked this cove with a grove of trees, a promise of life. Intending to discover this lost garden amid the icy shores, the *Beagle* had set out, all in the hopes of claiming new virgin territory for the Crown.

Only too late had they come to understand the true meaning of the map's markings. In the end, the whole venture had ended in horror and bloodshed, a journey that, by necessity, would be stricken from the records by mutual consent of all.

None must ever return here.

And if anyone dared try, the captain intended that they would find nothing. What was hidden here must never reach the larger world.

With the anchor freed, the ship slowly turned with a great cracking of ice from the rigging and a shiver of frost from the sails. FitzRoy had already gone off to see to the ship's battery of guns. The HMS *Beagle* was a *Cherokee*-class sloop of the Royal Navy, outfitted originally with ten guns. And though the warship had been converted into an exploration vessel, it still carried six cannons.

Another scream drew Charles's attention back to the deck, to the crewman writhing amid a nest of sailcloth.

"Hold him down!" the ship's surgeon shouted.

Charles went to the doctor's aid, joining the others to grasp a shoulder and help pin Rensfry in place. He made the mistake of catching the boatswain's eyes. He read the pain and pleading there.

Lips moved as a moan pushed out words. ". . . get it out . . ."

The surgeon had finished freeing Rensfry's heavy coat and split the man's shirt with a blade, exposing a belly full of blood and a fist-sized wound. As Charles stared, a thick ripple passed through the abdomen, like a snake under sand.

Rensfry bucked under all their weights, his back arching in agony. A screech burst from his clenched throat, repeating his demand.

"Get it out!"

Bynoe did not hesitate. He shoved his hand into the wound, into the steaming depths of the man's belly. He pushed deeper yet again, past his wrist and forearm. Despite the frigid cold, beads of sweat rolled down the doctor's face. Elbow-deep now, he sought his prey.

A loud boom shook through the ship, shaking more frost atop them.

Then another and another.

Distantly, echoing from shore, came a much louder retort.

To either side, massive crags of ice broke from the cove's coastline and crashed into the sea. Still, more of the ship's guns boomed out their destruction of fiery grapeshot and heated cannonballs.

Captain FitzRoy was taking no chances.

"Too late," Bynoe finally said, withdrawing his arm from the wound. "We're too late."

Only now did Charles note the boatswain's body lay limp under his grasp. Dead eyes stared toward the blue skies.

Sitting back, he remembered Jemmy's earlier words about this accursed continent: *Demons also haunted its dark depths, ready to eat the hearts of the living . . .*

"What about the body?" one of the crewmen asked.

Bynoe looked to the rail, toward the roiling ice-choked sea. "Make his grave here, along with whatever lies inside him."

Charles had seen enough. As the sea rocked and guns exploded, he retreated while the others lifted Rensfry's body. He slunk cowardly back to his cabin without bearing witness to the boatswain's watery burial.

Once below, he found the small fire in the oven was almost out, but after the cold, the room's heat stifled his breaths. He crossed to his journal, ripped out the pages he had been working on, and fed them to those meager flames. He watched the pages curl, blacken, and turn to ash.

Only then did he return to the chart desk, to the maps still there—including the ancient Fuegian map. He picked it up and stared again at the cursed grove of trees marking this cove. His gaze shifted to the freshly fed flames.

He took a step toward the hearth, then stopped.

With cold fingers, he rolled the map and clenched it hard in both fists.

I'm still a scientist.

With a heavy heart, he turned from the fire and hid the map among his personal belongings—but not before one last unscientific thought.

God help me . . .

FIRST
Dark Genesis

1

April 27, 6:55 P.M. PDT
Mono Lake, California

"Looks like the surface of Mars."

Jenna Beck smiled to herself at hearing this most common description of Mono Lake from yet another tourist. As the day's last group of visitors took their final snapshots, she waited beside her white Ford F-150 pickup, the truck's front doors emblazoned with the star of the California State Park Rangers.

Tugging the stiff brim of her hat lower, she stared toward the sun. Though nightfall was an hour away, the slanting light had transformed the lake into a pearlescent mirror of blues and greens. Towering stalagmites of craggy limestone, called tufa, spread outward like a petrified forest along this southern edge of the lake and out into the waters.

It certainly appeared to be an otherworldly landscape—but definitely not Mars. She slapped at her arm, squashing a mosquito, proving life still thrived despite the barren beauty of the basin.

At the noise, the group's tour guide—an older woman named Hattie—glanced in her direction and offered a sympathetic smile, but she also clearly took this as a signal to wind up her talk. Hattie was native Kutzadika'a, of the northern Paiute people. In her mid-seventies, she knew more about the lake and its history than anyone in the basin.

"The lake," Hattie continued, "is said to be 760,000 years old, but some scientists believe it might be as old as three million, making it one of the oldest lakes in the United States. And while the lake is seventy square miles in area, at its deepest it is barely over a hundred feet deep. It's fed by a handful of bubbling springs and creeks, but it has no outflow, relying only on evaporation during the hot summer days. That's why the lake is three times as salty as the ocean and has a pH of 10, almost as alkaline as household lye."

A Spanish tourist grimaced and asked in halting English. "Does anything live in this *lago* . . . in this lake?"

"No fish, if that's what you were thinking, but there is life." Hattie motioned to Jenna, knowing such knowledge was her specialty.

Jenna cleared her throat and crossed through the cluster of a dozen tourists: half Americans, the others a mix of Europeans. Situated between Yosemite National Park and the neighboring ghost towns of Bodie State Historic Park, the lake drew a surprising number of foreign visitors.

"Life always finds a way to fill any environmental niche," Jenna began. "And Mono Lake is no exception. Despite its inhospitable chemistry of chlorides, sulfates, and arsenic, it has a very rich and complex ecosystem, one that we are trying to preserve through our conservation efforts here."

Jenna knelt at the shoreline. "Life at the lake starts with the winter bloom of a unique brine-tolerant algae. In fact, if you'd come here in March, you'd have found the lake as green as pea soup."

"Why isn't it green now?" a young father asked, resting a hand on his daughter's shoulder.

"That's because of the tiny brine shrimp that live here. They're barely bigger than a grain of rice and consume all that algae. Then the shrimps serve to feed the lake's most ubiquitous hunter."

Still kneeling at the water's edge, she waved a hand along the shore's edge, stirring a floating carpet of blackflies. They rose up in a cloud of buzzing complaint.

"Sick," said a sullen redheaded teenager as he stepped closer to get a better view.

"Don't worry. They're not biting flies." Jenna motioned a young boy of eight or nine to her side. "But they are creative little hunters. Come see."

The boy timidly came forward, followed by his parents and the other tourists. She patted the ground next to her, getting the boy to crouch, then pointed to the shallows of the lakebed, where several flies scurried underwater, encased within little silvery bubbles of air.

"It looks like they're scuba diving!" the boy said with a huge grin.

Jenna matched his smile, appreciating his childish excitement at this simple wonder of nature. It was one of the best aspects of her job: spreading that joy and amazement.

"Like I said, they're resourceful little hunters." She stood and moved aside to allow others to get a look. "And it is all those brine shrimp and blackflies that in turn feed the hundreds of thousands of swallows, grebes, cranes, and gulls that migrate through here." She pointed farther along the shoreline. "And if you look over there, you can even see an osprey nest in that tall tufa."

More snapshots were taken as she retreated back.

If she had wanted, she could have expanded further upon the unique web of life at Mono Lake. She had barely scratched the surface of complexity of the alkaline lake's strange ecosystem. There were all matter of odd species and adaptations to be found here, especially in the mud deep in the lake, where exotic bacteria thrived in conditions that would seem to defy logic, in mud so toxic and void of oxygen that nothing should live.

But it did.

Life always finds a way.

Though it was a quote from *Jurassic Park*, the same sentiment had also been drilled into her by her biology professor back at Cal Poly. She had planned on getting her doctorate in ecological sciences, but instead she had found herself more drawn toward the park service, to be out in the field, to be actively working to help preserve that fragile web of life that seemed to be fraying worse and worse with every passing year.

She retreated to her pickup, leaned her back against the door, and waited for the tour to end. Hattie would take the group back in the bus to the neighboring hamlet of Lee Vining, while Jenna trailed behind in her truck. She was already picturing the pile of baby back ribs served at Bodie Mike's, the local diner.

From the open window behind her, a wet tongue licked the back of her neck. She reached blindly back and scratched Nikko behind the ear. Apparently she wasn't the only one getting hungry.

"Almost done here, kiddo."

A thump of a tail answered her. The four-year-old Siberian husky was her constant companion, trained in search-and-rescue. Pushing his head out the open window, he rested his muzzle on her shoulder and sighed heavily. His eyes—one white-blue, the other an introspective brown—stared longingly toward the open hills. Hattie had once told her that, according to Native American legends, dogs with different-colored eyes could see both heaven and earth.

Whether this was true or not, Nikko's gaze remained more pedestrian at the moment. A jackrabbit shot across a nearby slope of dry brush, and Nikko burst to his feet inside the cab.

She smiled as the rabbit quickly vanished into the dusky shadows.

"Next time, Nikko. You'll get him next time."

Though the husky was a skilled working dog, he was still a *dog*.

Hattie collected and herded the group of tourists toward the bus, gathering stragglers along the way.

"And Indians used to eat those fly larva?" the red-headed teenager asked.

"We called them *kutsavi*. Women and children would gather the pupae from the rocks into woven baskets, then toast them up. It's still done on special occasions, as a rare treat."

Hattie winked at Jenna as she passed by.

Jenna hid a grin at the kid's sickened expression. That was one detail of the web of life found here that she had left Hattie to impart.

While the bus loaded up for the return run, Jenna tugged open her truck door and climbed in next to Nikko. As she settled in, the radio squawked loudly.

What now?

She unhooked the radio. "What's up, Bill?"

Bill Howard was the service dispatcher and a dear friend. Bill was in his mid-sixties but had taken her under his wing when she had first started here. That was over three years ago. She was now twenty-four and had finished her bachelor's degree in environmental sciences in her spare time, the little that there was. They were understaffed and overworked, but over these past few years, she had learned to love the moods of the lake, of the animals, even of her fellow rangers.

"I don't know for sure what's up, Jen, but I was hoping you could take a swing up north. Emergency services relayed a partial 911 call to our office."

"Give me the details." Besides acting as curators of the parks, rangers were also fully sworn law enforcement officers. Their duties encompassed a wide variety of roles, anything from criminal investigations to emergency medical response.

"The call came from outside of Bodie," Bill explained.

She frowned. Nothing was *outside of Bodie*, except for a handful of gold-rush-era ghost towns and old abandoned mines. That is, except for—

"It came from that military research site," Bill confirmed.

Crap.

"What was the call about?" she asked.

"I listened to the recording myself. All that could be heard was shouting. No words could be made out. Then the call cut off."

"So it could be anything or nothing."

"Exactly. Maybe the call was made by mistake, but someone should at least swing by the gate and make an inquiry."

"And apparently that would be me."

"Both Tony and Kate are out near Yosemite, dealing with a drunk-and-disorderly call."

"All right, Bill. I'm on it. I'll radio once I'm at the base gate. Let me know if you hear anything else."

The dispatcher agreed and signed off.

Jenna turned to Nikko. "Looks like those ribs are gonna have to wait, big fella."

7:24 P.M.

"Hurry!"

Four stories underground, Dr. Kendall Hess pounded up the stairs, followed closely by his systems analyst, Irene McIntire. Red emergency lights strobed at each landing. A siren rang a continual warning throughout the facility.

"We've lost containment levels four and five," she gasped behind him, monitoring the threat rising up from below on a handheld bioreader.

But the screams that chased them were enough of an assessment.

"It must be in the airways by now," Irene said.

"How could that be?"

His question was meant to be rhetorical, but Irene still answered it.

"It can't be. Not without massive lab error. But I checked—"

"It wasn't lab error," he blurted out more sharply than he intended.

He knew the more likely cause.

Sabotage.

Too many firewalls—both electronic and biological—had failed for this to be anything but purposeful. Someone had deliberately caused this containment breach.

"What can we do?" Irene pleaded.

They had only one recourse left, a final fail-safe, to fight fire with fire. But would it do more harm than good? He listened to the strangled cries rising from below and knew his answer.

They reached the top floor. Not knowing what they faced—especially if he was right about a saboteur—he stopped Irene with a touch on her arm. He saw the skin on the back of her hand was already blistering, the same along her neck.

"You must go for the radio. Send out a mayday. In case I fail."

Or God help me, if I lose my nerve.

She nodded, her eyes trying to hide her pain. What he was asking her to do would likely end in her death. "I'll try," she said, looking terrified.

Burning with regret, he tore the door open and pushed her toward the radio room. "Run!"

7:43 P.M.

The truck bumped hard from the paved road onto a gravel track.

Leaning heavily on the gas pedal, Jenna took less than twenty minutes to climb from Mono Lake to the eight-thousand-foot elevation of Bodie State Historic Park. But she wasn't heading to the neighboring park. Her destination was even higher and more remote.

With the sun a mere glimmer on the horizon, she bounced down the dark road, rattling gravel up into her wheel wells. Only a handful of people outside of law enforcement knew about this military site. It had been rapidly established, with barely a word raised about it. Even the building materials and personnel had been airlifted into place by military helicopters, while defense contractors handled all the construction.

Still, that didn't stop some information from leaking out.

The site was part of the U.S. Developmental Test Command. The installation was somehow connected with the Dugway Proving Grounds outside of Salt Lake City. She had looked up that place herself on the Internet and didn't like what she had found. Dugway was a nuclear, chemical, and biological test facility. Back in the sixties, thousands of sheep near the place had died from a deadly nerve gas leakage. Since then, the facility continued to expand its borders. It now covered almost a million acres, twice the size of Los Angeles.

So why did they need this extra facility up here in the middle of nowhere?

Of course, there was speculation: how the military scientists needed the depths of the abandoned mines found here, how their research was too dangerous to be near a major metropolis like Salt Lake City. Other minds concocted wilder theories, proposing the site was being used for secret extraterrestrial research—perhaps because Area 51 had become too much of a tourist attraction.

Unfortunately this last conjecture gained support when a group of scientists had ventured down to Mono Lake to take some deep core samples of the lake's bottom. They had been astrobiologists associated with NASA's National Space Science and Technology Center.

But what they had been searching for was far from extraterrestrial; in fact, it was very *terrestrial*. She had been able to have a brief chat with one of the researchers, Dr. Kendall Hess, a cordial silver-haired biologist, at Bodie Mike's. It seemed no one came to Mono Lake who didn't enjoy at least one meal at the diner. Over a cup of coffee, he had told her about his team's interest in the lake's extremophiles, those rare bacterial species thriving in toxic and hostile environments.

Such research allows us to better understand how life might exist on foreign worlds, he had explained.

Yet even then she had sensed that he had been holding back. She saw it in his face, a wariness and excitement.

Then again, this wasn't the first secret military site set up at Mono Lake. During the cold war, the government established several remote facilities in the area to test weapons systems and carry out various research projects. Even the lake's most famous beach—Navy Beach—was named after a former installation once set up along its south shore.

So what was one more secret lab?

After a few more teeth-rattling minutes, she noted the fence cutting across the hills ahead. A moment later, her headlights swept over a roadside sign, faded and pebbled with bullet holes. It read:

DEAD END ROAD

NO TRESPASSING

GOVERNMENT PROPERTY

From here, a gate normally blocked the road, but instead it stood open. Suspicious, she slowed her truck and stopped at the threshold. By now, the sun had vanished behind the hills, and a heavy twilight had fallen over the rolling meadows.

"What do you think, Nikko? It's not trespassing if they leave the door open, is it?"

Nikko cocked his head, his ears up quizzically.

She lifted the handset and radioed park dispatch. "Bill, I've reached the base's gates."

"Any sign of problems?"

"Not that I can tell from here. Except someone left the gate open. What do you think I should do?"

"While you were en route, I placed a few calls up the chain of military command. I've still not heard any word back."

"So it's up to me."

"We don't have jurisdiction to—"

"Sorry." She bobbled the radio's feed. "Can't make out what you were saying, Bill."

She ended the call and re-hooked the radio.

"I'm just saying . . . we came all the way out here, didn't we, Nikko?"

So let's see what all the fuss is about.

She pressed the accelerator and eased past the gate and headed toward a cluster of illuminated buildings crowning the shadowed hill ahead. The small installation appeared to be a handful of Quonset-style huts and hastily constructed concrete-block bunkers. She suspected those buildings were nothing more than the tip of a buried pyramid, especially from the number of satellite dishes and antenna arrays sprouting from those rooftops.

Nikko growled as a low thumping reached her.

She braked and instinctively punched off her headlights, respecting her own intuition as much as her dog's.

From behind one of the Quonset huts, a small black helicopter rose into view, climbing high enough to find the last rays of the setting sun. She held her breath, hoping the sun's glare and the shadows below the hill kept her hidden. What especially stood the hairs on the nape of her neck was the fact that she noted no insignia on the bird. Its sleek predatory black shape definitely didn't look military.

She slowly let her breath out as the helicopter headed away from her position, whisking over the hills and vanishing from sight.

The squawk of the radio made her jump. She grabbed the handset.

"Jenna!" Bill sounded frantic. "Are you on your way back?"

She sighed. "Not yet. I thought I'd hang at the gate for a bit to see if anyone came out to say hello."

It was a lie, but it was better than the truth.

"Then get the hell out of there!"

"Why?"

"I received another call, relayed through military command. It was radioed by someone at the site.

Listen." After a pause, a woman's voice faintly came through, but there was no mistaking the panic and urgency. "*This is sierra, victor, whiskey. There's been a breach. Fail-safe initiated. No matter the outcome: Kill us . . . kill us all.*"

Jenna stared toward the cluster of buildings—when the entire hilltop erupted into a cloud of fire and smoke. The ground under her bucked hard, bouncing and rattling the truck.

Oh my God . . .

After a hard swallow to get breathing again, she slammed the pickup into reverse and pounded the accelerator, sending the truck careening backward.

A wall of smoke billowed toward her.

Even in her desperation, she knew she must not let that cloud reach her. She remembered all those sheep killed outside of Dugway. Her caution proved wise when a moment later a jackrabbit burst from that pall, took a couple of bounding hops, then collapsed on its side in a writhing seizure.

"Hang on, Nikko!"

She couldn't get enough speed in reverse, so she threw the truck into a fishtailing spin to right herself, sending gravel flying—then gunned the engine and tore past the open gate. In her rearview mirrors, she watched the cloud pursuing her.

Something black slammed into her truck's hood, making her gasp.

A crow.

Raven-dark wings fluttered as it rolled away.

More birds crashed into the brush to either side of the road, falling dead out of the sky.

Nikko whimpered.

She felt like doing the same, but all she could truly hear were that poor woman's last words.

Kill us . . . kill us all . . .

2

I am a lucky man . . .

Painter Crowe stared at his fiancée silhouetted against the fading blaze of the sunset over the Pacific. She stood at the edge of a bluff overlooking a stretch of sandy shore, staring out toward Rincon Point, where a few surfers still braved the day's last waves. From the beach directly below came the faint honking of harbor seals, their nesting area off-limits to tourists during the breeding season.

His fiancée, Lisa Cummings, surveyed the landscape through a set of binoculars. From his vantage behind her, Painter examined her in turn. She wore a yellow bikini covered by a thin cotton wrap belted at the waist. The sheer fabric allowed him to appreciate the curve of her backside, the angle of her hip, the length of her leg.

From his vantage, he came to a definitive conclusion.

I'm the luckiest man in the whole world.

Lisa interrupted his reverie, pointing below. "This beach is where I conducted research for my doctoral thesis. I was testing the diving physiology of harbor seals. You should've seen the pups . . . so cute. I spent weeks tagging the older ones with pulse ox sensors, so I could study their adaptation to deep-sea diving. The corollary to human respiration, oxygen saturation, endurance and stamina—"

Painter stepped to her side and scooped an arm intimately around her waist. "You know we could do our own research on endurance and stamina back at the hotel room."

She lowered the binoculars and smiled at him, using a pinkie to whisk a few windblown strands of blond hair. She arched an eyebrow at him. "I think we've done plenty of that research already."

"Still, you can never be too thorough."

She turned into him, pressing against him. "You may be right." She kissed him lightly on the lips, lingering there for a moment, then broke loose of their embrace. "But it's late, and we do have to meet the caterer in an hour and arrange the final menu for the rehearsal dinner."

He sighed heavily, watching the sun fade completely away. The wedding was in four days. It was going to be a small affair officiated on a local beach, attended by their closest friends and family, with a reception afterward at the Four Seasons Biltmore in Montecito. Yet, as that fateful day grew closer, the list of details only seemed to grow longer. To escape the chaos for a few hours, the two had taken a late afternoon walk along the Carpinteria Bluffs overlooking the Pacific, strolling across open meadows dotted with towering eucalyptus trees.

It was such moments that also allowed Painter to learn more intimate details about Lisa's childhood, about her roots out west here. He'd already known how she had grown up in Southern California and graduated from UCLA, but to experience her in her own element—reminiscing, telling stories, simply basking under her native sun—made him love her all the more.

How could he not?

From her long blond hair to the smoothest skin that bronzed with the lightest touch of the sun, she was the epitome of the Golden State. Still, only the most foolhardy would assume her looks were the extent of her assets. Behind that beauty was a mind that outshone all. Not only had she graduated top of her class from

UCLA's med school, but she had also earned a PhD in human physiology.

With such a connection out west, they had chosen Santa Barbara as the location for their wedding. Though the two of them now made their home on the opposite coast—in Washington, D.C.—a majority of Lisa's friends and family were still out here. So shifting the venue to California only made sense, especially as Painter had no real family of his own. He had been orphaned at a young age and mostly distanced from the Native American side of his family; his only blood relative was a distant niece, and she was going to school at Brigham Young in Utah.

That left only a handful of guests who would need to make the cross-country trek, namely Painter's innermost circle at Sigma Force. Not that such a journey was without hardship for those few. The group's lead field commander, Grayson Pierce, had a father slipping further into the mental fog of Alzheimer's, and—

"Did I tell you I heard from Kat this morning?" Lisa asked, as if reading his mind.

He shook his head.

"She managed to find someone to watch the girls. You should have heard the relief in her voice. I don't think she was looking forward to such a long flight with two young children in tow."

He grinned as they headed back across the darkening bluffs. "I also suspect Kat and Monk could use a vacation from diapers and midnight feedings."

Kathryn Bryant was Sigma's chief intelligence expert, and Painter's second-in-command, his proverbial right arm. Her husband, Monk Kokkalis, was a fellow Sigma operative, trained in forensic medicine and biotechnology.

"Speaking of diapers and midnight bottles . . ." Lisa leaned into him, entwining her fingers with his. "Maybe that's a chore we'll soon be complaining about."

"Maybe."

From her slight sigh, she must have heard the hesitation in his voice. They had, of course, spoken of having children, of starting a family. But dreaming was different from staring that reality full in the face.

Her hand slipped from his grasp. "Painter—"

A sharp and insistent bleat from his phone cut her off, saving him from any explanation—which was a good thing because he couldn't explain his reluctance even to himself. His back stiffened at the distinctive ringtone. Lisa didn't object as he answered, knowing that particular chime sounded only in the case of an emergency.

Painter lifted the phone to his ear. "Crowe here."

"Director." It was Kat Bryant. "We've got trouble."

For his second-in-command to be calling him now, it had to be *big* trouble. Then again, when did Sigma ever deal with small problems? As a covert wing for DARPA—the military's Defense Advanced Research Projects Agency—Sigma Force dealt with global threats of a scientific or technological nature. As director of the group, Painter had gathered a select group of Special Forces soldiers from across the different branches of service and retrained them in various scientific disciplines to act as field operatives for DARPA. If a problem landed in Sigma's lap, it was seldom a minor concern.

While normally such an urgent call would set him on edge, he could not discount the relief he felt, welcoming the distraction. *If I have to taste another piece of wedding cake or decide which centerpiece to go with which table at the reception . . .*

"What's wrong?" he asked Kat, bracing himself for the answer.

8:09 P.M.

"No, no, no!"

Jenna pounded the truck's brakes, throwing her hard into the seat belt's shoulder strap. Nikko tumbled off the seat next to her. As the husky scrambled back up, she stared into the rearview mirror.

The world behind her had become a smoky black wall, rolling relentlessly down from the highlands above. She had to get out of its path, but the road ahead turned in a hard hairpin, zigzagging down toward the distant basin of Mono Lake. To take that switchback would send them driving back *toward* the poisonous smoke. Twisting in her seat, she followed the curve of the road and saw the way did indeed lead back into that roiling cloud.

Despite the early evening chill, she wiped sweat from her brow.

Nikko studied her, trusting her to get them to safety.

But where?

She flipped on her high beams and studied the switchback ahead. She noted a faint pair of tire tracks aiming away from the gravel road and out into the open terrain of sagebrush and scrubby pinyon pines. She didn't know where that thin track led. Certainly tourists and local teenagers often made their own illegal paths, camping in neighboring box canyons or building bonfires beside creeks. Heaven knows, she had chased plenty of them off herself in her role as park ranger.

With no other choice, she gunned the engine and sped to the switchback. She bumped the truck over the shoulder and onto the thin off-road trail. She raced along the rutted track, rattling every nut and bolt in the Ford. Nikko panted beside her, his ears tall, his eyes everywhere.

"Hang on there, buddy."

The terrain grew more rugged, requiring her to reduce her speed. Despite the urgency, she couldn't risk breaking an axle or ripping a tire on one of the razor-edged boulders. Her gaze twitched constantly to the rearview mirror. Behind her, the pall of smoke swallowed the moon.

She found herself holding her breath, fearing what was coming.

The path began to climb, cresting toward the top of another hill. Her progress slowed to a treacherous crawl. She cursed her luck and considered abandoning the trail, but by now the surroundings had turned even rockier. No direction looked better than the one she was following.

Committed now, she pushed harder on the accelerator, testing the extremes of the truck's four-wheel drive system. Finally the slope evened out again. Taking advantage, she sped recklessly around a bend in the trail, clearing a shoulder of the hill—only to have the beams of her headlights splash across an old rockslide that cut directly across the trail.

She braked hard, but the pickup skidded on loose sand and rock. Her front bumper smashed into the closest boulder. The airbag deployed, slamming her in the face like a swinging bag of cement. It knocked the breath from her. Her head rang, but not loud enough for her to miss hearing the engine cough and die.

As her eyes filled with pained tears, she tasted blood from a split lip. "Nikko . . ."

The husky had kept his seat, looking no worse for the impact.

"C'mon."

She shoved her door open and half fell out of her seat to the ground. She stood on shaky legs. The air smelled burnt and oily.

Are we already too late?

She turned toward the smoke and pictured the jackrabbit bounding out of that pall and writhing to death. She took a few steps—unsteady for sure, but not from poison. *Simply dazed.* Or at least she prayed that was the reason.

"Just keep moving," she ordered herself.

Nikko joined her, dancing on his paws, his thick tail a waving flag of determination.

Behind them, the solid wall of smoke had grown ragged and wispy-edged. Still, it continued to fall toward her like an engulfing wave. She knew she'd never outrun it on foot.

She stared toward the top of the hill.

Her only hope.

She retrieved a flashlight from her truck and quickly headed upward. She picked a path through the rockslide, whistling for Nikko to stay close. Once through, she discovered a rolling meadow of bitterbrush and prickly phlox. The open terrain allowed her to move faster. She sprinted toward the crest of the hill, following the bouncing beam of her flashlight, climbing ever higher.

But was the hill *high* enough?

Gasping, she forced her legs to pump harder. Nikko raced silently alongside her, ignoring the occasional burst of a nesting sage sparrow or the bound of a black-tailed jackrabbit.

At last they reached the summit. Only then did she risk a glance over her shoulder. She watched that towering wave of smoke break against the shoal of the tall hill and spread outward, filling the lower valleys all around, turning the hilltop into an island within a poisonous sea.

But how long would this refuge remain safe?

She fled farther away from that deadly shore, toward the highest crown of the hill. Near the top, sharp-edged silhouettes cut against the stars, marking the dilapidated remains of an old ghost town. She counted maybe a dozen barns and buildings. Gold-rush-era outposts like this dotted the local hills, most forgotten and unmapped—with the exception of the nearby town of Bodie, a larger ghost town that stood as the centerpiece of Bodie State Historic Park.

Still, she hurried gladly toward that meager shelter, taking strength from the stubbornly standing walls and roofs. As she neared the closest structure, she pulled out her cell phone, hoping she was high enough to get a signal. With her truck's radio drowned in that toxic sea, her cell phone was the only means of communication.

With great relief, she noted a single glowing bar of signal strength.

Not great, but I'm not complaining.

She dialed the dispatch office. The line was quickly picked up by a breathless Bill Howard.

Though the connection was dodgy, she heard the relief in her friend's voice. "Jen, are you o . . . ay?"

"I'm banged up little, but I'm okay."

"What's . . . banged up?"

She bit back her frustration at the reception. She tried speaking louder. "Listen, Bill. You've got trouble rolling your way."

She tried to explain about the explosion, but the spotty signal made communication difficult.

"You need to evacuate Lee Vining," she said, almost shouting. "Also any of the area's campsites."

"I didn't . . . et that. What's that about an evacuation?"

She closed her eyes, exasperated. She took a couple of breaths.

Maybe if I get on the roof of one of these barns, I could get a better signal.

Before she could consider the best course, a low thumping sounded. At first she thought it was her own heart pounding in her ears. Then Nikko whined, hearing it too. As the noise grew louder, she searched the skies and spotted a blip of navigation lights.

A helicopter.

She knew it was too soon for Bill to have sent up a search-and-rescue team. With her nerves jangling a warning, she flicked off her flashlight and rushed toward the shelter of the ghost town. Reaching the outskirts, she ducked alongside an old barn as a helicopter crested into view.

She recognized the sleek black shape of the aircraft. It was the same bird she had seen lifting off from the military base just prior to the explosion.

Had they caught sight of my truck racing away from the blast zone and doubled back? But why?

Not knowing for sure, she kept out of sight. Reaching the gaping barn door, she hurried inside with Nikko. She rushed across the dark confines, halting only long enough to check her phone.

Her call to Bill had dropped, and the screen now showed no bars.

She was cut off, on her own.

Reaching the far side of the barn, she peered carefully out through the broken glass of a window. The helicopter lowered toward a meadow on that side. Once the skids were close enough to the ground, men in black uniforms bailed out on both sides. The rotor wash of the helicopter pounded the scrub brush around them.

Her heart thundered in her throat as she noted the shouldered rifles.

This was no rescue party.

She touched her only weapon, holstered at her hip. A taser. By law, California Park Rangers could carry firearms, but it was mostly discouraged when assisting with tours like today.

Nikko growled at the growing commotion outside.

She waved him silent, knowing that their only hope of surviving was to stay hidden.

As she slunk lower, the last man—a true giant— hopped out of the helicopter and strode a few steps away. He carried a long muzzled weapon. She didn't recognize it—until a jet of fire shot out the end, lighting up the meadow.

Flamethrower.

It took her a moment to understand the necessity for such a weapon. Then her fingers tightened on the sill of the barn's window, noting the dried and warped wood. She was hiding in a veritable tinderbox.

Outside, the cluster of armed men spread wide, preparing to circle the small outcropping of buildings.

They must know I'm here, hiding somewhere in the ghost town.

Their plan was clear. They intended to burn her out into the open.

Beyond the men, the toxic sea swirled around the hill's crown. There was no escaping this island. She sank to her heels, her mind feverishly running through her options. Only one certainty remained.

I can't survive this.

But that didn't mean she would stop being a ranger. If nothing else, she would leave some clue to her fate, to what really happened out here.

Nikko sidled next to her.

She hugged him hard, knowing it was likely for the last time. "I need you to do one more thing for me, buddy," she whispered in his ear.

He thumped his tail.

"That's a good boy."

3

April 27, 11:10 P.M. EDT
Takoma Park, Maryland

When it rains, it pours . . .

Gray Pierce sped his motorcycle down the wet suburban street. It had been storming solidly for the past week. Overtaxed drains left treacherous puddles along the road's edges. His headlamp cut a swath through the heavy drops as he aimed for his father's house.

The Craftsman bungalow lay midway along the next block. Even from here, Gray spotted light blazing from all the windows, illuminating the wraparound porch and the wooden swing that hung listlessly there. The home looked the same as it always did, belying the storm that awaited him inside.

As he reached the driveway, he leaned his six-foot frame into the turn and rumbled toward the detached garage in the back. A harsh bellow rose from behind the house, heard even over the roar of the Yamaha V-Max's engine.

It seems matters had worsened here.

As he cut the engine, a figure appeared from the backyard, stalking through the rain. It was his younger brother, Kenny. The family resemblance was evident, from his ruddy Welsh complexion to his dark, thick hair.

But that was the extent of the similarities between the two brothers.

Gray tugged off his motorcycle helmet and hopped off the bike to face his brother's wrath. Though they were the same height, Kenny had a beer gut, a feature well earned from a decade living the soft life of a software engineer in California, while nursing a drinking problem. Recently Kenny had taken a sabbatical from his job and returned here to help out with their father. Still, he threatened to head back west almost every week.

"I can't take it anymore," Kenny said, balling his fists, his face bright red with aggravation. "You have to talk some sense into him."

"Where is he?"

Kenny waved toward the backyard, looking both irritated and embarrassed.

"What's he doing outside in the rain?" Gray headed toward the rear of the house.

"You tell me."

Gray reached the yard. The single lamp above the kitchen back door offered little light, but he had no trouble spotting the tall man standing near a row of oleanders that bordered the fence. The sight stopped Gray for a moment as he tried to comprehend what he was seeing.

His father stood barefoot and naked, except for a pair of boxers, which clung damply to his bony physique. His thin arms were raised, his face upturned to the rain, as if praying to some storm god. Then those arms scissored together in front of the bushes.

"He thinks he's trimming the oleanders," Kenny explained, calmer now. "I found him wandering in the kitchen earlier. It's the second time this week. Only I couldn't get him back to bed. You know how stubborn he can be, even before . . . before all of this."

Alzheimer's.

Kenny would rarely say the word, as if fearful he might catch it by talking about it.

"That's when I called you," Kenny said. "He listens to you."

"Since when?" he muttered.

While growing up, Gray and his father had had a tumultuous relationship. His father was a former Texas oilman, rugged and hard, with a personal philosophy of grit and independence. That is, until an industrial accident at a drilling rig sheared one of his legs off at the knee. After that, his outlook soured into one of bitterness and anger. Much of which he directed at his eldest son. It eventually drove Gray away, into the Army and finally into Sigma.

Standing here now, Gray sought that infuriatingly hard man in the frail figure in the yard. He gaped at the ribs, the sagging skin, the map of his spine. This was not even a shadow of his father's former self. It was a shell, stripped of all by age and disease.

Gray stepped over to his father and gently touched his shoulder. "Dad, that's enough."

Eyes turned to him, surprisingly bright. Unfortunately it was old anger that shone there. "These bushes need to be cut back. The neighbors are already complaining. Your mother—"

Is dead.

Gray bit back a twinge of guilt and kept a firm grip on his father's shoulder. "I'll do it, Dad."

"What about school?"

Gray stumbled to match the old man's timeline, then continued smoothly. "I'll do it after school. Okay."

The fire dulled in his father's bleary blue eyes. "You'd better, boy. A man is only as good as his word."

"I'll do it. I promise."

Gray led him to the back porch and into the kitchen. The motion, the warmth, and the brighter light seemed to slowly help his father focus.

"Gr . . . Gray, what are you doing here?" his father asked hoarsely, as if seeing him for the first time.

"Just stopped by to check on how you were doing."

A thin hand patted the back of his arm. "How 'bout a beer then?"

"Another time. I've got to get back to Sigma. Duty calls."

Which was the truth. Kat had caught him en route from his apartment, asking him to join her at Sigma command in D.C. After he had explained about the situation with his father, she had given him some latitude. Still, he had heard the urgency in her voice and didn't want to let her down.

He glanced to Kenny.

"I'll get him up to bed. After episodes like this, he usually sleeps the rest of the night."

Good.

"But, Gray, this isn't over." Kenny lowered his voice. "I can't keep doing this night after night. In fact, I talked with Mary about this earlier today."

Gray felt a twinge of irritation at being left out of this conversation. Mary Benning was an RN who watched over their father during the day. The nights were mostly covered by Kenny, with Gray filling in when he could.

"What does she think?"

"We need around-the-clock care, with safeguards in place. Door alarms. Gates for the stairs. Or . . ."

"Or find a home for him."

Kenny nodded.

But this is his home.

Kenny must have read the stricken expression. "We don't have to decide right away. For now, Mary gave me the numbers for some nurses that could start covering the night shift. I think we could both use the break."

"Okay."

"I'll get it all arranged," Kenny said.

A twinge of suspicion rang through Gray, wary that his brother's sudden resourcefulness was driven more by a desire to wash his hands of their father and escape back to California. But at the same time, Gray recognized his brother was likely right. Something had to be done.

As Kenny led their father toward the stairs and the bedrooms above, Gray pulled out his cell phone and dialed Sigma command. He reached Kat almost immediately.

"I'm coming in now."

"You'd better hurry. The situation is growing worse."

Gray glanced toward the stairs.

It certainly is.

11:33 P.M.

Gray reached Sigma command in fifteen minutes, pushing his Yamaha to its limits on the nearly deserted streets, chased as much by the ghosts behind him as he was drawn forward by the urgent summons to D.C. He could have begged off on coming in, but he had nothing but worries waiting for him at his apartment. Even his bed was presently cold and empty, as Seichan was still in Hong Kong, working with her mother on a fund-raising project for impoverished girls in Southeast Asia.

So for the moment, he simply needed to keep moving.

As soon as the elevator doors opened onto the subterranean levels of Sigma command, Gray strode out into the hallway. The facility occupied long-abandoned World War II–era bunkers and fallout shelters beneath the Smithsonian Castle. The covert location at the edge of the National Mall offered Sigma members ready access both to the halls of power and to the Smithsonian Institution's many labs and research materials.

Gray headed toward the nerve center of the facility—and the mastermind who ran Sigma's intelligence and communication net.

Kat must have heard his approach and stepped out into the hallway to meet him. Despite the midnight hour and the long day she'd had, she was dressed in a crisp set of navy dress blues. Her short auburn hair was combed neatly in a boyish coif, but there was nothing boyish about the rest of her. She nodded to him, her eyes hard and focused.

"What's this about?" Gray asked as he joined her.

Without wasting a breath, she turned and headed back into Sigma's communication center. He followed her into the circular room, banked on all sides by monitors and computer stations. Normally two or three technicians manned this hub, and when an operation was in full swing, there could be twice that number. But at this late hour, only a single figure awaited them: Kat's main analyst, Jason Carter.

The young man sat at a station, typing furiously. He was dressed in black jeans and a Boston Red Sox T-shirt. His flax-blond hair was cowlicked and disheveled, like he'd just woken up, but more likely, the exhaustion on his face was from not having slept at all. Though only twenty-two, the kid was whip-smart, especially when it came to anything with a circuit board. According to Painter,

Jason had been kicked out of the Navy for breaking into DoD servers with nothing more than a BlackBerry and a jury-rigged iPad. After that incident, Kat had personally recruited him, taking him under her wing.

Kat spoke to Gray. "A little over an hour ago, a military research base out in California had some sort of disaster. There was a frantic mayday."

She touched Jason's shoulder.

He tapped a key. An audio feed immediately began to play. It was a woman's voice, stiff but plainly winded, struggling to maintain composure.

"This is sierra, victor, whiskey. There's been a breach. Fail-safe initiated. No matter the outcome: Kill us . . . kill us all."

Kat continued. "We've identified the caller as Dr. Irene McIntire, chief systems analyst for the base."

On the computer screen, an image of a middle-aged woman in a lab coat appeared, smiling for the camera. Her eyes twinkled with excitement. Gray tried to balance this image with the frantic voice he'd just heard.

"What were they working on?" Gray asked.

Jason interrupted, cupping a Bluetooth headphone more firmly to his ear. "They've arrived. Coming down now."

"That's what I'm hoping to find out," Kat said, answering Gray's question. "All I know is the research station must have been dealing with something hazardous, something that required drastic action to stop. Satellite imagery showed an explosion. Lots of smoke."

Jason brought up those photos, too, flipping through them rapidly. Though the images were gray-scaled and grainy, Gray could easily make out the flash of fire, the billow of an oily black cloud.

"We still can't see through the smoke to evaluate the current status of the base," Kat said. "But there's been no further communication."

"They must have razed the place."

"It would seem that way at the moment. Painter is looking into matters out west, tapping into local resources. He's tasked me with discovering more details about the base's operations." Kat turned to Gray, her eyes worried. "I already learned that the site is managed by DARPA."

He failed to hide his surprise. DARPA was the defense department that oversaw Sigma's operations—though knowledge of this group's existence was restricted to only a few key people, those with the highest security clearance. But he shouldn't have been so shocked to learn this base was tied to DARPA. The military's research and development agency had hundreds of facilities spread through several divisions and across the breadth of the country. Most of them operated with minimal oversight, running independently, tapping into the most unique minds and talents out there. The details of each operation were on a need-to-know basis.

And apparently we didn't need to know about this.

"There were over thirty men and women at that base when things went sour," Kat said. From the stiffness in her shoulders and hard set to her lips, she was furious.

Gray couldn't blame her as he stared at the monitor and the billowing black cloud. "Do you know which specific DARPA division was running that place?"

"BTO. The Biological Technologies Office. It's a relatively new division. Their mission statement is to explore the intersection between biology and the physical sciences."

Gray frowned. His own expertise for Sigma straddled that same line. It was dangerous territory, encompassing everything from genetic engineering to synthetic biology.

Voices echoed down the hall, coming from the direction of the elevator. Gray glanced over his shoulder.

"After getting Painter's permission," Kat explained, "I asked the director of the BTO—Dr. Lucius Raffee—to join us here to help troubleshoot the situation."

As the new party drew closer, their voices expressed tension at this midnight summons.

Two men appeared at the entrance to the communication hub. The first man was a stranger, a distinguished black man dressed in a knee-length coat over an Armani suit. He looked to be in his mid-fifties, with salt-and-pepper hair and a neat goatee.

"Dr. Raffee," Kat said, stepping forward and shaking his hand. "Thank you for coming."

"It was not like your man offered me much choice. I was just leaving a performance of *La Bohème* at the Kennedy Center when I was accosted."

The doctor's escort, Monk Kokkalis, pushed into the room. He was a bulldog of a man with a shaved head and the muscular build of a linebacker. The man cocked an eyebrow toward Gray as if to say *catch a load of this guy*. He then stepped over and lightly kissed his wife's cheek.

Monk whispered faintly to Kat. "Honey, I'm home."

Dr. Raffee glanced between the two, trying to comprehend them as a couple. Gray understood the man's confusion. They made a striking, if odd, pair.

"I assume my husband filled you in on the situation in California," Kat said.

"He did." Dr. Raffee sighed heavily. "But I'm afraid there's little concrete information I can offer you concerning what went wrong . . . or even the exact nature of the work that might have resulted in such drastic countermeasures at that base. I've telephoned several of my key people to follow up. Hopefully, we'll hear from them shortly. All I know at the moment is that the head researcher was Dr. Kendall Hess, a specialist in astrobiology with an emphasis on investigating shadow biospheres."

Kat frowned. "Shadow biospheres?"

He waved a hand dismissively. "He was searching for radically different forms of life, specifically those that employed unusual biochemical or molecular processes to function."

Gray had some familiarity on the subject. "Like organisms that use RNA instead of DNA."

"Indeed. But shadow biospheres could even be more esoteric than that. Hess proposed that there might be some hidden suite of life that uses an entirely different set of amino acids than what is commonly known. It was why he set up the research station near Mono Lake."

"Why's that?" Gray asked.

"Back in 2010, a group of NASA scientists were able to take a microbe native to that highly alkaline lake and force it to switch from using phosphorus in its biochemical processes to arsenic."

"Why is that significant?" Monk asked.

"As an astrobiologist, Hess was familiar with the NASA team's work. He believed such a discovery proved that early life on earth was likely arsenic-based. He also hypothesized that a thriving biosphere of arsenic-based organisms might exist somewhere on earth."

Gray understood Hess's fervor. Such a discovery would turn biology on its ear and open up an entire new chapter of life on earth.

Raffee frowned. "But he was also investigating many other possible shadow biospheres. Like desert varnish." From their confused expressions, he explained in more detail. "Desert varnish is that rust to black coating found on exposed rock surfaces. Native people in the past used to scrape it away to create their petroglyphs."

Gray pictured the ancient stick-figure drawings of people and animals found around the world.

"But the odd thing about desert varnish," Raffee continued, "is that it still remains unresolved how it forms. Is it a chemical reaction? The by-product of some unknown microbial process? No one knows. In fact, the status of varnish as *living* or *nonliving* has been argued all the way back to the time of Darwin."

Monk grumbled his irritation. "But how does researching some grime on rocks end up triggering a frantic mayday and an explosion?"

"I don't know. At least not yet. I do know that Hess's work had already drawn the attention of the private sector, that a portion of his latest work was a joint corporate venture, a part of the federal Technology Transfer Program." He shrugged. "That's what happens when you have so many budget cuts in R&D."

"What was this venture backing?" Kat asked.

"Over the years, Hess's investigation into shadow biospheres had uncovered a slew of new extremophiles, organisms that thrive in harsh and unusual environments. Such microbes are great resources for the discovery of unique chemicals and compounds. Couple that with the exploding field of synthetic biology, where labs are testing the extremes of genetic engineering, and you have potentially a very lucrative enterprise."

Gray knew that billions of dollars of corporate money were already pouring into such ventures, from giants like Monsanto, Exxon, DuPont, and BP. And when it came to such high stakes, corporations often placed profit ahead of safety.

"If you're right about private sector money funding Dr. Hess's work," Gray asked, "could this accident have been some form of corporate sabotage?"

"I can't say, but I'm doubtful. His corporate-funded research was fairly altruistic. It was called Project Neogenesis."

"And what was its goal?" Kat asked.

"A lofty one. Dr. Hess believes he can slow down or halt the growing number of extinctions on this planet, specifically those losses due to the actions of man. Namely pollution and the effects of climate change. I heard Dr. Hess once give a TED lecture on the fact that the earth is in the middle of a sixth mass extinction, one great enough to rival the asteroid strike that killed off the dinosaurs. I remember him saying how a mere two-degree increase in global temperature would immediately wipe out millions of species."

Kat knit her brows together. "And what was Dr. Hess's plan to stop this from happening?"

Raffee stared around the room as if the answer were obvious. "He believes he has discovered a path to engineer our way out of this doom."

"With Project Neogenesis?" Kat asked.

Gray now understood the name's significance.

New genesis.

He glanced to the smoking image still fixed on the screen. It was indeed a worthy goal, but at the same time, the man's hubris had possibly cost thirty men and women their lives.

And with a chill, Gray sensed this wasn't over yet.

How many more would die?

4

April 27, 8:35 P.M. PDT
Mono Lake, California

I can't hold out much longer.

Jenna lay flat on her belly beneath the rusted bulk of
an old tractor. She had a clear view of the helicopter idling
in the meadow beyond the ghost town. She took a flurry
of photos with her phone. She dared not use the flash feature for risk of being spotted by the assault team on the
ground. It had taken stealth and teeth-clenched patience
to creep from the barn to this meager hiding spot.

She craned her neck to track the broad-shouldered
man sweeping in a circle around the small cluster of dry
structures crowning the hill. His flamethrower roared,
shooting out a blazing ten-foot jet. He set fire to the
grass, to the bushes, to the closest buildings, turning

the hilltop into a hellish landscape. Smoke rolled high, reminding her all too well of the poisonous sea that kept her trapped here.

She might not be able to escape, but that didn't mean she couldn't leave something behind, some clue to her fate, to what happened here.

She wiped the sweat from her brow with the back of her hand. She had done her best to capture as many pictures of the helicopter and the armed men as possible. Hopefully someone would be able to identify the aircraft or recognize the few faces she had captured digitally. Using the zoom feature, she had gotten a close-up of the giant wielding the flamethrower. His features were burnished, possibly Hispanic, with dark hair under a military-style cap and a prominent purplish scar that split his chin.

As ugly as that guy is, he's gotta be in some law enforcement database.

Knowing she'd done all she could, she rolled to her side and found a pair of eyes shining back at her, reflecting the firelight. Nikko panted silently, his tongue lolling. She ran a hand from the crown of his head to his flank. His muscles trembled with adrenaline, ready to run, but she had to ask more of him.

She reached and secured the strap of her cell phone's case to his leather collar, then cupped his muzzle, meeting that determined gaze.

"Nikko, stay. Hold."

Reinforcing her command, she held a palm toward him, then clenched a fist.

"Stay and hold," she repeated.

He stopped panting, and a small whine escaped.

"I know, but you have to stay here."

She gave him a reassuring rub along both cheeks. He leaned hard into her palm, as if asking her not to go.

Be my big brave boy. One more time, okay?

She let go of his face. His head drooped sullenly, his chin settling between his paws. Still, his eyes never left hers. He had been her companion since she first started out as a ranger. She had been fresh out of school, while he had just finished his own search-and-rescue training. They had grown together, both professionally and personally, becoming partners and friends. He was also there when her mother had died of breast cancer two and a half years ago.

She shied away from the memory of that long, brutal battle. It had devastated her father, leaving him a faded shell of his former self, lost in grief and survivor's guilt. The death had become a gulf that neither could seem to bridge. Jenna had also secretly had a BCRA gene test performed, an analysis that confirmed she carried one of the two inherited genetic markers that indicate a heightened risk of breast cancer. Even now she hadn't fully come to terms with that information, nor shared the results with her father.

Instead, she dove headlong into her job, finding solace in the raw beauty of the wilderness, discovering peace in the turning of the seasons, that endless cycle of death and rebirth. But also she found a de facto family in her fellow rangers, in the simple camaraderie of like-minded souls. Most of all, though, she found Nikko.

He whined again softly, as if knowing what she must do.

She leaned close and touched her nose to his.

Love you, too, buddy.

A part of her desperately wanted to stay with him, but she had watched her mother bravely face the inevitable. Now it was her turn.

With her record of events secure and hidden with Nikko, she knew what she had to do. She gave Nikko a final rub, then rolled out from beneath the tractor. She needed to lead the others as far away from the husky's hiding place as possible. She doubted whoever hunted her knew about her service dog or would even worry about him if they did. The endgame of the hunters here was to eliminate any witnesses who could talk. Once that was accomplished, the assault team should leave. Hopefully after that, someone would come looking for her—and find Nikko and the evidence she had left behind.

It was all she could do.

That, and give her hunters a good chase.

She set off at a low sprint, aiming away from the flames toward the darkest section of the hilltop. She made it fifty yards—then a shout rose to her left, a triumphant bawl of a hunter who had spotted their prey.

She ran faster with one last thought burning brightly.

Good-bye, my buddy.

8:35 P.M.

Dr. Kendall Hess jolted at the staccato retorts of rifle fire. He sat straighter in his seat, straining his shoulders as he struggled to see out the helicopter's side window. The plastic ties that bound his wrists behind him cut painfully into his skin.

What was happening?

He struggled through a foggy drug haze. *Ketamine and Valium*, he guessed, though he couldn't be sure what sedative had been shot into his thigh after he was captured at the lab.

Still, he had witnessed what had transpired after the helicopter had fled the base. His entire body ached at the memory of the explosion, of the countermeasures he had managed to release as a last resort. He prayed such drastic action would contain what had escaped from the Level 4 biolab, but he couldn't be certain. What he and his team had created in that subterranean lab was an early prototype, far too dangerous to ever be released into the real world. But someone had let it loose, a saboteur.

But why?

He pictured the faces of his colleagues.

Gone, all gone.

Another burst of gunfire echoed across the fiery hilltop.

Kendall had been left with one guard in the helicopter, but the man stared out the other window, plainly lusting to join the hunt. If only the pilot had failed to spot the fleeing truck earlier—from its logo, a park ranger vehicle—Kendall might have held out some hope, both for himself and for anyone within a hundred miles of his former lab.

Again he prayed his countermeasures held. The smoke contained a noxious concoction engineered by Hess's team: a weapon-grade mix of VX and saxitoxin, a blend of a paralytic agent with a lethal organophosphate derivative. Nothing living could survive the slightest exposure.

Except for what I created.

His team had still not discovered a way to kill that synthetic microorganism. The engineered nerve gas was only meant to *contain* its spread, to kill any organism that might carry it farther afield.

As the barrage of gunfire continued out there, he pictured the unknown ranger doing his best to hold out, but the man was clearly outnumbered and outgunned. Still, the ranger kept fighting.

Can I do any less?

Kendall struggled through his drug-induced fog for clarity. He pulled at the snug plastic ties, using the pain to help him focus. One mystery occupied his full attention. The saboteurs had shot everyone at the base or left them to die with the explosion.

So why am I still alive? What do they need from me?

Kendall was determined not to cooperate, but he was also realistic enough to know that he could be broken. Anyone could be broken. There was only one way he could thwart them.

As another spate of gunfire erupted, Kendall twisted his arms enough to punch the release on his seat harness. As he was freed, he tugged the hatch open and fell sideways out of the cabin. He managed to catch one leg under him as he hit the ground. He used the support to propel himself away from the helicopter.

A shocked bellow rose from the cabin, coming from the lone guard—followed by a loud *crack*.

Dirt exploded near his left foot.

He ignored the threat, trusting that his captors wanted to keep him alive. He fled headlong, stumbling with his arms still tied behind him. His legs tripped on scrubby grass and ripped through snagging bushes. He aimed for the smoky darkness swirling around the lower slopes of the hill.

That path led to certain death.

He ran faster toward it.

It's better this way.

With the hunt for the ranger occupying everyone's attention, he grew more confident.

I can make it . . . it's what I deserve—

Then a shadow overtook him, impossibly fast, shivering across the landscape, lit by the fires blazing on the hilltop. A hard blow struck him in the lower back, sending him sprawling facedown into the scrub brush. He rolled over, scrabbling backward on hands and feet.

A massive shape stood limned against the flames.

Kendall didn't need to see the ragged scar to recognize the leader of the assault team. The figure stalked over to him, raised an arm, and slammed down the steel butt of a rifle.

With his hands still pinned behind him, Kendall couldn't deflect the blow. Pain exploded in his nose and forehead. He collapsed backward, his limbs gone rubbery and limp. Darkness closed the world to a tight, agonized knot.

Before he could move, iron fingers clamped on to his ankle and dragged him back toward the helicopter. Thorns and sharp rocks cut into his back. They might need him alive, but plainly it didn't matter in what condition.

He blacked out for several breaths, only to find himself waking as he was tossed into the cabin. Orders were barked in Spanish. He heard the words *apúrate* and *peligro*.

He translated through the daze.

Hurry up and *danger.*

The world suddenly filled with a dull roar, then teetered drunkenly. He realized the helicopter was lifting off.

He rolled enough to peer out the window. Below the skids, dark figures ran across the hellish landscape of the burning ghost town. It seemed the helicopter was abandoning the rest of the assault team.

But why?

The pilot gesticulated wildly toward the ground.

Kendall stared closer. He suddenly understood the threat. The poisonous cloud of nerve gas was beginning to waft upward from the surrounding valleys. At first he thought the smoke had been stirred by the passing craft's rotor wash, but then he understood.

Updraft!

The blazing firestorm here was pushing up a column of hot air. As it rose from the hilltop, it drew the deadly gas along with it, pulling it like a veil over the burning summit.

No wonder a swift evacuation had been ordered. Kendall stared at the hulking form of the leader seated across from him, a weapon across his knees. The other's gaze was also out the window, but he stared skyward, as if already writing off his teammates.

Kendall refused to be so callous.

He searched below for some sign of the beleaguered ranger. He held out no hope, but the fellow deserved some witness, or at the very least, a final prayer. He whispered a few words as the helicopter whisked away—ending with one last entreaty, staring down at that black, swirling sea of poison.

Let me be right about the gas.

Above all else—nothing must live.

5

April 27, 8:49 P.M. PDT
Mono Lake, California

Jenna crouched inside the dilapidated remains of an old general store. She hid with her back against the graffiti-scarred counter at the rear. Above her head, rows of wooden shelves frosted with cobwebs held a handful of antique bottles with age-curled labels. She fought not to sneeze from all the dust and did her best to ignore the pain in her upper arm. A trace of fire from a bullet had grazed her bicep.

Hold it together, she told herself.

She strained to listen for the approach of any of the armed men, a task made more difficult by the pounding of her heart in her throat. She was lucky to have held out as long as she had, playing cat and mouse among the few remaining buildings that had not yet been torched.

She had only made it to safety now because of the distraction of the helicopter's lifting off. The sudden departure confused the hunters long enough for her to make a mad dash into the store. But like the others, she was equally baffled by the change in circumstances here.

Why was the helicopter abandoning those on the ground? Or was it merely departing long enough until she was found and dispatched?

A moment ago she had caught a brief glimpse of a lab-coated figure being dragged back into the aircraft's cabin. The man was plainly a captive, likely one of the researchers from the military base. The distance was too far for her to pick out any details to identify the prisoner. Had the helicopter left to discourage another escape attempt?

She wasn't buying that.

Instead, something must have spooked the aircraft away.

But what?

She desperately wanted to pop her head up and search for whatever that new danger might be out there, but she couldn't trust that the armed men wouldn't complete their assignment. She had already gleaned these were hard men with military training. No matter the risk, these soldiers would stay on task—which meant eliminating her.

The crunch of glass drew her attention behind her and to the left. She pictured the open window on that side. Someone must have climbed through there versus using the front door. Earlier, using the roar of the helicopter as cover, she had shattered one of the antique bottles from the shelves overhead at every point of ingress: two windows and a door.

Using the noise as a guide, she popped up and aimed her only weapon. A shadow crouched ten feet away, silhouetted against the fiery glow outside. She pulled the trigger. A blue spark of brilliance shot from her gun and struck the figure. A sharp cry of incapacitating pain followed as the Taser's barbs struck home.

She vaulted over the counter as the assailant collapsed to the floor, writhing in agony. She aimed her Taser X3 and fired a second cartridge to silence him. She was taking no chances. Her weapon held a third round, but she knew it wasn't enough. It was why she had set up this ambush in the store.

She crossed to the man—now unconscious, maybe dead—and relieved him of his rifle. She holstered her Taser and quickly ran her hands over his assault weapon. While she rarely carried a side arm, she had taken the mandatory weapons training. The rifle appeared to be a Heckler & Koch, model 416 or 417. Either way, it was similar enough to the AR-15 she had practiced with on the shooting range.

She hurried to the door, dropped to a knee, and brought up her rifle. She studied the view. The cry of the soldier had not escaped the attention of the other hunters. Through the smoky firelight, men ran low among the burning remains of the ghost town. They were attempting to flank her. She aimed for the closest man and fired a burst of rounds. Dirt blasted at his toes, but one round struck the man's left shin and sent him crashing to the ground.

His teammates darted for cover. While it wouldn't stop them, her attack should slow them down. Return fire peppered the facade of the general store. Rounds ripped through the old wood like hot coals through paper. But she was already moving, dashing back to hide behind the thick-beamed counter. She would make her last stand here, intending to take out as many of the others as she could.

Once in position, she rested her rifle on the counter and searched through the night-vision scope for her next target. She kept a watch out both windows and the door. It took her a little time to adjust to the zoom. For a moment, she captured a view of a man in the distance, far out in the meadow. Though he wasn't an immediate threat, it was his frantic action that momentarily snagged her attention.

He ran toward the ghost town, his rifle tumbling out of his hands; then he fell to his knees. His back arched in a convulsive spasm before toppling on his side in full seizure. She remembered the jackrabbit and suddenly knew what had driven the helicopter away.

That poisonous sea must be rising, starting to swamp the summit.

Her finger trembled on the rifle's trigger, recognizing the futility of her foolish attempt to make a last stand here. No matter how many of the soldiers she killed, in the end they were all doomed.

She thought of Nikko, hiding under the tractor. She knew he would still be there, obeying her last command, ever loyal. She had hoped her sacrifice would at least protect him, allow him to be found by any rescuers dispatched by Bill Howard.

Nikko . . . I'm sorry.

A figure appeared through the window to her right. With a burning knot of anger in her gut, she fired a savage fusillade, aiming center mass, and watched with satisfaction as the man's body was blown out of sight. A renewed barrage of return fire tore through the store. It sounded like a thousand chain saws taking down a forest. Blasted fragments of dry wood rained down all around her.

She ducked lower but kept her rifle in position on the counter. Whenever she spotted a shadow move, she fired at it. At some point she had begun to cry. She only knew it when her vision blurred, requiring her to wipe her eyes.

She sank to her knees for a second, dropping out of view, struggling to comprehend her tears. Was it fear, desperation, anger, grief?

Likely all of the above.

You've done all you could, she thought, trying to reassure herself, but the thought brought no comfort.

8:52 P.M.

Kendall sat dully in his seat, strapped again in place. He studied the landscape below, trying to discern where he was being taken. They had finally crossed beyond the pall of nerve gas, leaving the mountains behind. They now appeared to be heading east over the Nevada desert. But the dark terrain below was featureless, offering no landmarks.

The large man seated across from him had been in a gruff conversation with the pilot for most of the flight. Kendall tried to eavesdrop as well as he could while feigning disinterest, but much of their communication had been in some obscure Spanish patois. Some phrases he could glean; others were gibberish.

If he had to guess the team's origin, he would plant a flag somewhere in South America. Colombia, maybe Paraguay. This conclusion was perhaps biased because of the assault team's appearance. They were clearly paramilitary, all of the same nationality. To a man, they were small of stature, with rounded faces and pinched eyes, their pocked skin the color of dark mocha with some freckling. The exception to this was their leader. He stood close to seven feet, a giant for any nationality.

From the conversation, Kendall was fairly certain the man's name was Mateo, while the pilot was Jorge.

As if drawn by his thoughts, the scarred man turned to him. He brandished a knife. Kendall quailed back, fearing his intent, but the man grabbed him roughly by the shoulder and turned him enough to slice free the plastic ties from his wrists.

Once his hands were freed, Kendall gladly rubbed the raw skin, wincing at the tenderness. He considered going for the rifle resting on the far seat, but he knew how fast the other could move. Any such attempt would likely only earn him another blow to his skull, and his head still ached from being butted by that rifle earlier, a lesson well learned.

The pilot reached back and handed Mateo a cell phone, which he in turn passed to Kendall. "You listen. Do as told."

Kendall saw a call had already been placed. The caller ID simply read UNKNOWN.

He lifted the phone to his ear. "Hello?" he asked, hating how sheepish he sounded.

"Ah, Dr. Hess, it's high time we talked again."

Kendall felt his blood sink.

It cannot be . . .

Still, he recognized the voice. The rich tenor and the British accent were unmistakable. Kendall had no doubt the man on the other end of the line was the one who had orchestrated the attack.

He swallowed hard, knowing that matters were a thousandfold worse than he had ever suspected. Despite the impossibility of it, he could not dismiss the truth.

I've been kidnapped by a dead man.

8:55 P.M.

At the center of a growing firestorm, Jenna crouched behind the counter of the general store. Holes riddled the walls. Wood dust filled the deafening space. The escalating blasts threatened to deafen her. All that kept her safe was the thick-planked bulk of the counter. But even that refuge could not last much longer under such a barrage.

Then a new noise intruded.

A heavy thump-thumping.

She pictured the assault team's helicopter returning, intending to extract the men here. But a moment later, a loud explosion burst from the location of the heaviest gunfire. She felt the concussion like a fist to the chest.

Then another blast to her right.

Dazed, she rose back up. The hail of rounds through the storefront had suddenly stopped, but not the gunfire. In fact the firefight grew more intense out there— but it was no longer aimed at her position.

Confused, she stood, keeping her rifle raised.

What was—

A dark shape leaped up directly in front of her. A hand grabbed the barrel of the rifle and yanked the weapon out of her surprised grip. It was the man whom she had Tasered earlier. Plainly he had been only unconscious, not dead. In her desperation, she had failed to check his status.

He lunged at her with a dagger.

She twisted away at the last second, but the sharp blade cut a line of fire across her collarbone. The momentum of the thrust carried the man's torso half-way over the counter. She snatched the X3 from its holster, jammed it against his eye, and pulled the trigger. The explosion of the weapon's last cartridge blew the man's head back.

He collapsed limply, sprawled across the counter.

Fueled by adrenaline, she rolled across the top and retrieved the rifle. Gasping, she stumbled toward the doorway. Already the gunplay outside had died down to sporadic bursts, and by the time she reached the doorway, even that had ended.

All that remained was the bell-beat of a helicopter's rotors.

She searched the smoky skies.

Shapes fell out of the night.

Parachutists.

They dropped toward the fires below. Night-vision gear obscured their faces; assault rifles were held in their hands. She watched a paratrooper fire into the ghost town, followed by a cry from below. Farther out, a military helicopter hovered into view and lowered toward the meadow.

Jenna could guess the origin of this rescue force. The U.S Marine Corps maintained their Mountain Warfare Training Center only thirty miles from Mono Lake. They must have been mobilized as soon as the mayday had been sent out from the base. Those last chilling words would have drawn a swift response.

Kill us . . . kill us all.

But how had the Marines found her so quickly? Was it the fires?

Then she guessed the more likely reason. She pictured her abandoned truck, the deflated airbag. The crash would have triggered an automatic GPS alert. Bill Howard must have picked it up after her last attempt to communicate with him was cut off. Knowing him, he would have sent out an immediate SOS with her last known location.

Relief swept through her, but she also remembered the convulsing figure of one of the assailants. The paratroopers were dropping right toward that rising tide of toxin. She had to warn them of the danger.

Regardless if there were any remaining enemy on the ground, she abandoned her shelter and ran out into the open. She waved an arm toward the closest parachutist. She cringed as his weapon swung toward her.

"I'm with the park rangers!" she shouted up at him.

The weapon remained fixed on her until the paratrooper landed. With one hand, he unhooked his chute and let it billow away. Others struck the ground all around the hilltop and out in the ghost town, preparing to mop up.

"Jenna Beck?" the Marine called to her, reaching her side. With his night-vision gear still in place, he cast a menacing figure.

She shivered, but not from fear of him. "It's not safe here."

"We know." He grabbed her forearm. "We're to escort you to the helicopter, get you to safety. But we need to move fast. The wash of the blades will only keep the gas at bay a little longer."

"But—"

Another Marine joined them and grabbed her other arm, squeezing painfully the bullet graze on that side. They manhandled her swiftly toward the waiting helicopter. The other paratroopers swept to either side.

"Wait," she said, struggling to free her arms.

She was ignored.

A shout rose to her left. One of the enemy rose out of hiding, a pistol in hand. She recognized him as the man whose leg she had shattered earlier. Rifles pointed, but they refrained from immediately shooting. One of the Marines rushed toward the man's blind side, clearly intending to take him as prisoner.

But the man put the pistol to his own head and pulled the trigger.

Jenna glanced away, sickened.

Clearly the assault team was under orders not to be captured or interrogated. Again she was struck by their unwavering sense of duty. Whoever they were, they were deadly earnest in their purpose.

Reaching the open meadow, the two Marines hauled her between them. Her toes barely touched the dirt. They reached the large transport helicopter, the powerful rotor wash half blinding her with blown dust and dirt.

No.

She tried to dig in her heels. Failing that, she kicked the paratrooper on her left. She struck him a glancing blow to his knee. Caught by surprise, he stumbled to the side, releasing her.

She swung around to the ghost town, raised her freed arm, and planted two fingers in her mouth. She whistled loudly and sharply, a piercing summons.

"We don't have any more time," the Marine clutching her said.

His companion returned and together they herded her toward the open passenger cabin. The other eight Marines came pounding up to join them. She struggled at the doorway.

"No! Wait! Just a few seconds more."

"We don't have those seconds."

She was lifted and shoved inside. The rest of the rescue team piled in after her. Amid the chaos, she kept a firm hold on a handgrip near the open doorway, searching the smoky meadow, the edges of the ghost town.

C'mon, Nikko.

She didn't have a clear view of the tractor where she had left her partner. Was he still alive? She remembered the thunderous blasts that had heralded the arrival of the Marines. They must have fired rocket-propelled grenades to soften the enemy. One of the curling ribbons of smoke was near where the rusted tractor was located.

In her attempt to save Nikko, had she gotten him killed instead?

With everyone on board, the helicopter's engines roared louder. The wheels lifted free of the grass.

Then she spotted movement, a shape racing through the scrub brush from the edge of the ghost town.

Nikko.

She whistled again for him. He sprinted even faster toward the rising helicopter, but the craft was already yards above the ground. Refusing to abandon him, she leaped out the open cabin door and landed in a hard crouch in the sandy dirt.

Angry shouts rose above her.

Then Nikko was there, leaping into her arms, knocking her down on her backside. He panted in her face, wriggling his relief. She hugged him tightly, ready to face whatever was to come—as long as they did it together.

Then hands grabbed her from behind, hauling her up. Without the wheels ever touching the ground, the helicopter had lowered enough to retrieve them.

She clung to Nikko, carrying him with her into the cabin. She landed on her back, Nikko on top of her.

The door slammed at her heels.

The Marine who had first grabbed her leaned over her. He had ripped away his night-vision gear, revealing a young, rugged face with a scrub of dark stubble. She expected to be admonished, to be dressed down for her foolhardy action.

Instead, he clapped her on the shoulder and pulled her to a seated position. "Name's Drake. Wasn't alerted about the dog," he said in an apologetic tone. "Marines never leave a soldier behind. Even a four-legged one."

"Thanks," she said.

He shrugged and helped her up into a seat, then gave Nikko a good scratching around his neck. "Handsome fella."

She smiled, already liking the guy. Besides, the same could be said for the Marine.

Handsome fella.

Nikko danced a bit on his paws, trying to look everywhere at once, but he kept one haunch firmly against her shin, refusing to be separated from her.

I feel the same way, buddy.

She stared out the window as the helicopter tilted to the side. She caught the distant silvery glint of Mono Lake, still free of the spreading cloud of toxin. If the Marines knew about the nerve gas, then likely word had reached Bill Howard and he was already instituting an evacuation of the immediate area.

The helicopter swung and headed away from the lake.

Frowning, she faced Drake. "Where are we going?"

"Back to MWTC."

She turned to the window. So they were flying back to the Mountain Warfare Training Center. Not a surprise considering the research base had been a military operation in the first place. Still, suspicions rang through her.

Drake stoked that worry with one final detail. "Apparently there's a man from D.C. who really wants to talk to you. He should be getting to the center about the same time as us."

Jenna didn't like the sound of that. She bent down and gave Nikko a good rub, while covertly freeing her cell phone from his collar. With her back turned to the group, she slipped it into her pocket. Until she understood more, she intended to play her cards close to her chest. Especially after all she had gone through, all she had risked.

"Once he debriefs you," Drake finished, "you should be able to go home."

She didn't respond, but she tightened her grip on her hidden phone, thinking of that Washington bureaucrat.

Whoever you are, mister, you're not getting rid of me that easily.

6

April 27, 9:45 P.M. PDT
Humboldt-Toiyabe National Forest, California

"We're on final approach," the pilot announced over the radio. "We'll be wheels down in ten."

Painter stared below the wings of the military aircraft as a meadow came into view, nestled high within the Sierra Nevada Mountains. A few lights shone from a cluster of buildings and homes down there, marking one of the most remote U.S. bases. The Mountain Warfare Training Center occupied forty-six thousand acres of the Humboldt-Toiyabe National Forest. It was literally in the middle of nowhere and at an elevation of seven thousand feet, the perfect place to train soldiers for combat operations in mountainous terrain and in cold-weather environments. Classes here were said to be the most rigorous and daunting anywhere.

"Have you heard anything new?" Lisa asked him, stirring from the jump seat next to him, a pile of research notes stacked on her lap. She looked at him over a pair of reading glasses, something she had taken to wearing of late. He liked the look.

"Gray and the others are still working with Dr. Raffee back at Sigma command. They're gathering intelligence about what was really going on at that station. It seems only a handful of people had intimate knowledge of Dr. Hess's secret research."

"Project Neogenesis," Lisa said.

He nodded with a sigh. "As project leader, Hess kept any details limited to a small circle of colleagues. And most of them were on-site when whatever containment was breached. The status of those at the base remains unknown. Until that toxic cloud dissipates or neutralizes, no one can get near the site."

"What about my request for a shipment of biohazard suits? Properly equipped, we should be able to survey the area on foot."

He knew she wanted to lead that expedition. It chilled him to picture her venturing into that toxic miasma wearing a self-contained isolation suit, like a deep-sea diver in hellish waters. "For now, until we know more, no one goes near there. Evacuations are still continuing with the help of local authorities and the military. We're cordoning off a fifty-mile hot zone around the site."

She sighed and glanced toward the small window next to her seat. "It still seems amazing that something like this could've happened. Especially with no one knowing what was going on at the deepest levels of that base."

"You'd be surprised at how common that is. Since 9/11, there's been a huge spike in biodefense spending, resulting in a slew of new Level 4 labs popping up across the country. Corporate-funded, government-backed, university-run. These labs are dealing with the worst of the worst, agents that have no vaccine or cure."

"Like Ebola, Marburg, Lassa fever."

"Exactly, but also bugs that are being engineered—weaponized—all in the name of preparing for the inevitable, to be a jump ahead of the enemy."

"What sort of oversight is there?"

"Very little, mostly independent and piecemeal. Right now there are some fifteen thousand scientists authorized to work with deadly pathogens, but there are *zero* federal agencies charged with assessing the risks of all of these labs, let alone even keeping track of their number. As a consequence, there've been countless reports of mishandling of contagious pathogens, of vials gone missing, of poor records. So when it comes to an accident like this one, it was not a matter of *if* but of *when* it would happen."

He stared out the window, toward the south, toward that pall of toxic smoke. He had already been informed about the countermeasures released by the base: an engineered blend of a paralytic agent and a nerve gas, all to thwart what might have escaped, to kill any living vector that might transmit it or allow it to spread.

"The genie's out of the bottle," he mumbled, referring not only to events here but also to the rapid escalation of bioengineering projects going on across the country.

He turned back to Lisa. "And it's not only these sanctioned facilities we must worry about. In garages, attics, and local community centers, homegrown genetics labs are sprouting up everywhere. For a small price, you can learn to do your own genetic experiments, even patent your creations."

"How very entrepreneurial. It sounds like the cyberpunks of the past have become the biopunks of today."

"Only now they're hacking into genetic code instead of computer codes. And again with little to no oversight. At the moment, the government depends on self-policing of these grassroots labs."

"The sudden escalation in the number of labs doesn't surprise me."

"Why's that?" he asked.

"The cost of lab equipment and materials has been plummeting for years. What once cost tens of thousands of dollars can be done for pennies now. Along with that, there's been a corresponding increase in speed. Right now, the pace of our ability to read and write DNA increases tenfold every year."

He calculated the implication in his head. That meant in ten short years, genetic engineering could be ten *billion* times faster.

Lisa continued. "Things are moving along at breakneck speeds. Already a lab has managed to create the first synthetically built cell. And just last year biologists engineered an artificial chromosome, building a functional, living yeast from scratch, with gaps in its DNA where they plan to insert special additions in the near future."

"Designer yeast. Great."

Lisa shrugged. "And there are darker implications about that genie getting out of the bottle. It's not just accidental releases we need to worry about. I was reading about this Kickstarter program—where for forty dollars, a group of enterprising young biopunks will send you a hundred seeds for a type of weed that incorporates a glowing gene."

"Glow-in-the-dark weeds? Why?"

"Mischief mostly. They want their funders to spread the seeds into the wild. They already have five thousand backers, which means over five hundred thousand synthetic seeds could be cast across the United States in the near future."

Painter knew such actions were merely the tip of a dangerous iceberg. General Metcalf—the head of DARPA and his boss—had expressed that one of homeland security's greatest fears was how vulnerable U.S. labs were to foreign agents. A terrorist organization could easily insert a graduate student or postdoctoral fellow into one of these bioweapon facilities, either to obtain a deadly pathogen or to get the necessary training to run their own labs.

Painter studied the fog-shrouded mountains in the distance.

Had something like that happened here? Had it been an act of terrorism?

To answer that very question—along with surveying the site firsthand—General Metcalf had ordered Painter to fly out to this remote Marine base. The Mountain Warfare Training Center had become the official staging ground for overseeing this disaster. He was to coordinate with the colonel who ran the center, where assets were already being gathered.

Painter could have left Lisa behind, but her knowledge and keen insight had already proved invaluable. Plus she had insisted on coming, her eyes aglow with the challenge. He reached his hand over to hers, their fingers entwining as if they were bound together forever. How could he refuse his future bride anything?

Such indulgence was part of the reason they had a third companion for this flight. Josh Cummings—Lisa's younger brother—sat up in the cockpit, carrying on an animated conversation with the flight crew. Josh was presently pointing to the airstrip below. It was the main airfield for the Marine base, a site the young man had visited often in the past, and the other reason he was along on this ride.

Like his sister, Josh was lean and blond-haired. He could easily be mistaken for a typical California surfer, but Josh's passion was less about sea and sun than it was about heights and sheer cliffs of rock. He was a renowned mountaineer, summiting a majority of the world's tallest peaks in his twenty-five years, garnering accolades for his skill and building a small business from several of his patents on equipment design.

As a result, he had developed a working relationship with this base as a civilian consultant. He even wore the red knit cap of a Mountain Warfare Instructor, known simply as Red Hats. Few civilians ever earned the right to wear that cap, to teach soldiers the ins and outs of working a mountain. It was a testament to Josh's skill.

But other than that cap, few would mistake Josh for a U.S. Marine. He wore his hair to his shoulders and had a casual disregard for authority. Even his garb was anything but military. Under a sheepskin jacket— something Josh had won from a Sherpa after a night of poker inside a tent on a slope of K2 during a snow- storm—he wore a gray expedition-weight thermal shirt with his company's logo. It was a silhouette of a set of mountains with the centermost one the tallest. It looked distinctly like a fist giving you the finger.

Definitely not military approved.

For most of the year, Josh lived out of his back- pack, but he had been in town for the wedding and had insisted on accompanying his sister to the base. Painter had agreed without reservations. Josh knew most of the personnel up here and could vouch for Painter, hopefully helping to smooth any ruffled feathers from Sigma's trespassing into their territory. Plus from Josh's training exercises in the past, he had intimate knowl- edge of the local terrain, which could prove useful.

Josh demonstrated that now, calling out loudly to be heard over the engines. "Land at the north end of the airfield. You'll cough up less sand. That's where the Marines do most of their V/STOL training."

Lisa glanced at Painter with a quizzical arch of an eyebrow.

"Vertical takeoff and landing," he translated. If the armed forces loved anything more than their guns, it was their acronyms.

Still, Painter couldn't dismiss a bit of excitement as their aircraft readied itself to land. They were flying aboard an MV-22 Osprey, courtesy of the Marine Corps Air Ground Combat Center at Twentynine Palms, , outside of Los Angeles. The unusual vehicle was known as a tiltrotor, named for its ability to transform from a traditional prop-engine plane into a helicopter-like craft by rotating the engine nacelles at the ends of each wingtip.

Twisting in his seat, Painter watched the propellers slowly swing from vertical to horizontal. The plane's forward speed rapidly slowed until it was expertly hovering over the airfield; then the massive craft lowered toward the ground. Moments later, their wheels touched down.

Lisa let out a breath she must have been holding with a loud sigh. "That was amazing."

Painter noted another two Ospreys parked farther away, with crews working around them, suggesting they'd just arrived, a part of the mobilization happening here. A bevy of other Marine helicopters dotted the field.

"Looks like everyone took up your invitation," Lisa said.

Before leaving the coast, Painter had laid down a rough sketch of the order of operations for this mission: search and rescue, evacuation, site quarantine, investigation, and finally cleanup. The first three duties were already under way, allowing Painter's team to proceed directly with their investigation.

He knew where he wanted to start. The first responders—a U.S. Marine search-and-rescue team—had saved the life of a witness, a local park ranger who had happened to be on-site when the base exploded. Painter had heard about the firefight atop a neighboring hill, which raised a substantial mystery: *Who were those hostiles and what did they have to do with what had transpired at the base?*

Only one person potentially had those answers.

And from what Painter had heard en route—she wasn't talking.

10:19 P.M.

Jenna didn't bother to check the doorknob. She knew she was locked inside. She paced the length of the space. Judging from the chalkboard in front and the rows of seats, she figured it was a small classroom. Out the third-story window, she spotted a dark ski lift in the distance, along with a row of stables. Directly below her, an ambulance slowly sidled away from the entrance to the building.

The departing EMS team had already seen to her injuries: wrapping her arm, suturing the small laceration across her collarbone, then finally injecting her with antibiotics. They offered to shoot her up with pain relievers, but she opted to simply pop some ibuprofen.

Have to keep my head clear.

But her growing anger wasn't helping.

Nikko, sprawled on the floor, watched her, his gaze tracking her as she stalked from one side of the classroom to the other. A bowl of water and an empty food dish rested beside him. A tray holding a cellophane-wrapped ham sandwich and a carton of milk sat on one of the desks. She ignored it, still far from having an appetite.

She checked her watch.

How long are they going to keep me here?

The Marine who had rescued her—Gunnery Sergeant Samuel Drake—had told her she would be debriefed by someone from Washington. Yet it had been over an hour since she had arrived here.

So where the hell is this guy?

The base commander had stopped to check in on her, asking her some questions, but she had stonewalled him. She would tell her story once, but only after getting some answers first.

A scuff and rattle drew her attention back to the door. *Finally . . .*

She withdrew a few steps and crossed her arms, ready for a fight. The door opened, but it was not the man she had been expecting. Gunnery Sergeant Drake entered. He looked refreshed, his dark brown hair wet and combed back. He wore a loose pair of khaki trousers and a matching T-shirt that clung tightly across his chest, exposing muscular arms.

While she wanted to be perturbed at the intrusion, she found her arms uncrossing, doing her best to look casual. She was sure she failed miserably.

He smiled at her, which didn't help matters.

"Just bringing a gift from a friend," he said, his voice a deep bass that felt warmer than before, no longer curt and hardened by the weight of command. "Thought maybe you'd be willing to share."

He lifted an arm to reveal a large brown paper sack, slightly damp along the bottom edge.

"What is it?" She took a step closer, then a familiar aroma struck her.

It can't be.

"Baby back ribs from Bodie Mike's Barbecue," he confirmed. "Also coleslaw and fries."

THE 6TH EXTINCTION • 103

"How . . . ?" she asked, stammering in confusion.

He grinned wider, showing perfect teeth. "We've got people flying back and forth between here and Mono Lake, coordinating the evacuation. It seems a friend of yours decided to send back a care package from Lee Vining before the town was evacuated. He thought you might be hungry after all of the excitement."

Only one person knew she was here.

She smiled for the first time in what seemed like ages. "Bill, I could kiss you."

Drake's dark eyes twinkled with amusement. "If you want, I'm sure I could relay that back to him?"

"How about I just split the fries with you instead?" She moved to one of the desks.

"What about the ribs?"

"Nope. They're all mine."

He shifted a desk closer and swung a leg over the chair to sit next to her. As he ripped open the bag, she quickly found her appetite again. She was halfway through the slab of the ribs, with Nikko firmly at her knee, a hopeful expression fixed on his face, when the door opened again.

A contingent of strangers entered. It had to be the party from D.C. After waiting for so long, she now wished they'd leave and come back later.

She wiped her fingers.

Drake stood quickly and stiffly as the base commander entered with the others. "Colonel Bozeman."

"At ease, Drake." The commander looked to be in his early sixties, with silver hair to match the eagle resting above rows of colorful ribbons on his khaki shirt. His eyes settled on the half-finished meal. "Didn't mean to interrupt, Ms. Beck, but this is Director Painter Crowe, an adjunct with DARPA. He has some questions before we get you back to your fellow rangers."

The man's two companions were introduced. They were clearly related, likely brother and sister, maybe even twins, but she concentrated on the man in front. The newcomer had black hair, with a single lock gone snowy white and tucked behind an ear. His complexion was clearly of Native American heritage, but his sharp blue eyes hinted at some European blood in there, too. She wanted to snap at him, but something in his manner defused her. Maybe it was the shadow of a welcoming smile or the intelligent glint to those eyes. This was clearly no meddling bureaucrat or condescending intelligence agent.

Still, she found her hand covering the phone in her pocket.

I want answers.

Crowe turned to the colonel. "Could we have some privacy?"

"Certainly." Bozeman waved to Drake. "Let's give them the room."

Drake followed him out, but not before bumping his fist with the blond man who remained leaning against the door. "Good to see you, Josh."

"Wish it was under better circumstances."

"Me, too." He grinned broadly. "But that's why they pay us the big bucks, isn't it?"

As the two Marines left and the door closed, Crowe turned his laser focus back to Jenna. "Ms. Beck, you've been through a lot, but I was hoping you could give us some additional information about what happened tonight. Run through events in as much detail as possible. I'm especially curious about the group of men who attacked you atop the hill."

She stood her ground. "Not before you tell me what really was going on inside that research station. It's put the entire basin at risk. Not only the fragile ecosystem here that took millennia to build, but also endangering my friends and colleagues."

"I wish I could tell you," he answered.

"Wish or won't?"

"To be honest, we don't know the exact nature of the work. The base was headed by Dr. Kendall Hess, a very secretive fellow."

Jenna frowned, remembering the astrobiologist who had come down to Mono Lake. She recalled her conversation with him over a cup of coffee at Bodie Mike's. Even back then, she'd been struck by how guarded he was, how carefully he chose his words.

"I met him," she admitted. "When he was collecting core samples of the mud at the bottom of the lake."

Crowe turned back to his companion, Lisa Cummings. He silently communicated with her, as if the two were judging if this detail was important or not.

Jenna glanced between them, her frown deepening. "What was Dr. Hess working on?"

Crowe faced her again. "All we know for sure is that he was studying and experimenting with exotic life-forms."

"Extremophiles," Jenna said with a nod, remembering the details of their brief talk. "He said he was looking for unusual organisms—bacteria, protozoa—anything that might have developed unique strategies to survive in harsh environments."

Lisa stepped closer. "More specifically he was investigating shadow biospheres, environments where nonstandard life might exist in secret. We believe his interest in this area came about after some NASA scientists found bacteria in Mono Lake that could be trained to live on arsenic."

Jenna understood. "So that's why Dr. Hess chose this location."

Crowe nodded. "Perhaps to continue that line of research, or even take it a step farther. We believe he might have been trying to engineer something new, something that never existed on this planet."

"And it got loose."

"That's what we believe, but we don't know if it was an industrial accident, lab error, or something more malicious."

Jenna rubbed Nikko. He remained calm and relaxed at her side, showing no tension. He plainly felt no wariness in the presence of these strangers. Over the years, she had grown to trust her partner's judgment of character. Along with that, she sensed no subterfuge in the trio's manner and appreciated their willingness to share information.

Taking a chance, she opened herself up a bit. "I don't believe it was an accident, Director Crowe."

"Painter is fine, but why do you think that?"

"I saw a helicopter leaving the base between the time the mayday was sent out and when everything went to hell. It was the same helicopter that offloaded a squad of mercenaries atop that hill. They must have spotted me fleeing from the toxic cloud."

"And went after you to eliminate the only witness."

She nodded. "They came darned close to accomplishing that."

"Can you describe the helicopter? Did you note any insignia or numbers?"

She shook her head. "But I did get a photo of it."

She took a small measure of enjoyment at his shocked expression. As she pulled out her cell phone, she related what had happened at the ghost town, going into as exacting detail as she could. She also called up the camera roll on her phone and went through the pictures. She stopped at the photo of the giant carrying a flamethrower.

"This guy seemed to be the leader of the assault team."

Painter took her phone and zoomed in on his features. "You caught a clear shot of him. Good job."

She felt a flush of pride. "Hopefully he's in some database."

"I hope so, too. We'll definitely run him through facial recognition software, both here and abroad. We'll also get the photo of the helicopter into law enforcement bulletins across the Southwest. They can't have gotten too far."

"They also have a prisoner," she warned. "One of the scientists. Or at least the man was wearing a white lab coat. He tried to escape, but that guy with the flamethrower recaptured him, dragged him back to the helicopter and took off."

Painter looked up from the phone. "Did you get a picture of their prisoner?"

"'Fraid not. By that time I had already hid my phone with Nikko." She patted the husky's side.

Painter studied her closer, then spoke as if reading her mind. "Let me guess. You hoped that once they killed you, the enemy would leave. Then later someone would find Nikko and your phone."

She was impressed. She had mentioned none of that, but the man had figured it all out anyway.

Lisa spoke up. "If they kidnapped someone, I'd lay money on it being Dr. Hess. He would be the highest-value target at that base."

Painter turned to Jenna.

She shrugged. "I couldn't say if it was him. It all happened so fast, and I never got a good look at his face. But it could have been Dr. Hess. Still, there's one other thing. Whoever it was, he was trying to run *into* that toxic cloud before he was recaptured, like he would rather die than be taken away."

"Which suggests the prisoner must have secrets he didn't want the enemy knowing." Painter sounded darkly worried.

"Secrets about what?" she asked.

"That's what we need to find out."

"I'd like to help."

Painter studied her for a long moment. "I'll admit we could use your eyes during this initial investigation. There may have been some detail you've forgotten or didn't think was important at the time. But I must warn you, it will be dangerous."

"It's already dangerous."

"But I believe it'll get much worse. Whatever was started here is likely the tip of something larger and far more deadly."

"Then luckily I've got help." Jenna placed her palm on Nikko's head. He thumped his tail, ready for anything. "What do we do first?"

Painter glanced to Dr. Cummings. "At first light, we go into that toxic wasteland. Look for clues to what went down."

"And perhaps to what got out," his companion added.

Jenna felt the blood coldly settle into her lower gut as she pictured reentering the trap she had just escaped.

What have I gotten myself into?

7

April 28, 3:39 A.M. EDT
Arlington, Virginia

"Why are we always stuck in a basement?" Monk
asked.

Gray glanced over to his best friend and colleague. They were presently buried in the sublevels
of DARPA's new headquarters on Founders Square
in Arlington, Virginia. They had accompanied Dr.
Lucius Raffee back here. The Biological Technologies
Offices took up a large swath of real estate on the
seventh floor. Upstairs, the director of BTO continued to make calls, trying to rouse someone in the
middle of the night who had more than a cursory
knowledge of the research going on at the facility in
California.

In the meantime, they had their own business down here.

"In your case," Gray answered, stretching a kink from his neck as he sat at a computer station, "you're destined to either be holed up in a basement or swinging from some bell tower."

"Is that a Quasimodo crack?" Monk scowled from a neighboring station.

"You *are* developing a bit of a hunch."

"It's from hauling two growing girls in my arms all day. It'd give anyone a bit of a hitch in their back."

The third member of their team made a small sound of exasperation and huddled deeper over his keyboard, typing rapidly. Kat had sent Jason Carter to run a digital forensics analysis on the base's files and logs, to cull through the mountains of data, inventory requests, and countless e-mails for some clue as to what was really going on in California.

The three of them were encased in DARPA's main data center, a small room with a window that overlooked banks of black mainframes, each the size of a refrigerator. The walls of the subbasement were three feet thick and insulated against any form of electronic intrusion or attack.

"I think I found something," Jason said, looking up bleary-eyed. An empty Starbucks cup rested by his elbow. "I ran a search crawler through the stacks, using both Dr. Hess's name and Social Security number. I cross-referenced that with the term *neogenesis.*"

"What did you find?"

"The search ended up still pulling out several terabytes of information. It would take days to sift through it all. So I refined the crawl to cross-reference with *VX gas.*"

"One of the toxins used as a countermeasure by the base?"

He nodded. "I figured those files might address whatever organism that poison was engineered to kill. But look at the first folder that popped up."

Gray crossed over to his station, joined by Monk. He read the file name.

D.A.R.W.I.N.

"What the hell," Monk muttered.

"The folder is massive," Jason said. "I glanced briefly through the first few files. They mostly reference the British Antarctic Survey. They're the major UK group involved in research on that continent. The first paper was highlighted and detailed the group's success in bringing a fifteen-hundred-year-old Antarctic moss back to life."

Gray could see why that would intrigue a scientist like Hess, a researcher interested in exotic life.

"But check out this subfolder titled *History*," Jason said. "I clicked on it, hoping it would offer some background about how this British scientific group was connected to Dr. Hess's research in California. But look what showed up instead."

Jason tapped the folder icon and a series of maps appeared. He clicked on the first one, listed as PIRI REIS _ 1513.

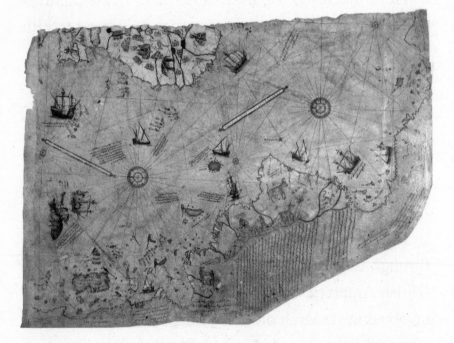

"I've heard about that map," Gray said, leaning closer. "It's got quite a history. A Turkish explorer,

Admiral Piri Reis, compiled this chart on a piece of gazelle skin back in 1513, showing the coast of Africa and South America, along with the northernmost edge of Antarctica."

Gray ran a finger along that coastline on the bottom of the screen.

"What's unusual about that?" Monk asked.

"Antarctica wasn't discovered—at least not officially—until three centuries later, but more mysteriously, some claim that his rendition shows the continent's *true* coastline, a coastline *without* ice." Gray looked up. "The last time the coast was likely free of ice was six thousand years ago."

"But all that's highly disputed," Jason added. "The landmass shown here is most likely not even Antarctica."

"What do you mean?" Monk asked. "The map's a fake?"

"No," Gray said. "The map is authentic, but the Turk admits in a series of notes in the margins that he compiled his map from more ancient charts. So the appearance of this Antarctic coastline is likely just a combination of mapmaking confusion and coincidence."

Monk scratched his chin. "Then what's it doing in a folder among Dr. Hess's files?"

Gray had no answer, but Jason apparently did.

The kid spoke while typing. "This map and several others in the folder are all tagged as coming from a Professor Alex Harrington."

Gray leaned closer.

Jason flashed through various windows rapidly. "I just Googled him. Says here he's a paleobiologist attached to the British Antarctic Survey."

"Paleobiologist?" Monk asked.

"It's a discipline that combines archaeology with evolutionary biology." With his fingers still tapping, Jason added, "And it looks like the professor exchanged a slew of e-mails and phone calls with Dr. Hess, going back almost two decades. They shared a common interest in unusual ecosystems."

Jason glanced up at Gray with one eyebrow high.

Gray understood. *If anyone knows intimate details about Hess's research, it might be this guy.*

"Good work," Gray said. "But we should run this past Raffee upstairs. Maybe the director knows something more about this relationship with the Brits. Can you print this file up?"

Jason scowled, reached down, and yanked a flash drive from a port. "Already copied everything here. It would take hours to print all of this. When you reach the director's office, all you have to do is find the USB port on his computer and—"

"I know how to use a flash drive. I'm not a dinosaur."

"Sorry. You're like twelve years older than me. In digital times, that's at least the Pleistocene era." He hid a grin behind his Starbucks cup as he tried to suck down the last dregs of coffee.

Monk clapped Jason on the shoulder. "I now get what Kat sees in this kid."

Gray pocketed the drive and headed toward the door. "Keep searching those files," he ordered. "See if you can dig up anything else while I talk to Director Raffee."

Gray strode down a short basement hallway, entered the security elevator, and inserted his black Sigma card, emblazoned with a silver Greek letter Σ, the mathematical symbol meaning the "sum of all," which was Sigma Force's credo for combining the best of body and mind to deal with global threats. The card also served as a skeleton key for most locked doors in D.C.

He tapped the button for the seventh floor. As the car rose smoothly upward, Gray pulled out his phone, looking to see if there was any message from Kenny about their father. It was Gray's first chance to check in the past hour, as the subterranean data center had no cell reception. He let out a sigh of relief when he saw no messages.

At least it should be a quiet night.

As the elevator opened, Gray hurried through the dark, deserted corridors. It was a maze up here, made tighter by the stacks of boxes standing outside doors. Scaffolding and paint cans also blocked the way. DARPA was still transitioning from its old headquarters a few blocks away to this one in Founders Square. Some divisions were still in the former building; others had either moved out or were in the process of settling in. He imagined the chaos during the day, but at this late hour, everything was hushed and calm.

Turning a corner, he spotted a cracked open doorway aglow with lamplight. It seemed Raffee had earned a corner office. Gray hurried toward it—when a harsh shout stopped him.

He faded against one wall.

The voice, muffled by distance, hadn't sounded like the director. Gray's hand reached to his service weapon, a SIG Sauer P226, from the shoulder holster under his jacket. As his fingers tightened on the grip, a distinct *pop, pop, pop* echoed to him.

The door to Raffee's office swung open, casting light far down the corridor. Gray slunk lower, sheltering behind a parked Xerox copier in the hallway. He peeked out enough to see four men—dressed in black camo and carrying pistols equipped with silencers— file out and sweep toward his position. Gray glanced behind him. The nearest door was yards away.

Too far.

He calculated quickly. His pistol held a dozen .357 rounds. He would have to make each shot count, especially if the combatants were equipped with body armor. His only advantage at the moment was the element of surprise.

He steeled himself to act, centering his breath.

The last man through the door barked into a radio. "The others are downstairs. Sublevel three. Take the stairs, we'll use the elevator."

He pictured Monk and Jason, ensconced in the small room, unaware of the firestorm headed their way.

Gray waited until the first two men passed his hiding spot. Focused on their goal, they failed to see him crouched behind the Xerox machine.

He fired twice, both head shots—then pivoted and rolled low into the open. He aimed back toward Raffee's office and the other two men. He shot the closest in the knee, dropping him—but even in pain and caught off guard, the man fired his pistol as he fell.

The round whistled past Gray's ear.

Damn . . .

These were plainly hardened professionals, likely former military. As the other's shoulder hit the floor, Gray blasted him point-blank in his face, not taking any further chances.

The final gunman retreated behind a piece of scaffolding, peppering rounds down the hall. Gray stayed flat on the ground, using the body in front of him as a shield. Shots pounded into the man's teammate or ricocheted off the linoleum.

Gray had to act before his target fled back into Raffee's office. From the way the man cast a glance in that direction, it was clearly his intent: to get to safety and call up reinforcements.

Can't let that happen.

Gray popped up and strafed at his adversary's position. Rounds pinged off the scaffolding or buried into the far wall behind his target. The man kept hidden as Gray kept pulling the trigger, his arm straight out, stepping over the body on the ground.

Finally he reached his twelfth shot—and his slide locked.

Out of bullets.

His adversary rose back into view, aiming his smoking weapon, a triumphant sneer fixed on his face.

Gray dropped his SIG Sauer. As the other's eyes twitched to follow its fall, Gray used the distraction to swing up his other arm, revealing the pistol he had hidden behind his thigh, a weapon he had confiscated from the dead man on the floor. He pulled the trigger twice—but once would have been enough.

A clean shot through the eye dropped the final combatant to the floor.

Gray rushed forward and burst into Raffee's office. He didn't hold out much hope that the director was still alive, but he had to check. He found the man in his chair, his jacket off, his sleeves rolled up. A bloom of crimson stained the center of his white shirt and a clean round hole pierced his forehead.

Biting back his fury at the callous execution, he grabbed the phone atop the desk, but he immediately saw the cord had been cut. He took a breath, considered searching for another phone; even if he found one, he wasn't familiar enough with the system to know how to reach the subbasement extension. And with no cell reception down below, the phone in his pocket was useless.

He had no way of warning Monk and Jason.

4:04 A.M.

"Maybe those debunkers are wrong about that Piri Reis map," Jason said, straightening his hunched shoulders from the monitor. He took a deep breath, hiding his nervousness about broaching such a conclusion on his own. He knew about the past exploits of Commander Pierce and his partner and felt out of their league.

I'm only a glorified tech geek.

Still, his gut told him that what he'd found might be important.

"What do you mean?" Monk asked, letting out a jaw-popping yawn. He sat with his boots up on the neighboring desk.

"You'd better check this out."

Monk grumbled under his breath—something about kids always waking him up. He shifted his feet to the ground and slid his chair next to Jason. "What did you find?"

"I've been looking through the other historical maps included in the folder from the British Antarctic Survey and reading through Professor Harrington's notes on them."

"The paleobiologist."

"That's right." Jason cleared his throat, swallowing hard. "Here's another pair of maps of Antarctica, both dating about twenty years after the Piri Reis map was drawn in 1513. One by a fellow named Oronteus Finaeus and the other by Gerardus Mercator."

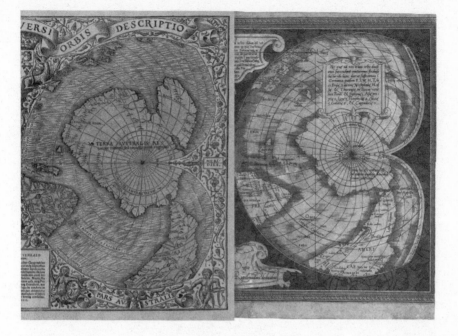

"Notice again that they both show Antarctica without ice," Jason said. "Harrington also notes that the maps reveal mountain ranges, peaks that are currently buried deep under glaciers and should not have been visible back in the sixteenth century. Likewise, the maps include fine details about the continent, like charting Alexander Island and the Weddell Sea."

Monk scrunched his brow. "And both of these maps were drawn centuries *before* the continent was ever officially discovered."

Jason nodded. "And many millennia *after* Antarctica's coastlines were ever free of ice. There's also this map from 1739 by a French cartographer named Buache."

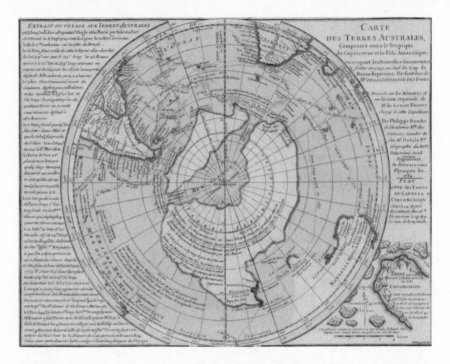

"See how this chart shows Antarctica being depicted as *two* landmasses, separated by a river or sea. That's true. While the continent appears to be one continuous landmass, strip away the ice and it's actually a mountainous archipelago broken up into two main sections: Lesser Antarctica and Greater Antarctica. This detail wasn't known until seismic mapping was done by the U.S. Air Force in 1968."

"And this map was from the eighteenth century?"

"That's right." He couldn't keep the excitement from his voice.

"But what does any of this have to do with Dr. Hess's research in California?"

The question deflated his enthusiasm. "I don't know, but there's a lot more from Professor Harrington in this folder, some files dating back to World War II. Much of it highly redacted. I'll need time to go through it all."

"Sounds like you're going to need a keg of coffee when we get back to Sigma command."

Jason resigned himself to this fact. "I suppose when it comes to mysteries surrounding Antarctica, it's better me than anyone else."

Monk stared harder at him. "What do you mean?"

"Kat . . . I mean Captain Bryant . . . never told you?"

"There's lots of things my wife doesn't tell me. Most of it for my own good." Monk pointed a finger at him. "So spill it, kid."

Jason stared at the man's raised hand, noting the slight unnatural sheen to its surface. It was a prosthetic, eerily lifelike, showing fine hairs on the back and knuckles. Jason knew the story of how Monk had lost the hand and respected the man all the more for it. Afterward, DARPA had replaced it with this marvel of bioengineering, incorporating advanced mechanics and actuators, allowing sensory feedback and surgically precise movements. Jason had also heard that Monk would detach the hand and control it remotely via contact points on the titanium cuff surgically attached to the stump of his wrist.

Jason would love to see such a performance someday.

"If you're done staring . . ." Monk warned, a slight growl in his voice.

"Sorry."

"You mentioned you had a connection to Antarctica."

"I once lived there, but it's been a while. My mom, stepdad, and sister are still there . . . near McMurdo Station."

Monk squinted at him, sensing there was more to his story, adventures left untold, but he left it there. "Then with your background, maybe you should be the one to interview this Harrington guy. Find out what the Brit knows."

Jason perked up. He always wanted to do fieldwork someday, and this might be the opening he needed. Anything to break free of motherboards, logic circuits, and code-breaking algorithms.

A door closed down the hallway, the sound echoing to them.

Monk stood up.

Jason glanced over his shoulder. "Sounds like Commander Pierce is back."

Hopefully with something more exciting to do than look at maps.

"Kid, do you have a side arm?"

Only now did he note how tense his companion had gone. All that easygoing manner had washed out of his form.

"No . . ." Jason squeaked out.

"Neither do I, but that was the stairwell door. Not the elevator. Don't think Gray needs the exercise at this late hour."

The heavy tread of multiple boots on concrete reached them.

Monk turned to Jason, his gaze dead serious. "I'm open to any bright ideas, kid."

4:06 A.M.

Gray worked swiftly, knowing every second counted.

As he swept along the seventh-floor hallway, he collected extra magazines from the dead, making sure they matched the weapon he had swiped. He didn't know how many others were downstairs, but he was taking no chances. In a firefight, the difference between life and death could be a single round.

"I'm heading below," he said, pinning his cell phone to his ear with his shoulder. After finding Raffee dead, he had placed a quick call to Sigma for help.

"I'll get units to you as soon as I can." Kat sounded tense, but even with her husband in harm's way, she stayed focused. "Be careful."

"Only as careful as I need to be."

He hung up as he reached the end of the corridor. He paused long enough to grab a hammer from a construction worker's toolbox. Despite Kat's efforts, he estimated it would still take law enforcement several minutes to arrive on-site.

Too late to help Monk and Jason.

Gray stepped to the fire alarm on the wall and yanked the red lever down. An alarm immediately rang out. His goal was to light a fire under the enemy, hopefully scare them into flight. Failing that, it might make them at least hurry, perhaps even make needless mistakes.

Plus the racket should help cover his own approach.

He crossed to the elevator bay, knowing the stairwell would be guarded, and entered the same cage he took to get here. He pressed one of the lower floor buttons, but as soon as he felt the cage descend half a floor, he hit the stop button. A buzzing alarm sounded as the cage came to an abrupt halt, but the noise was easily drowned out by the louder clamor of the fire system.

Using the claw-toothed hammer, he pried open the inner door of the elevator. As he'd hoped, the cage had stopped shy of the sixth floor, exposing the top half of the exterior door on that level. He reached and tugged the latch to manually release those doors. Once free, he ducked out of the cage—only to turn back and crawl beneath the stalled elevator.

The open shaft yawned below him.

With the cage above his head, he swung out onto the emergency ladder that ran down the wall to his left. Once mounted, he slid along its length, ignoring the individual rungs. He used his hands and feet to occasionally brake to control his speed, counting the floors as he fell past them. In twenty seconds, he had reached the subbasement doors marked L3.

Hanging by one hand, he pulled the latch to release those doors, then lunged out as soon as they parted. He landed and skidded on his knees across the floor, his body twisted to face the neighboring stairwell door. As he had suspected, a lone gunman stood guard, holding the way open with one foot, keeping an eye on the stairs.

Gray already had his stolen pistol out, still outfitted with a silencer. He shot the man in the head, the suppressed gunshot little more than a harsh cough. He quickly swung his gun toward the data center down the hall.

Shadows moved in there, along with hushed, angry voices.

"Maybe they were never here," he heard one assailant call out sharply. "That dead guy could've lied about someone being down here."

Gray let out a breath. So Monk and Jason hadn't been found. Maybe they'd already made it upstairs. But he had to be certain, especially after hearing a voice, full of command, bark out.

"We're out of bloody time!"

Another voice: "Done! Got the worm delivered into the servers. It'll delete all files here and any redundant backups elsewhere."

"Then get those last charges set and move out!"

With the fire alarm still ringing, Gray moved down the hallway to the data center's open door. He took a fast glance inside before ducking back out of sight.

Four men.

They were all staring through the window to the rows of mainframes in the neighboring room.

Must be more men in there, setting the final charges.

Their mission was clearly to compromise those servers. He pictured Lucius Raffee upstairs. He imagined the handful of security guards in the building had suffered a similar fate. Had the director simply been at the wrong time and place, or was his execution another goal of this assault team? An hour ago, he had heard from Painter about the attempt to eliminate the only witness to events in California. Was this attack a part of that, an attempt to erase all trails that led back to that base?

He had no way of knowing—except the one in command sounded like he had a British accent. He recalled Jason's discovery of the connection between Dr. Hess's work and a research team out of England.

Could just be a coincidence, but maybe not.

"All set!" a voice called from the server farm.

"Clear out," the leader said. "Double-time before we're pinned down here."

Gray kept to the side of the doorway, half hidden behind a trash can. He was still mostly in the open, but he hoped that in their mad rush to flee, they'd dash right past him.

As expected, men burst out of the control room and pounded down the hallway toward the stairwell— where the guard's body still lay in shadows.

Gray didn't have much time to act.

As soon as the last man barreled out, Gray rolled across the threshold and into the data center. He kicked the door closed behind him, swiping his black Sigma card to lock it from the inside.

A shout burst from the hallway outside.

Gray stood, staring through the bulletproof window in the door.

A flashlight clicked on down the corridor, revealing a cluster of men around their fallen teammate. The tallest of the lot—burly-chested, with chiseled aristocratic features—turned and stared back at Gray.

They made eye contact across the distance, the other glowering in fury.

A teammate touched the man's shoulder and pointed to his watch. They plainly had no time to force Gray out of the locked room, not with law enforcement closing a noose around the area and the charges about to blow.

With a silent growl fixed to his lips, the leader waved the others up the stairs, then fled with them.

Gray turned and opened the door that led into the server farm. A half flight of metal stairs led down to the air-conditioned, insulated space. From his perch, he searched the rows of tall black mainframes. He noted packages of C-4 affixed to the closest racks, their timers glowing, all counting down from 90 seconds.

He bellowed into the space. "Monk! Jason!"

Along the back row, a door to one of the towering refrigerator-sized mainframes swung open. Monk and Jason fell out, untangling their limbs.

Thank God . . .

Gray waved. "Move your asses!"

They came running, dodging down the rows of servers. The pair bounded up the metal stairs to reach the data center room.

Gray unlocked the door to the hallway with a swipe of his card.

Monk slapped Jason on the back. "Quick thinking, kid."

Jason got knocked a step forward but collected himself. "It's common for server farms to be overbuilt," he explained, "to leave empty racks for future expansion. Figured DARPA would do the same."

Gray led them out and sprinted for the stairs. "This way."

Reaching the stairwell door, he found no body, only a pool of blood.

"See you had some trouble reaching us," Monk said, noting the stain.

"More men were upstairs, too. They executed Dr. Raffee."

Monk swore as they rushed upward, sprinting from landing to landing. "Any idea who they were?"

"They took the body below, but there are four more on the seventh floor. We might be able to ID them."

That's if there's a building still standing after all of this.

They burst out onto the ground floor and ran across the lobby. Gray spotted the slack form of one of the building's security guards collapsed behind his desk. Anger fired through him anew. He pictured the face of the assault team leader, and silently promised to even the score.

But that would have to wait.

Gray shoved out the front doors and raced across the apron of patios with the others. As they reached the sidewalk along North Randolph Street, a low rumble shook the ground, accompanied by a deep boom. Several of the building's lower windows shattered outward. Moments later, black smoke began to roll out into the night.

In the distance, a chorus of sirens echoed, descending toward their location.

Monk sighed heavily. "So much for DARPA's big move."

Gray herded the others away, leaving the cleanup to the approaching emergency crews. He wanted to get back to Sigma command, but more important, he wanted answers.

Who the hell sent that team . . . and why?

8

April 28, 6:02 A.M. PDT
Sierra Nevada Mountains, California

I hope I'm doing this right . . .

Jenna stood in the staging tent at the rally point outside of the hot zone. Through the translucent walls, the sunrise was a muffled brightness to the east. The air inside the tent smelled of a slurry of acidic chemicals and body odor.

Something must have shown on her face because Dr. Cummings—*Lisa,* she reminded herself to call her—came over to her side. Both of them were already in their one-piece disposable Tyvek suits, which were said to be impermeable to most chemicals.

At least I certainly hope so.

As an additional safeguard, they were instructed to duct tape the ends of their gloves to the sleeves of their suits.

"Looks good," Lisa said, checking her over. "I'll help you into the next layer."

"Thanks."

They crossed to a row of bright red encapsulation suits that hung from a rolling rack. The second layer would cover them from head to toe, completely sealing them from the outside atmosphere. They would breathe inside via air masks and shoulder-harnessed oxygen tanks.

Together the two women helped each other into the respective suits. Jenna felt a claustrophobic moment of panic as the final seal was secured, gasping within her mask. Trying to hide it, she stood up and took a few steps, as if testing the weight of the tanks.

"Strutting the runway, I see." This came over the voice-actuated radio fitted into their air masks.

She turned to see Gunnery Sergeant Drake salute her, equally encased in what was euphemistically called a bunny suit.

"How could I not?" she responded back. "Especially when I'm wearing the height of fashion."

She tried to sound light, but it came out more doleful to her ear.

"You'll be fine," Drake said, reaching to give her a pat on the shoulder.

She shied away, fearful of ripping something.

"The suits are tougher than they look," Lisa assured her.

The woman's brother, Josh, stood behind her, also suited up. Another two Marines would be joining them in this expedition, but in her nervousness, she had already forgotten their names.

The radio gave a burst of digital noise, then a new voice intruded. "Transport's ready to move you all out."

It was Director Crowe. He was ten miles away, back at the Marine base, overseeing this mission and coordinating the emergency response teams around the region.

His other duty—and an important one—was to pet-sit Nikko.

She already missed the husky. His absence left her feeling unbalanced, but no one made biohazard suits for dogs.

"How's the video feed from the cameras?" Lisa asked, waving a hand in front of her face.

"Perfect," Painter replied. "With the satellite connection, I should be able to watch over your shoulders as you proceed. So be careful out there. Follow proper protocols and avoid any unnecessary risks."

"Yes, Dad," Josh mumbled under his breath, but it still came through clearly over their sensitive radios.

Painter ignored him and continued. "So far the margins of the hot zone seem to be remaining stable, but we don't know what other dangers are out there."

Jenna stared through the translucent walls of the tent, thinking about where they were going. The quarantine border was a mile off. The toxic gas had finally reached its maximum spread in the last few hours, settling to the ground. Chemical monitoring stations ringed the area, watching in case the winds shifted and stirred up the dirt and sand.

Their goal—ground zero of the blast site—was twenty miles off.

At this point, no one knew if whatever broke containment at the base had been neutralized. She tried to imagine anything surviving both the heat of the explosion and that toxic cloud.

She shivered in her suit at the very thought.

Their mission was simple enough: Collect samples, survey the damage, and look for any clues to what happened.

Painter had encouraged her to stay at the Marine base, to remotely observe the excursion into the hot zone alongside him. But she had always been a boots-on-the-ground sort of girl. It was why she had joined the park rangers, to get her hands dirty.

She had also insisted on coming along for another reason. A nagging worry had kept her up most of the night, tossing and turning: *If I had gotten to the base earlier, could I have done something to stop all of this?*

Perhaps it was a foolish conceit, born more of pride than reality, but she could not shake it. Especially after learning over thirty people had lost their lives at the station. As a park ranger, with a sworn duty to uphold the law, she refused to be sidelined in this investigation.

Not on my home turf.

"Okay, guys and gals," Drake said, leading the way, "let's mount up."

Jenna followed with the others, shifting the shoulder harness to better balance her tanks. It was already getting warm inside her suit. They exited the tent, like a group of astronauts stepping out onto an alien landscape. She recalled the tourist yesterday claiming how Mono Lake looked like the surface of Mars.

And here I am now . . . further proving his point.

Outside, a green military Hummer stood parked on the road heading into the hot zone. The vehicle had been configured as a troop carrier, with a crew cab in front and an open bed in the back with bench seats. One of their Marine escorts—Lance Corporal Schmitt, she suddenly recalled—climbed behind the wheel. The rest of them were assisted into the rear bed.

Once they were all seated, Drake patted his gloved palm on the cab. "All set, Schmitty."

The engine coughed to life and rumbled. Then they were moving, climbing toward the border of the quarantine zone. Jenna swallowed hard and kept checking the sealed zippers on her suit.

Lisa sat next to her. "Shouldn't be much to worry about. The majority of the toxin has settled and is rapidly losing potency."

Still, Jenna felt little relief, especially after seeing the cloud of dust kicked up by the wide tires over the gravel road. She fought to even her breathing, to preserve her oxygen supply. They had additional tanks loaded on board, but the goal was not to have to switch them out in the hot zone if possible.

After a couple of minutes, Lance Corporal Schmitt tapped his horn and pointed an arm out the open window.

A waist-high cylinder—one of the chemical monitors—sat roadside. A tall antenna sprouted from its top, along with a three-cup anemometer used to gauge wind speeds. Thankfully the small vane remained perfectly still.

Drake eyeballed it as the vehicle trundled past the marker. "Kiss the clean air good-bye, folks."

They were entering the hot zone.

The road climbed higher into the scrubby hills, the view interrupted by occasional stands of Jeffrey pines.

Everything looked fine at first, just another day-trip into the mountains. Then the first mule deer appeared alongside the shoulder of the road. It lay on its flank, its neck twisted from a final convulsion, a thick pink tongue protruding from soft lips.

Jenna gulped and looked away, but after another mile, there was no relief in any direction. Wildlife in the basin was notoriously shy, hard to find, especially during the day. But the explosion, the smoke, and the poison seemed to have driven everything out of their dens, warrens, and holes.

Soon their tires crunched over the broken bodies of seagulls, rock wrens, and ground squirrels. Furred lumps of cottontails and jackrabbits dotted the surrounding slopes. Larger shadows marked a felled herd of mule deer. Elsewhere one of the area's rare bighorn sheep lay crashed on its front legs, curled horns tangled in a thornbush.

A tear rolled down her cheek. She couldn't wipe it away. Even as a park ranger, she had never imagined there was so much hidden life in these hills.

Now all dead.

The truck made a stop every mile. Drake would take soil samples while Lisa gathered hair and tissue specimens from the dead animals. Jenna helped her try to collect a blood sample from a black bear. Unfortunately, when they rolled the bulk over for a jugular stick, Jenna found a small cub crushed under its mother's bulk.

Seeing this, Lisa stopped and strode away. "That's enough," she said. "That's enough."

The quiet banter among them died away with each successive mile, until the only noises were their own breathing, the rumble of the engine, and the crunch of the tires.

When they were about three miles out from ground zero, Drake finally spoke up again. "Look at the vegetation covering the slope up ahead."

Jenna rose from the bench for a better look.

Until now, the hills had looked normal enough, covered by sagebrush interspersed with monkeyflower, phlox, and a few stands of pinyon pines. But up ahead that all changed. On both sides of the road, the slopes were blackened, without a single shoot of green showing.

"Could the explosion have triggered a brush fire?" Lisa asked.

Jenna shook her head. She had plenty of experience with such blazes, some triggered by lightning strikes, others by careless campers. Between the dry grasses and combustible brush, flames could clear through acres in minutes. All that would be left would be ash and the burned trunks of some of the larger pines.

"This was no fire," Jenna said.

"Let's get a closer look." Lisa touched the gunnery sergeant's arm.

"Stop the truck," Drake ordered.

The driver braked at the edge of the blackened fields.

Drake turned to Lisa and Jenna. "Maybe you two should stay here until we're sure it's safe."

Jenna rolled her eyes.

There was nothing *safe* about any of this.

She crossed to the rear of the Hummer and hopped out. Lisa followed, accompanied by the others.

"Grab the collection kits," Lisa ordered her brother.

"Got 'em," Josh answered, leaping out of the bed and landing lightly.

With the driver staying behind the wheel, the group set off into the meadow. Jenna stepped carefully. So much that grew in this harsh, alkaline environment had evolved some nasty defenses: long thorns, hooked barbs, sharp branches. She feared puncturing or compromising the integrity of her suit.

They all edged carefully across a landscape of greens, purples, and reds toward the swath of darkness. It looked like a shadow had fallen over the upper half of the hill. The demarcation line between the two areas appeared crisp from a distance, but as they reached the border, it was less well defined, a mix of healthy and dead flora.

Lisa directed her brother. "Josh, you collect a plant that looks healthy in this zone. I'll bag up one of the charred-looking specimens." She pointed to Drake. "Let's get soil samples here, too."

As everyone set off to obey, Jenna kept to Lisa's side. Together they stepped into the shadowy fields and crouched beside a patch of tall, thin plants, each stalk crowned by black petals.

"*Castilleja*," Jenna said. "Desert paintbrush. Sometimes called prairie-fire because of its bright red flowers. They're just beginning to bloom this time of year."

She pointed to a healthy spread of paintbrush along the lower slopes, where the flowers budded in shades of crimson.

Lisa grabbed the base of one of the diseased plants and tugged it free of the soil, roots and all. But as she tried to fold it into a large plastic specimen bag, the stalk and leaves crumbled apart, like a sculpture made of sand.

Jenna helped hold open the bag to catch the detritus as it fell away. Once done, they both stood. Lisa gazed toward the summit of the hill.

"Let's go look," Jenna said, wanting to know the extent of the damage.

Placing each boot with great care, they scaled the slope to the ridgeline. Jenna gasped as the view opened up ahead. For as far as she could see, black hills spread outward, and a perfect stillness blanketed the area.

Off in the distance, a chain-link fence cut across the dead hills, marking the official border of the research station.

"Could that toxic cloud have caused this die-off?" Jenna asked. "Was the gas somehow extra deadly this close to the base?"

"Maybe, but I doubt it."

Jenna heard the fear in her voice and knew what troubled her.

Was this a sign that something had escaped the base? Jenna stared around her. *Worst of all, could it still be active?*

Lisa retreated from the sight, drawing Jenna with her. "Let's continue to ground zero. Search for any evidence and get back to the staging area with our specimens. Then maybe we'll have some answers."

Returning to the edge of the dark field, they found Drake and his fellow Marine pounding in a row of wooden stakes along the margin, delineating the border. To the side, Josh stood with all of the team's samples—both soil and plants—collected in a box.

Together they returned to the Hummer, climbed back into the bed, and continued their journey toward the blasted heart of the hot zone.

Jenna gaped at the destruction around them, noting the corpse of a coyote in a ditch, its fur mostly gone, its body as blackened as the fields.

She stared in the direction of the base.

What horror did you create, Dr. Hess?

6:43 A.M. PDT
Baja California, Mexico

Kendall Hess stood alongside the small prop plane as it was being refueled. He'd been allowed to stretch his legs. His towering guard Mateo passed a stack of hundred-dollar bills wrapped with a rubber band to a local man, his eyes wary under the brim of a cowboy hat.

Likely a drug smuggler, Kendall imagined. The unmarked airstrip and the lone refueling truck added weight to this deduction.

After the events in the mountains, Kendall had done his best to track their route south. Mateo had abandoned the helicopter in the Nevada desert and switched to a private plane at a small airfield. He changed again to this Cessna in Arizona and used it to cross the border just before sunrise. Since then, they had been traveling along the Baja peninsula. He guessed they were some-where south of the city of San Felipe.

In the distance, the Sea of Cortez shone brightly, an azure brilliance against the rolling dunes of the sur-rounding desert. It was a harsh, empty landscape, spiked by a few cacti.

He recognized the tall, spiny plants. *Pachycereus pringlei*, called elephant cacti for their sheer size. This particular species had garnered his scientific attention because of its ability to survive in such hostile lands. It grew to well over ten meters and was capable of living for over a thousand years, often on soil that was little more than rock. It accomplished that through a symbi-otic relationship with a unique bacterium. The micro-organism helped break down stone and fix nitrogen for the plant. The relationship was so successful that the cactus packed the bacteria into its own seeds.

Kendall had briefly studied that microbe as part of his research into extremophiles, but it proved to be a dead end.

Let's hope the same can't be said for me.

"Back in," Mateo ordered gruffly.

Knowing he had no choice, Kendall ducked under the wing and climbed into the cabin, shadowed by the bulk of his guard. The aircraft's pilot was the same man who had flown them from California. As soon as

Kendall was seated, the Cessna began rolling along the runway, then lifted off and aimed south yet again.

Where are they taking me?

He didn't know the answer to that, but he knew who waited for him at the other end. It was the same man who had orchestrated the attack, and who likely had been manipulating Kendall's research from afar for the past decade.

The bastard—once a colleague—had been declared dead eleven years ago. His plane had crashed in the Congo, and a week later, searchers found the wreckage, along with the charred remains of what appeared to be the flight crew and passengers. Kendall now knew that was a lie, a fabrication, but at the time, he had been secretly relieved to hear about the man's death, fearful of the dark path he had been following.

If he's still pursuing that line of research . . .

Kendall trembled with dread, knowing what he had created in his own lab, what had been unleashed in California. With a shudder, he could guess why he had been kidnapped.

God help us all.

6:46 A.M. PDT

Painter leaned closer to the monitor, shadowed by the base commander, Colonel Bozeman. The computer screen was broken up into five sections, the video feed coming from the various members of the expeditionary team. Through their cameras, he studied the blasted landscape as the truck approached the security fence around the former base.

"Don't get too close to the actual station," he radioed, warning the team. "Most of that base is buried underground. Who knows what's left of its structural integrity after that blast? The mass of the truck—even your own body weight—could trigger a collapse. We don't want you all accidentally dropping into a toxic sinkhole."

"We wouldn't like that either, sir," Drake answered.

Colonel Bozeman leaned over Painter's shoulder and spoke into the microphone. "Listen to the director, Drake. No lip. He's in command."

"Yes, sir."

As the colonel straightened, Painter continued. "From the schematics of the base, you should keep at least two hundred yards back. Any closer and you'll find yourself parked over the station itself."

"Don't think that's going to be a problem," Drake replied.

On the screen, the Hummer trundled through the open gate and up the entry road a short distance where it stopped.

"Are you seeing this?" Drake asked.

To get a better view, Painter tapped one section on the monitor, zooming in on that feed. It came from the camera built into Lisa's suit. She stood in the bed of the truck, giving him a good vantage of the road ahead.

Fifty yards away, a large crater had been blown out of the flank of the hill. A pall of smoke hung over the blast site. The span of destruction was much greater than he had anticipated. It seemed Dr. Hess had been taking no chances when he designed this fail-safe.

"I think more than just the base collapsed," Jenna radioed.

Nikko stirred at Painter's feet, rising to his haunches, one ear cocked to the sound of his master's voice.

"What do you mean?" he asked.

"Rumor has it that the military built this station inside an already existing mine. One from the gold rush era. Looks like when the station blew, it collapsed sections of the surrounding tunnels, too."

That can't be good.

Painter swung to Bozeman. "Do we have any map or survey of that old mine?"

"I'll go check." He rushed out, already bellowing commands to his staff.

Painter took a deep breath and spoke again. "Until we know the full extent of those old tunnels, you should pull back."

"What about investigating ground zero?" Lisa asked.

"From the looks of it, you're not going to find anything useful anyway. It's safer if you—"

The image shuddered on the screen.

Shouts erupted.

Painter watched as Lisa's hands grabbed the roll bar behind the cab. The front end of the Hummer tilted downward, the ground crumbling away beneath it. Fissures shattered outward toward the large crater.

On the screen, Drake slammed his palm repeatedly on the top of the cab. "Go, go, go!"

The engine roared into reverse. He heard tires tearing into gravel.

Nikko leaped to his feet, growling to match the timbre of the straining motor.

Slowly the truck retreated, the front end climbing out of the ever-widening hole. The driver drove backward, zigzagging for traction on the unsteady ground. A breathless moment later, they barreled in reverse through the gates and onto the outer road.

Ahead, the sinkhole crumbled and fell away into the abandoned mine, but it did not pursue them any further.

Drake spoke up. "I say we listen to the director and get our asses out of here."

No one argued.

Painter leaned back and patted Nikko on the flank. "They're okay."

He sought to calm the dog as much as his own pounding heart. He switched to another video feed—this one coming from Josh's camera. As the young man helped his sister down to the bench, Painter studied her face, her features partially obscured by the mask. He noted strands of hair plastered to her cheeks by sweat, but she appeared otherwise unfazed and more important—

She's safe.

That was victory enough for him.

The expedition might not have learned anything significant about the base, but hopefully the collected samples would help lead them in the right direction.

The truck began to turn around outside the gate when Jenna spoke up again. "Wait!"

Drake called for the driver to stop.

Painter sat back up.

"I just realized something. I don't know if it's important, but I forgot to mention it earlier." She pointed to the gate. "When I arrived last night, this was open. Like it is now. I didn't think too much of it at the time, but now it's got me wondering."

Painter followed her train of thought. *The enemy had departed by helicopter. Likely that's the way they arrived, too.*

"Who left the gate open?" Jenna asked. "What if it wasn't someone *entering* the base, but someone *fleeing* out?"

Painter considered the timeline. "When the mayday was dispatched by the base's system analyst, she mentioned the containment breach, but nothing about an attack."

"Which means someone—someone on the inside—likely sabotaged the base in advance, setting everything in motion. And knowing what was coming, the saboteur fled before all hell broke loose."

Painter weighed the likelihood of this scenario. "Makes some sense. The resulting chaos would've helped cover the arrival of the assault team, allowing them to land and nab Hess."

Jenna pointed to the crater. "And with this level of destruction, it would take weeks, if not months, to find and identify all the bodies. No one would know Hess had been snatched for quite some time."

"Which goes to explain why the enemy was so determined to silence *you*. They didn't know how much you saw and couldn't risk letting knowledge of the kidnapping get out."

"But they failed," Jenna added. "And now we know someone probably fled from here, too. The only road out of these hills passes through either Mono City or Lee Vining. Both towns have multiple traffic cameras. If we could track the saboteur down . . ."

We might learn what really happened here—and why.

Earlier, Painter had had a full rundown on events back in D.C., detailing the attack on DARPA's headquarters and the execution of Dr. Lucius Raffee. Someone was clearly trying to erase all ties to this base.

But now they had some hope of getting a jump on them.

Painter scratched Nikko behind the ear.

You have one smart owner.

He leaned to the microphone. "Okay, good job everyone. Let's get you all home safe."

6:55 A.M.

Lisa sat in sullen silence as the Hummer descended out of the hills. In her head, she reviewed the protocols for their return to the forward staging area.

At the border, a group of Marines—working with a team from the CDC—had already constructed a makeshift quarantine garage for the truck. After offloading inside there, she and the others would strip and go through multiple decontamination stages. Additionally, the team would be isolated for twelve hours to watch for any signs of contagion or contamination.

She stared at the rolling black hills, recognizing the seriousness of this threat. She estimated this dead zone covered at least fifty square miles.

But what did it mean? Had the explosion aerosolized whatever was growing in that lab, seeded it far and wide? If so, had Dr. Hess's toxic countermeasures managed to neutralize it?

The only answers lay back at the Marine base, where a Level 4 biolab was being set up within a hangar. She was anxious to get back there to study the samples and specimens.

Finally, green hills appeared ahead, softened by the morning light. It looked like they were traveling out of a black-and-white film toward something shot in Technicolor. She took hope from that beauty, from the resilience of nature.

Then she spotted all the bodies in the hills—birds, deer, even lizards and snakes—and a heavy despair settled over her shoulders. Or maybe it was these darned oxygen tanks. She shifted her harness trying to get more comfortable.

"Look over there." Jenna pointed toward the edge of the blackened swath.

Then Lisa saw it, too. "Stop the truck," she ordered Drake.

He obeyed, and the vehicle ground to a halt.

To the side of the road, the line of wooden stakes that marked the boundary of the dead zone was still where the Marines had pounded them into place earlier. Only now, that dark shadow had spread past that margin, edging farther down that green slope.

"It's still spreading," Jenna said, her voice hushed.

Drake swore.

Lisa swallowed away the dry fear in her mouth. "We should measure how far it's moved past the stakes." She ducked to check the clock on the dash of the Hummer. "We can calculate a rough estimate about how fast it's moving."

"I'm on it," Drake said.

The gunnery sergeant retrieved a tape measure from an equipment locker at the back of the bed and hopped down to the road.

Josh followed him. "I'll help you."

Lisa moved to join them, but Painter came on the radio. "Lisa, I've got you on a private channel."

She stopped, gripping the edge of the truck bed. She waved for the others to continue. "What is it?"

"If that organism is still alive, if it wasn't killed by the toxins in the gas, we might have to incinerate the area."

"But will fire actually kill it?"

"I think it might."

"Why?"

"The assault team arrived with a *flamethrower* as a part of their gear. It's an unusual choice."

Lisa understood. "Unless they were anticipating the need for such a weapon."

"Exactly. The team had been sent to raid a lab with a known contamination breach. Someone might have dispatched them with the means to blaze a safe path to reach Hess."

"I hope you're right." She looked toward the carcasses littering the landscape. "Maybe the secondary goal of the nerve gas—if the toxins failed to kill the organism—was to kill anything that could move, anything that might carry this organism out of the area."

"To keep the contagion localized."

She nodded to herself. This conversation made her even more anxious to get to that biolab, to test these theories.

A sharp cry drew her attention beyond the truck. Josh was down on one knee. Drake helped her brother up.

"Gotta watch those hidden rocks up here," Drake said.

Josh shook loose of the man's grip and backed a step. He was staring down at his left leg. "I got stabbed. A thorn, I think."

"Let me see."

Drake began to examine it—but Lisa yelled over to him. "Stay back!" She hopped down and hurried toward them. "Josh, don't move."

She reached the two men, noting her brother's face had gone pale.

She crouched and examined the tear in his suit and the sliver of branch pinned to his leg by an imbedded thorn.

The bit of stem and leaf were both black.

"Get duct tape!" Drake yelled to the other Marine; then to Lisa he said, "We can patch up his suit. It's not a big rip."

Instead, Lisa reached her gloved fingers and tore the hole larger. She got a peek at Josh's shin. The skin around the impaled black thorn had already gone a purplish red.

"Really stings," Josh said, wincing.

Lisa turned to Drake. "We need rope. A belt. Something to make a tourniquet."

Drake ran off.

"You're going to be fine," Lisa said, but even her words sounded rote and unconvincing. She stood with her kid brother, finding his hand and squeezing tightly.

Behind his mask, Josh breathed hard, his eyes narrowed by pain. He looked a decade younger, the fear turning him into a boy looking to his older sister for help.

Words echoed in her head.

Kill us . . . kill us all.

Drake came pounding back, dragging everyone but the driver with him. He had a length of climbing rope in his hands. She helped secure it around Josh's thigh.

"Make it as tight as you can," she said.

Jenna stood with her arms anxiously crossed, clearly recognizing the threat. "Will the tourniquet keep it from spreading?"

Lisa didn't answer, not wanting to lie.

Once the rope was secure, dug deep into the muscles of Josh's thigh, the Marines helped haul Josh back to the Hummer. As they lifted him into the bed, Lisa crossed to the equipment box and retrieved what she needed.

Painter came on over the private line. "Lisa . . ."

"It has to be done," she whispered back.

"At least wait until you get back here."

"We'll lose too much time."

Drake gaped when she turned, seeing what she was carrying. She passed him the fire axe.

"At the knee," she said. "Take it off at the knee."

9

"That's him," Gray said.

He leaned on his fists atop the computer station in Sigma's nerve center. He was alone with Kat, though Jason was in the neighboring room, visible through the window, working on the files they'd recovered from DARPA's servers.

Thank God I still had that flash drive with me.

Concentrating on the monitor, Gray stared at the photo of the man on the screen: his chiseled features, his pinched nose, his cropped blond hair. He remembered that same face glowering at him from the end of the hallway back at DARPA's headquarters.

"You're sure it's him?" Kat asked.

"Without a doubt. Who is he?"

Hours ago, after returning to Sigma command from Arlington, Gray had been debriefed by Kat. She also had him sit down with a sketch artist, while another team had collected the bodies from the seventh floor hallway of DARPA. They found no identification on the dead, but fingerprints were taken. It hadn't taken Kat long to determine they were all former British special forces soldiers, specifically SAS—22nd Special Air Service. Most likely they had become mercenaries for hire, some elite team that fetched a steep price.

Kat pointed to the screen. "Their leader here is Major Dylan Wright."

"Let me guess. He's also SAS."

"Close. He's British special forces, but he was with the SBS."

Special Boat Service.

Gray knew about that UK detachment. The unit was established in World War II to conduct raids on German targets, mostly in the Mediterranean, Aegean, and Adriatic seas. Now they were deployed worldwide as a counterterrorist group.

"If I had to guess," Kat said, "I'd say this group was made up of former members of the British X Squadron. That specialized unit formed in 2004, made up of volunteers from both SAS and SBS."

Same as the team that raided DARPA.

"X Squadron is considered the best of the best," Kat finished.

"So who hired these ex-soldiers?" Gray asked.

"Unknown, but I've got the word out across various intelligence services, along with some contacts in the shadowy guns-for-hire world. Hopefully we'll have some answers in the next few hours." Kat glanced his way, a sympathetic cast to her eyes. "In the meantime, if you want to attend to any personal matters, now should be a good time."

Gray sighed. He'd already had a nap and swung by his father's house. The day nurse had been there, and they had talked at length about installing door alarms and other security measures to help keep his father safe at night. But even she had admitted it was a stopgap plan at best, and that he and Kenny needed to think about taking that next step, which meant moving their father out of his home—if not into a memory care unit, at least into an assisted living facility.

"I think I'll go hit the gym instead," he said, needing to clear his head. "Work off some steam."

Kat stared at him a second longer, then slowly nodded. "I think Monk is down there now."

Knuckles rapped on glass behind them, drawing their attention around. Jason waved for Kat to join him. Curious, Gray followed her into the neighboring office.

Kat crossed behind the desk to join Jason. "Are you making any headway with those files?"

"Some. But I wish I had been able to recover more than this single folder of information about the base. It's like trying to get a complete picture of a room by peeking through a keyhole. If only I'd had more time to back up additional files . . ."

Kat touched him on the shoulder. "The first thing you have to accept in the intelligence business is that you *never* have the complete picture. You learn to deal with the facts at hand and do your best to infer from there."

Jason frowned, still plainly unsatisfied. From the shadowy bags under his eyes and the Rockstar energy drink by his elbow, it looked like the kid hadn't slept at all.

"I did put in a call to the British Antarctic Survey," Jason added, "to try to reach Professor Harrington, that paleobiologist who was in regular contact with Dr. Hess. He may be able to fill in a lot of the blanks in our investigation."

"Hopefully so," Kat said. "But why did you call us in here? Did you find something?"

"Maybe, but I wanted to run it past you. After so many hours buried in these files, I may be too close. I need fresh eyes."

"No worries. I've been there many times myself. Go ahead and use us as a sounding board."

Gray was struck by how gentle Kat was with the young man. It was a sharp contrast to her usual steely-eyed manner and no-nonsense sensibility. When he'd first met Kat, he felt like he always had to stand a little taller, his back a little straighter. She had that effect on people. Maybe it was the result of raising two girls, but here was a different side to her. While it was a far cry from warm and cuddly, she was clearly a good mentor.

Jason straightened in his seat, his manner more confident. "Okay, but you'll have to bear with me, as I've been neck-deep in what various British military and research teams were doing in Antarctica."

Kat glanced over to Gray, her meaning clear. *British military again.* Same as the team who had raided DARPA. *Could there be a connection?*

"Go on," Kat encouraged Jason.

"Before I get to the history, let's start with more current events. Back in 1961, the international Antarctic Treaty came into force, basically declaring that the continent was off-limits to territorial claims, that it was to be used for peaceful purposes only. Since then, a multitude of bases have been established across the breadth of Antarctica. Some are purely research outposts, but a majority—despite the treaty—are indeed joint military/research bases."

Similar to the one in California, Gray realized.

"But prior to that treaty, an ongoing turf war was waged on that continent by international communities. Everyone wanted to claim a piece of that frozen pie. This fighting came to a head during World War II, due to the use of the Southern Ocean as a haven for Nazi U-boats. But even prior to the war, Germany was very aggressive in attempting to stake a claim. In 1938, they established the Deutsche Antarktische Expedition to explore the continent and set up a base."

Jason tapped the keyboard and brought up an emblem of the German team.

"The official reason for this expedition was to look for a site to establish a whaling station, but most believed they were actually scouting locations for a German naval base. Oddly enough they even hired the famous American polar explorer, Richard E. Byrd, to lecture the group before they departed from Hamburg. Which is important."

"Why's that?" Gray asked.

"The Nazis eventually carved a territorial claim out of a section of Antarctica called Queen Maud Land, which was considered Norwegian territory at the time. The Germans named the new place Neuschwabenland. Apparently this stoked the Americans to lead their own expedition, one led by the same Richard Byrd. There was much mystery surrounding this U.S. expedition. Byrd had commissioned the construction of a massive snow cruiser, a fifty-five-foot monstrosity capable of climbing polar mountains or forging giant crevasses. The top deck could even hold a small exploratory plane. Here's a picture of it landing in Antarctica."

He clicked an icon to bring an image of the vehicle on the screen.

"An impressive beast," Gray admitted.

"It was built to carry enough equipment and supplies to last an exploration team a full year, to operate with total independence, making it basically a mobile base."

"What was its purpose?"

"Ah, now that's when it gets interesting. While there was much publicity about the construction and transportation of this beast, once that cruiser reached Antarctica, everything went silent. Not only were Byrd's orders for this expedition secret, but the very existence of those orders had been classified. Only years afterward did Byrd admit that the snow cruiser had explored nine hundred miles of unknown coastline, what he called the Phantom Coast. And that fifty-nine men had been left behind to carry on that exploration."

"What were they looking for?" Kat asked.

Jason shrugged. "There are a lot of theories, some mundane, others pretty far out there. But Professor Harrington had copious notes and collated historical documents from that time. He believes the Germans discovered something incredible, something buried under the ice."

"What?" Gray scoffed. "Like a UFO?"

"No, but you're not as far off as you might think. Some old accounts support that the Germans had found a vast underground cavern system of warm lakes, vast crevasses, and tunnels."

Gray must have let his skepticism show.

Jason glanced at Kat, who nodded as if allowing him to speak freely. "There's some precedent for it," he said, stammering a bit as if he had some personal knowledge of such matters.

Gray wanted to know more, but Kat waved Jason to continue.

He cleared his throat. "Actually recent geological surveys make the German claims seem less wild. Studies done over the past few years have revealed surprising anomalies deep under the ice. From ancient lakes and flowing rivers—both of which might be full of life—to trenches that dwarf the Grand Canyon. Even buried volcanoes have been discovered, some with lava flows melting a slow path miles beneath the ice."

Gray tried to picture such a strange landscape.

"Either way," Jason continued, "the belief in the existence of a Nazi base grew to national attention. Here's an article published in the *New York Times* in 1945."

Gray leaned over his shoulder and read the headline. "*Antarctic Haven Reported.*"

Kat made a small sigh of impatience. "Yes, but what does this have to do with Dr. Hess or the British Antarctic Survey?"

"Everything. Professor Harrington put great stock in these prior expeditions. You see the Brits were actually some of the most active explorers in Antarctica. They were the first to establish a base there, they named most of the major landmarks, and in the ten years after the war, they led a dozen expeditions across the continent, most of them conducted by an organization called the Falkland Islands Dependencies Survey." Jason looked up at them. "The group changed their name in 1962 to the British Antarctic Survey."

"So it's been the same group operating down there for decades," Kat said, her expression turning thoughtful, weighing this information. "But why did they conduct so many expeditions, especially after World War II?"

"You have to understand that at the end of the war, most of the major players in Nazi Germany ended up in British hands. Rudolf Hess, Heinrich Himmler, and most important of all, the head of the German navy, Grand Admiral Karl Dönitz. The Brits had unfettered access to interrogate these leaders and their confederates, well before we or the Soviets did."

Gray understood the significance in regard to their discussion. "And as navy commander, Dönitz would certainly have intimate knowledge of the U-boat activity around that southernmost continent."

"He did, including knowing the location of the Neuschwabenland base and what the Germans discovered on that continent. Apparently it was something incredible. Here's a quote from Admiral Dönitz during the Nuremberg Trials, where he boasted about Nazi discoveries in Antarctica. He says they found an *invulnerable fortress, a paradise-like oasis in the middle of eternal ice.*"

Jason let that fact sink in before continuing. "And what's even more unusual is that this admiral, one so high up the Nazi chain of command, ended up serving only *ten* years in Spandau Prison in Berlin. So while others were put to death, the Nazi fleet commander escaped with barely a slap on the hand. Why is that, do you suppose?"

"Let me guess," Gray said. "He made some sort of deal. A lighter prison sentence in exchange for information."

Jason nodded. "That's what Professor Harrington claims in his exchanges with Dr. Hess."

"And this British group has been searching for this lost cavern system for decades?" Kat said. "Why is it so important?"

Jason took in a sharp breath. "That's all there is about it in the history files, but Professor Harrington's private notes hint at some secret papers—maybe a map—something once in the possession of Darwin."

Gray couldn't hold back his shock. "As in *Charles* Darwin."

"That's right."

Gray pointed to the file name at the top of the computer screen.

D.A.R.W.I.N.

"Is that why the folder we copied from DARPA's servers is titled like that?" he asked.

"Maybe, but it's also apparently the acronym for the main philosophy shared by Harrington and Hess. They discuss it in several of their e-mails. It stands for *Develop and Revolutionize Without Injuring Nature.* The two researchers were united in an effort to seek a way to halt the current great extinction that's sweeping the globe."

The sixth extinction.

Gray remembered Dr. Raffee's description of Hess's mission: to try to engineer a way out of this mass extinction.

"But what does this past history have to do with Hess's current synthetic biology project?" Kat asked.

"I don't know, but I believe it all came to a head in 1999."

"Why then?"

"Both scientists kept referencing a discovery made in October of that year, describing it as a breakthrough in both their pursuits. Harrington described it more ostentatiously, as *the key to opening Hell's gate.*"

Gray didn't like the sound of that.

"They were both very cagey when writing about it. But they did reveal what that *key* was." Jason faced them. "It's why I called you in here. I thought it might be important in regard to what's happening in California."

"What was it?" Gray pressed.

"I confirmed this with independent sources. This particular detail is definitely true. Back in 1999, a group of researchers discovered a virus in Antarctica— one to which no animals or humans were immune. What's even odder is that this microbe was found far out on the desolate ice fields, where nothing else lived. Some of the scientists from that time speculated the virus could have been some form of prehistoric life that thawed out of the ice . . . or maybe it was part of an old biological weapons program. Either way, the discovery excited both Harrington and Hess."

Gray understood why this detail had provoked Jason. Considering what was happening in California, it could be significant.

Before they could discuss it further, the phone on Kat's desk rang. She picked it up. Gray hoped it was further news from California. He checked his watch; the expedition team should be on their way back out of the hot zone—hopefully with some answers.

Kat glanced to Gray. "I'm being connected to Professor Harrington."

He straightened. *Maybe this was even better.*

Kat put the call on speaker.

"*Hello, hello.*" The connection was faint, cutting in and out. "*This is Alex Harrington, can you hear me?*"

"We can, Professor. You're speaking with—"

"*I know,*" he said, cutting her off. "*You're with Sigma.*"

Kat glared at Jason.

He mouthed, "I didn't say a word."

"*I was good friends with Sean McKnight,*" Harrington explained.

Gray and Kat gave each other startled looks. Sean McKnight had founded Sigma Force. In fact, he had recruited Painter into the fold over a decade ago, and eventually the man gave his life in the line of duty, dying within these very walls.

"Sir," Kat said, "we've been trying to reach you. I don't know if you heard about the accident at Dr. Hess's lab in California."

There was a long pause, long enough that Gray worried the connection had been lost.

Then Harrington spoke again. He sounded panicked and angry. "*That fool. I warned him.*"

"We need your help," Kat pushed. "To better understand what Dr. Hess was researching."

"*Not over the phone. If you want answers, you'll have to come to me.*"

"Where are you?"

"*Antarctica . . . Queen Maud Land.*"

"Can you be more specific?"

"*No. Come to the Halley Research Station on the Brunt Ice Shelf. I'll have someone meet you there—someone I can trust—and they'll bring you to me.*"

"Professor," Kat continued to press, "this matter is time critical."

"*Then you'd better hurry. But first tell me this, is Dr. Hess dead or is he missing?*"

Kat's lips narrowed, clearly judging how much to say. Finally she opted for the truth. "We believe he may have been kidnapped."

Again there was a long pause on the line. Fear replaced anger in the professor's voice. "*Then you'd better get here now.*"

The line clicked and went dead.

A new voice spoke behind them. "Sounds like a road trip is in order."

Gray turned to find Monk at the threshold, standing in sweatpants and a sopping T-shirt with a basketball under one arm.

"Came up to see if you wanted to play some one-on-one," Monk said, "but it sounds like that'll have to wait."

"True," Kat said. "Someone needs to go down there and interrogate Harrington immediately."

Gray nodded to Monk. "We can handle it. It shouldn't take more than the two of us."

"You may be right," Monk said, "but this trip is not for me, buddy. Not this time. You need someone familiar with Antarctica at your side."

"Who's that?"

Monk pointed. "How about him?"

Gray turned to Jason. *The kid?*

Jason looked equally surprised.

"Monk's right," Kat said. "Jason has read through all the files and has spent time on that continent. He'll be a valuable resource on the ground out there."

Gray didn't bother arguing. He trusted Kat's operational assessment as much as he did Painter's. "Okay, when do we leave?"

"Right now. Before the professor changes his mind about cooperating. From his behavior just now, Harrington is clearly paranoid and terrified of something . . . or someone."

Gray agreed.

But who could that be?

10

April 28, 9:33 P.M. AMT
Roraima, Brazil

He always loved the jungle at night, as the day fell away, giving up its conceit of safety, leaving behind only darkness, shifting shadows, and the rustle of nocturnal creatures. Without the sun, the bright forest became a primordial dark jungle, where man had no place.

As Cutter Elwes stood on the balcony overlooking the compound's lake below and the rain forest beyond, a scatter of lines from a poem within the pages of Rudyard Kipling's *The Jungle Book* popped into his head. He read it often to his young son, appreciating Kipling's lack of sentimentality, while honoring the beauty of Nature.

Now Chil the Kite brings home the night
That Mang the Bat sets free—
The herds are shut in byre and hut,
For loosed till dawn are we.
This is the hour of pride and power,
Talon and tush and claw.
O hear the call!—Good Hunting, All
That keep the Jungle Law!

He closed his eyes and listened to the buzzing of gnats and flies, the ultrasonic swoop of funnel-eared bats, the warning cough of a spider monkey. He heard the breeze brushing through the leaves of towering kapoks, the whisper of wings from a flight of parrots. On the back of his tongue, he tasted the scent of heavy loam, of rotted leaf, accompanied by the sweetness of night-blooming jasmine.

Words interrupted from the open doors behind him. "*Viens ici, mon mari.*"

He smiled, knowing how hard Ashuu tried to speak French for him. He turned, leaned on the balcony rail, and stared at her naked, dusky skin, the fullness of her breasts, the long fall of ebony waves to the small of her back. She was of the Macuxi tribe; her name meant small, but it also was used to describe something as wonderful.

He crossed and palmed the slight swelling in her lower belly, heralding her second trimester.

Wonderful, indeed.

She ran her fingers from his shoulder to his back, the tips tracing the ragged scars found there, knowing how it excited him. He wore his wounds with pride, remembering the African lion's claws ripping through his flesh, marking him forever. Some nights he could still smell that fetid breath, full of blood and meat and hunger.

She drew him into their bedroom by the hand.

He turned his back on the forest, on his creations that were still learning Kipling's Law of the Jungle under that dark bower, knowing soon nothing would keep him from realizing his goal: to spark a new genesis for this planet, one driven not by the mind of God, but by the hand of man.

He squeezed Ashuu's fingers.

By my own hand, it will begin.

As he followed his wife inside, the dark forest called to him, the old scars burning across his shoulder and down his back, forever reminding him of the law of the jungle.

He remembered another bit of poetry, this time from Lord Tennyson, a distant relative on his mother's side, from his poem *In Memoriam A.H.H.* It spoke to the central tenet of survival of the fittest, speaking to both the magnificence and heartlessness of evolution, describing nature's truest heart as . . .

. . . *red in tooth and claw.*

No truer words had ever been written.

And I will make it my Law.

SECOND

The Phantom Coast

11

April 29, 7:05 A.M. PDT
Lee Vining, California

What's one more ghost town here in the mountains?

Jenna rode in the back of a military vehicle with Nikko. The husky panted next to her, excited to be home. Their two escorts sat up front: Drake in the passenger seat, Lance Corporal Schmitt behind the wheel again. The group had airlifted by helicopter to Lee Vining's small airport and was headed through the evacuated town to the ranger's station.

Usually this early in the morning, the tiny lakeside town bustled with tourists day-tripping from neighboring Yosemite or stirring from the handful of motels stretched along Highway 395. Today, nothing moved down the main drag, except for a lone tumbleweed rolling along the center yellow line, pushed by the growing winds.

While the sun was shining to the east, dark clouds filled the western skies, piling over the Sierra Nevada range, threatening to roll across the basin at any moment. The forecast was for rain and heavy winds. She pictured that deadly wasteland up in the hills and imagined runoff sweeping from the higher elevations to the lake level and beyond.

But it wasn't the VX gas that had everyone watching the skies. The latest toxicology report showed the potency of that nerve agent had rapidly diminished once in contact with the soil.

Instead, she pictured that blackened wasteland—and what was incubating there.

Thank God, no one is still in town.

The evacuation of Lee Vining—with its population of two hundred or so, not counting tourists—hadn't taken long. She stared at the yellow sign for Nicely's Restaurant, advertising a breakfast special that would never be served. A little farther, the Mono Lake Committee Information Center and Bookstore still had the American flag hanging out front, but the place was shuttered up tightly.

Would anyone ever be allowed to return here?

Finally the vehicle turned off the highway and onto Visitor Center Drive. The road wended its way up to the ranger station that overlooked Mono Lake. They didn't bother stopping at the parking lot and drove right up to the towering glass entrance. The building doubled as a visitors' center, with interpretive displays, a couple of art galleries, and a tiny theater.

A familiar figure opened the door as they drew to a stop. Bill Howard lifted an arm in greeting. He was dressed in blue jeans and a brown ranger's shirt and jacket. Despite being in his mid-sixties, he kept his body hard and fit. The only sign of his age was his thinning hair and the sun-crinkles at the corners of his eyes.

She was really glad to see him, but she wasn't the only one. Nikko hopped out and bounded up to Bill. The dog leaped for a bear hug from her fellow ranger. It was poor discipline, but Nikko only behaved this way with Bill, who more than tolerated it. Then again, Bill had three dogs of his own.

She crossed and hugged Bill just as warmly. "It's good to see you."

"Same here, kid. Sounds like you've had an exciting couple of days."

That was the understatement of the year.

Drake climbed out of the vehicle and joined them. "Sir, did you get the information sent by Director Crowe?"

Bill's back stiffened, going professional. "I did, and I've got all the traffic cameras and webcams pulled up. Follow me."

They crossed through the visitors' center and into the ranger station proper. The back office was small, with only enough room for a few desks, a row of computers, and a large whiteboard at the back. Jenna saw a long list of vehicles written on the board, along with license numbers, thirty-two of them in total.

Over the past sixteen hours, Painter Crowe had managed to get a full list of personnel working at the mountain research station. He also pulled up their vehicle registrations and any rental car information. It had taken an exasperatingly long time due to the level of security and the multiple government agencies involved—but most of the delay came from the simple fact that yesterday was a Sunday.

Who knew national security could be so dependent on the day of the week?

Bill Howard waved to a line of three computers. "I've cued up cameras from here and Mono City, and in case your target slipped past those unseen, I pulled feed from webcams around Tioga Pass headed to Yosemite and down 395."

"That should cover everything south of the lake," Jenna explained to Drake.

The gunnery sergeant nodded, satisfied. "Crowe has the sheriff's department up in Bridgeport searching roads to the north of here. If someone from that base is a saboteur and hightailed it out of there, we should be able to cross-reference the vehicle information with cars passing by one or more of those cameras."

Jenna pictured the open gates that led to the research station. It would take painstaking effort to check every car against that list, but it had to be done. It was their best lead. That is, if her theory of a fleeing saboteur even held water.

Maybe someone simply forgot to secure that gate.

Only one way to find out.

"Let's get to work," Jenna said.

Despite the mind-numbing task before them, she knew better than to complain. Others had it much worse.

7:32 A.M.

"How's he doing?" Painter asked the nurse.

The woman—a young Marine who was part of the MWTC's medical staff—snapped off a pair of surgical gloves as she stepped out of the air lock from the quarantined ward. She looked haggard after finishing the night shift, followed by an hour-long decontamination procedure.

She turned to stare through the glass window into the makeshift recovery room. The self-contained BSL4 patient containment unit occupied a corner of a large hangar. The isolation facility had been airlifted from the U.S. Army Medical Research Institute of Infectious Diseases in Fort Detrick and hastily installed in here.

It held a single bed and one patient.

Josh lay there, connected by tubes and wires to a plethora of medical equipment. His skin was pale, his breathing shallow. His left leg—what was left of it— was slung halfway up. A light blanket hid the end of his stump.

Two other figures moved inside—a doctor and nurse—both ensconced in biohazard suits, tethered to the wall by oxygen tubes.

"He's doing as best as could be expected," the nurse answered, peeling off a surgical cap to reveal auburn hair cut in a short bob. She was pretty, but worry darkened her features. "According to the doctor, he may need more surgery."

Painter closed his eyes for a breath. He pictured the fall of the axe, the bloody rush out of the hills, the frustrating time lost moving Josh safely from the forward staging area to here. Surgery had to be done under the same level of isolation, with surgeons suited up and struggling to repair the blunt trauma while wearing bulky gloves. Lisa shared the same blood type as her brother and donated two pints—more than she should have—while crying most of the time.

He knew how hard it had been for Lisa to make that decision in the field. Initially, she had kept her composure, knowing Josh needed a medical doctor at that time, not a sister. But once here, after Josh was taken into surgery, she broke down, nearly collapsing in despair and worry.

He'd tried to get her to take a sedative, to sleep, but she had refused.

Only one thing kept her sane, kept her moving.

Painter stared across the hangar to another cluster of white-walled structures. It was the Level 4 biolab installed by the CDC team. Lisa had been holed up with that group throughout the night. The loss of the leg was not the only concern.

"Has there been any sign of contamination?" Painter pressed the nurse.

She gave a small shake of her head, shrugging her shoulders. "We're doing regular blood work, monitoring his temperature, watching for some sign of a mounting immune response. Every half hour, we check his body for any outward lesions. It's all we can do. We still don't know what to be watching for, or even what we're dealing with."

The nurse looked in the direction of the larger suite of BSL4 labs on the far side of the hangar.

Everybody was waiting for more information.

Twenty minutes ago, Painter had heard from a team stationed up by the dead zone. The blight—whatever it was—continued to spread unabated, consuming acres in a matter of hours.

But what the hell was causing it?

He thanked the nurse and headed toward the best place to discover an answer to that question.

Over the past twenty-four hours, Washington had been flying in personnel, mobilizing specialists from multiple disciplines: epidemiologists, virologists, bacteriologists, geneticists, bioengineers, anyone who might help. The entire region had been quarantined to a distance of fifty miles from ground zero. News crews fought for coverage at the edges, setting up camps.

It was becoming a zoo out there.

Distantly a rumble of thunder echoed over the mountains, rattling the steel roof of the hangar.

Even Mother Nature seemed determined to make matters worse.

Painter strode more quickly toward the BSL4 complex.

We need to catch a break . . . even a small one.

7:56 A.M.

"Look at this," Jenna called out from her computer.

Drake rolled his chair over from his workstation, bringing with him a musky scent of his masculinity.

Bill stretched a kink from his lower back and stepped to join them. Even Nikko lifted his head from the floor, where he'd been working on an old Nylabone she kept in the station to distract him when she worked.

On the screen, she had captured the frozen image of a white Toyota Camry. The footage came from a weather camera along Highway 395, south of town. Unfortunately, the resolution was poor.

She pointed to the whiteboard on the back wall, which included a white Camry on the list of suspect cars. "I can't make out the license plate, but the driver was going fast."

She hit the play button and the vehicle in question zoomed down the stretch of highway.

"Seventy to eighty miles per hour," Bill estimated.

"The car's a common make and model," Drake commented skeptically. "Could be someone just heading home."

"Yeah, but watch as it passes another car in the opposite lane."

She reversed the footage and clicked through more slowly, frame by frame. In one shot, a minivan crosses its path, traveling the other direction. The headlamps hit the windshield at the right angle to fully illuminate the driver. Again the resolution didn't allow for much of an identification.

Drake squinted. "Dark blond maybe, medium to long hair. Still a blur."

"Yeah, but look at what she's wearing."

Bill whistled. "Either she likes wearing white suits or that's a lab coat."

Jenna turned to the whiteboard. "Which researcher is listed as driving a white Camry?"

Drake rolled his chair over and grabbed his tablet computer from the desk. He scrolled through until he found the matching government employee file. "Says here that it's Amy Serpry, biologist from Boston, recent hire. Five months ago."

"How about a picture?"

Drake tapped at the screen, studied it, then turned it to face them. "Blond, hair in a ponytail. Still, it looks pretty long to me." The Marine gave her a half-smile that made her feel much too warm. "I think this is when we say *jackpot*."

Jenna wanted more assurance. "What do we know about her?"

Painter had given them everything he could about each researcher: records, evaluations, their background checks, even any papers published under their name.

Drake scanned through the highlights of her bio. "She's from France, became an American citizen seven years ago, attended postdoctoral programs at both Oxford and Northwestern."

No wonder Dr. Hess employed her. Plus from the photo, the woman was quite pretty, an asset that probably never hurts when it comes to getting hired by the boys' club that was the scientific world.

Drake continued to read in silence, clearly looking for anything that stood out. "Get this," he finally said. "She was a major figure in a movement that encouraged open access to scientific information. They advocated for more transparency. She even wrote an op-ed piece, supporting a Dutch virologist who had posted online the genetic tricks to make H5N1—the bird flu—more contagious and deadly."

"She was okay with that being published?" Bill asked.

Drake read for a bit longer. "She was definitely not against it."

Jenna took in a deep breath. "We should relay this to the sheriff's department and Director Crowe. That Camry is an '09 model. Likely equipped with a GPS unit."

"And with the VIN number," Bill said, "we should be able to track its location."

"It's worth checking out," Jenna agreed.

Drake stood up and waved for her to follow. "In the meantime, we should get back to the helicopter. Be ready to move once we have a location."

Jenna felt a measure of pride at being included—not that she would've had it any other way.

"Go." Bill reached for a phone. "I'll set everything in motion and alert you as soon as I hear something."

With Nikko in tow, Jenna and Drake hurried out of the office and across the visitors' center to the front doors. As she exited, a few cold raindrops struck her face.

She studied the skies and didn't like what she saw.

A spatter of lightning lit the underbellies of a stack of black clouds.

Drake frowned, matching her expression. "We're running out of time."

He was right.

Jenna rushed for the waiting vehicle.

Somebody had better come up with some answers— and quick.

8:04 A.M.
Lisa studied the rat in the cage, watching it root in the bedding, pushing its pink nose through the wood shavings. She empathized with the tiny creature, feeling equally trapped and threatened.

The test subject sat in a cage that was divided into two sections separated by a dense HEPA filter. On the opposite side was a black pile of dust—debris from one of the dead plants.

She typed a note into the computer, a challenging task with the thick gloves of her BSL4 suit.

FIVE HOURS AND NO SIGN OF TRANSMISSION.

They had run a series of trials with various pore sizes and thicknesses of filters, trying to evaluate the *size* of the infectious agent. So far this was the only rat that continued to show no signs of contamination. The others were all sick or dying from multi-organ failure.

She struggled not to think about her brother, entombed in the patient containment unit across the hangar.

Hours ago, she had performed a necropsy with a histopathologist on one of the rats in an early stage of infection. Its lungs and heart were the worst afflicted, with petechiae on the alveoli and rhabdomyolysis of the cardiac muscle fibers. Its heart was literally melting away. With initial lesions manifesting so dramatically in the chest, it suggested an airborne mode of transmission.

It was why they started this series of filter tests.

She continued to type.

ASSESSMENT: INFECTIOUS PARTICLE MUST
BE UNDER 15 NANOMETERS IN SIZE.

So definitely not a bacterium.

One of the smallest known bacterial species was *Mycoplasma genitalium*, which topped off between 200 and 300 nanometers.

"Gotta be a virus," she mumbled.

But even the tiniest virus known to man was the porcine circovirus, which was 17 nanometers in size. The transmittable particle here was even smaller than that. It was no wonder they were still struggling to get a picture of it, to examine its ultrastructure.

Two hours ago, a CDC technician had finally finished setting up and calibrating a scanning electron microscope inside a neighboring lab in the hangar. Hopefully soon they'd get to confront the adversary face-to-face.

She sighed, wanting to rub the knot of a headache out of her temples, but suited up she could not even brush the few hairs away that were tickling her nose. She had tried blowing them to the side before finally giving up. She knew exhaustion was getting the better of her, but she refused to leave the suite of BSL4 labs that were conducting various stages of research.

The radio crackled in her ear, then the lead epidemiologist, Dr. Grant Parson, spoke. "All researchers are to report to the central conference room for a summary meeting."

Lisa placed a rubber palm on the plastic cage. "Keep hanging in there, little fella."

She stood, unhooked her oxygen hose from the wall, and carried it with her through the air lock that led out from the in vivo animal-testing lab to the rest of the complex. Each lab was cordoned off from the other, both compartmentalizing the research and further limiting the chance of an outbreak spreading through the facility.

She stepped into the central hub. Every other hour, the lab's scientists gathered in the room to compare notes and confer about their progress. To facilitate these meetings, a long table had been set up with additional monitors to aid in teleconferencing with researchers across the United States. A window behind the table looked out into the dark hangar.

She spotted a familiar face out there, standing at the glass.

She lifted an arm toward Painter and pointed to her ear. He wore a radio headpiece and dialed into a private channel.

"How're you doing?" he asked, resting his hand on the window.

"We're making slow progress," she said, though she knew he was asking about her personal status, not an update on the research. She shied away from that and asked a more important question. "How's Josh?"

She got regular updates from the medical staff, but she wanted to hear it from Painter, from someone who personally knew her brother.

"Still sedated, but he's holding his own. Josh is tough . . . and a fighter."

Painter was certainly right. Her brother tackled mountains, but even he couldn't battle what couldn't be seen.

"The good news is that it looks like the surgeons were able to salvage the knee joint," Painter added. "Should help his recovery and physical therapy afterward."

She prayed there was an afterward. "What about . . . is there any sign of infection?"

"No. Everything looks good."

She took little comfort from this news. Josh's contact with the agent had been via a break in the skin versus being inhaled. The lack of symptoms could just be due to a longer incubation period from that route of exposure.

A fear continued to nag at her.

Had I gotten his leg off in time?

Dr. Parson spoke up behind her. "Let's get this meeting started."

Lisa settled her gloved palm over Painter's hand on the window. "Keep an eye on him for me."

Painter nodded.

Lisa turned to join the other researchers. Some sat, others stood, all in their BSL4 suits. Over the next fifteen minutes, the head of each lab module gave an update.

An edaphologist—a soil scientist who studied micro-organisms, fungi, and other life hiding in the earth—was the first to report. Anxiety fueled his words.

"I finished a full soils analysis from the dead zone. It's not just the vegetation and wildlife that's being killed. To a depth of two feet, I found the samples to be devoid of any life. Bacteria, spores, insects, worms. All dead. The ground had been essentially sterilized."

Parson let his shock show. "That level of pathogenicity . . . it's unheard of."

Lisa pictured those dark hills, imagining the same shadow penetrating deep underground, leaving no life in its wake as it slowly rolled across the landscape. She had also heard about the inclement weather descending upon the Mono Lake Basin. It was a recipe for an ecological disaster of incalculable proportions.

A bacteriologist spoke up next. "Speaking of pathogenicity, our team has run through a gamut of liquid disinfection traps, seeking some way to sterilize the samples from the field. We've tried extremes of alkalinity and acidity. Lye, various bleaches, et cetera. But the samples remain infectious."

"What about extreme heat?" Lisa asked, remembering Painter's belief that they might have to scorch those hills to stop the blight from spreading.

The researcher shrugged. "We thought we initially had some success. We burned an infected plant to a fine ash—and at first it seemed to work, but after it cooled, it remained just as infectious. We believe the heat merely put the microbe into some type of spore or cyst-like state."

"Maybe it takes something hotter," Lisa said.

"Possibly. But how hot is hot enough? We've discussed a nuclear level of heat. But if the fires of an atomic bomb don't kill it, the blast could scatter and aerosolize the agent for hundreds of miles."

That was definitely not an option.

"Keep searching," Parson encouraged.

"It would help if we knew what we were fighting," the bacteriologist finished, which earned him many nods from his fellow scientists.

Lisa explained her own findings, confirming that they were likely dealing with something viral in nature.

"But it's exceedingly small," she said, "smaller than any known virus. We know Dr. Hess was experimenting with extremophiles from around the world, organisms that could thrive in acidic or alkaline environments, even some that could survive in the molten heat found in volcanic vents."

She looked pointedly at the bacteriologist. "Then to make matters worse, we know Hess was also delving into the very fringes of synthetic biology. His project—Neogenesis—sought to genetically manipulate the DNA of extremophiles in an attempt to help endangered species, to make them hardier and more resistant to environmental changes. In this quest, who knows what monster he created down there?"

Dr. Edmund Dent, a CDC virologist, stood up. "I believe we've caught a glimpse of that monster. Under the newly installed electron microscope."

All eyes turned to him.

"At first we thought it was a technical glitch. What we found seemed too small—unimaginably small—but if Dr. Cummings's assessment concerning the size of the infectious particle is accurate, then perhaps it's not a mistake." Dent glanced to her. "If you'd be willing to join us . . ."

"Of course. I think we should also bring in a geneticist and bioengineer. Just in case, we—"

A loud klaxon sounded, drawing all their gazes to the window. A blue light flashed in the darkness, spinning in time with the alarm. It came from the patient containment unit.

Panic drew Lisa to her feet.

12

April 29, 3:05 P.M. GMT
Brunt Ice Shelf, Antarctica

"Hold on tight!" the pilot called out.

The small Twin Otter plane bucked like an untamed stallion as it crossed high over the iceberg-choked Weddell Sea. The winds worsened as they neared the coast.

"These bastarding katabatics are kicking me in the arse!" the pilot explained. "If you're feeling lurgy, I got airsickness bags back there if you're going to chunder. Don't go messin' my girl up."

Gray kept a firm hold on the strap webbing of his jump seat. He was belted in tightly along one side of the cabin. At the back, crates of gear and supplies rattled and creaked. He was normally not prone to motion sickness, but this roller coaster of a flight was testing even his mettle.

Jason sat across the cabin, his head lolling, half asleep, plainly unfazed by the turbulence. Apparently he'd had plenty of experience with this storm-swept continent. Instead, the kid seemed more afflicted by the twenty-four hours of long flights to get to the south end of the world.

At least this was their last leg.

Earlier today, just after sunrise—which was *noon* this side of the world, the beginning of their dark winter—they had flown from the Falkland Islands to the Antarctic Peninsula, landing atop a rocky promontory on Adelaide Island, where the British maintained Rothera Station. That flight had been aboard a large, bright red Dash 7 aircraft, with *British Antarctic Survey* emblazoned on its side. At Rothera, they had switched to this smaller Twin Otter, similarly painted, and set off across the Weddell Sea toward the Brunt Ice Shelf: a floating hundred-meter-thick sheet that hugged the far coastline in a region of East Antarctica called Coats Land.

As they made their approach, the aircraft's twin props chopped into the polar airstream—called the katabatic winds—which rolled down from the higher elevations of the inner mountain ranges to roar out to sea.

Their pilot was an older UK airman named Barstow, who clearly had had plenty of arctic experience. He continued his ongoing commentary and tour. "Did you know the name of these winds comes from the Greek word *katabaino*, which means *to go down?*"

"Let's hope that doesn't happen to us," a voice grumbled behind him.

Joe Kowalski huddled in the back. His large frame was folded nearly in half to fit into the cramped space. He looked like a shaven-headed gorilla crammed into a sewer pipe. He kept his head ducked from the low roof—not that he hadn't hit it a few times during the bumpy ride over the Weddell Sea.

Kat had sent the big man along on this mission as additional support and muscle, while voicing another reason, too. *Get him out of here. After his breakup with Elizabeth Polk, all he does is mope around these halls.*

Gray wondered how Kat could tell the difference. Kowalski was never a beam of sunshine, even on his best days.

Still, Gray hadn't complained. The guy might not look or sound it, but the former Navy sailor had his own skill set, which mostly involved things that go *boom.* As Sigma's demolitions expert, he had proved invaluable in the past. Plus his cantankerous attitude sort of grew on you, like mold on bread. Once you got used to him, he was all right.

Not that I would ever admit that aloud.

"You can see Halley Station up yonder," Barstow called back. "It's that big blue centipede sittin' atop the ice."

Gray twisted to look out a window as the Twin Otter banked toward a landing.

Directly below, the black seas rode up against cliffs of blue ice, the walls towering as high as a row of forty-story skyscrapers. While the Brunt Ice Shelf appeared like a craggy coastline, it was actually a tongue of ice protruding into the sea, sixty miles across, flowing out from the higher glaciers of Queen Maud Land to the east. It moved at a rate of ten football fields every year, calving into bergs at the end, broken by the warmer waters of the Weddell and by the motion of the tides.

But what drew Gray's full attention was something perched atop those cliffs. It did indeed look like a centipede. The Halley VI Research Station had been established in 2012, using a unique design of individual steel modules, each colored blue, connected to one another by enclosed walkways. Each pod rested on stilt-like skis with the height controlled by hydraulics.

"That's the sixth version of Halley," Barstow said, bobbling the craft in the wind. "The other five were buried in the snow, crushed, and pushed into the sea. That's why we have everything on skis now. We can tow the station out of deep snow or keep it ahead of the drifting ice."

Kowalski had his nose to the window. "Then how come it's so close to that drop now?"

He was right. The eight linked modules, all lined up in a row, sat only a hundred yards from the cliff's edge.

"Won't be there much longer. Be movin' her inland in a couple more weeks. A group of climate eggheads have been doing a yearlong study of melting glaciers, tracking the speed of ice sliding off this bloody continent. They're just about done here, and the whole lot will be shippin' out to the other side of Antarctica." The pilot glanced back to them—which Gray didn't appreciate as the Twin Otter was in mid-dive toward a landing. "They're heading over to the Ross Ice Shelf. To McMurdo Station. One of your Yank bases."

"Eyes on the road," Kowalski groused from the back, pointing forward for extra emphasis.

As the pilot swung back to his duty, Gray turned to Jason, who had stirred at the jostling and noise. "McMurdo? You still have family there, right?"

"Near there," Jason said.

"Who'd want to live out here?" Kowalski said. "Freeze your goddamned balls off if you even tried to take a piss."

Barstow snorted a laugh. "Especially midwinter, mate. Then you'd likely lose your todger, too. Come winter, it's monkeys out there."

"Monkeys?" Kowalski asked.

"He means it's damned cold," Gray translated.

Jason pointed below. "Why's that one section of the station in the middle painted red and all the others are blue?"

"It's our red-light district down here," Barstow answered, fighting the plane to keep level as the ice rose up toward them. "That section is where all the fun happens. We eat there, raise a few pints on the rare occasion, play snooker, and have tellies for watching movies."

The Twin Otter landed and slid across a plowed surface that doubled as a runway. The entire craft rattled and thrummed atop its skis, finally coming to a stop not too far from the station.

They all exited. Though bundled deep in thick polar jackets, the winds immediately discovered every gap and loose fold. Each breath was like sucking in liquid nitrogen, while the reflected glare of the sun sitting low on the horizon was blinding off the ice. Sunset was only a half hour away. In another couple of days, it wouldn't rise or set at all.

The pilot followed them out, but he kept his coat unzipped, his hood down. He turned his craggy face up to the blue skies, as if basking in the last moments of sunlight. "Won't be this warm for much longer."

Warm?

Even Gray's teeth ached from the cold.

"Got to get your tan when you can," Barstow said and led them toward a set of stairs that climbed up to one of the giant blue modules.

From the ground, the sheer size of the station was impressive. Each pod looked as big as a two-story house and was elevated fifteen yards above the snow-swept ice by four giant hydraulic skis. A full-sized tractor could easily drive *under* the station, which from the parked John Deere nearby probably occasionally happened.

"Must be how they tow the modules," Jason said, eyeing the American-built piece of machinery. He then squinted at the ice-encrusted bulk of the station. "Whole setup looks like something out of *Star Wars.*"

"Right," Kowalski agreed. "Like on the ice planet Hoth."

Gray and Jason looked at him.

His perpetual scowl deepened. "I watch movies."

"This way, gents," Barstow said, motioning for them to mount the stairs.

As they clomped their way up, knocking snow from their boots, a door opened above and a woman in an unzipped red parka stepped to the top landing to greet them. Her long brunette hair was combed back from her face and secured against the wind in an efficient but still feminine ponytail. Her physique was lithe and muscular, her cheeks wind-burned and tanned. Here was a woman who clearly refused to stay locked inside the station.

"Welcome to the bottom of the world," she greeted them. "I'm Karen Von Der Bruegge."

Gray climbed to her and shook her hand. "Thank you for accommodating us, Dr. Von Der Bruegge."

"Karen is fine. We're far from formal here."

Gray had been briefed about this woman who served as both the station's lead scientist and base commander. At only forty-two, she was already a well-regarded arctic biologist, trained in Cambridge. In the mission's dossier, Gray had seen her photographs of polar bears in the far north. Now she was on the opposite side of the globe, studying colonies of emperor penguins that nested here.

"Come inside. We'll get you settled." She turned and led them through the hatch. "This is the command module, where you'll find the boot room, communication station, surgery, and my office. But I think you'll be more comfortable in our recreation area."

Gray took a look around as she led them through her domain, noting the small surgical suite with a single operating theater. He paused at a door leading into the communication room.

"Dr. Von Der Bruegge . . . Karen, I've been trying to reach the States since we reached Rothera Station over on Adelaide, but I keep failing to get a substantial signal."

Her brow crinkled. "Your sat phone . . . it must be using a geosynchronous connection."

"That's right."

"Those work poorly when you cross seventy degrees south of the equator. Which pretty much means all of Antarctica. We use an LEO satellite system here. Low earth orbit." She pointed to the room. "Feel free to make a call. We can give you some privacy. But I must warn you that we're in the middle of a solar storm that's been affecting our systems, too. Very bothersome, but it makes the aurora australis—our southern lights— quite spectacular."

Gray stepped into the room. "Thank you."

Karen turned to the others. "I'll take you to our communal area. I'm guessing you could use some hot coffee and food right about now."

"I never turn down a free meal," Kowalski said, sounding less mournful.

As they exited through a hatch into one of the enclosed bridges between the modules, Gray closed the door to the communication room and stepped to the satellite phone. He dialed a secure number for Sigma command and listened to the tonal notes as a scrambled line was connected.

Kat answered immediately. "Did you reach Halley Station?" she asked, not wasting any time.

"Probably shook a few fillings out of my molars, but we're here safe and sound. We still have to await the arrival of whomever Professor Harrington is sending here. Then maybe we'll start getting some answers."

"Hopefully that will happen soon. The news out of California has been growing grimmer over the past couple of hours. A storm front is moving into the area, with the threat of torrential rains and flash floods."

Gray understood the danger. Any containment of that quarantine zone would be impossible.

As Kat continued, some of her words were lost amid pops of static and digital drops. "You should also know that Lisa's brother is showing . . . signs of infection. He had a seizure twenty minutes ago. We're still trying to determine if it's secondary to his exposure or a surgical complication. Either way, we need to get . . . handle on this situation ASAP before all hell breaks loose."

"How's Lisa holding up?"

"She's working around the clock. Driven to find some way of helping her brother. Still, it's got Painter worried. The only good news is that we may have a possible lead on the saboteur of the base. We're following up on that right now."

"Good, and I'll expedite what I can here. But we still have an hour until Professor Harrington's contact is due to arrive to ferry us to his location."

Wherever the hell that was.

Kat's impatience rang through from a world away. "If only he wasn't so damned paranoid . . ."

Gray appreciated her frustration, but he was nagged by another worry: *What if Harrington had a good reason to be paranoid?*

3:32 P.M.

Back home again . . .

With the sun close to setting, Jason took advantage of the view. He sat at a table before a two-story bank of triple-glazed windows that looked out across the ice field to the expanse of the Weddell Sea. Massive ships of ice dotted those dark blue waters, sculpted by wind and waves into ethereal shapes that towered high into crests, arches, and jagged blue-white sails.

He had joined Sigma to do good, to keep the nation safe, but he had also hoped to see more of the world. Instead, he spent most of his time buried underground at Sigma command, and now on his first real field assignment . . .

I get sent home.

He had spent part of his childhood in Antarctica, with his mother and stepfather, who still worked near McMurdo Station on the other side of the continent.

Now I've come back full circle.

He sipped dourly from a cup of hot tea, listening to the chatter from the handful of base personnel who shared the recreation area. The red module was broken into two levels. The lower half contained the dining facilities, while a corkscrew staircase led up to a loft that held a small library, a bank of computers, and a conference area. There was even a rock-climbing wall that ran between the two floors.

Directly behind him, a trio of men played pool, speaking in what sounded like Norwegian. Though the site was a UK station, it drew an international group of researchers. According to Dr. Von Der Bruegge, the place normally housed fifty to sixty scientists, but they were downsizing of late as the dark winter months approached. Their numbers had dwindled to twenty, and only a dozen or so people would remain through what would eventually be perpetual night.

Due to this transitional period, the base hummed with activity—both inside and out. Beyond the windows, a pair of Sno-Cats dragged pallets of crates away from the station. But the most amazing sight was of the green John Deere tractor slowly hauling one of the unattached blue modules across the ice. It vanished ghostly into the fog that stuck close to the shelf, defying the higher winds as sunset approached.

The commander had said that over the next week—working 24/7—the station would be disassembled and dragged piecemeal inland, where it would be reassembled for the winter months.

In the sky, another Twin Otter flew low along the edge of the ice shelf, catching the last rays of the sun and looking as if it were coming in for a landing for the night. Rather than the cherry red of the British Antarctic Survey squadron, this one was painted chalk white. It was an unusual paint job for an arctic region, where bright primary colors were preferred in order to better stand out against the ice and snow.

Maybe it's Professor Harrington's contact.

Jason half stood, ready to alert Gray. Across the way, Kowalski was at the buffet, piling up a second plate of food, mostly slices of pie from the looks of it.

Then the plane tilted higher, turning away from the plowed airstrip. It looked to be leaving again. It must not be their contact after all, maybe a sightseer. Either way, it was a false alarm

Jason settled back to his chair.

He watched the plane bank on a wingtip. A door opened along its side. He spotted movement within— followed by the suspicious protrusion of a pair of long black tubes.

Fire spat from their ends, trailing smoke.

Rocket launchers.

The first blasts destroyed the lone Twin Otter on the ice. Then the plane swept toward the station.

Jason felt his arm grabbed.

Kowalski yanked him out of his chair. "Time to go, kid."

3:49 P.M.

Gray ran low down the elevated bridge that connected the command module to the recreation pod. The blasts still echoed in his head. He had just stepped into the enclosed span after finishing his call with Kat—when the first rockets exploded. Through the windows along the bridge, he watched the ruins of the Twin Otter burn.

Ahead, another figure rose from a crouched position in the passageway.

Gray ran up to her. "Karen, are you okay?"

The base commander looked dazed, momentarily stunned. Then her blue eyes focused, going angry rather than scared.

"What the bloody hell?" she blurted out.

"We're under attack."

She made to push past him. "We must get out a mayday."

Gray caught her around the midsection, stopping her. He heard the timbre of the aircraft's engines growing louder. He dragged her toward the recreation module.

"No time," he warned.

"But—"

"Trust me."

Gray didn't have time to explain, so he rushed her to the end of the bridge, half carrying her. As he reached the far door, it opened before him. Kowalski appeared, filling the threshold. It looked like he had Jason equally in hand.

"Back inside!" Gray yelled.

As Kowalski moved out of the way, Gray charged through and shoved Karen toward his partners. He slammed the door behind him—just as another pair of explosions shook the entire module. Glassware fell from shelves in the dining area, and several of the triangular panes of window cracked into splinters from the concussion.

Gray stared out the porthole window in the door. The far end of the connecting bridge had been blasted away. A crater also smoked in the flank of the command module.

Right where the communication room was located.

Karen had rejoined him, looking over his shoulder.

"They're isolating us," Gray explained. "First they took out the plane, eliminating the only way off the ice. Then when I heard the plane coming this way, I knew they would target communications next, to further cut us off from the outside world."

"Who are *they*?"

Gray pictured the team that had assaulted DARPA headquarters. The Twin Otter in the sky had been *white*, a common color for arctic combat operations. He imagined a ground assault was imminent.

"Do you have any weapons?" Gray asked.

Karen turned the opposite direction. "In the caboose. The last module of the station. But we don't have many."

He'd take *too few* versus *none*.

By now, others had gathered around, including Barstow, along with a handful of frightened-looking researchers.

"How many others are inside the station?" Gray asked, leading them across the dining hall.

Karen surveyed those with them, clearly doing a head count. "This time of year, no more than another five or six, not counting the work crew already outside."

Gray reached the far side and hauled open the door to the next bridge. "Keep moving! Module by module! All the way to the rear!" He waved everyone through, then ran alongside Karen. "Does the station have an intercom system, a way of dispatching a general alarm?"

She nodded. "Of course. It'll also radio to anyone out on the ice."

"Good. Then once we reach the last module, order an evacuation."

She glanced at him with concern. "With the sun down, the temps outside will drop precipitously."

"We have no other choice."

It had grown quiet outside. No further blasts. He pictured the Twin Otter circling to land. He had no doubt an assault team would be offloaded soon. Without any means of communication, they were unable to request help, while the attackers would have all night to search the station or merely set charges and blow each module to hell.

As Gray formulated a plan, his retreating group burst into the next module. It was the station's living quarters, made up of a series of small bedrooms painted in bright colors. They collected another station member there: a small panicked-looking young man wearing glasses. They continued onward, passing through two more research modules. Both had been packed up and closed down for the winter.

Finally they reached the last car of this icy train. It was clearly a storage space.

"Where are the weapons?" Gray asked.

"Near the back door," Karen said and tossed a set of keys to Barstow. "Show them."

While he obeyed, Karen stepped over to an intercom on the wall, quickly tapping in a code. Gray followed Barstow as Karen sounded a general alert, warning any other station members inside to evacuate. To those outside, she instructed them to stay away.

Barstow led them to a locker on the back wall and used Karen's key to open the double doors. Gray stared at the rows of rifles and handguns, trying not to show his disappointment at the meager number of weapons, but then again, what sort of threat would this base normally face? There were no land-based predators out here, nothing but penguins and some seals. The few rifles and guns were likely meant to deal with any unruly guests of the station—not a full-on assault.

Gray passed around the six Glock 17 pistols and shouldered one of the three assault rifles. It was an L86A2 Light Support Weapon. He passed another to Kowalski and the last to Barstow. To the side, Jason loaded his Glock with experienced skill.

Gray stepped to the window in the last door. Outside, night had fallen on this short day, dropping a blanket of darkness over them. Beyond the hatch, a small platform led to a ladder that descended down to the ice.

"Kowalski and Barstow, once we're on the ground, we'll try to discourage the plane from landing. Failing that, we'll move to a defensible position." Gray turned to Jason. "You lead the others away. Put as much distance between here and the station as you can."

The kid nodded. His eyes looked alert, frosted by a healthy fear, but ready to move.

Karen returned, bearing an armload of handheld radios. "Grabbed these, too."

Gray nodded at her resourcefulness, then took one and pushed it into his parka's pocket. "Pass the others around."

Once they were ready, Gray took the lead. He hauled open the hatch to the dark, frigid night. As the first blast of cold hit his face, he suddenly doubted the wisdom of his plan. Death was as certain out on the ice as it was inside the station. They would need to find shelter and fast—somewhere other than here.

But where?

Another blast erupted, shaking the station. The lights flickered once, then died.

Karen spoke behind him. "Must've taken out the generators."

Gray frowned. *Had the enemy eavesdropped on Karen's alert? Had it triggered this new attack? Or was this the assault team's final salvo to soften and unnerve their targets before landing?*

The continuing drone of the Twin Otter reminded him that any further reservations or hesitation would only worsen their odds. Knowing this, he hurried into the cold, pulling on his gloves, and mounted the ladder. He slid most of the way down and waved for the others to follow.

With the butt of his weapon at his shoulder, he used the scope to track the lights of the Twin Otter in the evening sky. It banked on the far side of the station. Then a flash flared from its hull. Another explosion echoed across the ice. A small island of light went dark out there.

"I think that was one of our Sno-Cats," Karen said, her voice strained with guilt. "I should've warned them to go dark."

Gray noted another Sno-Cat parked on the ice to the right of the station, along with a trio of Ski-Doos. "Can you get those snow machines started fast enough? If you keep the lights off, you'll be able to cover more ground than on foot."

She nodded.

"What if the enemy has night-vision?" Jason asked, joining them.

"If they do, they'll spot us just as easily on foot." Gray pointed to the thick banks of fog settling to the icy shelf all around the station. "Once you're moving, make for that cover as quickly as you can. It's your best chance."

Jason eyed that refuge doubtfully.

In a hope to better their odds, Gray turned to Kowalski and Barstow. "We'll buy the others as much time as possible." He motioned to the opposite side of the station from the parked snow machines. "If we fire from over there, we can keep the enemy's attention on us."

Kowalski shrugged. "I guess it's better than freezing our asses off."

Barstow also nodded.

With a plan in place, Gray ordered the two groups to split up.

Jason glanced over a shoulder as he led his party off. "One of the Ski-Doos is a three-seater." He eyed Gray's team. "I'll leave it with the engine running. Just in case."

Gray acknowledged this with a nod, impressed with the kid's quick thinking.

With the matter settled, Gray led Kowalski and Barstow under the caboose of the station. He heard the snow engines grumble to life on the other side—at first cold and choking, then with more throaty power.

Gray watched the group slowly depart, disappearing into the fog, one after the other.

Satisfied, Gray stepped out from under the shelter of the station, weapon at his shoulder. He followed the Twin Otter in the sky as it turned and swung in his direction, seeming to climb higher as if sensing the hidden snipers below.

Its strange actions worried Gray. Suspicions jangled up his spine.

Why hadn't it made any effort to land yet?

The plane continued a slow circle, like a hawk above a field. So far, the assault seemed targeted to isolate the base, to keep its occupants pinned down.

But to what end? What are they waiting for?

The answer came a heartbeat later.

A massive explosion—a hundredfold stronger than any of the prior rocket blasts—shook the world. At the far end of the station, a geyser of ice and fire blew high into the night. Then another detonation erupted, much closer, followed by yet another.

Gray and the others were knocked to their knees. He pictured a row of munitions buried deep in the ice. The line of charges must have been planted long ago.

The series of blasts continued on the far side of the station, running from one end to the other.

Gray stared beyond that line, toward the heavy fog bank.

As least the others got clear in time . . .

As Gray watched, fissures skittered outward, connecting the new craters together and extending yet again. He imagined the ice splitting downward as well, cleaving deep into the shelf of floating ice.

Gray suddenly understood the enemy's plan.

His stomach knotted into a cold fist.

Confirming his worst fear, a final loud *crack* erupted, sounding like the earth's crust shattering beneath them.

Slowly the ice shifted under his knees, tilting away from the new fracture and leaning out toward the dark sea. The buried bombs had succeeded in breaking loose a chunk of the Brunt Ice Shelf, calving a new iceberg— one that included Halley VI atop it.

The entire station shuddered and began to slowly slide across the slanting ice, skating atop its giant skis.

Gray stared upward in disbelief.

Kowalski watched it all, too. "Looks like I won't be patching things up with my ex after all."

13

April 29, 8:45 A.M. PDT
Yosemite Valley, California

"If you're going to hide," Drake said, "this isn't a bad place to hole up."

"Let's hope she's still here." Jenna climbed out of the SUV into the morning drizzle. She pulled up her Gore-Tex jacket's hood and appreciated the majesty that was the famous Ahwahnee Hotel, the crown jewel of Yosemite National Park.

Opened in 1927, the rustic mountain lodge was a masterful mix of Arts and Crafts style and Native American design, famous for its massive sandstone fireplaces, its hand-stenciled wood beams, and for its many stained glass windows. Though a night's stay was too pricey for Jenna's salary, she occasionally splurged for a brunch in the resplendent dining room, a three-story-tall space supported by massive sugar pine trestles.

But the main lodge wasn't their destination this morning.

The four-man Marine team had parked their nondescript vehicle in a back lot. Drake led the way toward the woods bordering the hotel, drawing Jenna and Nikko with him. They were all dressed in civilian gear, made bulkier by the Kevlar body armor under their clothes, and kept their weapons out of sight.

Jenna had her compact .40-caliber Smith & Wesson M&P belted at her waist, hidden by the fall of her jacket, along with a pair of handcuffs hanging on her other hip.

Ten minutes ago, the team had been airlifted by helicopter over the Sierra Nevada range, passing through some rough weather, to reach the Yosemite Valley. The wide meadow next to the Ahwahnee was a common landing spot for rescue choppers in the park, but Drake had feared they might spook their quarry, so he chose a site farther out—landing at nearby Stoneman Meadow.

"Car," Lance Corporal Schmitt said.

He pointed to a white Toyota Camry with Massachusetts plates. The license number was a match. The vehicle belonged to Amy Serpry.

An hour ago, Painter had expedited a GPS search for a vehicle matching the car's VIN number. They had discovered it here, in Yosemite Valley, not far from the region of the mountains that had been evacuated and quarantined.

Initially everyone thought the woman had abandoned the car, possibly switching vehicles. An inquiry to the hotel had revealed no record of an Amy Serpry checking in. But a photo was sent to the front desk. It seemed a woman matching her description had booked a room under an alias, arriving with false identification and credit cards.

An undeniable sign of guilt.

But why had the suspect settled here, so close to the border of the quarantine zone? Did she stay in the area to observe the aftermath of her handiwork?

Anger burned in Jenna's gut, picturing the wasteland, all the dead wildlife. She shied away from remembering the fall of the axe, the screaming. She had held Josh's shoulders when Drake did what had to be done. Afterward, the gunnery sergeant refused to speak during the return trip, his gaze lost in the hills.

"She must still be here," Schmitt said, as they filed past her car. "Unless she left in another vehicle from here."

Let's hope not. We need answers.

Drake marched in the lead, his face hard and stoic. He clearly wanted more than answers; he wanted payback.

The Toyota was parked near a small path that led back through a stand of Ponderosa pines. The Ahwahnee maintained twenty-four rustic rental cabins, all hidden in the woods. Amy must have booked one of those remote cottages in order to keep a low profile.

The team set off down the path. The scent of pine pitch swelled under the dripping canopy of the forest. At a fork, two of Drake's men flanked to the right. Steps later, the gunnery sergeant headed with another Marine into the woods to the left. They intended to circle the cabin, to lay a noose around the place.

As the Marines vanished, she and Nikko headed directly for the cottage. The plan was for Jenna to make the first approach. In civilian clothes with a dog at her side, she looked like any other tourist. The goal was to get Amy to let her guard down, to perhaps open the door to a lost hiker.

After a turn in the pathway, a quaint cedar-plank cottage appeared, nestled among the pines. It was painted green to better blend into the forest. A wet stone patio framed a door with two sidelights. The windows were all draped shut, as were the glass panes in the door.

Looks like somebody sure wants her privacy.

Jenna felt no misgivings about striding forward on her own, knowing the Marines had her back. Still, she gave her armored vest a surreptitious tug. Nikko kept to her knee, as if sensing her tension.

As she reached the door, she shook back her hood, ignoring the rain, and plastered on a feigned look of confusion. She knocked firmly, then stepped back.

"Hello," she called out. "I was wondering if you could tell me how to get to the Ahwahnee's lobby?"

A faint sound reached her.

So somebody was inside.

She leaned closer, bringing her ear near the door. "Hello!" she tried again, louder this time.

As she listened, she realized the noise was the muffled ringing of a phone. From the tone, it had to be a cell phone.

She took in a breath to call again when somebody responded, hoarse, barely audible.

"*. . . help me . . .*"

Reacting instinctively to the plaintive cry, Jenna pulled out her Smith & Wesson and used the butt of her pistol to smash the side light next to the doorknob. As the window shattered, she yanked the cuff of her jacket lower over her hand, brushed the worst of the glass out of the way, then reached through and tugged on the door latch inside, disengaging the lock.

She heard boots pounding up behind her.

A glance back revealed Drake running her way. "Wait!"

Now unlocked, the door swung open on its own.

Jenna kept sheltered to the side and raised her pistol in both hands. Drake reached her, taking a position on the other side.

A single bedside lamp glowed inside the shadowy room. It revealed a figure in the bed, half covered by a comforter. From the blond hair, it had to be Amy Serpry—but the woman's face was swollen and blotched, her skin blistering, darkening the edges of her lips. Vomit stained the top of the quilt, while the sheets were tangled as if she had fought within them.

Earlier, Jenna had heard about Josh having a seizure.

She suspected Amy had suffered similarly.

No wonder she hadn't escaped too far. She must've gotten sick and went to ground where she could.

Jenna felt little sympathy for the saboteur, knowing how many had died because of the woman's actions.

Amy's head tilted on the pillow, falling in the direction of the door. Her eyes were an opaque white, likely blind. Her mouth opened, as if to again plead for help.

Instead, blood poured forth, swamping the pillow and soaking the mattress. The body sagged in the bed, going slack and still.

Jenna took a step to go to her aid, but Drake blocked her at the threshold with his arm.

"Look at the rug," he warned.

At first Jenna could make no sense of the small shapes dotting the floor. Then her mind snapped to what she was seeing.

Mice . . . dead mice.

She had heard stories of the tiny trespassers who often shared these cottages with the hotel guests. A friend of hers from college had stayed in one of these cabins last year. Afterward, all she could talk about was how mice bounded across her bed at night, rooted through her luggage, even deposited a few droppings in her shoes.

To deal with the vermin problem, the hotel maintained an ongoing war, especially after cases of mouse-borne hantavirus broke out in the valley.

But the war inside *this* cottage was already over.

Or almost over.

A lone mouse hopped feebly across the carpet, its body shaking.

Jenna reacted too slowly, too focused on the horrors inside.

Nikko burst past her, the motion igniting his hunter's instinct.

"Nikko, no!"

The husky stopped at her command, but he already had the mouse in his teeth. He turned back, his tail dropping, knowing he had done something wrong.

"Nikko . . ."

The dog dropped the mouse and came sheepishly toward her, his head bowed, his tail tucked.

Drake pushed Jenna back with one arm—then reached and closed the door. What lurked inside that room was something far worse than any hantavirus.

On the opposite side of the door, Nikko whined, pleading to be let out.

9:01 A.M.

Lisa waited inside the air lock for the pressure to stabilize before she could open the inner door that led into the lab complex. Through the walls, she heard the light *tin-tinning* of raindrops on the metal roof of the cavernous hangar.

It reminded her that time was running short.

According to the local meteorologists, the massive storm front continued to push into the region. As of yet, the dead acres surrounding ground zero remained dry, but it was only a matter of time before those dark skies opened up over the area. A logistical group had been tasked to figure out how far this disease might spread, employing computerized modeling programs to calculate runoff patterns based on topography and local geology.

Their initial reports were harrowing.

Painter was currently teleconferencing with various state and federal officials, trying to stay one step ahead of this disaster. Unfortunately, a new arrival in the middle of the night had proven to be a headache. The technical director from the DTC—the U.S. Army Developmental Test Command—had flown in from Dugway Proving Grounds in Utah, which handled the nation's defense against nuclear, chemical, and biological threats. In the few short hours since the man had arrived, he'd already become a pain in Painter's ass.

The light above the inner door turned green, and the magnetic lock released with an audible pop of pressure. Lisa stepped through, all too glad to leave the political hassles to Painter. She had a greater challenge that needed her full attention.

She glanced over a shoulder toward the patient containment unit on the hangar's far side. Josh was resting again, on a diazepam drip. The cause of his brief seizure remained unknown, but she feared it was a possible sign of infection spreading to his central nervous system.

She pictured the thorn sticking out of his leg.

I hope I'm wrong.

But until she knew for sure, she intended to keep working.

"Dr. Cummings, you're back. Fantastic."

The voice came through her radio earpiece. She turned and spotted Dr. Edmund Dent, the CDC virologist, on the far side of a window, standing in his lab. He lifted an arm in greeting—then waved for her to come inside.

"Thanks to your work, I think we've made some significant progress in isolating the infectious particle," he radioed to her. "Once we knew to look for something so small, we've started to make good headway. But I'd love to get your input on what we've found so far."

"Of course," she said.

Excited for even a measure of progress, Lisa hurried through the smaller air lock to reach his lab. His section of the BSL4 suite was all shiny with steel hardware: high-speed centrifuges, a mass spectrometer, a Leica ultramicrotome and cryochamber, along with a pair of electron microscopes.

She discovered another suited figure seated at one of the computer stations, bowed over a monitor. She failed to recognize him until he turned. She kept the surprise out of her face as best she could.

It was Dr. Raymond Lindahl, the technical director from the U.S. Army Developmental Test Command. Through his face shield, the man looked to be in his early fifties, with dyed black hair and a matching goatee. Since his arrival, he had been sticking his long nose into all of Painter's work, making snap judgments, ordering changes when it was in his prerogative to do so—which, frustratingly for Painter, was all too often.

Now it seemed Painter's pain was about to become her own.

Of course, it was not inappropriate for the man to be here. Lisa had heard about Lindahl's background as both a geneticist and a bioengineer. He was brilliant in his own right and had the arrogance to go along with it.

"Dr. Dent," Lindahl said stiffly, "I'm not sure we need Dr. Cummings's expertise in medicine and physiology here. Her time is better spent with clinical work, concentrating on her animal studies, not at this level of research."

The virologist did not back down, which made Lisa like him all the more. Edmund was ten years younger than Lindahl and had a bohemian attitude, likely honed from his time spent at Berkeley and Stanford. Though she had never seen the virologist out of his protective suit, she always imagined him in Birkenstocks and a tie-dyed T-shirt.

"It was Lisa's work that enabled our progress here," Edmund reminded Lindahl. "And it never hurts to get another pair of eyes on a problem. Besides, when is honey ever made with only one bee in a hive?"

An exasperated sigh escaped Lindahl, but he let the matter drop.

Edmund rolled a chair next to the DTC director. "Lisa, let me catch you up. I mentioned at the earlier meeting that I thought I might have caught a glimpse of the monster in play here. Here's a transmission electron micrograph of a cross section of alveoli from the lungs of an infected rat."

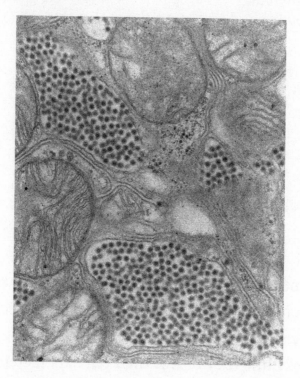

Lisa leaned closer, studying the pockets of tiny particles densely packed into the lung's small air cells.

"Those definitely look like virions—viral particles," Lisa admitted. "But I've never seen anything so
small."

Edmund nodded his head. "I took measurements
from some particles budding along infected cardiac
muscle fibers. This is from a scanning electron micrograph, offering more of a 3-D view."

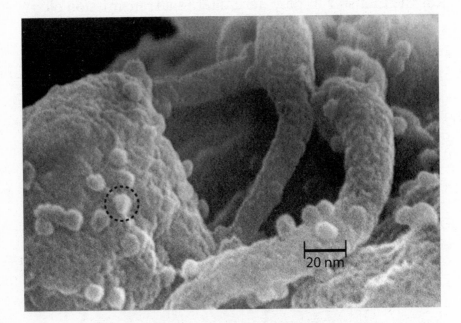

The new picture revealed individual viruses attached
to branching muscle bundles and nerves. A scale had
been included to offer some measure of size.

"Looks like they're less than *ten* nanometers," Lisa
commented. "That's *half* the size of the smallest known
virus."

"Which is why I stepped in to help." Lindahl elbowed Edmund out of the way. "To get a clearer picture, I collated the protein data from the team's molecular biologist. From that data and using a program I patented, I worked up a three-dimensional representation of the virion's capsid, its outer shell."

Lisa studied the spherical modeling of the infectious particle. She was impressed at Lindahl's skill, almost to the point of accepting his arrogance.

"That's the outer face of our monster," Edmund said. "Henry is already in the midst of doing a genetic analysis on what's hidden *inside* that shell."

Dr. Henry Jenkins was a geneticist from Harvard.

"But we can still extrapolate plenty from this capsid," Lindahl said. "Enough to say this is an *artificial* construct. Beneath that protein coat, we found carbon graphene fibers—each only two atoms thick—woven in a hexagonal pattern."

He brought up another image alongside the last one, showing that protein coat removed this time, leaving a tangled webbing behind.

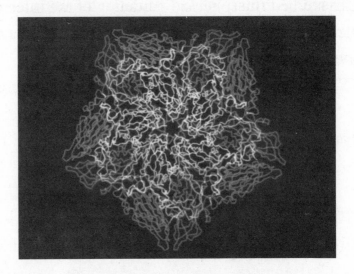

It definitely looked artificial. Lisa pondered the significance of those man-made fibers. Graphene was a remarkably tough material, stronger than spider's silk.

"It almost looks," she said, "as if Hess was trying to engineer the equivalent of a Kevlar layer under that shell."

Lindahl turned to her. "Exactly. Very insightful. This additional substructure could account for the virion's stability, how it's proven resistant to bleaches, acids, even fire."

Yet, none of this answered the bigger question: *What's that tough coat protecting?*

Lindahl continued. "It seems Dr. Hess engineered a *perfect* shell, one that is small enough to penetrate any tissue. Animal, plant, fungus. Its unusual size and nature might explain why it's so universally pathogenic."

She nodded, remembering how the organism had sterilized the soil to a depth of two feet.

"But why did Hess create it?" Lisa asked. "What's its purpose?"

"Are you familiar with eVLPs?" Lindahl asked.

She shook her head.

"We were discussing the subject just before you arrived," Edmund explained. "It stands for empty virus-like particles. It's a new field of experimental study, where you strip the DNA out of a virus until only its outer shell remains. There are advantages to this in regards to vaccine production."

She understood. *Those empty particles would stimulate a strong antigenic or protective response without the risk of the vaccine agent making you sick.*

"But that's the least of it," Lindahl said. "Once you have an empty shell, you can build from there. Add organic or even inorganic compounds, like those graphene fibers."

"And once you create that shell," Edmund added, "you can fill it with whatever wonders or horrors you want. In other words, the perfect shell becomes the perfect delivery system."

Lisa stared again at the face of that monster.

What was *hidden inside there?*

"And you think Dr. Hess accomplished something like that?" Lisa asked. "That he built this virion from scratch in his lab and put something inside it."

Lindahl leaned back. "We already have the technology. Way back in 2002, a group of scientists at Stony Brook synthesized a live polio virus from nothing but chemicals and a known genetic blueprint."

Edmund huffed. "The project was sponsored by the Pentagon."

Lisa heard the not-so-veiled accusation in his voice. Dr. Hess's work was funded by the military, too.

Lindahl ignored the implication. "And in 2005, a larger influenza virus was synthesized in another lab. In 2006, the same was accomplished with the Epstein-Barr virus, which has the same number of base pairs as smallpox. But that's child's play compared to today. We can now manufacture organisms a hundred-fold larger and at a fraction of the cost." He snorted dismissively. "You can even buy a DNA synthesizer on eBay."

"So what exactly did Dr. Hess put in there?" Lisa asked.

Before anyone would hazard a guess, Lisa's radio buzzed. From the reactions of the other two men, they heard it, too.

It was Painter. The urgent stress in his voice quickened her heart. "We just heard word from Yosemite," he reported. "The suspected saboteur is dead."

Dead . . .

Lisa closed her eyes, thinking of Josh. Amy Serpry had been their only lead, the only way to discover more details about Dr. Hess's work.

"From the initial report," Painter continued, "she likely died of the same disease we're battling here. The National Guard, along with an outbreak response team, is en route to lock down the grounds around the Ahwahnee. We also possibly have new exposure victims. Ranger Beck and Gunnery Sergeant Drake. Along with the ranger's dog."

Oh, no . . .

Painter continued with additional instructions and safeguards. The CDC was to set up another quarantine area in the hangar, in time to accept the incoming victims.

Once he was done, Lisa switched to a private channel.

"How badly were they exposed?" she asked.

"Jenna and Drake never stepped inside the cabin, and according to Drake, it was raining with the wind at their backs, so they may be okay."

"And the dog?"

"He went inside the cabin and snatched up a mouse that may have been sick."

So the husky likely had mucosal contact with the virion.

She stared again at the monster on the screen.

Poor dog.

14

April 29, 4:04 P.M. GMT
Brunt Ice Shelf, Antarctica

As ice groaned and cracked beneath him, Gray gaped at the sight of the massive bulk of Halley Station passing overhead. Its giant skis scraped down the slanting surface of ice, beginning the slide toward a tumble into the frigid Weddell Sea.

On the far side of the station, that blasted fracture line still smoked and steamed from the fires of those buried munitions. The chunk of the ice holding the station continued to tilt away from the larger expanse of the Brunt Shelf.

Gray pushed to his feet and yanked the British pilot up. "Move it! Both of you!"

Kowalski gained his legs unsteadily, searching around. "Where?"

"Follow me!"

Gray took off, digging his boots into the snow-swept ice, climbing the ever-steepening slope as the station slid behind him. The surface was rough enough for adequate traction, but a few times, he slipped to a knee or a hand. Using the steel butt of his assault rifle as a crutch, he fought to move faster. They had only seconds to act. He shouldered his way into the fog of steam and smoke billowing down from the blast zone. Visibility dropped to an arm's length.

He prayed his sense of direction held true.

Another few steps, he let out a breath of relief—but only a small one.

The shape of a Ski-Doo appeared ahead. The rumble of its engine grew louder as he stumbled toward it.

Thank God, Jason had the foresight to leave it warmed up.

Gray reached the three-man Ski-Doo and swung his leg over the seat—but before he could settle into place, Barstow waved him back.

"Who's the expert here? I'll drive. You and your buddy ride shotgun."

Gray didn't argue, trusting the arctic pilot had more experience than he did with these snow machines. As Kowalski climbed on behind him, Gray pointed over the nose of the Ski-Doo, toward the widening fracture ahead.

"We'll have to—"

"Got it," Barstow said and gunned the engine.

Snow and shredded ice shot from behind the rear treads, and the Ski-Doo leaped forward. Their only hope was to try to vault over that gorge and reach the solid ice on the far side. The odds were slim, especially with their vehicle overloaded, but to remain here was certain death.

Gray hunkered lower.

Kowalski swore loudly.

Then Barstow made an abrupt sharp turn, catching Gray by surprise, almost throwing him out of his seat. The back end of the Ski-Doo skidded into a fish-tail until the nose was pointed away from the fracture zone. The engine roared louder, and Barstow sped the craft *down* the steep slope. They cleared the steamy fog and burst into the open. It now looked like they were chasing the slowly sliding station.

Gray yelled, "What're you—?"

"Let a man drive!"

Barstow hunched over the handlebars, trying to eke out more speed. Gray had no choice but to follow his example.

But they weren't alone out here.

The only warning was a flicker of navigation lights in the dark skies overhead. The enemy's Twin Otter sped past—then the ice exploded ahead of them in a fiery blast of rocket fire.

"Bloody hell!" Barstow hollered. "Hold on to your arses, gents!"

The pilot swerved around the smoking crater and sped toward the only shelter. He made another fast turn, casting up a rooster tail of ice and snow—then skidded sideways under the sliding station, passing cleanly between two of the four giant hydraulic skis holding up that module.

Kowalski groaned. "Just tell me when it's over!"

It wasn't.

Barstow had lost momentum after his rash maneuver, but he now raced along the underside of Halley VI, expertly keeping them out of direct sight of the Twin Otter. With the station still careening down the slanted shelf, the Ski-Doo regained some of its speed.

By now Gray understood Barstow's earlier maneuver, why he had done a 180, turning them about-face. There was no way the Ski-Doo—going *uphill*—could've gained enough speed to hurtle over that widening gorge, especially overloaded. But by going *downhill*, Barstow could gain momentum, transforming the Ski-Doo into a tread-driven rocket.

Only one problem with this plan . . .

They were running out of ice.

Ahead, the foremost module of this skidding centipede reached the cliff's edge and fell, twisting free of the remainder of the station, and plunged toward the dark seas far below.

"Time to go, boys!"

Barstow angled away, flying between two of the towering skis and back out into the open. They fled slightly upslope now, racing away from the station as it fell—piece by piece—into the Weddell Sea.

Ahead, their small section of dislodged ice teetered at a steep angle away from the flat expanse of the larger Brunt Ice Shelf. Barstow raced up that tilting chunk of ice, aiming for where the piece broke away from the greater shelf, picking a spot where the gap was the smallest.

He opened full throttle.

But a certain stubborn hawk was not about to lose its prey. The Twin Otter burst out of the smoky steam ahead of them, swooping low, its propellers ripping through the fog. It turned and lifted up on one wingtip, exposing the cabin hatch on that side—along with an assailant holding an RPG launcher to his shoulder.

The enemy was taking no chances.

The next shot would be at nearly point-blank range.

Gray twisted in his seat, elbowing Kowalski back. He freed his rifle and brought it up one-handed, his arm outstretched. He pulled hard on the trigger, strafing in full automatic mode, dumping all thirty rounds in three seconds. He concentrated his first volley on that dark doorway. With a scream, the gunman tumbled out the open hatch. Gray unloaded the rest of his rifle into the lowermost prop as the plane swept past.

"Hold on!" Barstow yelled.

Kowalski knocked Gray low into the seat, piling on top of him.

The Ski-Doo reached the last of the ice—and went airborne.

It flew high off the upraised lip of fractured ice, corkscrewing in midflight. Gray had a clear view down into the gap for a harrowing breath. Then they plummeted and hit the far side crookedly, landing on the edge of one tread.

The snow machine jolted hard and rolled, throwing them all clear.

Gray tumbled across the ice, losing his weapon, hugging his limbs in tight. He finally came to a stop. The Ski-Doo took another few bounces, then came to a rest. The other two men rose from the ice.

Kowalski patted himself, as if confirming he was still alive. "Didn't exactly stick that landing."

Barstow joined them, cradling one arm, his face bloody. He glanced over to the broken bulk of the

Ski-Doo. "As they say, any landing you can walk away from . . ."

"They were talking about airplanes," Kowalski admonished, "not friggin' snowmobiles."

The pilot shrugged his good shoulder. "We were *flying* there for a bit. So it still counts."

Gray ignored them and searched the skies. He watched a small cluster of lights fall out of the darkness, disappearing beyond the edge of the cliff as the broken-off corner of the Brunt Shelf slid into the sea. He wasn't positive he'd damaged the Twin Otter enough to make it crash or if the plane was merely limping away. Either way, the enemy could have radioed for additional support.

Gray didn't want to stick around to find out.

He turned to the Ski-Doo.

Barstow must have read his expression. "Sorry, mate, she's tits up. Looks like we'll be walking from here."

Gray pulled up the hood of his parka, already cold.

Kowalski voiced the question foremost in his own mind. "Where the hell do we go from here?"

4:18 P.M.

"It's gone . . . all gone."

Jason heard the despair in the station commander's voice—or rather *former* station commander. He and

Karen stood atop a hillock of ice. It was tall enough for them to see beyond the patches of cold fog all the way to the coast. The shattered section of the shelf's edge remained misty, but there was no mistaking a feature missing from that distant landscape.

The Halley VI Research Station was gone.

Those earlier blasts still filled Jason's head. While fleeing aboard one of the Ski-Doos, he had watched that coastline shatter away amid flashes of fire and concussive blasts. The shock wave of those detonations had traveled through the ice to his position a kilometer away. It had taken another few agonizing minutes to find a high enough vantage to get a good look at the outcome.

Now they knew.

. . . all gone.

Karen took a deep breath, shaking off her initial shock. "We should keep going," she warned, eyeing the thick polar fog.

The temperature seemed to be dropping tens of degrees every minute.

Or maybe it's hypothermia already settling in, Jason thought.

Thirty yards off, their lone Sno-Cat idled among the cluster of snowmobiles. They had rescued a dozen members of the station, but how long could they stay out here? Caught unprepared, most were poorly dressed for these frigid temperatures, and the group of snow machines would only get them so far on their single tanks of gas. Even the heater on the Sno-Cat wasn't working. It was why the vehicle had not been in use at the time of the attack.

"We need to find shelter," Karen said. "But we're still hundreds of miles from any base or camp. Our best chance is to stay here, hope someone heard those explosions and comes looking. But it could take days."

"How long can we last out here on our own?"

She snorted. "We'll be lucky to make it through the night. Sunrise is still another eighteen hours off. And the coming day will be only two hours long."

Jason considered their options. "If anyone does come looking for us, they'll have a hard time spotting us in the dark."

"Maybe we could devise some signal. Siphon some of the petrol from one of the vehicles and ignite it if we hear a plane."

Jason recognized one clear problem with this plan. "What if it's not *rescuers* that come looking for us first?"

Karen hugged her arms around herself. "You're right," she mumbled. "Then what do we do?"

"I think I know where we can go."

Karen lifted both eyebrows, but before she could question him, a squawk rose from her coat. She visibly startled at the sudden noise. She tugged down her parka's zipper and removed a portable radio, one of the set she had distributed before exiting the station.

". . . *hear us? Does anyone copy?*"

"That's Gray!" Jason said, struggling past the impossibility of it.

Karen passed Jason the radio.

He pressed the button. "Commander Pierce?"

"*Jason, where are you? Are you safe?*"

He did his best to explain his situation, while getting a brief description from Gray about his escape from that calving berg of ice. But Gray's team still remained stranded out there, and like Jason, he feared the enemy might return soon.

"I can take a couple of Ski-Doos and go fetch them," Karen offered.

He nodded.

She faced him, her expression doubtful. "But, Jason, do you truly know somewhere we can find shelter?"

He stared out across the dark, featureless ice.

I hope so.

5:22 P.M.

Gray shivered inside his jacket and hunched farther over the handlebars of his Ski-Doo. He had a thick wool scarf frozen over the lower half of his face. His gloved fingers felt molded onto the grips by the cold.

He squinted against the wind, his aching eyes fixed to the glow of the Ski-Doo's headlamp as it tunneled weakly through the swirling fog. He kept his gaze locked onto the snow machine in front of him, driven by Karen Von Der Bruegge. The station commander had arrived an hour ago, dragging a second empty Ski-Doo behind hers. She now carried the injured Barstow on her vehicle, while Kowalski huddled behind Gray.

Gray had to trust that Karen knew where she was going. She seemed to be following the treaded tracks of the group led by Jason. The kid had taken the others deeper into the fog-patched expanse of the Brunt Ice Shelf, retreating from the Weddell Sea—hopefully far enough away that the enemy couldn't find them.

If we're lucky, maybe they'll believe we were all killed.

The Ski-Doo in front suddenly slowed. Distracted in thought, Gray came close to rear-ending the other, but he braked in time to avoid a collision. After another ten yards, the reason for that sudden deceleration appeared out of the gloom.

A massive shadowy silhouette filled the world ahead of them. It looked like a flat-topped mountain rising from the icy plain. As they approached closer, details emerged: the towering skis, the bulk of the blue module, and the lone John Deere tractor.

It was a detached section of the destroyed station.

Earlier, Jason had noted this module being towed into the fog just before the assault broke out. He had hoped that the enemy, focused on the bulk of the Halley VI Research Station, might not have spotted its departure.

Looks like the kid was right.

Though dark, the module looked unmolested. He spotted a Sno-Cat and a scatter of snow machines parked nearby. Karen drove her vehicle up and stopped alongside them. Gray trundled his Ski-Doo next to hers.

A hatch in the rear of the high module opened, and Jason stepped onto the small back deck. He waved them forward to the ladder that led up to him. Gray needed no such encouragement. The steamy breath of warm air from that open hatch was invitation enough.

The group hurried toward the shelter and its promise of heat. The temperature had dropped to thirty below zero, and with the katabatics kicking up more fiercely as the night deepened, the wind chill made the freeze all the more bone numbing.

Gray assisted Barstow up the ladder. The pilot had dislocated his arm when they crashed the Ski-Doo, and while they'd managed to pop it back into place, the limb was still painful and weak. After a bit of effort, everyone got inside.

Gray slammed the hatch against the polar freeze and took a moment to bask in the warmth. His face burned painfully as it thawed. Frostbite was certainly a worry, but at least he could still feel the tip of his nose.

He followed the others into the heart of the module, which appeared to be one of those residential pods, broken into bedrooms, a communal bathroom, and a gymnasium. Everything was decorated in primary colors, designed to compensate for the endless monotony of this frozen world. As his nasal passages continued to thaw, he also smelled the cedar scents from the wall planks, another psychological trick to mitigate for the lack of plants and greenery.

They all gathered in a small central common room, which held a table and chairs. Several of the rescued researchers had already retreated to various bunkrooms, likely shell-shocked and exhausted. Others leaned on walls, wearing dour, worried expressions.

They had full right to look that way.

Jason spoke, "We were able to catch up with the John Deere. Think we spooked the tractor driver as we all piled up on his tail. But at least his path was easy to follow. Once we got here, we fired up the module's generator." The kid waved to the smatter of lights. "Unfortunately we have no way to radio out."

Kowalski clapped Jason on the back. "You found this goddamned place. That's more than enough to win you a cigar." Proving himself a man of his word, he pulled a cellophane-wrapped stogie from an inside pocket of his parka and handed it to Jason. He then looked around. "It's okay to smoke in here, right?"

"Not normally," Karen said. "But considering the circumstances, I'll make an exception."

"Then I could get used to this place." Kowalski stalked off, perhaps looking for a quiet place to light up.

Gray turned to more practical matters. "What's the status of food and water?"

"No food in the module," Jason answered. "Only what the tractor driver brought with him. It was meant to last him several days in case he got stranded, but his reserves are not nearly enough to cover our numbers. Water shouldn't be a problem, though. We can always melt snow or ice."

"Then we'll have to ration what food we have." Gray turned next to Karen as she sank to a seat, her face wan and tired. "About what happened . . . those munitions that blew off that chunk of ice must have been buried for some time. How could that be?"

"I can only hazard a guess. The bombs could've been drilled into place and frozen over long before the station arrived."

"Is that possible?"

"It wouldn't be that hard," she speculated. "We shifted Halley VI closer to the sea about three months ago, so the climate scientists could complete their study of the accelerating thaw of the continent's ice sheets. Our move had been mapped out and scheduled a full year in advance, including picking the coordinates for our new location."

Gray considered this. "So somebody with such foreknowledge could've easily laid this trap, ready to destroy the station at a whim."

"Yes, but it still doesn't explain why."

"Perhaps it has something to do with Professor Harrington's research. Your station acts as the gateway to Queen Maud Land, where the professor's group set up shop. If somebody wanted to suddenly isolate that secret site, getting rid of Halley VI would be an important first step."

She looked even more ashen.

He asked, "Do you have any idea *what* Harrington was working on?"

Karen shook her head. "No, but that doesn't mean rumors didn't spread about what was going on out there. Stories ranged from the discovery of a lost Nazi base to the secret testing of nuclear weapons—which was done in this region by your own country, I might add, back in 1958. But all of this is wild conjecture at best."

Still, whatever the truth was, it was clearly worth killing over.

And likely still is.

He glanced to one of the triangular windows. "We'll need to post lookouts. All sides of the module. And at least one person patrolling outside, watching the skies."

Karen stood from the table. "I'll begin arranging shifts."

"One other thing," Jason said before she left. He pointed to a figure in oil-stained coveralls. "Carl says he can stay with the John Deere."

The man nodded. He must be the tractor driver.

"Its cabin is heated," Jason added. "Carl can tweak our position to keep the module under the fog flowing down from the coast. It should help hide us."

Gray admitted it was a solid plan. But how long could they hold out?

And more worrisome: *Who would find them first?*

11:43 P.M.

As midnight approached, Jason pulled into his parka and gathered his gloves, scarf, and goggles. He was scheduled for the first shift of the new day. They changed patrols on the hour, to avoid anyone standing watch for too long out in the frigid weather.

While he had taken a nap in preparation for his shift, he felt far from rested, nagged by worries.

And I'm certainly not looking forward to the next sixty cold minutes.

Once suited up, he headed to the hatch. He found Joe Kowalski leaning against the frame. He had the smoldering stub of cigar between his back molars, looking like he'd been chewing on it for a while.

"Shouldn't you be catching some shut-eye?" Jason asked. Sigma's demolitions expert was scheduled to relieve him at 1 A.M.

"Couldn't sleep." He took out his cigar and pointed its glowing tip at Jason. "You be careful out there. From what I hear, Crowe's got big hopes for you. Don't go getting yourself killed."

"Wasn't planning on it."

"That's just the thing, *planning's* got nothing to do with it. It's the unexpected that'll bite you in the ass every time. Blindside the hell out of you."

Jason nodded, recognizing the practical wisdom buried behind those gruff words. He stepped to move past Kowalski, when he noted a small photo clutched in the man's thick fingers. Before Jason could get more than a glimpse of the woman in the picture, Kowalski tucked the photo away.

As Jason hauled open the door, he wondered if the man's warning was less about the dangers of a mission and more about the pitfalls of a romantic life.

But such thoughts vanished as the cold struck him like a hard slap to the face. The wind came close to shoving him off the high deck. He half slid his way to the ladder and climbed down. He found one of the researchers sheltered on the leeward side of one of the giant ski towers.

The man crossed, patted Jason on the shoulder, and with a voice quavering from the bitter cold said, "All quiet. If you get too frozen, hop into Carl's cab to warm up."

With those few words, the researcher headed up the ladder and toward the promise of a warm bed.

Jason checked his watch.

Only fifty-nine minutes to go.

He slowly paced the station, staying out of the wind as much as possible. He studied the skies, searching for any telltale lights of an approaching plane. All remained dark out there; not even the stars were visible through the ice fog rolling across the shelf from the distant coast. The only light came from the south, a slight yellow glow, marking the John Deere's location. He used its position like a compass as he made his rounds.

After a while, the howl of the wind seemed to fill his head, rattling around inside his skull. His eyes began to play tricks on him, seeing phantom lights in the gloom. He blinked or rubbed them away.

As he circled yet again, he considered hopping into the tractor's cabin—not for the warmth, but to escape the monotony of the darkness and the perpetual howl of the katabatic winds. He moved out from under the hulking module and stepped toward that patch of yellow light, only to have a vague glow catch his eyes to the far left, to the west.

He tried blinking away that dull light, only to have it become *two* eyes shining out of the gloom. Through the roaring in his head, a lower grumbling intruded—accompanied a moment later by the *crunch* of ice.

It took him another half breath to realize it wasn't a trick of the night, but something huge, barreling through the winds toward the lone module.

Jason hauled out his radio and brought it to his lips. "I've got movement out here. On the ice. A big vehicle approaching from the west."

"Copy that," the lookout inside said. The man shouted to others inside the station before returning to the radio. "I'm seeing it now, too!"

Jason moved behind the cover of one of the ski supports, the radio still at his lips. "Tell Carl to douse his lights out there!"

After another couple of seconds, that island of warm light extinguished. The only illumination now came from those twin beams of light that rapidly grew larger and brighter. Jason estimated that what approached was the size of a tank. This particular guess was heightened by the sound of treads grinding across ice.

Jason heard the hatch slam shut above. Then Gray and Kowalski came clambering down the ladder, pistols in hand. Only then did Jason think to remove his own weapon from inside his parka.

"Over here!" Jason called to them.

The two men joined him.

Gray pointed to the other hydraulic towers. "Spread out. Stay hidden. Let them get close. Offload even. Any signs that they're hostiles, we'll use the darkness to wage a guerrilla war on the ground. Barstow is on the roof with Karen, armed with our last two rifles, to help cover us from above."

After getting acknowledgment from Jason about this plan, Gray headed to one pillar, Kowalski another. They ran low, trying not to be seen.

The lumbering vehicle had slowed, its engine changing timbre.

Then it stopped forty yards off.

The winds shifted the fog enough to reveal a strange sight. The arctic machine was the size of a massive tank and looked like one, too. Giant belt treads flanked both sides, each rising taller than an elephant's back. They supported what appeared to be an armored bus topped by what looked like the wheelhouse of a tugboat.

Lights flared up top, along with shadowy movement from within.

A door opened in that wheelhouse, and a dark figure stepped out onto the open deck that circled the upper structure. A shout cut through the wind's howl. It was not loud enough to discern any words, but it sounded like a query, a challenge.

Another figure passed something to the one on the deck.

From the sudden increase in volume of the speaker, it must have been a bullhorn. "HELLO! WE INTERCEPTED YOUR RADIO COMMUNICATION EARLIER! WE KNOW ABOUT YOUR TROUBLE!"

The speaker was clearly a woman, British from her accent. She must have eavesdropped on Gray's earlier radio call to Karen.

"WE FOLLOWED YOUR TRACKS AND CAME TO HELP!"

Gray bellowed from his hiding place, needing no bullhorn to be heard. "Who are you?"

"WE REPRESENT PROFESSOR ALEX HARRINGTON. WE WERE EN ROUTE TO

COLLECT A GROUP OF AMERICANS WHEN WE HEARD OF THE ATTACK."

Jason bit back his shock and considered this possibility. Painter had told them that the professor's contacts would be *flying* over to Halley. But after eavesdropping on the station's attack, had they turned back and come overland instead?

"WE MUST HURRY! IF THE AMERICANS ARE HERE, THEY MUST COME WITH US RIGHT AWAY."

"And who exactly are you?" Gray pressed, plainly wanting more proof. "What is your name?"

"I'M STELLA . . . STELLA HARRINGTON."

Jason took in a sharp breath, recognizing the name from the mission files. The speaker confirmed this in the next breath.

"THE PROFESSOR IS MY FATHER—AND HE'S IN DIRE TROUBLE!"

15

If they poke me with one more damned needle . . .

Jenna paced the length of her section of the newly expanded patient containment unit. She'd been quarantined here for the past twelve hours.

Inside the hangar, the CDC team had added new pods to the original quarantine hospital. Through a window on one side, she could see Josh, unconscious on his bed. He had suffered two more seizures during the past afternoon, fading in and out of delirium.

From her pod, she watched the young man being subjected to another battery of tests. A nurse held him rolled up one side, while a doctor performed a spinal tap. There remained little doubt Josh had become septicemic with whatever microbe was out there. But from what Jenna had been told, they hadn't been able to isolate the presence of the infectious virus in any of his tissues or blood as of yet.

They kept taking samples from her, too, looking for the same.

On the other side of her pod—*my cell*, she thought angrily—another window revealed Sam Drake in the neighboring section. Like her, he was dressed in a hospital gown and looked no happier as he sat in his bed. They had both been thoroughly scrubbed upon arriving here, a humiliating procedure that included having to huff through a pressurized nebulizer that delivered an aerosolized dose of a powerful broad-spectrum antimicrobial. It was a precaution in case they had inhaled any of the infectious particles at the Yosemite cabin—not that the drug had yet to be proven effective.

But better than nothing, I suppose.

Since then, she and Drake had been swabbed, scraped, poked, and had every bodily fluid collected. So far neither of them suffered from any of the clinical symptoms Josh had shown within the first twelve hours: namely a spiked fever and muscle tremors. Because of that, the doctors believed she and Drake might have escaped exposure at that cabin. Still, as an additional precaution, they had to stay quarantined for another day. If they remained asymptomatic, they could be discharged.

Could be being the operative message.

Very little was certain at the moment.

With one exception . . .

She paced another lap in her cell. Worry kept her moving, agitated, unable to sit or lie down for long. There was a third member of the Yosemite team whose fate was less uncertain.

Nikko.

Her partner had been whisked over to the suite of research labs across the dark hangar. Lisa assured her that he would be well taken care of, that she would keep Nikko kenneled in her own lab. Unfortunately, Nikko was spiking a fever already, accompanied by vomiting and diarrhea.

My poor boy . . .

Jenna longed to break out of here, to go to him. If only to comfort Nikko, to let him know she loved him. Anger fought with grief, leaving an ache in her chest. She hated to think of him suffering alone, wondering where she was, believing he'd been abandoned. But worst of all, she could not fathom losing him.

"You're going to wear a rut right through the floor."

She turned to see Drake at the window, his finger on the intercom button. He smiled softly, sadly, plainly knowing she was hurting.

She crossed and pressed the intercom's talk button. "If only I could go to him."

"I know, but Lisa will do everything she can." Drake's gaze moved past her shoulder to the window behind her. "Especially since she's got a personal stake in all this."

Jenna felt a twinge of guilt. What was the loss of a dog compared to a brother? Maybe she needed to gain a better perspective about all of this, to stay professional. After all, Nikko was just a dog.

But she refused to accept that.

To her, Nikko was just as much of a brother.

"What we can do while we're waiting," Drake said, lowering his voice, "is to figure out *what* we're all fighting. If we knew what was brewed up in that damned lab, then both Josh and Nikko would have a better chance of surviving."

Thunder boomed overhead, rattling the hangar, reminding her that it wasn't just Josh and Nikko who were at risk. The storm had finally reached Mono Basin, and the rain had begun to fall in the highlands beyond. According to Director Crowe, emergency crews were using helicopters to dump piles of sandbags into all of the lower streams and dry creek beds, to try to limit the contagion's spread.

Not that anyone expected total containment.

Even if the initial sandbagging efforts were effective, how long would those makeshift dams hold? And what if the organism reached the subterranean aquifers that drained throughout the region, contaminating the very water table?

Drake was right.

She kept her thumb on the talk button. "But how can we help find out anything more about that damned microbe? Especially locked up inside here. With the saboteur dead, that was our last direct lead."

"Then what about *indirect*?" Drake offered.

Jenna took a deep breath, trying to push back her anxiety and frustration. With the base blown up, with Hess kidnapped and still missing, the trail seemed cold. As far as anyone knew, Hess's inner circle of researchers was present at the lab at the time of its destruction. Amy Serpry had been their only hope.

With more time, maybe another clue could be found.

But they didn't have that time.

"Is there something we missed?" Drake asked, plainly racking his own brain.

She reviewed everything in her head: from the initial SOS received by Bill Howard to watching Amy

Serpry's body being airlifted away, sealed in a body bag. Her corpse had become the focus of attention over at the suite of BSL4 labs across the hangar.

Jenna closed her eyes, walking herself through the horrors of the past forty-eight hours. It was hard to believe only two days had passed since that call from Bill Howard.

That call . . .

She opened her eyes, letting the shock show.

"Jenna?" Drake asked.

"I have to reach Painter Crowe! Now!"

8:12 P.M.

For the moment, Painter had Colonel Bozeman's office to himself. It was a rare moment of privacy in what had become the command center for emergency operations in the area. In the past two days, a hurricane of political, military, and law enforcement agencies had crashed down upon this area, mostly falling upon Painter's own head. If an agency had an acronym, they were here, needing to be pacified, directed, or consulted.

As was usual with such matters, it had quickly threatened to become an ineffectual clusterfuck. Luckily, due to past efforts by Sigma, the president had personally intervened and granted Painter emergency authority, tapping him as the top dog here.

But be careful what you wish for . . .

Painter was still struggling to rein in the various agencies, to get everyone moving as a team. It had left little time for him to think, only react, to put out fires where he could.

So he took advantage of this momentary calm, while knowing this was only the proverbial eye of the hurricane.

I should go down and check on Lisa.

It had been hours since he'd last visited her. Not that talking through a window was the same as holding her. She had looked a ghost of herself even back then. He knew what drove her to such a ragged edge. Josh was getting worse, and there remained no effective treatment on the horizon.

He shoved his chair back, ready to comfort her as best he could—when the door opened. It was the Marine who had been assigned as his aide, a straight-laced young woman in a crisp uniform and cap named Jessup.

"Director Crowe," she said, "I have Ranger Beck on the line. She said it's urgent."

"Patch the call through."

He had spoken only briefly to Jenna and Drake after they returned from Yosemite. So far, the pair remained in good health and had likely avoided exposure. It was a small bit of good news in an otherwise bad day, especially as there remained no word from Gray's team in Antarctica, not since he had reached that British ice station. So far Kat was not overly worried, reporting that a massive solar flare was compromising communication across most of the southern hemisphere.

Hopefully they'd hear something from Gray soon.

In the meantime . . .

He picked up the phone. "Director Crowe here."

"Sir!" Jenna did sound agitated. "I just remembered something that might be important."

He sat up straighter. "What is it?"

"Back at the cabin, before I broke in, before I heard Amy's last plea for help—I heard a cell phone ringing inside. After everything that followed, I forgot to mention it."

"Are you sure it was a cell and not the cabin telephone?"

"I'm sure. Maybe it was someone checking up on her. An accomplice, someone who hired her. I don't know."

"But that makes no sense. We recovered Serpry's cell phone and personal belongings from the cabin before it was sealed up. Everything was thoroughly examined. I personally reviewed the LUDs pulled from her phone, hoping for some outside connection like you mentioned."

"And?"

"And there was nothing significant. A few calls to relatives and friends. But more important, there was not a single incoming or outgoing call placed in the past twenty-four hours from that cell phone. Even if she hadn't picked up, that call attempt would've shown up in those line-usage records."

There was a long pause on the line. "I'm sure it was her cell phone," Jenna said firmly. "Someone was attempting to reach her."

Painter had learned a healthy respect for the ranger and took her at her word. "I'll have a technician look over that phone again."

If Jenna was right and if those records had somehow been erased or corrupted, such an action had to be significant. It would certainly suggest that last call had been placed by one of Serpry's cohorts, possibly even by whoever was pulling her strings.

"You may have given us a new lead," Painter admitted.

"Good. Then if anything turns up, I want to be involved in following it up."

In the background, he heard a brash voice echo that sentiment, coming from Gunnery Sergeant Drake. "Me, too!"

Painter knew how determined the pair was to help, especially after what had happened to the ranger's dog.

"Let's see where this leads first," he said noncommittally.

"We're not sick!" Drake yelled in the background. "We're going! Even if I have to take a scalpel and cut our way out of here."

Painter understood their determination. He saw the same in Lisa's eyes each time he visited her. But sometimes all the determination in the world wasn't enough. Sometimes only one path was left open.

To make hard and difficult choices.

8:22 P.M.

"Dr. Cummings, I believe we should put the dog down."

Lisa swung toward Dr. Raymond Lindahl. The director from the U.S. Army Developmental Test Command crouched in his biosafety suit before the stainless steel cage that housed the husky.

Nikko lay on his side, breathing shallowly, an IV in place. He had been given a slight sedative to keep him calm, along with antiemetics to control his vomiting and a cocktail of antivirals.

Still, the dog continued to decline.

"He's suffering," Lindahl said, straightening to face her. "You'll be doing him a favor. And at his current level of infection, a necropsy would allow us to get a better understanding of the disease in these early stages. It's a rare opportunity."

Lisa kept her voice even, despite the anger seething inside her. "We can learn just as much by monitoring the patient's clinical signs, to measure his responses to various therapies."

The man rolled his eyes. "Until we better understand *what* we're dealing with, any therapy is just shooting in the dark. It's a foolish waste of resources and time."

Lisa stepped between Lindahl and Nikko's cage.

The director sighed. "I don't want to have to order you, Dr. Cummings. I thought you'd listen to reason."

"I don't take orders from you."

Lindahl stared her down. "I've been given full authority over these labs by military command. Besides, I thought you'd want to do everything humanly possible to help your brother."

She bristled at his accusation. "There's nothing *human* or humane about what you're proposing."

"You can't let sentimentality cloud your professional judgment," he argued. "Science by necessity must be dispassionate."

"Until I'm pulled from this lab by security, I won't let anyone harm my patient."

The fate of Nikko was interrupted by the hiss of the air lock as it released. They both turned to find the virologist, Edmund Dent, stepping into the lab, accompanied by the team's geneticist, Dr. Henry Jenkins, a towheaded wunderkind at the young age of twenty-five.

From Edmund's expression behind his face shield, he had bad news. "I wanted you to hear this in person," the virologist started. "We have the latest tests on your brother."

Lisa felt a sinking feeling in her gut, along with a measure of release, suspecting what Edmund had come to tell her. She had been waiting all along for this other shoe to drop.

"While we're still not finding active viremia in Josh's blood—which is a good sign—we spun down the latest sample of his cerebrospinal fluid."

Edmund motioned his companion to her computer station. Henry logged in and brought up Josh's medical file. Her brother's picture flashed up on the screen briefly, taken from his driver's license, his face smiling and wind-burned from a recent mountaineering trip.

Her heart tightened at the sight.

It was quickly replaced with an electron micrograph.

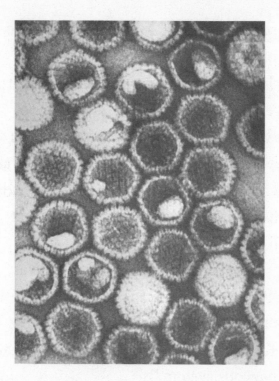

It showed a tight cluster of virions—collected from the sediment of her brother's CSF after it had been run through the lab's ultracentrifuge. By now, Lisa had no trouble recognizing the characteristic shape of the enemy.

She had difficulty balancing her brother's smiling face with the horror showing on the screen now. Tears welled up. She could not speak.

Edmund must have sensed her distress. "We think the progression of Josh's disease has been so protracted because the virus traveled up a nerve bundle in his leg to reach his central nervous system. Similar to the pathway taken by the rabies virus. It might also explain why we still find no active viral presence in his blood and why it took so long to detect its presence."

Henry clarified the significance. "When you amputated his leg in the field, the blood loss that followed likely washed any viral particles that had begun to establish in the limb's circulatory and lymphatic system."

"But not from the peripheral nerves," Edmund added. "A few particles must have reached the tibial or perhaps the common peroneal nerve before the amputation. There it took refuge and slowly spread up to his central nervous system."

She must have looked sickened.

Edmund touched her arm. "Still, this proves your quick actions in the field succeeded in buying your brother some valuable time."

She knew Edmund was trying to assuage her guilt, but she knew the fundamental truth here.

I should have taken off Josh's entire leg.

Instead, she had attempted to leave her brother with a functional knee joint, which would allow him better mobility with a prosthetic. As active as her brother was, she had wanted to give him the best chance to return to a full life.

If only I'd adhered to Lindahl's philosophy from a moment ago . . .

Out in those fields, she had let sentimentality cloud her professional judgment. And now it might cost Josh his life.

Possibly to distract her, Edmund pointed to the computer screen. "You should know that Henry has also learned a bit more about what makes this engineered monster tick."

Lisa fought through her despair, knowing it would do Josh no good.

Henry explained. "I've been working with the team's molecular biologist to do a genetic analysis of what lies *inside* the virion's synthetic capsid."

Lisa pictured that spherical protein shell, supported by an underlayment of tough graphene fibers. At the time she had wondered what lay hidden inside that hard exterior.

"We macerated and centrifuged samples of the virus to free the nucleic acids that make up its genetic—"

Lindahl stepped forward, waving impatiently. "We don't need to know how the sausage is made, Dr. Jenkins. We're not first-year biology students. Just tell us what you learned."

Edmund gave the director a scolding frown. "Henry was attempting to explain the difficulty in gaining such knowledge. It bears significance on what he's discovered."

"What difficulty?" Lisa asked.

Henry stared at her, looking exceptionally boyish with his thick-rimmed black eyeglasses and his tow-headed smooth looks. "Our initial attempts to extract any DNA failed. In fact, using a diphenylamine indicator, we failed to detect any DNA at all. We tried other techniques, too, with no better luck."

"What about RNA?" Lisa asked.

She knew that viruses fell into two categories: those that used deoxyribonucleic acid, DNA, as their genetic base versus those that used ribonucleic acid, RNA.

"We didn't find any RNA either," Henry said.

"That's impossible." Lindahl let his irritation ring out. "Then what did you find?"

Henry looked to Edmund, who answered for the more timid geneticist. "He and the molecular biologist found a form of XNA."

Lisa frowned, not understanding.

Edmund explained, "After successfully extracting nucleic acids from the virion's tough shell, they discovered no deoxyribose or ribose. Instead they found something foreign making up that genetic backbone."

"The X stands for *xeno*," Henry said. "Meaning alien."

"But he doesn't mean extraterrestrial," Edmund quickly added. "We believe this genetic material was engineered. Scientists have been dabbling with creating exotic types of XNAs for over a decade, demonstrating in their labs that these molecules can replicate and evolve, just like our DNA."

"But in this virion's case, what's different?" Lisa asked. "What's replaced the deoxyribose or ribose in these genetic molecules?"

Henry chewed his lower lip, then spoke. "We're still working on that, but so far we've detected traces of arsenic and abnormally high levels of iron phosphate."

Arsenic and iron . . .

Lisa crinkled her brow, remembering that Dr. Hess had come to Mono Lake because of the discovery of arsenic-loving bacteria in its mud. Was there some connection?

"But what was Hess trying to create with all of this?" Lindahl asked. "What was the purpose of this project?"

Edmund shrugged. "We can only guess. But there's one significant detail concerning those known XNAs created in various labs. They've all proven to be more resistant to degradation."

In other words, tougher.

"Just like that outer shell," Lindahl said. "No wonder we can't destroy the damned thing."

"At least not yet," Henry countered. "But if we could get a better handle on what makes up that exotic molecule—basically discover what that X stands for in this XNA—then we might be able to devise not only a viricide to kill the organism, but also a therapeutic regimen for anyone infected by it."

Lisa pictured Josh across the hangar and allowed herself a measure of hope—but only a small one.

"There's one other detail about XNAs that might be important," Edmund added. "It ties to the origin of life. The current research into XNA's ability to replicate and evolve suggests that a more ancient genetic system may have once existed on this planet, a genetic system *older* than DNA or RNA, one that predates the modern world."

Lisa considered this possibility and its implication. "The core of Dr. Hess's work had to do with engineering our way out of this current mass extinction. Could this experiment with synthetic life have something to do with that? Could he have been seeking to build a hardier ecosystem, one based or supported by XNA, something that could withstand pollution or survive the overheating of the globe?"

"Who knows?" Edmund admitted. "You'll have to ask him, if we ever find him. But Henry here has one last concern in regards to the problem at hand."

"What's that?" Lindahl asked.

Henry faced them. "I don't think this virion is an artificial construct . . . at least not entirely."

"Why do you think that?" Lisa asked.

"To date, no one's been able to successfully construct a fully functional XNA *organism*. The number of variables to accomplish that is astronomical. It seems like too much of a scientific leap forward, even for Dr. Hess."

Lindahl pointed to the monitor and the micrograph still on the screen. "But he succeeded. There's the proof."

Henry gave a small shake of his head. "Not necessarily. I think he made that leap by using a template. I think he found something exotic—a living XNA organism—and simply manipulated it into this current form, creating a hybrid of natural and synthetic biology."

Lisa slowly nodded. "You could be right. Hess had a great interest in extremophiles. Searching the world for the unusual or the bizarre. Maybe he found something."

Was that why he had been kidnapped?

"And if we could discover what that was," Edmund added, "then maybe we'd know what that X stands for and could begin to turn the tide on this whole mess."

Lisa's radio crackled and Painter came onto her private channel. She was excited to talk to him, to share what she had just learned—both the grim and the hopeful.

"I think we may have another lead," Painter said before she could speak. "Jenna suggested we take another look at Amy Serpry's cell phone. It looks like someone went to great lengths and sophistication to erase their communication with Serpry, to clear the local usage details from her service provider. But not everything got washed away completely, not if you know where and how to look deeper."

"What did you learn?" she asked, stepping away from the others.

Painter explained, "We were able to reconstruct enough of those records to know a call had been placed to her from South America. From the city of Boa Vista, the capital of the northern Brazilian state of Roraima."

Lisa knelt by Nikko's cage. The husky lifted his head, his eyes glassy as they rolled in her direction. He thumped his tail once.

That's a good boy.

"Before that trail gets any colder," Painter said, "I'm going to lead a team down there to investigate. I'll keep in contact with Colonel Bozeman, who will be running the show here in my absence."

Lisa wanted to go with him, to keep close to Painter's side, but she met the husky's pained gaze and knew her place was here. She also remembered Lindahl's warning.

You can't let sentimentality cloud your professional judgment.

She would not make that mistake again. Still, that didn't keep her from worrying. As Painter signed off, a question weighed on her.

What or who would be waiting for Painter down in Brazil?

16

April 29, 11:35 P.M. AMT
Airborne over Brazil

Dr. Kendall Hess ducked lower in his seat as another bolt of lightning shattered across the underbellies of the black clouds, lighting the dark forests far below. The thunderclap shook the helicopter, while rain slashed the window canopy of the small aircraft.

In front, the pilot swore in Spanish, fighting through the storm. Kendall's hulking escort sat in the back cabin with him, looking unperturbed, staring out the window on his side.

Kendall swallowed back his terror and tried to do the same. He pressed his forehead against the window. The flash of lightning had revealed little but the endless expanse of green jungle below. They had been flying southwest over this rain forest for the better part of the day, landing once at a refueling dump, which had been hacked out of the forest and camouflaged with netting.

Wherever they're taking me, it's beyond remote.

He despaired at ever seeing the larger world again.

He knew he must be somewhere in South America, likely still north of the equator. But he knew little else. Last night, his kidnappers had landed their Cessna for a final time outside a small town. He was taken to a ramshackle house with a corrugated tin roof and no running water and was allowed to sleep on a mattress on the dirt floor. They'd kept him hooded as they ferried him from the plane so he got no chance to figure out the name of that town. He had heard voices, though, from the streets, speaking in Spanish, some English, but mostly Portuguese.

From that, he guessed he was in Brazil, likely one of its northern states. But they hadn't stayed long enough for him to determine anything else. At dawn the next day, they transferred him to this small helicopter, which looked weathered and barely airworthy.

Still, it had gotten them this far.

Another burst of chain lightning crackled across the clouds. A dark silhouette appeared near the horizon, rising starkly from the forest, like a black battleship riding a green sea. Kendall shifted higher, trying to get a better view—especially as Mateo stirred, gathering a pack from the floor.

Was that their destination?

As the helicopter droned onward, the rain slowed but the rumbling thunder continued, accompanied by occasional bolts of brilliance, each one revealing more details of the mountain ahead.

And it was a *mountain*—rising from the forest floor in sheer cliffs, thousands of feet tall. Its flat summit, shrouded in heavy mists, pushed above the lowermost clouds.

Kendall recognized this unusual geological formation. It was unique to this region of South America. Towering blocks of ancient sandstone like this— called tepui—lay scattered across the rain forests and swamps of northern Brazil, extending into Venezuela and Guyana. They numbered over a hundred. The most famous was Mount Roraima, rising almost two miles above the forest floor, with its summit—a flat plateau—spread over ten square miles.

The tepui ahead was much smaller, maybe a quarter of that size.

But long ago, these hundreds of mesas had once been connected together into a single giant sandstone massif. As the continents broke apart and shifted, that ancient massif fragmented into pieces, where rain and wind eroded the broken blocks into this collection of scattered plateaus, lonely sentinels of another time.

Though Kendall had never visited any of these tepuis, he knew about them from his research into unusual forms of life. The tepuis were some of earth's oldest formations, going back to Precambrian times, older than most fossils. These islands in the sky, isolated for ages, were home to species found only atop their summits, animals and plants unique unto themselves. Due to the remoteness of the region and the sheer cliffs, many of the plateaus had never been walked by man. They represented some of the least-explored areas on the planet, remaining unpolluted and pure.

The helicopter climbed higher, buffeted by stronger winds, and swept toward the mountain—which from a bird's-eye view looked dark and forbidding, untouched by man.

As they crested the plateau, the surface of the tepui wasn't as flat as it appeared from a distance. A large central pond dominated the summit, reflecting their navigation lights. Along its southern bank, storm-flooded waters spilled down to a lower section of the plateau, a shelf covered by a dense, stunted forest, a mockery of the rich life far below. North of the pond spread a labyrinth of rock, sculpted by wind and rain into chasms, caves, and a forest of unearthly pillars, all of it covered by a spongy dark-green moss or a gelatinous-looking algae. But between the cracks, he spotted flourishes of orchids and flowering bromeliads, a magical garden bathed by the mists.

The helicopter lowered for a landing on a flat section of stone near the pond, its lights sweeping the plateau. Only then did Kendall see signs of human occupation. Built within one of the larger caves—filling it completely like an overflowing cornucopia—was a magnificent stone home with balconies, gables, even a hothouse conservatory. The home's surfaces were all painted shades of dark green to match its surroundings.

He also noted a neighboring corral, which held a couple of Arabian horses, alongside a parked row of golf carts, which looked distinctly out of place, though the vehicles were also painted green. Beyond the house, a handful of tall wind turbines blended perfectly with the stone pillars.

Someone plainly wants to keep a low profile.

That someone stood nearby, under an umbrella.

Once the skids touched down, Kendall's guard opened the cabin door and hopped out. He kept his tall height bowed from the blades overhead. A handful of men stood nearby with camouflage netting in hand, ready to hide the aircraft after it shut down. The group shared the same dark complexion and round faces as the guard and pilot. Likely they were all from the same native tribe.

Knowing he had no choice, Kendall climbed out into the misty drizzle. He shivered at the clammy coldness at this elevation, a distinct difference from the swelter of rain forest below. He stepped toward the man who the world believed had died eleven years ago.

"Cutter Elwes. For a dead man, you are looking well."

In fact, Cutter appeared *better* than the last time the two had spoken. It had been ages ago, at a synthetic biology conference in Nice. Then Cutter had been red-faced, full of youthful fury at the poor reception his paper had received from Kendall's colleagues.

But what had he expected?

Now the man appeared fit, relaxed, a calm purposefulness to his blue-steel gaze under dark black hair. He was dressed in crisp linen pants and a white shirt, with a beige safari vest on top.

"And you, my dear friend, look tired . . . and wet." Cutter held out his own umbrella.

Angry, Kendall ignored the offering.

Cutter voiced no offense and returned the umbrella to above his own head. He turned, clearly expecting Kendall to follow, which he did.

Where else am I going to go?

"I imagine you've had a hard trip getting here," Cutter said. "It's late and Mateo here will see you to your bed. There is a cold dinner, along with hot coffee— decaffeinated, of course—waiting for you on the nightstand. We have a long day ahead of us tomorrow."

Kendall stepped faster, drawing abreast of his host, trailed by his hulking escort. "You killed . . . murdered so many people. My friends, colleagues. If you expect me to cooperate after all you've done . . ."

Cutter dismissed this concern with a wave. "We'll hash out the details in the morning."

They reached the four-story home and passed through double doors into a cavernous entry hall. It was floored in hand-scraped planks of Brazilian mahogany, the ceiling arched high, the walls decorated in French tapestries. If Kendall hadn't known about the Elwes family wealth, he would have suspected as much from the many millions it must have cost to build this home in secret.

Kendall searched around, knowing that there must be more to this place. Cutter's passion had never been about finance or the accumulation of wealth. His passion had always been about the planet. He had started as a dedicated environmentalist, using family money to fund many conservation causes. But the man was also brilliant, with a Mensa score that pushed him beyond genius. Though Cutter was French on his father's side, he had studied at both Cambridge and Oxford. The latter was where his mother was educated and where Kendall had first met Cutter.

After the man graduated, he took that big brain of his and bottomless wealth and started a grassroots movement to democratize science with the establishment of teaching labs around the world, many delving into the early fringes of genetic engineering and DNA synthesis. He quickly became the proverbial king of the biopunk community, those heady entrepreneurs who were hacking their way into genetic code with delightful abandon.

He also nurtured a great following by fiercely advocating for an overhaul to environmental policy. Over time, he made extremist groups like Earth First! and the Earth Liberation Army seem conservative in comparison. People were drawn to his iconoclastic personality, his uncompromising purpose. He supported civil disobedience and dramatic protests.

But then everything changed.

He studied Cutter's back, noting how he slightly favored his right side. While on a mission to thwart poachers in the Serengeti, Cutter was mauled by an African lion, one of the very creatures he had sought to protect. He had almost died—*did* die, at least for a minute on the operating table. His recovery had been long and painful.

Most people would have taken such a horrible, disfiguring event as a reason to turn their back on their causes, but instead, Cutter only became that much more dedicated. It was as if by surviving the raw fury of that lion—that literal representation of nature's tooth and claw—he had somehow been infused with even more passion. But it also changed him. While he remained an environmentalist, his fervor became driven by a more nihilistic philosophy. He founded a new group, one of like-minded individuals, called Dark Eden, whose goal was no longer conservation, but to accept that the world was falling apart and to prepare for it, to perhaps even help it along, to look beyond the current mass extinction to a new genesis, a new Eden.

Over a short period of time, his actions became more radicalized, his followers manic. Eventually he was convicted in absentia on multiple charges, by multiple countries, and was forced to flee underground. It was while running from authorities that he suffered his plane crash.

Though now it was plain that his death had been a ruse all along, part of a greater plan for Dark Eden.

But what did he intend?

Cutter led him to an impressive stone staircase that swept upward. A woman descended toward them, dressed in a simple white shift that showed off the beauty of her burnished skin as it did her curves.

Cutter's voice softened. "Ah, Kendall, let me introduce you to the mother of my children." He held out a hand and helped her off the last step. "This is Ashuu."

The woman gave a small bow of her head, then turned her full attention upon Cutter, her dark eyes almost glowing in the lamplight. Her voice was a silky whisper. *"Tu fait une promesse à ton fils."*

Kendall translated the French.

You made a promise to your son.

"I know, my dear. As soon as I get our guest settled, I'll see to him."

She tenderly touched Cutter's cheek with the back of her soft hand, then nodded to Mateo. *"Bienvenue, mon frère."*

She then turned and headed back up the stairs.

Kendall frowned and stared back at Mateo.

Frère.

Brother.

Kendall searched the scarred countenance of the giant shadowing him. From the woman's sheer beauty, he would never have fathomed that these two were brother and sister, but now brought to his attention, he could see a vague family resemblance.

Cutter touched Kendall's elbow and pointed to the back of the hall. "Mateo will take you to your room. I'll see you in the morning. I have important business of my own to attend to before I retire." He shrugged with his usual rakish charm. "As my dear wife reminded me . . . *une promesse est une promesse.*"

A promise is a promise.

Cutter followed Ashuu up the stairs.

As Mateo roughly grabbed Kendall's shoulder and manhandled him away, he kept his eyes on Cutter's back, picturing the scars that had so radically transformed the man—both inside and out.

Why did you bring me here?

He suspected the answer already.

And it terrified him.

11:56 P.M.

Small fingers clutched Cutter's hand as he descended the steps carved into the sandstone floor of the tunnel.

"Papa, we must hurry."

Cutter smiled as his son dragged him faster, with the heedless abandon that only came with youth. At only ten, Jori found wonder in everything, his raw curiosity shining from every inch of his handsome face. He had his mother's soft features and mocha skin, but his eyes were his father's, shining a clear blue. Many a local witch doctor had touched the boy's face, staring into those eyes, and declared him special. One Macuxi elder described his son the best: *This one was born to see the world only through cloudless skies.*

That was Jori.

His blue gaze was always open for the next wonder.

It was what drove the pair of them for this midnight hike through the subterranean tunnels. They were headed to the living biosphere he had established on the tepui—or rather *inside* it.

Most of these sandstone summits were riddled with old caves and tunnels, formed as the soft rock was worn away by eons of rain and running water. It was said the cavern systems found here were the oldest in the world. So it was only appropriate that these ancient passageways had become the forges for what was to come.

The bare bulbs running along the tunnel roof revealed a steel door ahead, blocking the way forward. Cutter stepped to the electronic deadbolt and used a keycard from around his neck to unlock it. With a quiet whirring, a trio of wrist-thick bolts wound out of the doorframe.

"Ready?" he asked and checked his watch.

Three minutes before midnight.

Perfect.

Jori nodded, bouncing a bit on the balls of his feet.

Cutter hauled open the door to another world—the *next* world.

He led his son onto the landing outside the hatch. Overhead a light misty drizzle fell out of the sky and down into the depths of the massive sinkhole before him. Their overlook jutted fifteen feet below the lip of that cylindrical hole. A corkscrewing wide ledge ran along the sinkhole's inside walls, skimming from the plateau summit all the way to the base of the tepui. The hole was massive, three hundred meters across, but it was still a third smaller than its cousin, the giant sinkhole at the Sarisariñama tepui in Venezuela.

Still, this smaller confined ecosystem served his purposes beautifully.

The hole acted as an island within an island.

It was these same tepuis that inspired Sir Arthur Conan Doyle to write *The Lost World*, populating these islands among the clouds with the living remnants of a prehistoric past, a violent world of dinosaurs and pterodactyls. To Cutter, the reality was more thrilling than any Victorian fantasy. For him, each tabletop was a Galápagos in the sky, an evolutionary pressure cooker, where each species struggled to survive in unique ways.

He stepped to the wall, festooned with a riotous growth of vegetation, dripping with dampness, soaked in mists. He gently pointed to a small flower with white petals. Its tendril-like leaves were covered by tiny stalks, each tipped with a glistening sticky drop.

"Can you name this one, Jori?"

He sighed. "That's easy, Papa. That's a sundew. Dro . . . dro . . ."

Cutter smiled and finished for the boy. "*Drosera.*"

He nodded vigorously. "They catch ants and bugs and eat them."

"That's right."

Such plants were the foot soldiers in an evolutionary war up here, evolving distinctive survival strategies to compensate for the lack of nutrients and scarce soil found atop these tepuis, becoming carnivorous in order to live. And it wasn't just sundews, but also bladderworts, pitcher plants, even some bromeliad species had developed a taste for insects on this island in the sky.

"Nature is the ultimate innovator," he mumbled.

But sometimes nature needs a hand.

As midnight struck, a soft phosphorescence bloomed along the walls, flowing from the top toward the dark bottom.

Jori clapped his hands. This is what his son had come to see.

Cutter had engineered the glowing gene of a jellyfish into the DNA of a ubiquitous species of orchid that grew upon this tepui, including instilling a circadian rhythm to its glow cycle. Besides the pure beauty of it, the design offered illumination at night for the workers who tended to this unnatural garden.

Not that my creations need much nurturing at this point.

"Look, Papa! A frog!"

Jori went to touch the black-skinned amphibian as it clung to a vine.

"No, no . . ." Cutter warned and pulled the boy's hand back.

He could understand his son mistaking this sinkhole denizen for its common cousin up top, a frog unique to this tepui. The native species found above, *Oreophrynella*, could not hop or swim, but had developed opposable toes for a better grip on the slippery rock surfaces.

But the specimen here was not *native*.

"Remember," Cutter warned his son, "down here, we must be careful."

This frog had a potent neurotoxin engineered into the glandular structure of its skin. He had culled the sequence of genes from the Australian stonefish, the most venomous species in the world. One touch and a painful death would soon follow.

The frog had few enemies—at least in the natural world.

Disturbed by their voices, it skittered farther up the vine. The motion drew the attention of another predator. From under a leaf, diaphanous wings spread to the width of an open hand. The leaf fluttered free of its hold on the stem, revealing its clever bit of mimicry.

It was part of the *Phylliidae* family, sometimes called walking leaves.

Only this creation didn't walk.

Its wings fluttered through the mists, its tiny legs scrabbling at the air as it fell silently toward the frog.

"Papa, stop it!" Jori must have sensed what was about to happen. His son had a boyish affinity for frogs. He even kept a large terrarium in his bedroom, holding a collection of several species.

Jori moved to swat at the gently fluttering wings, but Cutter caught his wrist—not that the modified insect would do anything worse than sting the boy, but here was another teachable moment.

"Jori, what did we learn about the Law of the Jungle, about prey and predator? What's that called?"

He hung his head and mumbled to his toes. "Survival of the fittest."

He smiled and gave his son's hair a tussle. "Good boy."

Landing on the frog's back, the insect sank its sharp legs through the toxic skin and began to feed. As son and father watched, those pale outstretched wings slowly turned rosy with fresh blood.

"It's pretty," Jori said.

No, it's nature.

Beauty was simply another way Mother Nature survived, whether it be the sweet-smelling flower that drew the bee, or the wings of a butterfly that confused a hunter. All of the natural world had one goal: to survive, to pass its genes on to the next generation.

Cutter stepped to the edge of the landing and stared down that mile-long drop to the bottom. Every tens of meters the ecosystem changed. Near the top of the sinkhole, it was clammy and cold; down at the bottom, hot and tropical. The gradient in between allowed for the creation of test zones, unique ecological niches, to challenge his works in progress. Each level was color coded, running from lighter shades above to darker below, each separated by biological and physical barriers.

Black was the deepest and most deadly.

Even under the glow of the orchids, he could barely make out the dark humid jungle that grew along the bottom, its loam enriched by the detritus that rained down from above. That patch of isolated rain forest made a perfect hothouse furnace—where his greatest creations took shelter, growing stronger, learning to survive on their own.

The native tribes of this region feared these mist-shrouded tepuis, claiming dangerous spirits lurked here.

How true that was now.

Only these new spirits were his creations, designed for what was to come. He stood at the edge, looking across the expanse of the sinkhole.

Here was a new Galápagos for a new world.

One beyond the tyranny of humankind.

THIRD

Hellscape

17

April 30, 10:34 A.M. GMT
Queen Maud Land, Antarctica

"Where's the damned sun?" Kowalski groaned.

Gray understood the big man's frustration. He stood in the pilothouse of the massive treaded vehicle and studied the landscape beyond its tall windows. Though it was midmorning, it was pitch-black outside. With the moon already down, bright stars twinkled coldly across a cloudless sky. Occasional ethereal waves of brilliance rolled across the starscape, in hues of emerald and crimson, amid splashes of electric blue.

This dramatic storm of the aurora australis—the southern polar lights—had chased them across the frozen expanse of Queen Maud Land during their overnight trek. The fierceness of the display reflected the severity of the solar flare that compromised satellite communication across Antarctica. Each dazzling dance of the aurora reminded Gray how isolated they were out here.

He studied the terrain for some clue to where they were going. After abandoning Karen and the other researchers at the lone remaining Halley module, Gray and his team had headed east in the large vehicle, trundling across a flat sea of snow and ice. According to the dynamic map display above the pilot's station, their path paralleled the distant coastline. But out the window, there was no sign of sea or ocean, just a frozen world of white and blue. The only feature that broke up the monotonous landscape rose to the south of their position. A line of black craggy peaks poked out of the ice, marking the tops of buried mountains. Razor-sharp, the crags looked like a row of fangs and were in fact named Fenriskjeften—or the Jaws of Fenris, named after the mythic Nordic wolf.

Conversation drew his attention back to the control deck behind him—and to their host, Stella Harrington, daughter of the reclusive professor they were headed to meet.

"We actually designed our CAAT after the prototype built by DARPA," Stella explained to her avid pupil.

Jason stood next to her at the helm station, looking at a set of schematics for their strange vehicle. He plainly could not get enough information about their unique mode of transport.

Or maybe it was his teacher.

In her early twenties, Stella was the same age as Jason, with a pixie blond cut, stunning green eyes, and curves that showed even through her heavy wool sweater and thick polar pants. She was also whip-smart, holding a dual master's in botany and evolutionary biology, a challenging match for Sigma's resident computer genius.

"I remember seeing a video of that DARPA prototype," Jason said. "It was one-fifth this size. Can you still travel over water in this larger craft?"

"Why do you think it's called a Captive Air *Amphibious* Transport?" Stella teasingly rolled her eyes. "Each individual tread of the belts is made of a buoyant foam, allowing us to travel over both land or sea. And out here, that's important."

Jason frowned, glancing out to the frozen expanse. "Why do you need to be amphibious out here?"

"Because we use the CAAT mostly—" She suddenly stopped, perhaps knowing she was speaking too freely.

It had been that way since they boarded. Any conversation was laced with gaps and silences. She still hadn't told them what sort of trouble her father was in, only that he needed their help.

She looked away, her voice lowering guiltily. "You'll see."

Jason didn't press the matter.

"But the CAAT is still useful over the ice," Stella continued more confidently. "We can get her up to eighty miles an hour on flat terrain, and her length allows us to forge narrow crevasses."

Jason studied the schematics. "The vehicle reminds me somewhat of Admiral Byrd's snow cruiser, the big polar truck built just after World War II. Are you familiar with it?"

Gray remembered seeing a picture of that fifty-foot-long polar truck, capable of carrying a small plane on its back. The photo had been found in Professor Harrington's files that had been recovered from DARPA's servers.

"I . . . I am," Stella said, again speaking tentatively, as if she were walking on thin ice. "My father believed the CAAT could serve a similar role."

Jason nodded. "Makes sense."

The kid cast Gray a surreptitious glance. Gray suddenly realized Jason had been quietly testing Stella, using information from her father's files to see how open she would be with them.

Maybe he wasn't so moonstruck after all.

"How many people can this CAAT hold?" he asked.

"We're specked to carry a twelve-person team, including the bridge crew. But in a pinch, we could squeeze in another six or seven."

It was why they had to abandon Karen and the others. Gray had seen the cramped quarters down below. It seemed the vehicle's engine and mechanics took up most of the available space. The crew's quarter held a tiny mess hall and bunkroom, and Stella had come with a full complement of British soldiers, all armed, expecting they might run into trouble. There was no way the CAAT could carry Karen and all twelve of her fellow researchers.

But that was never an option.

Stella made it clear that Professor Harrington would allow only Gray and his two men to be ferried across Queen Maud Land to his secret base. It seemed the man's paranoia had only grown worse upon hearing about the attack. Stella had been en route by air when she picked up their radio chatter after Gray escaped from the destroyed base. She promptly turned around and sought out the CAAT, which was already out on the ice for a different mission. She made an emergency landing and rerouted the treaded tank for her rescue mission.

In a small concession, she had left two British soldiers with Karen and the others—along with rocket launchers and heavy weapons—in case the enemy managed to hunt down that roving module. It was the best that could be made of the situation.

Gray joined Jason at the helm. "How much longer until we reach our destination?"

Stella glanced over to the map on the dynamic positioning system above the pilot's head. She studied it for too long, plainly trying to weigh how much to say.

Jason interceded, applying a boyish lightness to his words. "It's not like we can tell anyone."

She kept staring at the map, but Gray noticed the ghost of a smile edge her lips. "I suppose that's true." She pointed to the DPS screen. "See that small peninsula shaped like a half-moon? About twenty miles away. That's Hellscape."

"Hellscape?" Jason asked, bunching his brows at the ominous-sounding name.

Her smile broadened. "You misunderstand. Not hellscape. It's Hell's *Cape*. As in Cape of Hell."

"Like that's much better," Kowalski commented dourly from across the pilothouse. "You're not gonna sell a lot of time-shares with that name."

"We didn't name it."

"Then who did?" Gray asked.

Stella hesitated—then finally broke down and spoke freely. "It was Charles Darwin. Back in 1832."

After a stunned moment of silence, he asked the obvious question. "Why did he name it Hell's Cape?"

Stella stared at the map, then shook her head. She repeated her noncommittal response from a moment ago. Only now her voice was frosted with dread.

"You'll see."

10:55 A.M.

It doesn't look that bad for Hell.

Jason watched the CAAT grind its way over the last mile toward the icy cape that jutted into the Southern Ocean. By now his eyes had adjusted to the darkness, seeing well by starlight and the glowing tides of the aurora australis in the dark sky.

Ahead, the curve of the shoreline—a mix of blue ice and black rocky cliffs—sheltered a small bay. At the bottom of the cliffs, waves crashed against a beach filled with boulders. This was one of the rare areas of the coastline free of ice.

"So where's this base?" Kowalski asked.

It was a good question.

Stella stood behind the pilot, leaning down and whispering into his ear. The man slowed the CAAT to a crawl as the vehicle approached the coast. He guided the giant belted treads up to the edge of a cliff—

—and then over it.

"Hold on to something," Stella warned.

Jason grabbed for the rail along one wall while Gray and Kowalski clutched the edges of a chart table.

The CAAT crept farther out until half its length jutted beyond the cliff. Then it began to fall, its front end tipping forward. Jason tightened his grip, expecting to plunge nose-first down to the rocky beach. Instead, the front treads hit a slope hidden below the precipice. The CAAT teetered, the back end lifting. Then they were trundling along a steep grade made of loose scree, heading to the boulder-strewn beach far below.

He let go of his hold and shifted forward to join Stella.

The slope looked man-made, likely bulldozed into place, made of the same loose stone as the beach. But to the casual passing eye, the construction would be easy to miss, especially sheltered by the curve of the cape.

At the bottom of the incline, the CAAT hit the beach and followed alongside the base of those towering sea cliffs, its treads churning across the sand. Ahead, a cavern opening appeared, cut like an axe blow into that ice-rimed rock face. The CAAT slowed and made a sharp turn toward that dark mouth. Its twin head lamps speared into the blackness. The tunnel ended after only thirty yards, blocked by a wall of cold blue steel. It rose five stories high and stretched a hundred yards wide. Along the edges, the barrier looked cemented into place with concrete.

As the CAAT entered, a massive set of double doors opened in that wall, pulling to either side on tracks. Bright light—blinding after the hours of darkness—flowed out, bathing over them.

"Welcome to Hell's Cape," Stella said.

Beyond the wall, a cavernous space opened, floored in steel but with natural stone walls. It looked like a cross between the deck of an aircraft carrier and the world's largest industrial hangar. Another full-sized CAAT sat parked alongside six smaller ones, each half the size of their big brother. There were also two prop planes fitted with floats being serviced on the other side. Elsewhere, a trio of forklifts moved crates, while overhead a track-and-pulley system drew a shipping container along the roof.

The pilot drove their vehicle into that chaos and drew abreast of its twin, as the giant doors sealed behind them. The CAAT came to a halt with a heavy sigh of its diesel engines.

As soon as they stopped, Stella waved them to the stairs leading below. "Let's disembark. My father has been anxious to meet you all."

She led the American team down to the lower level and out a ramp that dropped from the stern. The air was unusually warm, smelling of oil and chemical cleaners. Jason gaped at the sheer size of this installation.

Stella spoke to a thin British officer who had run up to them, breathless, his eyes worried. Once finished, she faced them and pointed across the cavern. "He's up on the observation deck."

On the far side of this massive hangar, a giant steel structure filled the entire back end of the cavern. It climbed eight stories, with interconnecting stairs and bridges. The very top level held a row of tall glass windows.

There was something vaguely familiar about the layout.

Gray noted it, too. "Is that the superstructure from a naval ship?"

Stella nodded. "From a decommissioned British destroyer. It was brought here piecemeal and reassembled."

Similar to the outer doors, the repurposed super-structure had been sealed along all its edges by concrete, like caulking a window into a frame.

"Follow me," Stella said, turning on a heel. "Stick close."

As Jason obeyed, he was distracted by her backside.

Kowalski caught him looking and nudged him with an elbow. "Just keep walking, kid. Nothing but trouble there."

Feeling his cheeks heat up, Jason stared anywhere but at Stella. The group passed through staggered rows of sandbags, stacked waist high, with three machine gun mounts holding American-made Browning M2s, all pointed toward the outer doors.

Overhead, he watched the shipping container pass along the trolley tracks above and vanish into the superstructure. For the first time, he noted that the container had thick *windows*, like an armored ski gondola. And that a bubble on the underside looked distinctly like a gun turret.

Jason hurried to keep up with the others.

What the hell is this place?

11:14 A.M.

Gray followed Stella through a door into the bottommost level of the steel superstructure. She herded them to a nearby freight elevator and hit the button for the top floor.

As it rose, Gray asked, "How long ago was this place established?"

From his perspective as he crossed the outer hangar, the construction of the British station had a certain slapdash quality to it, like somebody had built it in a hurry.

"Construction started six years ago," Stella answered. "It's slow work. We're still refining and adding to it when budgets and circumstances allow. But the search for this place goes back centuries."

"What do you mean by—?"

The elevator doors chimed open, cutting off his query.

She waved them out. "My father will explain . . . if there's enough time."

They stepped into what was once the bridge of the former destroyer, with a line of tall windows that overlooked the busy hangar space below. Most of the bridge had been converted and expanded into a group of offices centered around a warm library space. Persian rugs softened the steel floor, while wooden shelves rose on all sides, packed tightly with books. Elsewhere desks and tables held more stacked volumes, along with magazines and scattered papers. He also noted plinths holding various artifacts: chunks of fossils, odd crystalline rocks, older books that stood open, exposing hand-drawn biological diagrams or sketches of animals and birds. The largest tome was a massive volume of fanciful illuminated maps that appeared to be centuries old, the metallic inks glowing from the pages.

The renovation looked more like a museum, like something out of the natural history wing of the Royal British Society.

On the far side of the room, a thin distinguished man with salt-and-pepper hair stepped from a draped alcove between two bookcases. Though he looked to be in his late sixties, he strode briskly toward them. He wore gray pants held up with suspenders, polished shoes, and a starched white shirt. He paused only long enough to pull on a jacket that hung from a chair behind a broad desk that held a steaming tea service on top. He donned the coat quickly and stepped to greet them.

"Commander Pierce, thank you for coming."

Gray recognized Professor Alex Harrington from the mission dossier. He shook the man's hand, finding it bony but still with plenty of strength. He suspected this professor spent more time out in the field than in a classroom.

"Stella told me about your troubles over at Halley," Harrington said. "I imagine our problems are one in the same. Namely Major Dylan Wright, a former X Squadron leader."

Gray remembered the burly man who had commanded the assault team on DARPA, with his steely eyes and cropped white-blond hair. Back at Sigma command, Kat had identified the leader as Dylan Wright.

"How do you know him?" Gray asked.

"Wright and his handpicked team were assigned as security detail for the base in the early days. Then somebody got to him, or maybe he was a plant all along. I'm guessing the latter because he was always a major arse, came from some aristocratic family that had fallen on hard times, even carried around an antique English hunting pistol. Either way, we started to run into issues here, evidence of sabotage, along with missing files, even stolen samples. About a year and a half ago, he was caught on-camera but eventually escaped with his team, killing three other soldiers in the process, all good and loyal men."

Gray pictured Director Raffee, executed in his own office.

"If he destroyed Halley," Harrington continued, "I can't imagine he's not gunning for us here, especially picking such an opportune time when communications are down across the continent. And most worrisome, the man knows every detail about Hell's Cape."

"Why do you think he would be returning? What's he after?"

"Maybe simply revenge. The man had always been vindictive. But I think he means to do far worse. Our

work here—besides being sensitive and confiden-
tial—is very dangerous. He could wreak great havoc."

"And what's the nature of your research here?"

"*Nature* itself, actually." Harrington sighed, his eyes
tired and scared. "It's best we start at the beginning."

He stepped to his desk, waving them to crowd
around him. He then pressed his palm upon the corner
of a glass insert built into the desktop. A 40-inch LCD
screen glowed to light, bringing the very modern into
this Royal Society museum.

Harrington swiped and tapped its touchscreen surface. With a flick of his fingers, he scattered various
photographs across the screen, as easily as if he were
dealing physical cards on a game table.

Gray noted the file name that glowed near the top of
the screen.

D.A.R.W.I.N.

He had seen it before, remembering the acronym
stood for Develop and Revolutionize Without Injuring
Nature. It was the core conservation philosophy shared
by Harrington and Hess. But he stayed silent, letting
the professor control the story.

"It all goes back to the voyage of the HMS *Beagle*
and the journey of Charles Darwin through this region.

And a fateful encounter with the Fuegian tribesmen of Tierra del Fuego. Here's an old pencil sketch of that first meeting, near the Straits of Magellan."

He tapped and enlarged a photo showing the old British sloop and a group of natives in boats.

"The Fuegians were skilled sailors and fishermen, hunting the seas around the tip of South America and beyond. According to a secret journal written by Darwin and kept under guard at the British Museum, the captain of the *Beagle* obtained an old map that showed a section of Antarctic coastline, along with a hint of a possible region that was free of ice. Seeking to claim it for the Crown, the *Beagle* sought this location—but what they discovered so scared them that it was forever stricken from the record of that voyage."

Jason studied the picture. "What did they find?"

"Bear with me," Harrington said. "You see, Darwin could not let that knowledge completely vanish, so he preserved the map along with his secret journal. Only a select few scientists were ever allowed access to it. Most considered his story too fanciful to be believed, especially as the site would never be found for another century."

"Hell's Cape," Gray said. "This place."

"For most of the past century, thick ice shelves hid the true coastline. It was only after the recent decades of thawing that we were able to rediscover it again. Even still, we had to use bombs to break loose the remaining ice to reach this place and set up our base. It was only afterward that we came to realize we weren't the *first* ones to come since Darwin's fateful visit. But I'm getting ahead of myself."

Harrington brought up more maps. Gray recognized the one drawn by the Turkish explorer Piri Reis, along with the chart by Oronteus Finaeus. "These old maps suggest that sometime in the ancient past, some six thousand years ago, much of the coastline may have been free of ice. The Turkish admiral who drew this first map claimed he compiled it based on charts of great age, some dating back as far as the fourth century B.C."

"That long ago?" Jason asked.

The professor nodded. "During that time, the Minoans and the Phoenicians were astounding sailors, building giant oared warships that plowed far and wide. So it's possible they had reached this southernmost continent and recorded what they discovered. Admiral Piri Reis compiled his chart from maps secured at a library in Constantinople, but even he suspected some of his most ancient source material might have come from the famed Library of Alexandria before it was destroyed."

"Why did he think that?"

"He mentions that some of the maps he reviewed in Constantinople had notations that suggested an Egyptian origin. And according to archaeologists, the ancient Egyptians were plying the seas as far back as 3500 B.C."

"So close to six thousand years ago," Gray said. "When the coasts may have been free of ice. But what do these charts have to do with Darwin?"

"After returning to England, Darwin grew obsessed with discovering more about what he had encountered at the place he named Hell's Cape. He collated ancient maps and searched records of great antiquity, looking for any other mention of this place. He also tried to understand its unique geology."

"What's unique about it?" Kowalski asked. "Looks like a big cave."

"It's much bigger than you can imagine. All of it warmed by geothermal activity. In fact, when Darwin found the mouth of this cavern, it was stained bloodred with iron oxides that steamed forth out of the opening, rising from a boiling sea of iron-rich salt water found deep below. On the other side of the continent you can find a similar geological formation—called Blood Falls—in the McMurdo Dry Valleys, near your American base."

Gray could only imagine what that ominous sight must have looked like to those Victorian-era men aboard the *Beagle*.

"Darwin's obsession overtook his life, so much so that it delayed the publication of his famous treatise on evolution, *On the Origin of Species*. Did you know it took him almost twenty years after his voyage aboard the *Beagle* to publish his groundbreaking work? We know it wasn't fear of controversy that delayed the publication. It was something else."

Harrington waved his hands over the set of maps. "It was this obsession. Additionally, what he discovered in these caves, I believe, may have even been instrumental in helping him formulate his theory: of species evolving to fit an environmental niche, of survival of the fittest being the driving force of nature. Such a theory is certainly proven out here."

Gray's curiosity piqued even stronger.

What is hidden here?

"How large is this cavern system?" Jason asked.

"We can't say for sure. Ground-penetrating radar is useless due to the miles of ice that cover the continent farther inland. Any such surveys are further complicated by the fact that this system extends beneath the coastal mountains."

Gray pictured the fanged ridge of the Fenriskjeften crags.

The professor continued. "But we've sent drones with radar equipment as far as we could into the system. I estimate that the tunnels and caves could span much of the continent, maybe reaching as far as Lake Vostok, or even the Wilkes Land crater, which opens up some intriguing possibilities about the origins of what we found. And we may have some corroboration of its massive size from historical sources."

"What historical sources?" Jason asked.

"The Nazis . . . specifically the head of the German navy at the time."

"Admiral Dönitz." Jason cringed as soon as the name left his mouth, inadvertently revealing that they had previous access to some of these D.A.R.W.I.N. files.

But Harrington never responded. Maybe he assumed such knowledge was commonplace. Though Stella did cast the young man a curious glance.

Harrington continued. "Dönitz claimed the Nazis had discovered an underwater trench that tunneled through the heart of this continent, formed by an interconnecting series of lakes, rivers, caves, and ice tunnels."

Gray recalled Jason sharing the German admiral's words from the Nuremberg trials, of the Nazis' discovery of *a paradise-like oasis in the middle of eternal ice.*

Jason spoke again, more slowly, plainly cautious after his slip-up. "You think the Nazis discovered this cavern system during the war?"

"They weren't the only ones. Did you know the U.S. government set off nuclear bombs in this area? They claimed they were merely doing atomic testing, but it makes me wonder if perhaps they were trying to clean up a mess, trying to kill something they had inadvertently let loose. It was in that same area that a unique virus was discovered in 1999, one that seemed universally pathogenic."

Gray remembered how that discovery had intrigued both Hess and Harringon, who described it as *the key to Hell's gate.*

"It was Dr. Hess who recognized the unique genetic code found in that virus, something very different from our own. It was a marker that led us to eventually discover this place, though it still took another eight long years to find the mouth of this cavern system."

"Until the continent melted enough to reveal its secrets," Gray said.

"Precisely."

Jason cleared his throat. "But how are you so sure the Germans and Americans were ever here?"

"Because—"

A loud *boom* shook the world, rattling the windows in their frames. Everyone initially ducked, expecting the worst, but as the superstructure held, Gray ran low toward the row of windows overlooking the giant hangar. He reached it in time to see one of the giant steel doors fall free of its track and crash into the space, flattening one of the parked floatplanes.

Black smoke billowed into the hangar. Shapes in snow-white polar armor rushed through the cover of that cloud.

It had to be Major Wright's team.

Gunfire erupted.

A couple of British soldiers dropped, but one reached a machine-gun mount and began firing at the enemy. The chugging of the weapon was loud enough to reach the top of the superstructure—until a rocket struck the man's position with a thunderous explosion.

"Let's go!" Harrington said, tugging on Gray's sleeve. "We can't let them unleash hell upon the world!"

Gray allowed himself to be led to the opposite side of the bridge, chased by the sounds of the ongoing battle below. At the back wall, the professor ducked through the same set of drapes through which he had entered.

Gray followed, drawing everyone with him.

Beyond the drapes, a long passageway extended toward the rear of the superstructure. Their boots pounded along the steel floor. The tunnel ended at a glass-enclosed observation deck on the back of the station. It was attached to the cavern roof. From the gondola parked beside it, this glass-and-steel perch also served as a trolley stop for the overhead track system.

Gray reached the deck at Harrington's heels.

As the view opened up before him, he drew to a stop, too stunned to move, to speak.

The same could not be said of everyone.

"Okay," Kowalski said, "now the goddamned name makes sense."

18

April 30, 7:20 A.M. AMT
Boa Vista, Brazil

It's like tracing the steps of a ghost . . .

Jenna followed Drake and Painter down the swelter-
ing streets of Boa Vista, the capital city of the Brazilian
state of Roraima. The temperature was already climbing toward ninety degrees, but the humidity had to be
a hundred. Her lightweight blouse clung to her armpits
and stuck to her ribs under the backpack slung over her
shoulders. She had to keep tugging her shirt down as
it tried to ride up from her shorts. She also wore a cap
against the bright sun, her ponytail hanging out the back.

Drake and Painter were also dressed casually, as
were the two Marines—Schmitt and Marlow—who
trailed them, passing themselves off as tourists, a

not-uncommon sight in the city. Apparently Boa Vista was the jumping-off point for any adventurous traveler who wished to visit the northern Brazilian rain forest, or the neighboring tablelands of Guyana or Venezuela.

The fact that Boa Vista was a gateway city also complicated their search for Amy Serpry's last steps. From the forensics on the saboteur's phone, they knew Amy had received a call from this city. Jenna heard the ringing of that phone in her ears. She flashed back to the woman's ravaged body in the bed . . . and to Nikko.

She shied away from this last thought. She hated to abandon her partner in California, but her best chance of helping him was out here, hunting for answers to that monstrous disease.

The team had landed an hour ago, just as the sun was rising. From the air, the city was laid out like the spokes of a wheel. They had traveled by taxi down one of those radiating spurs and were now on foot to reach a small guesthouse off the main road. It lay nestled amid a quiet treelined neighborhood.

"That should be it," Painter said, pointing toward a quaint colonial-style clapboard hotel midway down the street.

As they crossed toward the guesthouse, Drake silently signaled for the two Marines to drift to either side of the road, to covertly secure a perimeter.

Jenna headed with Drake and Painter toward the hotel steps. A wooden porch ran along the front, supporting flowerboxes bursting with blooms. There was even a small swing, currently occupied by a fat orange tabby, who stretched upon seeing them and paced along its length.

"Must be the proprietor," Drake said, pausing to give the cat a scratch under the chin.

Caught off guard, Jenna let slip a small laugh, but quickly stifled it, blaming her outburst on the tension.

The hotel was their only concrete lead. While they knew Amy's last call had originated from this city, they could not isolate it any further. Painter believed the caller had employed a crude satellite mirroring system to hide his or her exact location.

So that meant they had to put boots on the ground in Brazil, employing good old-fashioned footwork, which was fine by her.

Sometimes old school is best.

As Painter pulled open the door to the guesthouse, she adjusted her backpack, running her palm over the grip of the Glock 20 holstered on the underside of her bag. Painter had supplied them with weapons shortly after landing, found hidden in an airport storage locker. He never told her how that had been arranged, and she didn't care to ask.

Though armed, she still felt naked without Nikko at her hip.

Jenna followed Painter inside, while Drake remained on the porch with the cat. As they approached the reception desk, which was little more than a raised bench, Painter scooped an arm around Jenna's waist.

An older Brazilian woman, wearing a housecoat and a welcoming smile, stood up from a cushioned chair before a small television and greeted them. "*Sejam bem-vindos.*"

"*Obrigado,*" Painter thanked her. "Do you speak English?"

Her smile widened. "Yes. Mostly I can."

"This is my daughter," Painter said, drawing Jenna forward. "She is looking for a friend of hers, someone she was supposed to meet in the city. But they never showed up."

The woman's face grew more serious, nodding her head at their concern.

Jenna felt a slight pressure on her lower back as Painter urged her to continue. "Her . . . her name is Amy Serpry," she said, putting as much worry into her voice as possible, which wasn't hard.

I am *worried . . .*

"My friend has been traveling in the area for the past month, but when she first came here, she stayed at your beautiful hotel."

With no way to trace the call in any greater detail, Painter had tried to track the last steps of the saboteur, searching bank records, tracing additional phone calls from her home apartment in Boston, even mapping the GPS log recovered from her Toyota Camry. It was like filling in the life of a ghost, bit by digital bit, constructing her steps over the past months.

The investigation also revealed more about the woman's volatile youth, before she settled into her postdoctoral program and was hired by Dr. Hess. In her late teens, she had been part of a radical environmental movement called Dark Eden, which advocated for a natural world beyond humankind, promoting acts of ecoterrorism to make their point.

Then shortly after 2 A.M. last night, Painter had received a call from D.C. Jenna had been in Painter's office with Drake at the time, both of them just released from quarantine. Painter had put the call on speakerphone. The woman on the other line—Kathryn Bryant—had made a breakthrough.

We found no hits on her U.S. passport, so we thought she was stateside all of this time. But then I found out she still kept her French passport.

Apparently, Amy had become a U.S. citizen seven years ago, but having been born in France, she still maintained a dual citizenship. Tracing that original passport, Bryant discovered that Amy had taken a flight five weeks ago, paid for in cash, from Los Angeles to Boa Vista. The timing and location couldn't be a coincidence.

It hadn't taken long to discover that Amy had used a French credit card, issued from Crédit du Nord, to pay for Internet services at this hotel in Boa Vista.

That thin lead led them to be standing here now, hoping for some additional clue to follow the steps of their ghost.

"I have a picture of her," Jenna said.

She took out a copy of Amy's driver's license photo. Again, Jenna had difficulty looking at that smiling face, knowing the horrors the woman would unleash, remembering the state of her body at that Yosemite cabin.

The proprietor studied the photograph, then slowly nodded her head. "I remember. Very pretty."

"Did she come with someone?" Jenna pressed. "Or meet someone here."

"Someone who might know where she is now?" Painter added.

The woman chewed her lower lip, plainly trying her best to recall anything. Then she slowly nodded.

"I remember. A man come at night. He was very . . ." She struggled for the word and instead forked her fingers and pretended bolts were shooting out of her eyes.

"Intense?" Jenna asked.

"*Sim*"—she nodded—"but scary, too. Senhor Cruz no like him. He hiss and hide."

Senhor Cruz must be the tabby out front.

If that nighttime visitor was Amy's accomplice or boss, maybe the cat was a good judge of character. He certainly had taken a shine to Drake.

Painter stepped forward, pulling out a sheaf of photographs. "Maybe you could recognize him. These are some of Amy's friends."

He spread the pictures across the reservation table. They showed various colleagues and associates of Amy's. But a majority of the photographs came from when Amy was young, from Dark Eden's old website, which still had pictures of the early members of that group. It was the most likely connection. There was even one that showed a teenaged Amy smiling in a group photo.

The woman bent lower over the pictures, slipping on a pair of reading glasses. She shifted through them and gave each a good look. On the group photo, she tapped one face.

"This the man. He smiles in picture, but not when he was here. He was very"—she glanced up to Jenna—"*intense.*"

Painter retrieved the photograph and studied the man in the picture. Jenna looked over his shoulder. The suspect had ebony black hair, combed back from a handsome pale face with piercing blue eyes.

"Did you overhear them speaking at all?" Painter asked.

"*Não*. They go to her room. He leave, but I no see him."

"And no one else came?"

"*Não*."

Painter nodded and passed her a few bills of Brazilian currency. "*Obrigado*."

She pushed the bills back with a shake of her head. "I hope you find your friend. I hope she not with that man."

Jenna patted the woman's hand atop the bills. "For Senhor Cruz, then. Buy him some nice fish."

The woman smiled, then nodded, her fingers crinkling the bills off the bench. "*Obrigado*."

Jenna headed with Painter out onto the porch.

"Did you learn anything?" Drake asked, waving for Schmitt and Marlow to close in.

Painter sighed. "Someone came to visit her, someone from her past, from Dark Eden."

Drake glowered. "Then that must be our guy."

"Who is he?" Jenna asked.

"He *was* the founder of Dark Eden." Painter did not sound happy and explained why. "According to all reports, he died eleven years ago."

Jenna glanced back to the guesthouse.

So it seems we're still chasing ghosts.

7:45 A.M.

"Isn't the view beautiful?" Cutter Elwes asked.

Kendall wanted to argue, to lash out, but even he could not find the gumption as he stared beyond the wrought-iron rails of the balcony.

The sun was just cresting the rim of the tepui. The thunderstorm had cleared during the night, leaving the skies a dazzling blue overhead, but mists still clung to the summit, adding to the illusion that this was an island in the clouds. The morning light cast those mists into shades of honey amber and dusky rose. The plateau itself seemed to glow with the new day, glistening in every shade of emerald, while the pond was a perfect reflection of the cloudless sky.

It was tempting to let his guard down in the face of such inspiring beauty, but he remained steadfast. He sat stiff-backed across the table from his host, a breakfast spread between them: a kaleidoscope of colorful fruits, dark breads, and hot platters of eggs and lentils.

No meat . . . not for Cutter Elwes.

Kendall had picked at the offering, but he had no appetite, his stomach churned at what this day surely held for him. Cutter intended to make Kendall cooperate, to share his knowledge, but he would refuse.

At least for as long as I can.

In the past, few people successfully withstood Cutter, and Kendall doubted that reality had changed. He had envisioned all manner of torture during the night, the fear allowing him little sleep. Any thought of escape—of even throwing himself off this mountain—was dashed by his ever-present shadow.

Even now Mateo's hulking form stood guard by the balcony door.

Trying to steer the conversation away from what was to come, Kendall eyed his escort. "Mateo . . . he's native to these jungles. As is his sister, your wife. What tribe are they from? Akuntsu? Maybe Yanomami?"

From his days searching rain forests and jungles for extremophiles, Kendall was familiar with several of the Brazilian indigenous tribes.

"You look upon them with the eyes of a Westerner," Cutter scolded. "Each tribe is very distinct, once you've lived among them. Mateo and my wife are actually members of the Macuxi tribespeoples. Their tribe is a subgroup local to this region. They've lived in these forests for thousands of years, as much a part of nature here as any leaf, flower, or burrowing snake. Their people are also unique in another way."

"How?" he asked, hoping to keep the conversation along this track.

"The tribe demonstrates an unusual number of twin births, both fraternal and identical. In fact, Ashuu was born in triplet grouping. A very unusual one. She has an identical sister—*and* a fraternal brother, Mateo."

Kendall crinkled his brow. *Two identical girls and a boy.* He had heard of such unusual cases—of women who gave birth to identical twins along with a fraternal third, called a singleton. While births like that did occur naturally, it was more often the result of the use of fertility drugs.

Kendall lowered his voice, curiosity getting the better of him. "Do you think Mateo being born a singleton . . . could it account for his unusual size?"

"Possibly. Maybe a genetic anomaly secondary to just a strange triplet configuration. But what I find more fascinating is the tribe's unusual record of multiple births. It makes me wonder if there isn't some naturally occurring analog to a fertility drug in the local rain forest, some undiscovered pharmaceutical."

It *was* an interesting proposition. The rain forests were a source of a great number of new drugs, from a cure for malaria to some powerful anticancer medications. And there were surely hundreds of other discoveries still to be made. That is, if the rain forests continued to thrive, instead of being slashed and burned for farmland or cut down by logging companies.

But this raised another question.

"You know a lot about this tribe," Kendall said. *Even recruited them into working for you.* "So how did you gain that level of cooperation? Especially up here. As I recall, most natives fear these tepui."

"Not so the Macuxi. They revere these plateaus as the home of the gods, believing that the ancient tunnels, caves, and sinkholes are passageways to their underworld, where great giants pass on the wisdom of ages." Cutter stared beyond the balcony toward the lower forest—toward a vast dark sinkhole that was visible in the daylight. "Maybe they were right."

Kendall imagined Cutter thought of himself as one of those godlike giants, a keeper of great knowledge.

Cutter continued. "Did you know my great ancestor, Cuthbert Cary-Elwes, was a Jesuit priest? He lived among the Macuxi for twenty-three years and was greatly loved by these people. He's still remembered in stories, a part of the tribe's oral histories."

Kendall suspected the calculating and persuasive man seated across from him had used that past to sway these local tribesmen to his cause. Did he marry Ashuu for the same reason, to cement that bond by marrying into the tribe? Kendall knew how fiercely these natives respected both family ties and old obligations, even debts that spanned generations. To survive in the harsh jungle, a society had to be close-knit, to watch each other's back.

Cutter stood up abruptly, brushing his palms together. "If you've had enough to eat, we should get to work."

Kendall had been dreading this, but he forced his legs to push himself up. If nothing else, he intended to learn what Cutter planned—then fight him as fiercely as he could.

Cutter led him back indoors and over to an elevator cage wrapped in French wrought iron, like something out of an old hotel. Once Kendall and Mateo joined him inside, Cutter pressed the lowermost button.

Through the bars of the iron door, Kendall watched the floors drop away. They passed through a vast library, then a parlor with a huge fireplace, until finally they reached the ground floor with its cavernous entry hall—but the elevator didn't stop there.

It continued descending.

Walls of rough sandstone passed by outside, closing around them. They were sinking into the core of the tepui, into that labyrinthine world described by

Macuxi myth. The cage fell for another twenty long seconds, then dropped into a brightly lit space.

Kendall's brain took a few additional snaps of its synapses to make sense of what he was seeing. Gone were any signs of stone walls. Instead, a huge laboratory space opened ahead of him, shining with stainless steel and smooth disinfected, spotless surfaces. A handful of white-smocked workers busied themselves at various stations.

"Here we are," Cutter said and led Kendall out. "The true heart of Dark Eden."

Kendall stared at the state-of-the-art equipment. Down one wall ran a long series of fume and flood hoods, intermixed with shelves that held autoclaves, centrifuges, pipettes, beakers, graduated cylinders. Along the other wall stood huge steel doors that hid massive refrigerators or freezers. He also spotted the dark glass door of what must be an incubator.

But the bulk of the central space was made up of rows of workstations, holding multiple genetic analyzers, along with thermal cyclers for performing polymerase chain reactions and DNA synthesizers used to create high-quality oligonucleotides. He also identified equipment for carrying out the latest CRISPR-Cas9 technique for manipulating DNA strands.

This last scared him the most. It was a new technology, one so innovative that a novice could run it, but powerful enough that several research groups in the United States had already used it to mutate every single gene found in human cells. Some had nicknamed it the evolution machine. The potential abuse of that technology in the wrong hands already worried national security agencies, fearful of what might be released as a consequence, either purposefully or by accident.

How long has Cutter possessed this technology?

Kendall didn't know, but he recognized that this lab far outshone his own in both size and sophistication. Additionally, more rooms branched off from here, expanding Cutter's research to unknown ends.

Kendall found it hard to talk, his voice cracking. "What have you been doing, Cutter?"

"Amazing things . . . free from government regulation and far from oversight. It's allowed me to reach the farthest fringes of the possible. Though to be humble, I would say I'm actually only five to six years ahead of some of your colleagues. But what I was able to achieve already . . . to create . . ." Cutter faced Kendall. "And you, my dear friend, can teach me much more."

Kendall swallowed down his terror. "What do you want from me?"

"In your lab, you created the perfect eVLP, a hollow shell so small that it can enter any living cell. It's brilliant work, Kendall." He shook his head with respect. "You should be proud."

At the moment he felt anything but proud.

"Your creation makes for an ideal Trojan horse," Cutter said. "Anything could be put inside of it, and nothing could resist it. It's a flawless *genetic* delivery system." A scolding tone entered his voice. "But you engineered that empty shell using an otherworldly genetic blueprint, from something beyond DNA, didn't you?"

Kendall tried to hide any reaction from Cutter's intense ice-blue scrutiny. *Did the bastard know what he and Harrington had discovered in Antarctica? Did he know the origin of the XNA used to engineer that viral shell?*

Kendall decided it was time to take a stand. He straightened his shoulders, refusing to be swayed. "Cutter, I won't share my technique with you. The method for making that viral shell will die with me."

Cutter laughed—which chilled Kendall to the bone.

"Oh, no need, my friend. One of your young colleagues was kind enough to send me a sample five months ago, and I was able to reverse-engineer it. I've mass produced a supply that could last me years."

Kendall struggled to keep up with his adversary. "Then . . . then what do you want from me?"

"It's more about what I can do *for* you."

"What do you mean?"

"I want to help you stop the plague that's sweeping through California. Since you've been under my wing, your synthetic organism has spread, breaking out of its initial containment, pushed far and wide by recent flooding. It won't be long until it's everywhere, eating its way across your country—and beyond."

Kendall had feared such an outcome, but now to hear it come true . . .

"But there's no way to kill it," Kendall admitted in a hushed, frightened voice. "I tried everything."

"Ah, that's because you are locked inside a box." Cutter tapped his own skull. "Sometimes you must crack that shell of established scientific dogma. Look for new or creative solutions. In fact, I'm surprised you didn't figure it out yourself by now. It's been staring you and Professor Harrington in the face this entire time."

Cutter's words left little doubt that he knew about Harrington's work. With every statement, hope died a little more inside of him.

"And what do you want in exchange for this cure?" Kendall asked.

"Only your cooperation, nothing more. While I was able to re-create that clever viral shell of yours, I've continued to fail to *fill* it, to turn that empty shell into a living organism."

Kendall understood his frustration. It had taken his team years of trial and error to come up with that process. Afterward, he refined it personally and kept the technique guarded from everyone. But what weakened his knees now was the fear of *what* Cutter intended to seed into that viral shell, what he planned to unleash upon the world.

Cutter must have read the trepidation in his eyes and held up a palm. "I swear that what I intend to do will not kill a single human being or creature on this planet."

Kendall wanted to doubt his honesty, but he knew Cutter was a man of his word. He had a strange sense of honor in that regard.

"But if you don't cooperate, with every passing hour, the situation will grow worse in California. Soon it may grow beyond even my cure to resolve. Help me and you save the world. Refuse and the world will die by your own hands, by your own creation. That will be your legacy."

"You swear you have a cure."

Cutter kept his palm up, staring him in the eye. "I do, and I've tested it. It will work, but like I said, there may be limitations if you wait too long."

"And if I cooperate, you'll give me this cure, let me share it with the proper authorities."

"I will. I have no desire to see your creation wreak such havoc. I want to stop it as much as you do."

Kendall believed him. Despite his dark turn, Cutter remained an environmentalist. He would not want to see the world die. Still . . .

"Then why did you sabotage my lab?" Kendall asked, some of the heat reentering his voice. "Why kill everyone, and let that virus loose?"

Cutter stared at him as though the answer was self-evident.

Kendall suddenly understood and quailed at the sheer audacity of this man. "You did all of that as simple leverage, didn't you? To get me to reveal what I know."

"See, my dear friend," Cutter said, turning away. "You're already thinking outside the box. Now let's get to work."

But after taking a couple of steps, a cell phone rang from a pocket of Cutter's safari vest. He plucked it out, spoke briefly in what must be the Macuxi language. The only sign of Cutter's consternation was a single crease that formed in his perfect forehead.

Once finished, he sighed. "Seems like there is another problem, something that's followed you down here from California. Somebody has been making inquiries where they shouldn't be."

Kendall felt a flicker of hope, but it died as Cutter shook his head, clearly pushing this new worry behind him.

"No matter. It's a simple matter to quash."

8:07 A.M.

"The fool can't be serious," Painter said on the phone.

He paced outside a café near the central district of Boa Vista. The others were inside getting coffee and breakfast. He had already called Kat to gather as much intelligence as she could about Dark Eden's former founder, a dead man named Cutter Elwes. While he waited for her to call back, he placed a call to the Mountain Warfare Training Center to get an update.

"It's gotten bad here," Lisa said. "Last night's storm washed contamination well past many of the barriers. We've got pockets blooming miles away from the original site, connected by tendrils of die-offs along the drainage routes we weren't able to successfully block."

Painter pictured a cancerous black inkblot seeping in all directions across those mountains.

"They've pulled the quarantine zone back another twenty-five miles in all directions. Yosemite has been emptied out. It's only a little after five in the morning here, but at daybreak a more thorough search will commence. Depending on what they find, a decision will have to be made. To make matters worse, more inclement weather is expected to hit over the next three days. Storm after storm."

Painter had hoped for some break, but that didn't appear to be the case. Mother Nature seemed determined to confound his efforts.

Lisa continued. "Fearing that this contagion could get a wider and deeper foothold in California, Lindahl has placed the nuclear option on the table. It's seriously being considered."

Painter suddenly regretted coming here.

I should've known Lindahl would try something stupid like that.

"How *seriously* is this option being considered?"

"Very. Lindahl already has the support of the team that's been looking for a way to kill the organism. Their consensus is that the firestorm and radiation from a medium-yield blast could be the best hope. Models are being worked up, and worst-case scenarios are being calculated."

"What do you think?"

There was a long hesitation before she responded. "Painter, I don't know. In some ways, Lindahl is right. Something has to be done, or we'll reach a critical mass out here and we lose everything. If the blast could be controlled to limit the fallout, it might be worth risking it. If nothing else, such a drastic measure could at least knock this agent back on its heels, buy us more time to come up with a new strategy."

Painter still could not believe such an option was their only viable recourse.

"Or maybe I'm just tired," Lisa added. "Not thinking straight. Josh has continued to decline. The doctors put him into a medically induced coma in an attempt to control his seizures. And Nikko isn't doing much better. Like I said, *something* has to be done."

Painter ached to reach through the phone and hold her, reassure her. Instead, he had to put more pressure on her. "Lisa, you have to buy us more time. Keep Lindahl reined in. At least for another twenty-four hours."

"If we have that long . . ."

"We'll find something," Painter promised, but his words didn't come out as convincingly as he had hoped. "If not our team, then Gray's."

"Has Kat heard anything from the others?"

"No, not yet. But she says the solar storm is dying down, and satellite communications will hopefully resume later today. So let's at least try to hold back that nuclear option until we regain contact with Gray."

"I'll do my best."

Me, too.

He said his good-byes and stepped back to the café door when a bullet clipped his arm and shattered the restaurant window.

He fell to a knee while more rounds strafed the front of the café. Glass exploded over him as he rolled for cover behind a trash bin.

He caught a brief glimpse of his team inside, ducking for cover—he also saw three men in black camouflage burst from the kitchen behind them, assault weapons blazing into the morning diners. Across the street, another trio of assailants came charging, rifles smoking.

Pinned down, Painter had time for only one thought, recognizing the direness of their situation.

Gray, you'd better be having more luck.

19

April 30, 12:09 P.M. GMT
Queen Maud Land, Antarctica

"Everybody get aboard the lift!" Harrington shouted, as he rushed to the gondola that hung from its tracks alongside the observation deck of the beseiged Hell's Cape station. "Now!"

Gray had a hard time obeying, his gaze fixed to the dark netherworld beyond this glass-enclosed perch. Floodlights along the backside of the steel superstructure illuminated the immediate area below. But even those powerful xenon lamps failed to penetrate very far into that inky, cavernous blackness.

After fifty yards, the rock floor disappeared into a vast lake. The black surface bubbled and belched a yellowish steam, creating a toxic haze over the water.

A higher shelf of wet stone hugged the lake's right bank. Muddy tread tracks ran from the base of the superstructure out to that natural bridge.

Gray pictured those smaller CAATs parked in the hangar. He now understood the necessity for amphibious craft in the frozen arctic.

"Hurry!" Harrington barked.

The professor had opened the double set of doors that allowed access to the gondola and ducked through them. He crossed to a panel inside and hit a large red button. A siren ignited, blaring loudly, echoing from inside the steel superstructure and beyond.

Gray pushed Kowalski toward the waiting cage. "Go!"

Jason followed them with Stella.

Gray cringed at the noise as he climbed inside. As the doors closed, the din of the emergency klaxon died to a muffled ringing, proving how solidly insulated the gondola was.

"What're you doing, Professor?" Gray asked. "What's your plan?"

"To get somewhere safe."

Harrington pulled a lever and the cage began moving. But the gondola didn't head back through the superstructure toward the battle being waged in the hangar. Instead, it rode *forward*, out into that vast cavern.

Ducking a bit and craning his neck, Gray saw the black steel tracks continuing along the cavern roof, supported by trestles in places to create a relatively even run.

"Where are we going?" he asked as he straightened.

"To the Back Door." Harrington waved ahead with one arm; his other hand remained on the long red lever. "It's a substation about four miles out. It leads back to the surface, just beyond the Fenriskjeften crags."

Gray pictured that line of jagged peaks near the coast.

"There's a radio there," Stella added. "And a garaged CAAT."

"So we're just going to run?" Kowalski asked.

"No." The professor pointed to the red button he had struck. "I just sounded a general evacuation alarm. The British forces will hold off Dylan Wright's commandos for as long as possible, but after thirty minutes, they know to run. To get clear of this area."

"Why?" Gray asked.

"The entire backside of this station is packed full of bunker buster bombs, including an American-made thirty-thousand-pound Massive Ordnance Penetrator. It will destroy the base and seal up the mouth of the cavern system, bottling up what's down here."

"When's it set to blow?"

Harrington looked worried.

Stella answered, "It can only be deployed from the Back Door. Only my father has the blast code."

Gray frowned. *So the British forces will flee out the front while we sneak out the back door, blowing everything behind us. What the hell required such a level of security?*

Before he could ask, Gray felt a mother of all headaches flaring behind his eyes—but it wasn't only him.

Kowalski clutched the sides of his head, groaning. "Motherfu—"

Jason leaned on his knees, looking ready to vomit.

Harrington spoke through a tight jaw. "We'll be through the worst of it in another few seconds."

Gray breathed deeply, close to losing his breakfast, too. Then slowly the pain subsided; his back molars stopped vibrating in his skull. He could now guess the source of the sudden agony.

"LRAD?" he asked.

Long Range Acoustic Device.

Harrington nodded. "We have a series of sonic cannons pointed continually into the cavern at the edge of the station. As a buffer to keep everything as far back as possible. We've found a mix of ultrasonic and infrasonic frequencies to be an effective deterrent down here. Better than guns."

Gray leaned a hand against the wall, steadying himself, glad the gondola was so well insulated. He could only imagine the raw intensity of that sonic deterrent outside.

Jason pointed between his feet to a glass hatch in the floor. Through the window, a chair could be seen below, bolted inside an enclosed undercarriage canopy. A weapon with a large conical dish was racked in front of the seat.

"That's another LRAD cannon, isn't it?" Jason asked.

Stella nodded. "You can also swap it out for a machine gun, if need be."

"Once we're beyond the buffer zone," Harrington warned, "we may need both to protect the lift if we run into any serious trouble."

Trouble from what?

Out the windows ahead of them, the world was pitch-black. Behind the gondola, the station's lamp-lit bulkheads continued to recede into the darkness, reflected in the boiling lake. Then the tracks followed a bend in the cavernous tunnel and even that last light vanished.

Harrington stepped to a cabinet and opened a door. From hooks inside hung a row of heavy goggles—night-vision gear. "Put these on. I'm going to extinguish our cabin lights before we attract any attention. Then I'll ignite our exterior infrared lamps."

Gray tugged the gear over his eyes as Harrington doused the lights inside the gondola. His goggles picked up the small specks of light from diodes on the conveyor's control panel, but beyond the windows, the world remained dark. In this sunless and moonless underworld, even night-vision was useless.

Then the professor kicked on the exterior lamps, and beams of infrared penetrated that endless darkness. Though the wavelength was invisible to the naked eye, the goggles turned those beams into the brightest spotlights—illuminating what the darkness had hidden a moment ago.

Gray gaped as the view opened ahead of him.

Kowalski simply shook his head. "Something tells me we're gonna need bigger guns."

12:14 P.M.

Jason pressed his palms against the glass, taking in the sights as the armored gondola slowly rode its rails across the roof of this new world.

"Have you ever seen anything like this?" Stella asked.

"No . . . not like this."

The cavernous tunnel was tall enough to hold the Statue of Liberty without her torch ever scraping the rows of stalactites that hung from the roof like jagged fangs. Below, a snaking river slowly churned, fogged in steam. All around the gondola, a forest of massive columns formed a maze.

As their cage passed one, Jason noted stone branches jutting up from the pillar and joining the roof like support buttresses. Up close, the pillar's rough surface appeared strangely corrugated, almost like bark.

Then he looked even closer.

"It *is* bark," he suddenly realized aloud, glancing back as the column receded behind him.

"We're moving through a petrified forest," Stella said. "Remnants of a lost time when Antarctica was green and flush with life."

"They're *Glossopteris*, semitropical trees," Harrington said. "Over the past decades, archaeologists have uncovered three such ancient forests on the surface of the continent. Massive petrified stumps with scatters of fossilized leaves around them."

"But nothing as well preserved as down here," Stella added with a small note of pride.

Jason remembered a detail about Darwin's tale of the ancient Fuegian map: how on that chart, this place was marked by a grove of stylized trees. It was that promise of green life in this icy land that drew the *Beagle* to its ill-fated journey here.

Could this be that forest? Were these petrified trees what the Fuegians had actually drawn on their map?

Fascinated, Jason continued his bird's-eye survey of the terrain. As he watched the river below, something large humped out of the water and vanished. At first he thought it was a trick of the eye; then another appeared, and another.

"Something's in the water," he said.

Gray joined him. "Where?"

Before Jason could point, a large pale crustacean-like spider climbed out of the shallows and up onto a bank. It was the size of small calf, with a pair of large pincers in front and spikes along its carapace. Then those *spikes* scurried off the creature's back and appeared to be scouring the black algae from the damp rocks.

A dark shadow swooped down from a hidden nest among the stalactites and landed atop the tips of its clawed leathery wings. A sharp beak speared down and plucked up one of those small feeders, then stabbed down for another.

The larger crustacean defended its young and scrabbled after the attacker, its claws snapping. Avoiding a fight, those wings snapped out again, and with a single beat, the aerial predator burst upward. It flew in a wide arc, passing close to the gondola. It had a six-foot wingspan, its body covered in fine black scales; its head looked crocodilian, except for the sword-like beak.

"That's a smaller example of the species," Harrington commented. "We named them *Hastax valans*, Latin for flying spear. We've encountered individuals three times that size. That pale lobster is *Scalpox cancer* or chiseled claw."

"What else is out there?" Commander Pierce asked.

"So much more, an entire complex ecosystem. We're still trying to classify much of it. So far, we've identified over a thousand new species, from the lowly *Lutox vermem*—"

"A type of mudworm," Stella interjected.

"—to the elephant-sized *Pachycerex ferocis*."

Jason could not keep the mix of wonder and horror from his voice. "Amazing."

Gray knew Harrington's partner—Dr. Hess—had been scouring the globe for examples of shadow biospheres, looking for radical new forms of life.

Looks like he found it in spades here.

"This is the first environment of its kind," Harrington declared. "A unique xenobiological ecosystem."

Jason frowned. "Xenobiological?"

Stella explained, revealing her master's degree in evolutionary biology. "It's an ecosystem based on a biological system *foreign* to the rest of life on this planet. It's why we established a taxonomic classification system that incorporates an *X* into all the Latin names, to distinguish the various new species as *xenobiological.*"

Jason could not take his gaze from the sights below.

Outside the gondola, the flying predator had circled and looked ready to dive again upon that pale *Scalpox* and its young. It swept low over the water, stirring the mists. From the river—as if drawn upward by its wake—luminous globes the size of bowling balls shot upward. Jason shifted off his night-vision goggles for a moment. The globes scintillated in electric shades in the darkness, reminding him of the bioluminescent creatures found in deep-sea trenches. Only these glowing lures rose from larger bodies hiding underwater: huge eel-like creatures undulating through the river.

The aerial predator flew through a patch of those globular balloons, tangling and snagging them with its wings. Where they touched, flesh sizzled and burned. The *Hastax* writhed in agony and tumbled into the water. Through the dark surface, Jason watched those monstrous eels close in on their prey.

The attack reminded him of the hunting technique of an anglerfish, which used a similar bioluminescent lure to hunt for food.

Stella named this new predator, her voice frosted by dread. "*Volitox ignis.*"

Jason had taken enough Latin to guess the translation. "Floating fire."

"They're one of the nastier inhabitants down here. With their python-like bodies, they're very fast underwater, capable of casting out those burning tethers to nab prey out of the air or off the riverbank. They're also incredibly prolific, giving birth to great volumes of carnivorous young. To make matters worse, their offspring are born with vestigial limbs for climbing onto land. There's no escaping them."

"The *Volitox* are also very intelligent," Harrington added, looking equally grim. "They hunt in packs, employing a multitude of ambushing techniques. Even our sonic weapons are useless against them."

Stella scowled. "We lost three men in our early expeditions . . . before we knew better."

"It's a harsh, alien world down here," Harrington conceded. "The survival strategies that have evolved are clever and terrifying."

Jason stared down at the waters, gone black again, hiding what lurked below.

Sounds like we could use some clever survival strategies of our own.

12:16 P.M.

"They're gone, sir," his second-in-command stated.

"I can see that."

Major Dylan Wright stared at the empty tracks leading out from the observation deck. Fury heated his face, burning as hotly as the bullet graze across his upper thigh. He had lost two men during the raid, all in a rushed attempt to reach Harrington before he could escape.

Bertram and Chessie, he reminded himself, intending to honor the pair when the time was right. But he still had another fifteen men under his command, looking to him for the next move.

"The bombs," Dylan asked. "What's the word from Gleeson?"

His second-in-command, a muscular Scotsman named McKinnon, shook his head. "Looks like the base installed a new system after we left. Gleeson might be able to work out a way to defuse them, but not likely in the next half hour."

It won't take Harrington that long to reach the Back Door.

Dylan cursed the fact that his team's activities were exposed sixteen months ago, requiring a fast escape from

Hell's Cape to avoid capture. It had made the rest of his mission troublesome and problematic. Luckily he had the foresight to rig the ice shelf supporting the Halley station with incendiary bunker busters of his own. Hopefully it had taken out the American team. He pictured the man firing at the Twin Otter, smoking out the plane's starboard engine. His team had barely made it back to their base. Still, they had maintained their schedule.

Until now . . .

"I could send a team overland," McKinnon offered. "We could ambush them out there."

"If the base upgraded the security here, they would've done the same out there."

Besides, the Back Door substation was on the far side of the forbidding coastal crags. No team could get there in time to stop Harrington from blowing this place to kingdom come.

And that must not happen.

At least not before I've completed my mission.

Failure was not a word in his employer's vocabulary. Cutter Elwes had paid dearly for his team's services, including placing hefty bribes and pulling the right strings to get his group assigned to the station as a security detail. Since then they had been feeding Elwes intelligence about this place for years, obeying his every instruction.

And now the endgame was in play.

If successful, the windfall for his team would set them up for life.

McKinnon shifted his feet. "What's the next step?"

He ran various scenarios through his head, staring out into the dark cavern. Harrington had hightailed it out of here, like a fox before his father's hounds. But Dylan had never failed in a hunt—not on his family's country estate, and certainly not now.

His palm came to rest on the holstered nineteenth-century Howdah pistol, one of the rare treasures still in his possession, despite the family falling on hard times these past decades. The gun was a double-barrel weapon, over eighteen inches long, loaded with custom-made .577 cartridges and fired with rebounding twin hammers. The pistol dated back to the time of the British raj, when his family once lived as kings in India. Its name—*howdah*—came from the saddle worn by elephants, and the large-bore weapon had been used back then to defend against tiger attacks or to hunt large game.

He had even tested the gun here, against the denizens of Hell's Cape.

His fingers tightened on the grip, preparing for yet another hunt through these dark caverns.

"Gear the men up," he said. "Load the packages into the CAATs. We're going after them. Top speed."

"The professor has a good lead on us," McKinnon warned.

Dylan sneered, appreciating the challenge.

"Then we'll have to do something about that."

12:17 P.M.

A heavy silence had settled across the gondola, each passenger lost in his or her thoughts. All the while, Gray watched the mileage indicator click down. They were only a quarter of the way to this secondary station, the Back Door.

He studied the world beyond their meager refuge. With a long way still to go, he wanted as much information as possible before they reached the end of the line.

"So where did this all come from?" he finally asked, breaking the tense silence. "How could this ecosystem have survived down here for so long without any sunlight?"

"I don't have an answer to your first question," Harrington said, "but I have my theories. As to *how* this ecosystem could have survived, the situation here is not all that different from those oases of life found growing and thriving alongside deep-sea hydrothermal vents. No one expected to find life at those depths, in that eternal darkness, at such extreme temperatures. But nature found a way. The same down here, but on a grander scale."

Harrington waved a hand to indicate the steaming water. "The ecosystem down here is not driven by the sun, or photosynthesis, but by chemicals—by chemo-synthesis. It all starts with chemoautotrophic bacteria that feed on hydrogen sulfide or methane, chemicals continually spewing into this cavern system from all of the local geothermal activity. Those bacteria grow into thick mats—serving a similar role as the grasses of the sunlit world above—fueling the web of life found down here."

Stella cautioned, "But even chemosynthesis cannot fully explain how all this formed. Like my father mentioned, life down here is xenobiological, foreign to anything seen on the surface."

"How is it specifically foreign?" Jason asked.

"The life found in this ecosystem is not based on DNA, but on a variant using a different genetic backbone, namely XNA."

Gray had heard the reports out of California, about how the synthetic organism released by Dr. Hess was an organism engineered with XNA, replacing the normal sugar molecule in DNA with some toxic combination of arsenic and iron phosphate. Here must be the source of that unique genetic element.

"Why does XNA make such a difference?" he asked.

"It makes all the difference," Harrington expounded. "Richard Dawkins described our DNA as *selfish*, that our genes are driven by evolutionary pressures to multiply themselves above all else. If I had to describe XNA, I would depict it as *predatory*."

"Predatory?"

"From our studies of this natural landscape—and verified in labs that have synthetically created versions of XNA—these genes are opportunistic and highly mutagenic, far more than regular DNA, allowing for accelerated evolution. XNA genes are not merely selfish but focused toward total domination. Even the phenotypic expression of those genes reflects that core drive, creating organisms that are extremely hardy, resilient, and highly adaptable. Expose them to any environmental niche, and they will evolve a way to take it over."

"And Dr. Hess was experimenting with such a volatile genetic code?" Gray asked. *No wonder his creation has proven so hard to kill.*

"I warned him not to pursue this line of inquiry, or to at least conduct his experiments here, but he would not listen."

"What was he trying to do?"

"Kendall believed he could harness the best features of XNA, build it into a shell that could be used to vaccinate endangered species—maybe *all* species—to make them hardier, more adaptable, able to withstand the global forces that are driving us toward this sixth mass extinction."

"And that's possible, to incorporate XNA into our DNA?"

"Yes. In labs working with XNA now, they've already proven that xenobiological products could replace almost any living organism. So yes, it's theoretically possible. But there's also great risk."

Gray only had to stare out at the savage world below the gondola to recognize that truth. "Professor, you also said you had a theory about *how* life might have started down here."

Harrington nodded. "It's only a conjecture at this point. If I had more time, I might be able to substantiate it."

"What's your theory?"

"Do you remember how I mentioned this cavern system might cross a majority of the continent?"

"Through an interconnecting system of rivers, lakes, and ice tunnels."

"Don't sound so doubtful. While the surface of Antarctica is frozen and seemingly unchanging, it's warm and moist miles below, forming marshes and wetlands that have been hidden from the world for millennia. Take Lake Vostok, for example. It's as large as any of your Great Lakes and twice as deep and has been sealed away for fifteen million years. Then there's the amount of geothermal activity occurring below the ice. Did you know that one of my colleagues, a glaciologist with the BAS, discovered an active volcano almost half a mile under the Western Antarctic ice sheet, with evidence of lava flowing below? That's how strange and wonderful the true face of this continent is."

"So if this cavern system does transverse the continent, how does it explain how this ecosystem originated?"

"If you extrapolate what we've successfully mapped so far, the general direction of these tunnels seems to point toward a massive crater on the far side of East Antarctica, in a region called Wilkes Land. It was discovered back in 2006 and measures three hundred miles across. To create an impact crater that size, it's estimated that the meteorite would have been four times larger than the one that wiped out the dinosaurs. Some believe that impact here may have triggered the earth's *third* mass extinction: the Permian-Triassic extinction that wiped out almost all marine life and two-thirds of all terrestrial life."

"Okay, but why's that significant?"

"First, that meteoric impact could have cracked this cavern system into being. Then as most of the planet's species died off, some seed of XNA could have taken root in this empty ecosystem and grown to fill it, preserved in perfect isolation. But this scenario raises one other intriguing possibility."

"What's that?"

Surprisingly the answer came from Jason. "Panspermia."

Harrington smiled. "Very good."

Gray was familiar with the theory of panspermia, that life could have come to this planet on the back of a meteor, carried from afar to seed this world.

"Keep in mind that it would take a tough and resilient molecule to survive that long journey through the void of space," Harrington said.

"Like XNA," Gray said.

"Precisely. But as I said, it's only a conjecture. Though an intriguing one, I would say. Could this shadowy biosphere be a peek into an alien landscape, or at the very least, an alternate genetic pathway to life?"

Before this could be debated, the gondola rocked as it began to glide down a gentle slope, like an alpine ski lift descending back to earth.

It was too soon to be approaching the substation.

"It's the Squeeze," Harrington reassured him.

Gray stared out the window. Ahead, the cavernous tunnel tightened toward a bottleneck. The gondola swept into the narrower passageway. The cage now rode only three stories above the churning river. The banks to either side gave off a soft phosphorescence, that glow seeping into the water's edges, too, revealing shelves of strange bivalves and flashes of darting shapes in the shallows. Life teemed in those hot waters.

Harrington drew his attention forward. "Earlier you asked how I knew others had discovered these tunnels before our team. Look there."

The gondola rode around a bend in the Squeeze, and a gray shape appeared ahead, tall enough to scrape the roof. It was the conning tower of a sub. A line of broken stalactites marked the vessel's passage this far into these narrows. A majority of the submarine's cigar-shaped bulk was visible above the surface of the river, looking like a beached iron whale.

As their cage drew abreast of the old ship, Gray noted an emblem on the tower's side.

It was a black cross with a white submarine over it.

"German," Harrington said. "From the tenth flotilla of the Kriegsmarine."

A Nazi U-boat.

"These tunnels must've been more deeply flooded at one time," Harrington explained. "From evidence we found, the Germans blasted their way into here with torpedoes, but they could only penetrate so far. Afterward, a roof cave-in sealed the way behind them and was frozen over. Even if the crew tried continuing on foot or by rowboat, I can't imagine they got very far."

As the gondola drifted quietly past this somber grave marker, Gray could only imagine the terror of those submariners trapped here. Thankfully, the conning tower vanished into the darkness behind them, and their cage began to rise, climbing out of the Squeeze.

Before it could get very far, the gondola lurched to a stop, swinging from its overhead tracks for a frightening breath. Harrington worked the red lever, trying to get them moving again.

"What's wrong?" Gray asked.

Harrington glanced back in the direction they had traveled. "Dylan Wright. He must have reached the control box."

"Can you get us moving again?" Gray asked.

Without his laying a hand on the controls, the gondola began to run backward, returning slowly toward the base.

Wright must be trying to reel us back in.

Harrington reached overhead to a red plastic handle and pulled hard. A loud grinding pop sounded and the gondola swung to a stop again. "I disengaged us from the pulley cable."

The professor's eyes shone brightly with terror.

They were now dead in the water.

20

April 30, 8:18 A.M. AMT
Boa Vista, Brazil

Panicked at the sudden ambush, Jenna huddled behind an overturned table as gunfire ripped apart the café.

A moment ago, a trio of masked men had burst out of the kitchen, rifles at their shoulders. At the same time, the front plate glass window had shattered behind them, blown out by someone shooting from the street.

It was only because of Drake's fast reflexes she was still alive. As the first shots rang out, Drake had kicked the chair out from under her, then caught her as she fell and rolled her body under him. One of his fellow Marines—Marlow—tipped the heavy wooden table on its side, giving them temporary shelter. His partner, Schmitt, fired at the assailants.

"Painter . . ." Jenna gasped.

The director was still out on the street.

"On it," Drake said. "Stay here."

He shoved up, trying to get a fast glance through the blown-out window. Out on the street, the sudden staccato retorts of a pistol blasted away, in contrast to the louder rifle fire.

Has to be Painter putting up a fight.

"Looks like he's hurt, pinned down," Drake reported as he ducked back down. "Malcolm, Schmitt, cover me and hold the fort."

Not waiting for a response from his teammates, Drake leaped out of hiding. Both Marines kept up suppressive fire as the gunnery sergeant dove headlong out the window.

Jenna reached to her pack, to her own weapon, preparing to help.

As her fingers tightened on her pistol's grip, the firefight both inside and outside grew more intense. One of the gunmen toppled over a table; the other two dropped behind a counter, firing from a well-protected spot.

Malcolm swore, ducking back into shelter, his ear bleeding.

Jenna rose up and took his place, knowing any sign of weakness, any lessening of return fire, risked the enemy gaining the upper hand and overpowering them. She fired her Glock, driving back a gunman who had been starting to rise.

She took that fraction of a second to survey the café. Bodies littered the floor, blood spreading over the tiles. She noted a few small movements. Some of the half-dozen patrons and waitstaff were still alive.

But it was another movement that held her full attention.

A mirror behind the counter had been shattered by the first volley of rounds, but in the fractured reflection in the remaining pieces, she saw one of the enemy on his knees, reloading his rifle.

There won't be a better chance . . .

She fired again toward the position of the first gunman. "Now!" she yelled to the two Marines.

She didn't have time to explain more, so she simply dashed from behind the table and sprinted for the counter, hoping they would understand.

They did.

Malcolm and Schmitt flanked her, firing at the rifleman who was still an active threat. Under such a sustained volley, a bullet ricocheted off a rim of a metal chair and struck the assailant, knocking him back.

Jenna reached the counter and vaulted high, feet-first, sliding her hip through the broken plates and scattered utensils on the top. All the while, she kept her gaze fixed on the reflection of the hidden enemy. He had already finished reloading and was rising up to go to his partner's defense.

As he popped into view, she already had her left leg cocked and snapped a boot heel into his masked nose. His head cracked back with a satisfying *crunch* of teeth and bone. His body collapsed limply, out cold.

To the side, Schmitt placed a round through the other enemy's ear as the gunman tried to bring his rifle around.

The sudden cessation of gunplay inside the café left only the ringing in her ears, muffling the firefight outside.

Malcolm stalked low to her side as Schmitt poked his head and shoulder into the kitchen, leading with his pistol.

"All clear back here!" he called out, falling back to them.

Red-faced with fury, Malcolm lifted the muzzle of his weapon toward the cold-cocked man on the floor.

"Don't," Jenna said. "We may need him to talk."

Malcolm nodded.

She kept her Glock on the downed man. "I'll watch him. Go help Painter and Drake."

From the escalation of rifle fire out there, they were in trouble.

8:20 A.M.

"They're flanking us," Drake said.

Painter recognized this, too. He crouched shoulder to shoulder with the Marine behind a metal trash bin. The shelter barely offered enough cover for the two men as they fired from either side at the trio of gunmen across the road.

Unfortunately, the enemy had a distinct advantage. A row of cars lined the far sidewalk, offering plenty of cover and maneuverability. Their side of the street was a no-parking zone.

Still, if Drake hadn't come flying out the café window, Painter would likely be dead already.

The gunnery sergeant's sudden and opportune arrival drove the three assailants from the street and into cover behind the parked cars. But now those three had begun to split up. Two men ran low behind the vehicles, heading left and right along the street, while the third kept up a continuous barrage, the rounds ringing and ricocheting off the trash bin.

Trapped, Drake and Painter could barely move. It would take only another few seconds before the two flanking gunmen reached positions far enough along the road to get a clear, unobstructed bead on them.

"I'll cover you," Painter said, slapping in a fresh magazine. "Get back inside. Try to make it out the rear with the others."

Painter noted it had gone quiet inside the café—but was that a good sign or a bad one?

Then fresh gunfire erupted, blasting out from the shattered window of the café and strafing the row of cars across the street.

Caught off guard, the gunman to the left took a round through the neck, spinning away with a spray of blood. The assailant on the right suffered a similar fate, taking a bullet to the forehead.

The third had dropped low behind an old-model Volvo, plainly recognizing the tides had turned.

Drake rose to his toes, glancing to Painter, to his wounded shoulder. "We got this last one," he said, getting a confirmatory nod from his two teammates as they climbed out to the street. "This is what Marines are built for."

Painter knew better than to protest. "Try to take him alive."

As if sensing his coming demise, the hidden man started shouting—not at them, but from the sounds of it, into a phone or radio, likely calling for help or backup.

Painter caught a few words in Spanish, but the rest was a mix of some unknown native patois. One word in Spanish caught his attention. It was repeated again, more urgently.

Mujer.

Painter tensed, glancing back to the café.

Mujer meant *woman.*

"Where's Jenna?" Painter asked, his heart pounding harder.

Malcolm kept his gaze on the Volvo across the street. "Inside. It's all clear."

Or maybe not.

Disregarding the threat of the shooter, Painter bolted for the door and rushed inside. He held his pistol up with his good arm and scanned the tables, the bodies, and waded through the aftermath of the gun battle. He checked behind the counter, the kitchen.

A spat of gunfire echoed to him from the street.

A moment later, Drake burst into the café through the front door. His face looked stricken, scared, revealing a depth of emotion beyond the simple concern for a teammate.

"Jenna?" he asked.

"Gone." Painter nodded toward the street, knowing they had one chance of discovering who had taken her. "What about the third shooter?"

Drake understood the significance of his question, going paler. "He shot himself."

Dead.

Painter breathed heavily.

Then we lost her.

8:22 A.M.

The world returned to Jenna on waves of pain. Blackness shattered into light that was too bright, sounds too loud. She lifted her head from the rattling floor of a van, igniting a lancing stab that ran from a knot above her left temple to her neck.

Oww...

She bit back a groan, fearful of attracting the attention of her kidnappers. She took a fast assessment of her situation, her heart pounding in her throat. From her vantage, all she could see out the window was the upper floors of buildings sweeping past and the tangles of power lines.

A trickle of blood traced fire down her left cheek.

She remembered the ambush, allowing anger to hold back the terror icing at the edges of her self-control. She had been crouched behind the café counter, watching Malcolm and Schmitt cross to the window and start shooting into the street. The deafening barrage covered the approach of her attacker from the kitchen area. The only warning was a soft honeyed scent.

She turned to find a dark woman with shadowy eyes crouched a yard away, the balls of her bare feet positioned perfectly to avoid the broken glass on the floor—not to avoid getting cut, but in a feral level of stealth.

Before Jenna could react, the woman lunged, her arm sweeping wide whip-fast. The butt of a pistol cracked against Jenna's skull. Her vision flared brightly, then collapsed into a black hole, dragging her consciousness away with it.

How long was I out?

She didn't think it was long. Not more than a minute or two, she guessed.

From the front passenger seat, a face turned to peer back at her. Long black hair framed a darkly beautiful face. Her skin was the color of warm caramel, her black eyes aglow. Still, an edge of threat shone through those handsome features, from the hard edge of her full lips to the glassy-eyed menace in her gaze. It was like confronting the cold countenance of a panther in a tree, displaying nature at its most beautiful—and deadly.

Jenna wanted to retreat from that gaze, but she held the other's stare, refusing to back down. Not that Jenna could do anything more. Her wrists and ankles were secured with plastic ties.

The bright tinkle of a ringtone interrupted the standoff. The woman twisted back around as the driver passed her a cell phone.

She brought it to her ear. "*Oui*," she answered, her voice as silky dark as her complexion. She listened for a long breath, then glanced back to Jenna. "*Oui, j'ai fini.*"

Jenna knew she must be the topic of this conversation. Someone was confirming that she'd been captured, or at the very least that one member of the American team had been grabbed. She strained to eavesdrop on the rest of the conversation, but she didn't speak French. Still, she could guess who was on the other end of that line.

Cutter Elwes.

Apparently he must have had someone watching that guesthouse, making sure any trail that Amy had left in Boa Vista was continually under surveillance. Or maybe that kindly proprietor was not as *kindly* as she appeared and had sent word of the Americans who had come calling. Either way, Cutter must have ordered a local team to apprehend one of them, someone he could interrogate to find out how much the world knew about him, about his operations.

As a dead man, he plainly wished to remain in his currently deceased state.

The van fled faster as it broke free of the central district of Boa Vista. Jenna craned over her shoulder, fearful for Drake and the others. Had they survived the firefight? She prayed so, but she held out no hope that they would be able to track or follow her.

She faced around again, recognizing a hard truth.

I'm on my own.

After several more minutes, the van braked hard, sliding Jenna forward a couple of feet. She scooted up. Out the front window spread a rusted slum, the homes densely packed, clearly fabricated from whatever could be scavenged. But this wasn't her kidnappers' destination.

An old helicopter rested on a dirt pad. Its rotors already chopped at the air, preparing to depart.

Jenna despaired.

Where are they taking me?

8:32 A.M.

Still in Cutter's main lab, Kendall stood at the threshold to a neighboring Level Four biosafety facility, where a few technicians labored inside, their suits tethered with yellow air hoses. A moment ago, Cutter had stepped away to take a call. Kendall breathed deeply, still struggling to decide whether to help the bastard or not.

If I don't, the entire world could be destroyed.

If I do, would the end result be the same?

He balanced on a dagger's edge, his decision teetering upon one unanswered question: What was Cutter's plan for Kendall's synthetic eVLP? He remembered the man's worrisome description of that perfect empty shell.

A Trojan horse . . . a flawless genetic delivery system.

Cutter clearly planned on filling that Trojan horse—but with what?

Can I trust him when he says no one would be killed from whatever he planned to engineer into that empty shell?

Kendall's mind spun around and around, glad for whatever call allowed him the additional time to come to a decision. He used the delay to study the quarantined space before him. Like the main genetics facility behind him, the Level 4 lab contained the latest in DNA analysis and gene manipulation equipment. The back wall held a large refrigerated unit with glass doors. Rows of vials glowed behind that window.

A chill traced up his spine as he tried to imagine what was stored in there. But it was the four adjacent rooms flanking the refrigerator that truly terrified him. Each chamber contained a different piece of medical equipment. He recognized a simple X-ray machine in one room and a CT scanner in the next. The last two rooms held a magnetic resonance scanner for looking deep into tissues and a PET—positron emission tomography—scanner, for developing three-dimensional images of biological processes.

The presence of these pieces of equipment left no doubt.

Cutter had advanced to animal testing.

But how *advanced* was that testing?

Cutter finally returned, his manner more relaxed, as if he'd had good news. "Looks like we may be entertaining a guest before much longer. But we have much work to do before that, don't we, Kendall?"

Cutter lifted a curious brow, expecting an answer.

Kendall stared into the BSL4 lab. "And you swear, if I cooperate—if I teach you my technique—that no one will die as a result?"

"I can promise you that what I plan to use this technique for is entirely non-lethal." Cutter frowned as he must have read the distrust still shining on Kendall's face. "Maybe I can ease your mind with a short excursion. Won't take but a few minutes."

Cutter turned on a heel and headed away.

Kendall hurried after him, more than happy for the additional delay. Mateo followed behind, his ever-present shadow.

"Where are we going?" Kendall asked.

Cutter smiled back at him, a boyish enthusiasm glowing from his face. "A wonderful place."

Still, as Cutter turned back around, Kendall noted the drawn pull of his left shoulder. He imagined the thick scars binding that side. It was a reminder that despite appearances, that *boy* was long gone. He died on that African savannah ages ago. What was left was a hard and twisted genius with dark ambitions, deeply embittered at the world.

They exited the main genetic hall and followed a long natural tunnel. Kendall imagined they were crossing toward the middle of the plateau.

Cutter strode along, taking large steps. "We are not so different, you and I."

Kendall didn't bother disagreeing.

"We both care for this planet, are concerned where it's headed. But where *you* seek to preserve the status quo through your conservation efforts, I believe the world is too far gone. Man is incapable of reversing what its industry has wrought. Our appetites have grown too gluttonous, while our vision has grown narrower and narrower. Conservation is a lost cause. Why save a species here or there when the entire ecology collapses around your ears?"

"It was just such a calamity that I was trying to solve in California," Kendall countered. "To find a system-wide solution."

Cutter scoffed. "By attempting to engineer XNA hardiness and adaptability into various species as a whole? All you're doing is stealing from one biosphere in order to preserve another that is dying."

Kendall's back stiffened. So Cutter knew what he had been attempting to accomplish. The scientific term for it was facilitated adaptation, to fortify DNA in order to make a species more resistant to disease or make it more robust to survive in a harsh environment. He refused to apologize for his work. His research had the potential to protect many species against the ravages to come, but his work was still in its early stages. Unfortunately, what he had created so far was unrefined, dangerous, consuming all it touched, destroying any DNA it encountered.

It was never meant to be released.

As anger flared anew, Kendall confronted Cutter. "Then what would you have us do? Nothing?"

Cutter turned to him. "Why not? Get out of nature's way. Nature is the greatest innovator of all. It will survive us . . . maybe not in the form that you like or are familiar with. In the end, evolution will fill all those gaps created by a major die-off. All five past extinctions triggered an explosion of evolution afterward. Look at humankind. The dinosaurs had to die so we could rise. It is only through death that new life can grow."

Kendall had heard this central tenet of Dark Eden often enough to recognize it here. He boiled it down to its essential. "The great extinction holds the promise to bring about a new genesis."

Cutter nodded. "The beginning of a new Eden."

From the ardor in the other's voice, it sounded like he could not wait for that to happen.

Kendall sighed. "There remains a fundamental flaw to your reasoning."

"And what is that?"

"Extinction is fast. Evolution is slow."

"Exactly." Cutter stopped, looking close to hugging him for a moment. "That's exactly right! Extinction will always outpace evolution. But what if we could *speed* evolution up?"

"How?"

"I'll show you."

Cutter had reached a thick steel door that blocked the tunnel. He pulled a keycard from around his neck. "Conservation must worry less about *preserving* the life that was, and focus on *nurturing* what will come next."

"But how do we know what's coming?"

"We create it. We *direct* evolution toward this new genesis."

Kendall was stunned into silence.

Cutter swiped his card, and thick bolts began to slowly unlock.

"That's impossible," Kendall whispered, but even he couldn't convince himself. Genetic engineering and DNA synthesis were already at that threshold.

"Nothing's impossible," Cutter countered, as he pulled open the door. "Not any longer."

Bright daylight flooded the dimly lit tunnel, accompanied by a sweet mélange of scents undercut with the familiar muskiness of loam and rotted leaf. Drawn by that light, by the fresh air, Kendall followed Cutter gladly out of the passageway and onto a metal scaffolding that protruded from the side of a cliff.

As his boots clanked across the grating, Kendall craned up at the blue sky. The perch was fifteen feet from the lip of what appeared to be a huge sinkhole. The walls had been terraced into various levels of gardens, bursting with orchids, bromeliads, leafy vines, and blossoms of every hue and size. Each tier was connected by a winding road that corkscrewed along the inside walls.

Kendall watched an electric golf cart glide silently along that road, climbing toward their position, passing by gates that opened automatically before it. A triangular yellow sign with a black lightning bolt hung on the neighboring fence, indicating that each level's barrier was electrified.

Worry dampened his momentary wonder.

Cutter stood to the side, scanning the nearby walls, as if searching for weeds growing in his fantastical garden. "Ah," he finally said. "Down here. Come see for yourself."

He opened a gate along the landing's railing and climbed down a steep set of metal stairs to the stone road winding by at his level. Kendall kept his gaze away from that long central drop. It was so far down that he could barely see the bottom, especially with the morning sun still low on the horizon. Still, he noted what appeared to be the crowns of giant trees down there, possibly a piece of the Brazilian rain forest trapped below.

With great care, Kendall stepped from the steel stairs to ancient sandstone. He retreated from the edge of the road, away from that yawning precipice. On the far side spread a series of raised beds, about ten yards deep. They rode up against the cliffs, merging with the thick cascade of green growth that draped the walls. Narrow walkways crisscrossed those plantings. It all could be easily mistaken for some organic vegetable garden, but Kendall suspected what grew here was something far more insidious and anything but organic.

He noted a string of long-legged ants, each the size of his thumb, parading along the edge of one box.

"*Paraponera clavata*," Cutter named them. "Commonly known as bullet ants. Those little buggers got their nickname because their bite is considered one of the worst stings. The very top of the Schmidt sting pain index. Victims compare it to getting shot, and the pain can last for up to twenty-four hours."

Kendall took a step back.

"I was able to double their venom load."

Kendall glanced harshly at Cutter.

"A bite from one of these will leave you paralyzed and in excruciating pain. One of my workers accidentally got stung. He broke his back molars from the grinding pain. But that's not all. Come a little closer."

No thank you.

Kendall stayed rooted in place.

Cutter picked up a broken piece of a branch. "Bullet ants—like all ants—are ground-locked members of the Hymenoptera order, which includes bees and wasps."

He poked a reddish-black straggler, which responded by flaring out small membranous wings, all but invisible before. It flew a few inches away, then landed amid its stinging brethren, stirring them up.

"It was easy to return their wings to them," Cutter said. "Just a matter of splicing in genes from a tarantula hawk wasp. Especially as the two species share the same genetic heritage."

"You created a *chimera*," Kendall finally choked out. "A genetic hybrid."

"Precisely. I haven't been able to give them full flight yet, so far just those little buzzing bursts like you saw, but hopefully with time and environmental pressure, nature will do the rest, getting them flying as readily as their waspish cousins."

"How?" Kendall sputtered for a moment. "How did you accomplish this?"

"It was not all that difficult. You know as well as I that the technology is currently available. It was just a matter of having the will and resources to do it, free of oversight and regulation. You already saw my lab is equipped with multiple stations that use the latest CRISPR-Cas9 technique. A process I've refined further, by the way."

That was chilling news. CRISPR-Cas9 could already engineer any part of a genome with such precision that it had been likened to editing individual letters in an encyclopedia without creating a single spelling error.

"And you're certainly familiar with the MAGE and CAGE processes developed by George Church."

Kendall felt the blood drain into his legs. Like CRISPR, those two new techniques—multiplex automated genome engineering and conjugative assembly genome engineering—were sometimes referred to as evolution machines. These two gene-editing technologies were indeed just that, capable of automating thousands of genetic changes at the same time. They could introduce millions of years of evolution within minutes.

MAGE and CAGE held the promise to alter synthetic biology forever, taking it to new heights—*but where would those heights take us?*

He stared in horror at the row of large ants.

Cutter twiddled the small twig in his hand, seemingly disappointed by Kendall's reaction. "I read in a piece you wrote last year that you advocate using MAGE and CAGE as tools for resurrecting lost species."

He was right. These new gene-editing technologies held great promise. Researchers could take the intact genome of a living animal—then start making edits and alterations to the DNA, slowing converting it to the genome of a related species that had gone extinct.

"Start with an elephant and you might be able to resurrect a woolly mammoth out of its genes," Kendall mumbled aloud.

Not only was it theoretically possible, a Russian had gone so far as to create an experimental preserve in Siberia—called Pleistocene Park—where he hoped to allow these soon-to-be-created woolly mammoths to roam free.

"*De-extinction* was the word you used in the article," Cutter said with disdain. "It's such a sad distraction. To use such promising technology for this narrow preservationist agenda. All you're doing is choking nature's ability to respond to the damage wrought by humankind."

"And this is your answer?" Kendall mocked, waving to the line of marching black ants.

"Only a small part of a larger picture. Where you and your colleagues dwell in the past, looking to de-extinction for salvation, I turn to the future, to prepare for what's to come with a plan for *rewilding*."

"Rewilding?"

"To reintroduce keystone species—animals and plants that have the most impact on the environment."

"Like your ants."

"I've engineered my creations—all my creations—to be stronger, with the necessary tools to survive us. Along with newer innovations."

Cutter took his twig and encouraged one of the ants to climb atop its tip. Before it could clamber up and bite him, he flicked it into a neighboring planter box. The ant landed on a wide leaf of a bromeliad and scrambled along its length. Thin wings vibrated in irritation.

Then from a pore in the leaf, a glistening bubble erupted, enveloping the ant in a thick gelatinous sap. The squirming insect fought, but in seconds its legs dissolved away, followed shortly thereafter by the rest of its body. After that, the jelly bubble quickly lique-fied, trickling down the inside of the leaf to feed the root ball at the base.

"Here I engineered in a sequence of genes from the carnivorous sundew," Cutter explained. "Including intensifying its digestive enzymes."

Kendall's stomach churned as he turned to stare at the dark garden spread below. "How many others?"

"Hundreds of species. But they're just the first wave. I also took the step to genetically bind each alteration to sequences of DNA retrotransposons."

Kendall began to fathom what Cutter intended. Retrotransposons were also called jumping genes, named for their ability to leap between species in a process called horizontal gene transfer. Geneticists had come to believe these jumping genes were potent engines of evolution, passing traits across species lines. Recent studies of cattle DNA showed that a full quarter of their genome came from a species of horned viper, proving that Mother Nature had been shuffling genes for millennia, creating hybridized species since the dawn of time.

But it was no longer just nature.

"This is how you plan to speed up evolution," Kendall realized aloud. "You intend to use these traits tied to jumping genes to spread what you've created far and wide."

"Each species will be like a seed cast to the wind. One hybrid will lead to two, two to four. In all that shuffling, can you imagine what new species will arise? What new combinations will appear? All of them fighting to survive in this damaged world we created."

Kendall pictured a great conflagration spreading through the rain forest and across the world.

If Cutter could accomplish so much already, why does he need my engineered armor shell? What does he plan to put inside it?

There had to be another step to this madman's scheme.

"A new Eden beckons," Cutter continued, his voice exultant. "We are at the threshold of a new world. A genesis so dramatic we could witness it in our lifetime. I want to share that with you. Will you help me achieve it?"

Kendall faced the raw passion standing before him and did the only thing he could. He had to survive long enough to stop the man.

"Yes . . . I'll help you."

8:44 A.M.

"We have to go after her," Drake said, stomping back through the carnage left in the wake of the firefight, followed by his two teammates.

Painter knelt over one of the survivors, a young waitress. He had a towel pressed to her side, stanching the blood from a round through the lower abdomen. His own shoulder burned from the bullet that had torn a chunk from the back of his arm. Earlier,

Malcolm had quickly bandaged it from a med-kit in his backpack.

The three Marines had already swept the streets behind the establishment, but there was no sign of Jenna.

Painter understood the frustration he heard in Drake's voice.

In the distance, sirens descended toward this location. They would lose even more time dealing with local authorities.

A groan sounded from behind the counter.

So somebody finally decided to wake up.

Painter waved Schmitt to take his place. "Get a pressure wrap on this woman."

As the Marine obeyed, he crossed to the source of the noise. A figure lifted his head from the floor. His hands were tied behind his back. Blood soaked the mask that hid his features. It was the gunman who Jenna had cold-cocked during the fight. In their hurry, Jenna's kidnappers must have believed he was dead, especially from all of the blood.

Painter stepped over and ripped away the mask, earning a satisfying cry of pain. More blood poured from his shattered nose. His eyes were already nearly swollen shut.

"Take him," Painter ordered Drake.

The sirens were louder now.

He saw that Schmitt had finished securing a tight wrap around the waitress's belly. She should survive.

"Let's go," Painter said and waved everyone out.

Drake and Malcolm headed for the back door, the groggy gunman slung between them. Their SUV waited in the rear alley. It had been moved there by the Marines to facilitate a swift evacuation.

Drake manhandled their prisoner into the backseat. "What if this bastard doesn't talk?"

Painter used a knuckle to wipe up a drop of the man's blood from the car seat. "Maybe he won't have to. But we'll need help."

21

April 30, 6:02 A.M. PDT
Sierra Nevada Mountains, California

Hang in there, Josh . . .

Lisa sat on an uncomfortable stool in the patient containment unit. She held her brother's hand, wishing she could shed her gloves and truly touch him. Though he was right here, she felt a gulf between them. And it wasn't just the barrier of the polyethylene suit that separated them. The medically induced coma had stolen Josh from her: his raspy laugh, his ready joke, his blushing bashfulness in the presence of a pretty girl, his studious frown when hanging on a rope from a cliff face.

All gone.

Josh had been placed on a respirator a few minutes ago as his condition deteriorated. Each inhalation was too sharp, too regular. Off to the side, monitors clicked, hummed, and gently beeped. That was all that was left of her brother's energetic and full life.

The radio inside her suit buzzed, drawing her back straighter. She girded herself for more bad news. Then a familiar and welcome voice filled her head. She squeezed Josh's hand harder, as if trying to urge her brother to keep fighting, that Painter would save him.

"Lisa," Painter said, "how are you holding up?"

How do you think I'm doing?

Tears suddenly sprang to her eyes and ran down her cheeks. She had no way to wipe them away. She swallowed a few times to hide them from her voice.

"It . . . it's not good out here," she said, struggling to hold it together. "Every hour things get worse. I don't know if you heard, but Lindahl has ordered a nuclear device to be shipped to the mountains. It's en route and should arrive by this afternoon."

"And there's no way to deter him?"

"No. At daybreak, a whole team of surveyors mapped the contaminated areas—or at least those areas actively showing die-offs. It's worse than the overnight reports indicated. The organism is still spreading, approaching what Lindahl calls critical mass, the point where even a nuclear option might not work. Nuclear scientists are still doing calculations of load and the radiation levels necessary to achieve the highest level of lethality."

Lisa put as much urgency into her voice as she could muster in her exhausted state. "We need answers to stop this nuclear juggernaut. Or at least, some hope of a solution."

She stared at Josh's face, at his waxen complexion.

Please.

"We may have a good lead," Painter admitted, though he sounded hesitant, plainly worried. He gave her a fast update of his situation in Brazil.

Lisa found herself standing by the end of his story. "Someone kidnapped Jenna . . ."

She let go of Josh's hand and turned toward the complex of BSL4 labs across the hangar. Nikko was doing no better than Josh. The dog was on a plasma and platelet drip, growing moribund with every passing hour. In fact, the poor husky would already be dead if not for the herculean efforts of Dr. Edmund Dent. The virologist was using every medical tool in his arsenal to support Nikko and Josh. And while Edmund hadn't been able to reduce the viral load in his patients, his palliative treatments seemed to slow the progression of clinical signs.

Painter offered one glimmer of hope. "We're on our way to a facility in Boa Vista run by the Federal

University of Roraima and tied to the Genographic Project. For years, they've been gathering genetic information from all the various indigenous Brazilian tribes, using autosomal markers to calculate migration patterns and subgroups of the various tribes. They've put together an extensive database. With a blood sample from the man we apprehended, we might be able to find out what tribe he belongs to."

"Why does that matter?"

"Remember those photos Jenna took of the assailants who attacked her at the ghost town near Mono Lake?"

"I remember."

"It appears that group that attacked us here were of the same native tribe. Makes me wonder if Cutter Elwes hasn't gone all Heart of Darkness on us out in the rain forest, woven himself into that same tribe and bent them to his will. If we can find that tribe, we might find not only Elwes . . . but hopefully Jenna and Kendall Hess, too."

A silvery surge of optimism cut through her dark exhaustion. She took in a deep, shuddering breath. "You have to find something," she pressed. "Something I can take to Lindahl to halt or delay his plans."

"I'll do my best."

"I know you will. I love you."

"Same here, babe."

She wasn't satisfied with his reflexive response. "Just say it back, so I can hear it."

He laughed, which stoked that silvery shine inside her. "Not in front of the boys."

She pictured Drake and his teammates and found a smile dawning on her lips. She heard the same smile in Painter's voice.

"Okay," he said. "I love you, too."

After they said their good-byes, Lisa felt reinvigorated, ready to tackle anything. Her radio buzzed again. She hoped it was Painter, having forgotten to tell her something—anything to hear his voice again—but it was Edmund Dent.

"Lisa, you need to get back to your lab ASAP."

"Why?" She glanced in that direction. "Has Nikko gotten worse?"

"I was changing a bag of plasma for the big guy, and Lindahl left his radio mike open, broadcasting to the team here. He plans to have the nuclear research team experiment on Nikko. They want to know the effects that radiation will have on the organism when it's deeply entrenched in living tissue, to calculate a dosage that's high enough to kill it inside a body."

"They're planning to irradiate Nikko?"

"In ever-escalating dosages while taking biopsies of his kidney and liver, to see how much radiation it will take to eradicate the virus."

All the shining optimism from a moment ago ignited into a fiery anger. Jenna had put her life at risk to help them all, and they planned on killing her dog, torturing him, when the ranger's back was turned.

Over my dead body.

She rushed to the air lock of the quarantined ward.

"You'd better hurry," Edmund warned. "I just over-heard another order from Lindahl on the radio."

"What now?"

"He's commanded the Marine security team to bar you from your lab if you show any resistance."

That bastard . . .

She yanked the air lock door open and began the decontamination process. As the jets sprayed the exterior of her suit, she struggled to find a solution, a way of saving Nikko. By the time the green light flashed the all clear, allowing her to exit, she had come up with only one possibility—a gambit that would require great personal risk.

But she would take that chance.

For Nikko . . .

For Jenna . . .

She owed them both that much, but a worry nagged at the edges of her resolve as she stepped out of the air lock and crossed the dimly lit hangar toward the suite of BSL4 labs.

How much time did Nikko have? How much time did any of them have?

She knew only one thing for sure.

Somebody needed to find an answer—and fast.

22

April 30, 1:03 P.M. GMT
Queen Maud Land, Antarctica

"We can't just keep hanging around here," Kowalski commented, looking ready to kick the side of the stalled gondola.

Gray understood his teammate's consternation. He adjusted his night-vision goggles as he surveyed the landscape beyond their small cage in the sky. Their gondola hung four stories above the cavern floor. Dark waters washed against a shore of rock directly below. There was no going back the way they'd come, and the infrared illuminators along the undercarriage of the cage failed to penetrate very far ahead, revealing only a few of the ubiquitous petrified trunks, like pillars holding up the roof.

Who knew what horrors lay beyond that darkness?

Because what was visible here was terrifying enough.

The slow-moving river below churned with hidden life. Sleek fins broke the surface occasionally. He watched a turtle-shell-backed creature lumber through the shallows, its head spiked like the tail of a *Stegosaurus*. A crocodilian beast slithered on its belly from the algae-covered bank to avoid this hulking trespasser and vanished into the waters. Higher on the shore, clouds of batlike birds, looking little larger than thumb-sized sparrows, swirled up in tidy eddies and whorls, like smoke rising from their guarded nests. As Gray's eyes adjusted, finer details emerged. Patches of mossy growths sprouted from the algal beds; mists of tiny gnats or other midges swirled among the trunks of the petrified forest; pale white slugs inched up the walls, leaving glowing trails, like slow-moving graffiti artists.

Stella spoke to her father, drawing his attention around. "He's right." She nodded to Kowalski. "We can't stay here. Dylan Wright must know where we are and that we're trying to reach the Back Door. By now, he must have discovered that you reengineered the bunker busters to be shut out from the main station. After failing to reel us back in, he'll send a team after us."

"Through this *hellscape?*" Jason asked, purposefully mispronouncing the British installation's name for emphasis.

"He could use our CAATs," Professor Harrington said dourly. "Come by ground transport. We're only a mile or so away."

And three miles from the Back Door, Gray thought.

The older man hooked his arm around his daughter. Fear and worry etched the lines of his face deeper. She leaned into him, just as anxious about her father.

The lights grew incrementally dimmer. At first Gray thought it was his own terror narrowing his vision, but Kowalski swore, tapping at his goggles.

"When I decoupled us from the cable," Harrington explained, "it cut us off from the power conduit running along the roof. We're running on a battery charge right now."

"How long until we're out of juice?" Gray asked.

"A couple of hours at best."

Gray gave his head a slight shake. He did not want to be sitting here in the dark, waiting for Wright's team to discover them trapped in the dead gondola.

"What about that German sub?" Jason offered. "It's only two hundred yards back. Is there any way we could make it over to that shelter? Perhaps hole up inside there?"

Gray turned to Harrington. "Is that possible? Can we evacuate out of this gondola?"

Stella slipped from her father's arms and stepped to the hatch that blended into the floor. She tugged it open. A folded wire-and-metal ladder was stored inside. "If you pull that red lever, an emergency escape door will drop below and the ladder will deploy. It should reach the ground."

"No friggin' way I'm going down there," Kowalski said.

Harrington looked like he agreed, glancing apprehensively toward his daughter. Still, he turned and opened another cabinet along the wall. Inside, racked one atop the other, were three rifle-like weapons with barrels twice as thick as those of a 12-gauge shotgun.

"Directed stick radiators," Harrington explained. "Or DSRs. Built by the American Technology Corporation. They use a stacked series of disks in their barrels to amplify a pulse, producing the equivalent of a sonic bullet."

Kowalski snorted and mumbled under his breath. "Give me *real* bullets any day of the week."

Harrington ignored him. "The DSRs can also transmit speech or in reverse operation, be used as a directional microphone." He tapped what looked like a rifle sight on top. "I added portable IR illuminators for deployment down here."

"And these sonic rifles can protect us?" Gray asked.

"Mostly. They're not as potent as the larger LRAD units, but they'll send most life-forms down here scurrying away. But you need to be careful. The kinetic recoil of these guns is strong enough to knock you on your butt."

Gray stepped forward and picked one up, examining it thoroughly. Once done, he passed it toward Kowalski, who looked like he'd been offered a rattlesnake. Jason took the weapon instead.

Stella moved forward and grabbed a rifle for herself.

"She's a good shot," Harrington commented with pride. "Bloody things give me migraines if I try to use one."

Gray hauled out the last weapon, slinging it over his shoulder.

Harrington wasn't done yet. He stepped over and opened the hatch that led down to the canopied bubble on the underside of the gondola. Dropping to his knees, he reached inside. When he straightened, he had a more familiar weapon in his arms, struggling under its weight.

"I heard what you said earlier," he told Kowalski. "Thought you might like this instead."

Kowalski grinned, lifting the M240 machine gun from the professor's arms. He cradled it like a baby. He then dropped to a knee next to the professor and hauled out a long belt of 7.62x51mm NATO cartridges and flung the bandolier over his shoulders like a deadly scarf.

He stood up, puffing out his chest. "Now this is more like it."

Jason eyed the folded ladder, looking suddenly less sure of the wisdom of his plan. "So we try to make it over to the German sub?"

"No," Gray answered. "If found, we'd be trapped inside there. And even if Wright misses us, we'd leave the path open for his team to reach the Back Door first."

"Then where are we going?" Jason asked.

An old Churchill slogan popped into Gray's head.

If you're going through hell, keep going.

He pointed ahead. "We're going to strike out for that substation, try to reach the Back Door."

Kowalski's grin faded back to its usual scowl. "How the hell are we going to do that?"

He had no better answer—but somebody else did.

"I know what we can do," Harrington said, still sounding none too happy. "But we'll still have to trek some distance first."

1:22 P.M.

Hell became all too real, striking his every sense.

Jason descended cautiously down the rungs of the swinging ladder with his DSR slung across his back. Since lowering out of the gondola, the harsh world swallowed him whole.

Each breath brought in the reek of sulfurous brimstone, belched out from the volcanic forces underpinning this world. He could taste the foulness on the back of his tongue, while moist heat burned his skin, drawing beads of sweat from every pore. The silent world now whispered with creaks, croaks, laps of water, and a faint continual buzzing coming from a mix of nattering insects and a vague sense of ultrasonics bouncing off the walls, cast out by the life found down here.

The last set his teeth on edge, tickling the hairs on the back of his neck—or maybe it was simply the fear.

He stared below his feet. Gray and Kowalski had already reached the stone bank of the river. They had their weapons at their shoulders. The IR illuminator atop Gray's rifle cast out a pool of illumination into the darkness. Kowalski held his machine gun up, its belt of ammunition dragging all the way to the ground.

Jason watched Harrington step off the last rung of the ladder and join the other two men. They spoke in whispers, following the instructions given to them by the professor: *In this world of eternal darkness, sound is vision.*

It was why the sonic weapons employed here were so effective.

At least I hope they are.

Jason shifted his DSR more securely over his shoulders and continued his descent along the shaking ladder. He eyeballed the river below. He might survive a fall from this height if he hit the water—but getting out *alive* from that river would be the true challenge.

Harrington had shared another nugget of wisdom before they vacated the gondola: *Whatever you do, stay clear of the water.*

The ecosystem down here was dependent on that main river and its lakes, all of it fed by geothermally melted ice from the miles of glaciers overhead, and drained under the continent to parts unknown.

Before the gondola had stalled, the professor had educated them about the primordial world down here, how it was mostly *amphibious* in nature, thriving at that boundary between solid ground and the flowing rivers and pools. Many of the life cycles had evolved to incorporate stages that transitioned between those two extremes: juveniles sheltering along the rocky banks, adults living in the water, or vice versa.

Harrington had described the ecosystem as being stuck in the Carboniferous Period, an era when the topside world was dominated by primordial swamp forests. The professor had noted parallels in the evolutionary pathways taken by the life down here. Only this isolated and insulated world had become stagnant, never experiencing the radical changes wrought upon the world above by the breakup of the supercontinent of Pangaea or by the ravages of meteoric impacts. Still, the highly adaptable XNA genetic matrix had compounded the inventiveness of life dwelling inside this cavern system.

Soft words reached him from below, another warning from Harrington, directed mostly at Kowalski.

"Careful with your gun," the professor said. "Besides noise, *scent* is a strong trigger, especially blood. The racket of that weapon and resulting bloodshed could trigger a feeding frenzy."

Jason pictured the angry thrashing of sharks through spilled chum.

"To your right," Stella called quietly but urgently from above, drawing his attention in that direction.

At first he didn't see any threat. The massive bole of a fossilized tree rose twenty yards off. Then a veil of movement caught his eye, wafting around the trunk as if on a slight breeze—but there was no wind down here. He hooked an arm around a rung of the ladder and brought his gun around, clicking on its IR beam. The cone of brighter illumination revealed what Stella's sharper eyes had picked out.

Around the tree, a tangle of threadlike worms squirmed through the air toward them. Each floated on small parachutes of silken strands. Jason knew how some spiderlings and caterpillars used a similar technique, called kiting or ballooning, using either wind or the earth's static electric field to hold themselves aloft.

The flotilla drifted toward them.

"Move faster," Stella warned.

Jason obeyed, trusting her experience. He shouldered his DSR and began clambering more quickly down the ladder. Brought to his attention, he had no trouble continuing to track the threat.

Looking up as he climbed down, he failed to note a lone scout, coasting ahead of the others. The threadlike worm brushed against his cheek and clung there, burning into his flesh like the butt of a cigarette. Stifling a cry of pain, he tried to scratch it away, but the gossamer of silk settled over his skin, as sticky as Super Glue, pasting the larva to his cheek.

He dug harder.

"Leave it!" Stella urged, more loudly now, nearly on top of him. "We must get off the ladder. Now!"

Jason forced his hand back to the rungs, his eyes tearing up from the burning agony. He hurried down. Stella kept right above him. Beyond her body, the drifting mass collided into the length of the emergency ladder. Silk and flesh enmeshed into the steel, coating it thickly. Curls of sizzling smoke rose from the rungs and cables, as the creatures' corrosive acids reacted to the metal.

One of the individual wires in the tightly corded cable running through the rungs snapped with an audible *twang.*

Oh, crap . . .

Jason moved faster, almost sliding his way down now. He was still a good ten yards above the ground when Stella called out again.

"Your left!"

He twisted that way, bringing his rifle around one-handed, responding to the panic in her voice. Something large sprang off the trunk of the neighboring fossilized pillar. The creature must have been perfectly camouflaged as it worked into position, possibly drawn by the earlier passage of the three men.

Wings spread wide as it dove, revealing its nature.

Hastax valans.

A flying spear.

The sharp beak aimed for his chest, moments from impaling him. He pulled the trigger on the DSR, firing out a bullet of sound. The sonic burst struck the beast head-on. The *Hastax* screamed, its wings seizing up, sending it cartwheeling to the side.

While the spear missed its intended target, the recoil of the gun came close to throwing Jason off the ladder. One foot lost its rung, but his fingers clenched hard to keep himself perched. A glance below revealed the ladder's end sweeping from shore and dragging into the water as they swung out over the river.

Jason held his breath, waiting for the pendulum to swing them back again—when the cable running down the left side of ladder snapped, weakened by the corrosive acids and stressed by the sudden swing.

Jerked around, he lost his footing entirely but still hung by one hand.

Someone else wasn't as lucky.

A body tumbled past him.

Stella.

1:24 P.M.

Gray rushed to the shoreline as the young woman splashed into the river, vanishing underwater.

Harrington cried out and waded into the shallows, ready to go to his daughter's defense.

Gray grabbed and pushed him toward Kowalski. "Stay . . . I'll go."

But he was already too late.

A shape hurtled down from above, dropping feet-first into the river.

Jason followed Stella underwater.

Gray held his breath, letting two seconds tick past—then both came sputtering up. Stella struggled, her lips barely above water. Jason fought to pull her forward, but she seemed stuck. The young girl's eyes were wide with terror.

Jason called out. "Something's got her leg!"

Gray dropped his rifle, bent down, and yanked a dagger from a boot sheath. He sprang from his crouch and shot out over the water, diving smoothly under. His night-vision goggles picked up the glow from the weapon still tangled around Stella's torso. He kicked toward the light as schools of silvery fish scattered from his path. Small fist-sized shells burst away with whips of tentacles.

He prayed all the marine life remained equally spooked.

He reached Stella and followed the length of her body down to where a knot of leafy vine was bound around her calf. Tendrils of dark blood seeped from her leg. He grabbed a fistful of loose vine near her ankle and sawed at it with his dagger. The razor-sharp edge cut quickly through the vine.

Freed, Stella accidentally kicked him in the side of the head. He didn't blame her panic. He twisted back to the surface.

"Get the hell out of there!" Kowalski bellowed.

As Stella and Jason splashed for shore, Gray followed, still facing the river. A trio of large shapes humped out of the water, undulating toward them.

Luminous globes rose from the waters, lifted on dark stalks.

He remembered those same gelatinous orbs searing through the wings of the aerial predator, burning with acid fire.

Volitox ignis.

Jason reached the shore, twisting his weapon up and firing. Water cannoned out of the wide barrel, along with a sound that shot past Gray's shoulder. The passage left his head ringing like a bell struck with a sledgehammer.

Still, the deafening blast did nothing to deter the forms barreling toward Gray.

"Sonics don't work against that species!" Harrington yelled. "Run!"

With clothes waterlogged and heavy, Gray sloshed toward shore, but he knew one certainty.

I'll never make it.

Ahead of him, fiery orbs lowered, skimming the water, as if drawn by his flailing efforts.

Then a new series of blasts erupted behind him—coming not from a sonic weapon this time, but from the heavy chugging of a machine gun.

Kowalski fired from shore, but his aim was too high.

The rounds flew over the luminous globes and the hunters below—and struck a dark shape circling several meters above the river. It was the *Hastax* that Jason had stunned earlier. Bullets shredded its dazed form and sent it tumbling in a spray of black blood down into the waters, crashing amid the hunters.

The *Volitox* swarmed upon it, possibly first in a defensive reflex at the seeming attack, then in an escalating bloodlust.

Gray reached shore and joined the others.

"That should keep them busy . . . along with other scavengers," Harrington said. "But we should take advantage of the situation and get as far from here as possible."

"Go," Gray said, breathing hard and clapping Kowalski on the shoulder in silent thanks.

The big man lifted his machine gun and rested its bulk against his shoulder. "Like I said before, give me *real* bullets any day of the week."

As a group, they crossed along the bank, cautious of its slippery coating of algae and moss, keeping well clear of the water's edge.

Gray led with his weapon at his shoulder, flanked by Stella and Jason. Harrington followed, with Kowalski keeping up a rear guard. The professor eyed his daughter's limp. The woman's right leg remained shrouded by the severed coil of leafy vine. Her bottom pants leg was bloody.

"Do we need to take care of that?" Gray asked.

Harrington glanced behind them. The group had cleared a spur of rock, putting them out of direct view of the feeding frenzy. "We should," the professor said, drawing them farther out of the way. "Over here."

A slab of broken rock served as a seat for Stella. Her father gently unwrapped the vine, drawing bloody thorns, each an inch long, from her skin. Once removed, the muscular coil continued to squirm in the professor's grip, but Harrington kept hold.

Following the older man's instruction, Gray cut a seam along his daughter's pants, then administered first aid using antiseptic and a bandage from a small emergency med-kit taken from the gondola.

"Do we need to worry about poison?" he asked as he worked.

"No." Harrington lifted the length of vine. "*Sugox sanguine* is no worse than kelp. Only a little more aggressive."

"No kidding," Kowalski commented.

Vine in hand, the professor moved toward Jason.

The kid took a step back.

"Hold still," the professor said. "Let me see your face."

Jason turned his cheek, revealing a black gash.

Harrington lifted the writhing plant. Bright red blood dribbled from the cut end. Gray eyed those thorns anew, horror growing.

Had that muscular vine been sucking Stella's blood?

The professor tilted Jason's head farther back and hovered a fat crimson droplet over the wound.

What is he—?

From the gash, a fat white larva squirmed out, stretching toward that fresh blood. The professor speared it with one of the vine's thorns, pulled out the rest of its body, then threw the vine and the impaled parasite into the river.

Jason fingered his wound, his face sickened.

"Do you know about botflies?" Harrington asked.

Jason shook his head and looked like he didn't want to know.

Harrington elaborated anyway. "*Cuniculux spinae* are similar, a type of flesh-burrowing parasite. They burn their way deep into tissues and sprout oviparous spines."

"Oviparous?" Jason asked, looking more pale.

"Egg-laying. The eggs hatch into carnivorous larvae that spread far and wide. After that, they mature into—"

"I think that's enough of a biology lesson," Gray said, saving Jason from more details, while helping Stella back to her feet. "Let's keep going."

2:32 P.M.

Jason slogged beside Gray. They had been trekking for nearly forty-five minutes, but by his estimate, they had crossed no more than half a mile.

If even that.

"Not much farther," Harrington said behind them, but Jason wasn't sure if that was the truth or if the professor was merely trying to convince himself.

During their hike, the tunnel had been steadily descending, falling in a broken series of steps, each no more than a meter high. Waterfalls cascaded from level to level, echoing up and down the tunnel. They were able to follow the banks along the western wall, but a few times, it required winding past stagnant ponds or fording streams by hopping from rock to rock.

Yet, it wasn't the terrain that slowed them the most.

Life down here continually pressed against their small party, like a steady headwind. The sonic rifles deterred a majority of the larger creatures. But with every step, something squirmed, crawled, or flapped around them. All the while, biting flies continued to plague them, oblivious of their sonic discharges, an ever-present nuisance.

By now, it seemed every breath burned worse than the last.

Every yard harder to cross.

Sweat soaked through his clothes. His eyes felt swollen and on fire under his goggles.

The only bright side was Stella had drifted closer to him, marching at his shoulder, each taking turns keeping his or her rifle up. Initially, she or her father would try to educate them about what they encountered, classifying various species, but eventually it boiled down to a simple question for each new life-form.

Kowalski asked it now. "Should we shoot them?"

Jason stared ahead. Their path was blocked by what could only be construed as flocks of featherless emus, their numbers easily topping two hundred. Each birdlike creature stood on tall thin legs, likely evolved for wading among the series of ponds that dotted the immediate area. A cluster of nests held speckled eggs the size of grapefruits.

"If you move slowly, they shouldn't bother us," Harrington said. "They have no natural fear of people. As long as you don't get too near one of their nests, we should be able to pass unscathed."

"And if we do piss them off?" Gray asked.

"*Avex cano* have a flock mentality. They'll attack en masse. See that hooked claw at the back of their legs. It's used for gutting prey."

"But mostly they're docile," Stella said. "Even friendly, sometimes curious."

She demonstrated by stepping near one and holding out her hand. It hopped closer, cocking its head to one side, then the other. Only now did Jason notice it was eyeless. Small nostrils above a long paddle-shaped beak opened and closed.

She reached a little farther and ran her fingertips along the underside of that beak, earning a soft ululating noise from its throat. The sound spread to its neighbors, like a wave traveling outward from a pebble dropped into a pond.

Stepping forward, Stella followed those reverberations, easily passing through the flock, leading the way now. Jason was drawn in her wake, as much by the wonder of it all as his appreciation of the woman before him.

Nearby, an *Avex* stalked high-legged into one of the ponds, stirring up a phosphorescent wake in its passage, the glow rising from the thick jellylike growth floating atop the stagnant water. The creature scooped up a gullet full of that slime.

"They graze on those bacterial mats," Stella said. "Very nutritious."

"I'll stick to a T-bone," Kowalski commented, though he stared hungrily at the *Avex* flock as if trying to judge if they tasted like chicken.

The group passed unmolested, which perhaps is what made Jason let his guard down.

"Stop!" Harrington barked.

Jason froze. He had been about to step over a rock—only to have it sprout jointed legs, hard and chitinous, and scurry to the side. As it turned away, a curled tail came into view, tipped by a trio of six-inch-long stingers. From the glistening dampness to those spines, they must be venomous.

Harrington confirmed this by naming the scuttling creature. "*Pedex fervens.*"

Or roughly translated: *hot foot.*

Stella waved him onward.

He continued alongside Gray, but much of the momentary wonder from a moment ago had dried up.

After another long slog across the next hundred yards, the tunnel fell one last time and dumped into a massive space. The group gathered at the mouth of it. The sheer size boggled the senses.

"We call it the Coliseum," Stella said.

That was an understatement.

The roof was beyond the reach of their meager pool of IR emitters. The walls to either side yawned ever wider, stretching like open arms into the distance. The river they had been following broke into thousands of small creeks, rivers, and streams, turning the place into a massive stony delta. Farther out, large lakes reflected their lamps, revealing the shadows of darker islands.

But closer at hand, the handful of petrified tree trunks that they had previously traveled past became a virtual stone forest ahead. The specimens found here dwarfed the largest redwoods, but instead of being merely trunks, the trees in this gargantuan cavern were perfect stone replicas, including intact branches and tinier stems, weaving an arched, leafless canopy overhead.

It was a fossilized sculpture of an ancient world.

Overhead, strange luminous creatures floated through those branches, possibly held aloft on some internal reservoir of hydrogen gas or helium. They looked like Japanese lanterns adrift on a breeze.

The group entered the vast space, necks craning at the sheer size. Jason had read about the discovery of a trench under the Western Antarctic ice, twice as deep as the Grand Canyon. This space could be its cavernous equivalent.

"Over this way," Harrington urged.

The professor led them to the right, toward a wide shallow tributary of the delta. He splashed through the ankle-deep flow. Jason followed, but he had to fight the urge to tiptoe through the stream, still wary of the water. He watched for any new threat, while taking cues from Stella, who swept her IR beam ahead of her. He noted a double row of broken pillars, each as thick as Kowalski's thigh, running alongside their path. At first he thought they were natural formations, but the rows were too uniform. Closer inspection revealed they were actually the stubs of wooden pylons, anchored by mold-blackened steel spikes.

The construction looked too old to be the handiwork of the British.

Stella noticed his attention. "They're supports for a series of old bridges that fell apart long ago."

"Who built them?"

Harrington called out, drawing them all forward. The answer—and their destination—lay ahead. It was parked askew, sitting on an isthmus of rock amid this dark delta. The huge vehicle's bulk stood two stories tall, resting atop massive new tires. A handful of shiny ladders leaned against its side.

"We found it early on," Stella said. "A team of British mechanics recently got her working again."

Jason stared in awe.

It was Admiral Byrd's old snow cruiser.

3:14 P.M.

Dylan Wright stood near the rear ramp of the largest CAAT. Irritated, he adjusted his body armor with one hand; with the other, he kept the long double barrels of his Howdah pistol balanced against his shoulder, prepared to challenge any threat found down here.

A smaller CAAT flanked his own, engines idling. The two vehicles' headlamps shredded the darkness. On the roofs, Dylan's teammates manned large LRAD units installed on top. One dish pointed forward, the other backward, ready to be deployed if necessary.

Dylan cursed under his breath as he stared up at the stalled gondola overhead. From its undercarriage, the remains of a ladder hung down.

So Harrington and the others had gone to ground— but where?

The growl of an engine drew his attention behind him. A second small CAAT came rumbling across the river atop its flotation treads, reached the nearby bank of rock, and climbed out of the water, demonstrating the craft's amphibious nature.

It trundled up to Dylan's vehicle and came to a stop. A window rolled down. His second-in-command poked his head out.

"The professor's not holed up in that Kraut sub," McKinnon said. "We checked it from stem to stern."

Dylan had sent the Scotsman back to make sure Harrington hadn't gone into hiding inside the German vessel.

Knowing this for sure now, Dylan faced forward.

Then they truly set off on foot.

Earlier, one of his scouts had found tracks along the riverbank, but Dylan had wanted to make certain someone hadn't laid a false trail. He couldn't believe Harrington had the bollocks for such an overland trek.

Seems I keep underestimating you, old man.

Unfortunately, it had also taken his team too long to get the CAATs loaded for the mission—especially after a hidden clutch of British soldiers ambushed his team at Hell's Cape. In Dylan's mad rush to reach Harrington at the outset of the raid, he had failed to properly clear the station. A handful of soldiers had gone into hiding, only to waylay his team, pinning them down for a furious ten minutes. Eventually they were dispatched.

Still . . .

We lost too much time.

But now he would make up for it. Harrington could not have gotten too far on foot. He straightened, shrugging away his irritation, and climbed into his CAAT.

He holstered his pistol and called to the others, "Mount up! Move out!"

Time for the real hunt to begin.

23

"Now this is interesting," Dr. Lucas Cardoza said, straightening from his hunched position over his computer.

Painter rose from a stool and crossed over to his side.

The Brazilian geneticist headed the Genographic Project in Boa Vista. He was a portly fellow, with dark hair, a thick black mustache, and studious eyes behind thick-rimmed glasses. Cardoza and his team had been collating and recording DNA from the native tribes of South America for the past decade. Using a proprietary algorithm, he compiled the gathered data to trace the ancient migration patterns for hundreds of tribes who made the Brazilian forests their home.

Painter and Drake had joined Cardoza in his office at the Universidade Federal de Roraima, the city's main university. The researcher had agreed to perform a DNA analysis on the blood sample from the only surviving gunman from the assault at the café. As expected the prisoner, now under police custody, had refused to talk, even tried to hang himself in his cell in a failed suicide attempt. Such a desperate act spoke to the fervency of Cutter's followers and the tight tribalism among his group.

But what tribe was it?

"I think I might have found something," Cardoza said, waving Painter closer to his computer.

Drake bent down, too, grumbling under his breath. "About time."

Painter checked his watch. Jenna had been kidnapped roughly three hours ago. Her captors had a significant lead, and as time ticked away, her trail grew colder. He knew his team only had a narrow window in which to find her. Cutter Elwes had kidnapped her for a reason, likely to question her, to discover what the Americans knew about him. But after that, he would have no further use for her.

Knowing that, Painter had sent Malcolm and Schmitt to the Brazilian air base, prepping for the arrival of their new transport. The aircraft was flying in from a U.S. warship located in the South Atlantic. Kat had expedited all the arrangements, applying pressure through contacts in the Brazilian government and military to gain their cooperation. Also, staying one step ahead, Kat had made provisions to supply additional support to Painter, which was already en route. That was Kat's main strength: always anticipating what was needed versus passively waiting for orders.

He especially appreciated that now.

We can't lose any more time.

And not only for Jenna's sake.

Kat had also shared the news that a medium-yield nuclear device had reached the Mono Lake region and was being readied for deployment. Her assessment of the aftermath was grim. A hundred square miles would be firebombed, while the burst of radiation and fallout could contaminate over four hundred square miles, including all of Yosemite National Park. Worst of all, there continued to be no guarantee such a drastic tactic would eradicate the bioorganism.

So Painter needed answers—and the Brazilian geneticist was their best hope.

"What did you find?" Painter asked.

"I'm sorry this has taken so long," Cardoza apologized. "DNA analysis has gotten much swifter over the past few years, but the level of details necessary for such a genetic study takes painstaking precision. I didn't want to make a mistake and send you in the direction of the wrong tribe."

Painter placed a hand on the man's shoulder. "I appreciate your willingness to help on such short notice."

The researcher nodded gravely and pointed to the monitor. "Look at this."

On the screen glowed multiple rows of vertical gray-scale bars. It looked like a bar code, but this *code* actually mapped the prisoner's genetic legacy.

"I've identified twenty-two markers unique to natives of northern Brazil, which normally wouldn't help much, as the number of tribes in this area is rather large and their peoples scattered. But this sequence right here—" He circled a group of bars with his finger on the screen. "It's a unique mutation found in a subgroup of the Macuxi tribe, a tribe within a tribe, if you will. This particular group is notorious for their isolation and inbreeding, including a strange history of multiple births."

"And the prisoner belongs to this tight-knit group?"

"I'm almost certain."

It was that *almost* that made Painter nervous. "How sure are you?"

He adjusted his glasses. "In the ninety-ninth percentile. Maybe a fraction more than that."

Painter hid a smile. Only a scientist would qualify a 99 percent match as *almost*.

"Where does this tribe live?" Drake asked, leaning closer.

Cardoza tapped at his keyboard and brought up a topographic map. A red dot appeared about a hundred miles southeast of Boa Vista, deep into the rain forest.

Painter blew out a frustrated breath. That was still a lot of territory to cover. "What do you know about this section of the rain forest?" he asked, hoping for some break.

Cardoza shook his head. "Very little. It's almost impossible to reach overland due to the fractured nature of that geology. The terrain is broken into deep chasms, choked with vegetation. Few have ever ventured there."

"No wonder that tribe was inbreeding," Drake commented.

"Here's a satellite image of the area." Cardoza toggled from the topographic map to a panoramic photo taken from low orbit, showing the spread of dense canopy.

It looked impenetrable. Anything could be hidden under that dark green bower, but Painter had a gut instinct.

From reading everything he could about Cutter, Painter had begun to build a profile of the man's personality. Cutter had a flair for the dramatic, coupled with an ego that would make it hard for him to hide his head in the sand . . . even when playing dead.

"Can you zoom out?" Painter asked, remembering an unusual feature found on the topographic map.

"Certainly."

The image widened, panning out to include a larger chunk of the rain forest. The red dot marking the village lay close to the only significant break in that emerald sea. A tall mountain pushed high out of the rain forest to the south. The cliffs were sheer, looking unscalable. Its summit lay shrouded in mists.

"What's that?" Drake asked.

"A tepui," Cardoza explained. "A fractured piece of an ancient tableland. The towering plateaus of this region are centers of myths and legends, full of stories of vengeful spirits and lost passageways to the underworld."

Painter straightened.

And maybe a good place for a dead guy to return to the living.

Drake glanced over to him. "Think that's the place?"

"If not, it's close enough to the village marked on the map. We could always drop in on them for a visit."

Drop in, being the best description.

Painter added, "If we find nothing at that mountain, hopefully someone at that village would know something about Cutter Elwes."

"Then let's go." Drake turned swiftly without a thank-you or good-bye for Dr. Cardoza.

Painter understood the Marine's haste but took the time to shake the geneticist's hand. "You may have saved a young woman's life."

As he hurried after Drake, he prayed that was true.

11:38 A.M.

Jenna stood at the edge of civilization.

The jungle spread before her, buzzing with insects, whistling with birdcalls, while behind her, the helicopter's engine ticked and knocked as it cooled in the forest clearing.

A pair of bare-chested natives in stained shorts hand-pumped fuel into the grounded aircraft from giant black barrels. On the far side, hammocks hung from between the trunks of trees, tented with mosquito netting. Piles of cigarette butts littered the forest floor beneath the slings. A pornographic magazine lay atop the mounds, looking quickly dropped, likely after hearing the approach of the helicopter. The air stank of oil, tobacco smoke, and human waste.

She had moved to the edge of the clearing to escape it, imagining what it must smell like when the camouflage netting was drawn back over this festering pit of man's corruption. Currently the net drooped from the canopy, waiting to be pulled back into place after the helicopter departed, to once again hide this refueling station.

She stared up into the face of the noon sun, at the bluest of blue skies. The heat was blistering, already burning her winter-pale skin, made worse by the appalling humidity. She stepped into the shade of a mahogany tree, drawing the attention of her guard. The pilot had a rifle across his knees and glanced in her direction. Her captors hadn't bothered to keep her tied up.

Where could I go?

Even if she tried to run, these tribesmen knew this jungle far better than she did and she'd be quickly recaptured.

At the rain forest's edge, she inhaled the perfume of the jungle, trying to push down her terror. A breeze stirred leaves, bringing the scent of forest blossoms, damp soil, and green life. As a park ranger, she found it hard to ignore the raw beauty here and the miracle of life in all its myriad forms: from the towering trees leading up to the thick emerald canopy, to the whispering passage of a troop of monkeys through the lower branches, even the parade of ants up the bark of her shade tree. She had read how the naturalist E. O. Wilson had counted over two hundred species of ants on a single rain forest tree. It seemed life was determined to fill every nook and niche in this resplendent Eden.

Something larger stirred closer at hand in the jungle, stepping free of the shadows only yards away, startling her.

The ebony-haired woman strode forward, as barechested as the men. Her only clothes were a pair of dark brown shorts that blended with her skin. She carried a bow over one arm, with a quiver of arrows strung across her back. Over her shoulders, she balanced the limp body of a fawn. It had a gray head and black legs, with fur of reddish brown. Large black eyes stared glossily out at its former home.

She passed by Jenna without even a glance.

The woman had only been out in the forest for fifteen minutes. She dumped the carcass near the hammocks, leaving it for the two natives who must live at this refueling station. For the woman, it looked like the hunt had not been for meat or skin, but only for the personal sport.

Jenna noted how the men avoided staring at the woman, even though her breasts—which were quite spectacular—were exposed.

The woman slipped back into the blouse hanging from a branch and spoke to the pilot in a low, relaxed voice. Her dark eyes flicked to Jenna, then back to the man before her. The pilot nodded, yelled at the pair of natives, and waved for them to clear their gear out of the way.

Apparently it was time to go.

Minutes later, Jenna was back in her seat in the rear cabin. The rotors spun up to a roar and the helicopter leaped skyward, breaking free of the jungle and out in the blaze of the midday sun. Tilting its nose slightly down, the helicopter sped over that endless expanse of green canopy.

She stared ahead.

A dark shadow rose near the horizon, still a long ways off.

Is that where we're headed?

She had no way of knowing. All she knew for sure was that whatever waited for her at the end of this trek would not be pleasant. She closed her eyes and leaned back, girding herself against what was to come, missing her usual source of strength and resilience.

Nikko . . .

But her partner had his own battle to fight.

8:40 A.M. PDT
Sierra Nevada Mountains, CA

Lisa wheeled the gurney toward the air lock that led out of her in vivo lab. The one surviving rat stirred in its test cage, coming forward to watch her pass, its pink nose twitching.

Sorry, I can only save one passenger on this sinking ship.

Nikko lay on his side on the cushioned stretcher, barely breathing after the light sedation. His left front leg was splinted stiffly out, hooked to IV lines running to two bags: One contained fluids infused with a cocktail of antivirals and the other held platelet-rich plasma. The bags rested on the cushion next to the dog, waiting to be re-hung on poles.

Nikko's stretcher was a patient containment transport gurney, sealed tightly under a clear hood with its own oxygen supply, flowing from tanks secured on the underside.

She pushed the gurney into the air lock, waited for the pressure to equilibrate, then as the green light flashed, she nodded to the figure outside. Edmund Dent hauled open the air lock door on his side and helped her draw the gurney into the small conference room at the center of the BSL4 labs.

"We must hurry," Edmund said. "Don't have much time."

She knew this, too.

Lindahl and his cronies had all gone to oversee the arrival of the nuclear device to the mountain base, taking with him the entire team of nuclear and radiation scientists. For a brief window, the lab was mostly empty. The researchers still present were colleagues of Edmund, who had agreed to turn a blind eye to their current actions. They had all met Jenna, knew about her kidnapping and Lindahl's plan to irradiate the dog.

Still, who knew how long that silence will last under pressure?

Edmund helped manhandle the containment gurney to the main decontamination air lock. A Marine stood guard on the far side. Edmund lifted an arm as the guard turned, as if what they were doing was totally normal.

Lisa entered the air lock alone, leaving Edmund behind to help cover for her. In her wake, he was going to sabotage the air lock into her lab, to delay Lindahl for as long as possible from discovering Nikko had gone missing.

The decontamination process started. Sprays bathed her suit and the outer shell of the gurney, followed by ultraviolet radiation, then another round of spraying and air drying. The entire process took an agonizing twenty minutes.

The Marine outside would glance in her direction every now and then. Lisa avoided eye contact.

Finally the light flashed green, allowing her out. In the anteroom beyond the air lock, she shed out of her containment suit. Sweat pasted her clothes into every bodily crevice, mostly from the heat inside her sealed suit, but also from fear of discovery. She grabbed the gurney's handles and, with some effort, wheeled it out into the main hangar.

"Ready?" the guard asked.

She nodded. "Thanks."

Corporal Sarah Jessup—an auburn-haired Marine in a perfectly pressed uniform—had been assigned as Painter's personal aide. She had come with the highest praise from the base commander.

"You didn't have to do this," Lisa said as the two of them whisked Nikko through the cavernous space.

The woman shrugged. "I'm not breaking any rules. Director Crowe was assigned to be my direct superior. He verbally approved your actions. So I'm following orders like any good Marine." Still, she smiled softly back at Lisa. "Besides, I have a chocolate Lab at home. If anyone ever tried to hurt Belle, they'd sorely regret it."

Lisa took a deep steadying breath, thankful for the corporal's cooperation. If Jessup had not agreed and had not arranged to cover this guard shift, stealing Nikko out of the lab would have been impossible.

The corporal had facilitated matters in one other way.

"I set up the temporary quarantine area per your instructions," Jessup said. "In a place few would think to look."

"Where's that?"

Again that soft smile. "Back room of the base chapel. The chaplain has agreed to keep our cover, to deflect any inquiries."

"You got a priest to lie for us."

Her smile widened. "Don't worry, he's Episcopalian—and my boyfriend. Plus he loves Belle as much as I do . . . which he'd better or I'd never consider marrying him. Belle and I are a package deal."

Lisa heard the young love in the corporal's voice, reminding her of her own postponed nuptials. Missing Painter more acutely, she tamped down an ache in her heart.

She let Corporal Jessup lead the way, knowing this escapade would only buy them so much time. Eventually someone would talk or Nikko's hiding place would be discovered. Even barring that, the larger nuclear threat loomed over all.

With another storm due to hit after midnight, Lindahl had set a timetable for detonation as early as nightfall.

She pictured a fiery mushroom cloud blooming over these mountains.

Despair settled over her. Someone had to find a way to stop all of this before it was too late.

But who . . . and most important, how?

11:43 A.M. AMT
Roraima, Brazil

For the past two hours, Kendall had labored under the intense scrutiny of Cutter Elwes inside his facility's BSL4 lab. Both of them were encased in bright white biosafety suits with yellow air hoses coiling up to the wall.

Kendall held up two vials and read the labels.

25UG OF CRISPR CAS9-D10A NICKASE MRNA
1UG OF CRISPR CAS9-D10A NICKASE PLASMID

The small glass ampules contained the essential ingredients for editing genes. With these tools, a researcher could precisely break the double strands of DNA at specific target sites, allowing changes to be introduced. These specific vials were used mostly for transgenic applications: for inserting a foreign gene—called a transgene—into another organism's genetic code.

Like adding *new* wings to a bullet ant.

Cutter had plainly been playing God for some time, mixing foreign genes into established species. The act itself was not that shocking. The technology had been around for close to a decade, used to create transgenic creatures in labs all around the world. From bacteria to mice to even a colony of glow-in-the-dark cats. In fact, Cutter's work here was not all that advanced, especially considering he had access to the latest MAGE and CAGE processes, techniques that could introduce *hundreds* of mutational changes at once.

Unfortunately, while Cutter's creations were monstrous, Kendall didn't have the moral high ground to truly malign his work. At Mono Lake, Kendall had used the contents of these same vials to design his synthetic virus. His creation had also been the result of transgenic engineering. Only the transgenes he inserted were even more *foreign*, coming from one of the XNA species found in the shadow biosphere beneath Antarctica.

That last detail was critical to his success at Mono Lake. It led to the breakthrough that allowed him to finally crack the key to turning an empty viral shell into a living, multiplying organism.

God, help me . . . I can't let Cutter know how I did it.

Cutter returned from the tall refrigerators at the rear of the lab. Through the glass windows, the rows of test tubes and vials glowed. It was the genetic library for his creations—both those in the past and what he wanted to create in the future.

He returned now with two glass tubes, each half full of cloudy solution.

"In my right hand," he said, lifting that arm, "is the eVLP you engineered. Your perfect empty shell."

Kendall had already seen proof of Cutter's claim, spending the first hour in the lab examining his data, making sure the man had indeed recreated the exact same protein shell.

Cutter raised the other tube. "And this is *my* creation, a prion-sized piece of unique genetic code."

So this is what the bastard wants to seed into my shell.

Cutter's use of the word *prion* was worrisome. Prions were infectious proteins responsible for such maladies as mad cow disease in bovines and Creutzfeldt-Jakob in humans. The clinical symptoms of such infections were invariably neurological in nature, usually affecting the brain. Worst of all, these diseases were incurable and often fatal.

Cutter lifted the vials higher. "Now you must show me how to combine our work. *Your* shell and *my* genetic code." He put the two tubes into one hand and passed them to Kendall.

He reluctantly accepted them. "What does your code do?"

Cutter chided him with a wave of a gloved finger, then pointed to the workstation. "First you show me proof of concept. Show me that your success in California wasn't a fluke."

From this statement, Kendall could tell how galling it must be for Cutter to come begging for his help. Rather than accept that someone had accomplished what he could not, he would rather dismiss Kendall's accomplishment as dumb luck or a fluke. As much as Cutter had been changed after his mauling by a lion, his conceit remained perfectly intact.

"It will still take some time," Kendall stalled. "I'll need a complete DNA analysis of your code to find a way to insert it into the shell."

"It's already stored on the computer at your station."

"I'd like to do a complete analysis myself."

Suspicion lowered Cutter's left eyebrow. "Why repeat what's already been done?"

"It's a necessary part of my procedure. I'll likely have to alter your code, add a key sequence to unlock that shell."

At least that much was true.

Perhaps recognizing the logic of his statement, Cutter sighed and nodded. "Then get to work."

Before the man could turn away, Kendall stopped him. "I've agreed to cooperate. Can't you tell me how to stop the contagion in California?"

Before it's too late.

Cutter looked like he was actually considering this request. Finally, his eyes settled on Kendall. "I'll give you part of the solution, if you tell me more about how this *key* unlocks your shell. I have to say that intrigues me enough to perhaps show a little goodwill."

Kendall licked his dry lips, knowing he had to tiptoe carefully. He had to give Cutter enough information to be believed—the man was no fool—but not enough to show his hand completely.

Kendall cleared his throat. "Are you familiar with the media attention given to the Scripps Research Institute back in May 2014? After they announced the creation of a living, replicating colony of bacteria that contained new letters of the genetic alphabet?"

Cutter squinted in thought. "You're referring to them inserting artificial nucleotide bases into a bacterium's DNA."

He nodded. It was groundbreaking work. All of life's diversity on this planet—from slime mold to human beings—was based on a simple genetic alphabet of only four letters: A, C, G, and T. It was from the jumbling of those four letters that the riotous bounty of species arose on earth. But for the first time, the researchers at Scripps engineered a living bacterium with *two* additional letters in its genetic code: naming them X and Y.

"What about it?" Cutter asked.

"I did something similar," Kendall admitted. "Using the CRISPR technique, I was able to clip out sections of old viral DNA and replace them with foreign pieces of XNA. It is that *exact* sequence of XNA genes—and no other—that acts like a key to unlock the shell."

"Giving life to your creation." Cutter smiled. "That's why I kept failing. I didn't have that key."

And I hope you never get it.

"I should've thought of it myself," Cutter said. "That viral capsid, that perfect shell . . . you engineered its unusual configuration by producing proteins from XNA genes. So naturally to insert genetic material into that shell, it might take a specific sequence of XNA markers for the shell to accept it."

"A key to match the lock," Kendall said. "That was my breakthrough."

Or at least part of it.

"Ingenious, Kendall. You impress me."

"So if you're satisfied, can you share more details about the cure?"

It was Kendall's only hope. If he could figure out the solution on his own, then maybe he wouldn't have to give that bastard the recipe for arming the viral capsid.

"Fair enough," Cutter agreed. "First, you may remember how I mentioned earlier that the solution to annihilating your creation—to neutralizing it—was staring you and Harrington in the face all along. Like your solution with the key, it's all about XNA."

"How so?"

"What you sadly have failed to ask yourselves is *why* that exotic shadow biosphere has remained encapsulated in Antarctica for millennia, especially when there is an entire world out there almost defenseless against its aggressive and unique nature."

"What's the answer?"

"You hand me the key, and I'll give you that answer . . . and the method to turn it to your advantage in California."

Kendall didn't press the matter, knowing that was as much as he would get out of the man.

Cutter swung away again. "I'll leave you to your work. We have a guest arriving soon to whom I wish to speak." He glanced back at Kendall. "But I'll expect results when I get back. Trust me when I say, you don't want to disappoint me."

Kendall watched him leave through the room's air lock. In the main lab beyond, the hulking figure of Mateo stood guard, making sure Kendall stayed put.

With no other choice, Kendall began his study of Cutter's unique piece of genetic code, the very material he wanted to insert into Kendall's perfect genetic delivery system.

But what was it? What was its purpose?

If I could discover that, I might find a way to stop him.

And if nothing else, working on this code would put off the moment when he must eventually tell Cutter the truth: that the key he wanted so badly was out of his reach. Kendall could not reproduce it here. To engineer that key, he would first need the lymphocytes from a singular species in that biosphere. Its XNA was so unique that it couldn't be synthesized in any lab. It required a living sample to build that key.

But how long can I keep that secret?

For now all he could do was delay for as long as possible.

But to what end? he wondered. *Who can help me?*

11:55 A.M.

Painter stood on a remote tarmac of the Boa Vista international airport under the blaze of the midday sun. He shaded his eyes with his good arm, watching the skies. His other arm rested in a sling, his wound freshly rebandaged.

The airport lay only two miles outside the city and shared its facilities with Base Aérea de Boa Vista, the local contingent of the Brazilian Air Force. This corner of the grounds was rarely used, as evident from the weeds growing in the cracks in the blacktop. There was no runway, only a parking lot lined by a ramshackle row of old hangars and outbuildings, long gone to seed.

The current air base had moved to more modern facilities on the airport's far side. But this location served Painter's needs, as it was far from regular traffic and out of sight of most eyes. A small group of Brazilian airmen guarded the entrance to this area, keeping the curious away.

Drake paced impatiently behind him, while his teammates, Malcolm and Schmitt, lounged in the shade of one of the hangars.

"Here they come," Painter said, spotting a silver-gray aircraft cutting across that achingly blue sky.

"What took them so goddamned long?" Drake griped.

Painter didn't answer, knowing it was frustration that had trimmed the Marine's fuse so short. Drake clearly felt responsible for Jenna's kidnapping, having abandoned her inside that café. Not that it was his fault, but saying so made no difference. The Marine had an uncompromising code of honor. Still, Painter suspected the true source of Drake's anxiety was more personal than professional in nature. He and Jenna had grown close during this trial by fire.

Drake joined him, shading his eyes against the sun's glare.

Across the sky, the blip raced toward them. The plane had flown in from the USS *Harry S. Truman*, a *Nimitz*-class supercarrier conducting exercises in the South Atlantic.

As Painter watched, the aircraft's twin props swung from vertical to horizontal, slowing the plane and transforming it into a helicopter. The craft was similar to its larger brother, the MV-22 Osprey, that had ferried Painter from the coast of California to the Marine base in the Sierra Nevada Mountains. This aircraft was the new Bell V-280 Valor, sometimes called the Son of Osprey because of its smaller, sleeker design. It functioned mainly as a scout plane and could race at close to three hundred knots, covering a range of eight hundred nautical miles.

Perfect for where they needed to go.

The Valor hovered overhead and began to lower. Painter and Drake retreated across the cracked tarmac—or more accurately they were *pushed* back by the rotor wash from the twin props. The Valor landed as delicately as a mosquito on a bare arm. The noise was not as loud as would be expected, due to the stealth technology incorporated into the design, which muffled the engine's roar.

The side hatch opened.

True to her word, Kat had sent them additional men; another trio of Marines hopped out, dressed in body armor and helmets. Drake and his teammates greeted their comrades, clasping forearms in a brotherly fashion.

The swarthy leader of the support team strode up to Painter. "Heard you had some trouble, sir," he said with a slight Hispanic accent. "I'm Sergeant Suarez." He waved his arm to the two men flanking him, a muscular black Marine with eyes of steel and a red-haired mountain of a man. "Lance Corporals Abramson and Henckel."

Painter shook each soldier's hand. "Thanks for your help."

Suarez faced the aircraft. "The Valor's a great little bird. It'll be a tight squeeze aboard her, but we'll manage." The sergeant looked up at the blazing sun. "Hot one today, isn't it?"

He nodded.

And it'll likely get even hotter . . . in more ways than one.

24

Gray stood in the front cab of the massive snow cruiser, leaning on the back of the driver's seat. The wide windshield offered a panoramic view of the passing terrain of the cavernous Coliseum. For the past hour, they had been slowly traversing the heart of this stone delta, working their way through the petrified forest that towered all around.

Presently the cruiser skirted along the edge of a large lake, so wide the far side could not be discerned, even under the blaze of the cruiser's six headlamps, each the size of a manhole cover. Their path was lit brightly enough that they no longer needed their night-vision goggles.

Fringing the lake grew tall corpse-white reeds, crowned by waving, glowing filaments. Only these plants—or maybe they were animals—would rise on stilted legs and wade farther away as they neared. Stella said the bioluminescent bulbs of the reeds would attract insect life, snaring the unwary in those acidic tendrils.

And it wasn't only these reeds that avoided the cruiser.

Their blazing passage drew the attention of life down here, but the sheer size and the loud rumbling roar of its engines seemed to intimidate most predators or scatter the more timid species.

Kowalski manned the wheel. Normally riding shotgun with the big man in any vehicle was an unnerving experience, but Kowalski had the most history with driving semis and plainly had some mad skills with the cruiser, already proving his adept talent at maneuvering the monstrous rig through this harsh terrain. The guy might not have much luck with the ladies, but his affinity for engines certainly made up for it.

Clenching the stub of a smoldering cigar in his teeth, Kowalski concentrated on working the gears as he rode the cruiser over a fall of boulders, tipping its fifty-foot-long bulk sideways as the gargantuan tires chewed through the rockfall.

"Careful," Gray warned.

"Don't need a backseat driver," Kowalski grumbled. "Go find out how much farther we have to go. Forget miles per gallon . . . this thing gets *yards* per gallon. We'll be running on fumes before much longer."

To prove it, he tapped a thick finger on a gauge, showing it approaching an ominous red line.

Not good.

While life down here mostly ignored the cruiser, its lumbering passage stirred up everything in its wake, making it even riskier now to leave its shelter.

As the vehicle climbed free of the boulder pile, Gray left Kowalski to his driving and ducked down a short ladder into the main hold of the rig. The lower space had once been split into two floors, but apparently someone had gutted it long ago into this one big cabin. Still, the original bench seats lined both sides, leading to a rear ramp that could be dropped open to allow troops to bail out the back.

He found Stella and Jason sitting close together, talking softly, discussing what sounded like a biology lesson. He crossed to Harrington, who sat sullenly across the cabin, his elbows resting on his knees, his head hanging.

"Professor," Gray said, "we're running low on diesel. How much farther is this Back Door substation?"

Harrington lifted his face, his complexion wan and tired, his eyes glassy with anxiety. It looked like he had aged decades during the journey from Hell's Cape. "Not far. The Back Door is at the opposite end of the Coliseum. Can't miss it."

Something screeched loudly, then struck the top of the cruiser. Claws dragged along the roof—before falling away again.

We'd better reach it soon.

Harrington cast a worried glance toward his daughter—then leaned over, clutched Gray's knee, and whispered with some heat. "If something goes wrong, you'll get her out of here."

"I'll do my best," he promised.

His words seemed to offer Harrington little solace. To distract the man, he sat next to him.

Gray motioned to indicate the bulk of the cruiser. "So what was Admiral Byrd doing down here?"

"I think he came looking for a secret Nazi sub base—and found this place instead. All I can say for sure is that he arrived in Antarctica in 1946, a year after the end of World War II. He was accompanied by thirteen ships, over twenty aircraft, and almost five thousand men."

"Five thousand . . . why that many?"

"It was called Operation Highjump. The official story was that Highjump was a polar training exercise, coupled with a mission to map the continent, but most of his expedition's objectives were kept top secret. It led later to a series of atomic blasts down here. I think the bigwigs who oversaw Byrd's expedition had been trying to bottle this place up. It's said that Byrd was never really the same after that expedition, that he was a changed man, more reclusive, sickly. Some blamed it on the time he spent alone on the ice years before, but I wonder if it wasn't this place."

One only had to stare at Harrington's haunted, scared eyes to understand what he meant.

"Maybe we should never have found these caverns again," the professor said. "Maybe we should have heeded Darwin's wisdom to keep this secret buried and untouched."

Kowalski hollered from up front. "Better come see this!"

The urgency in his voice drew them all to their feet. They piled up into the front cab. Harrington dropped heavily into the passenger seat.

Past the windshield, a vast swampland blocked the way ahead, flowing with streams, pools, and a scatter of waterfalls. The great petrified forest behind them dwindled down to a handful of lonely sentinels out there. Overhead, stalactites pointed down from the roof.

Across this swampland spread vast fields of the phosphorescent reeds, lighting even the darkness beyond the reach of their headlamps. Strange creatures moved everywhere across this macabre field. Wading birds took off on leathery wings, fleeing the arrival of the growling, smoking beast of a cruiser. Lumbering shadows slumped through the reeds, their presence only discernible by their passage. Along the banks, other creatures slithered, hopped, or crawled out of their way. All the while, screams, caterwauls, and piping songs pierced their steel cocoon, as if life down here continually challenged this noisy trespasser into their midst.

But none of this was what caused Kowalski to call out.

Gray gaped at the sight before him.

My God . . .

Throughout this flooded savannah moved a herd of massive beasts, a hundred or more in number, each the size of a woolly mammoth. They moved mostly on all fours, though occasionally one would rise up on its hind legs and lumber in an ursine fashion for a few steps, likely surveying its surroundings for danger, before dropping back down. Their faces had short proboscises, like dwarf trunks of an elephant. These prehensile appendages would snatch at the reeds, pulling them up and gnashing them slowly, methodically, like a cow chewing a cud.

"See that moss growing along their flanks," Stella said.

Gray squinted. He had thought the great shaggy mats hanging from their muscular bodies were fur, like found on mammoths. Only this growth softly glowed in a kaleidoscope of colors.

"We believe the moss has a symbiotic relationship with these beasts, which we named *Pachycerex ferocis*. The *Pachyceri* use their body heat to trigger those changes in colors, using it as a way to communicate among the herd."

"Like fireflies in a meadow," Jason said, earning a smile from Stella.

Kowalski was less enamored. "Only looks like these fireflies could stomp you to death." He glanced over to the professor in the neighboring seat. "What about us? Is it safe to continue?"

"Just go slow. The headlamps will likely confuse them enough to let us pass."

For a species that communicated in soft glows, the herd probably thought the cruiser was yelling at them, like some tone-deaf and deformed member of their species.

"They've never truly bothered us in the past," Harrington continued. "But I've never seen such numbers in one place. We've spotted a few here and there, and they leave us alone, especially if we stay brightly lit."

"Maybe it's mating season," Stella said. "And this is their breeding ground."

"In that case," Kowalski said, "nobody out there better get the wrong idea about us and decide to put the moves on this boxy lady of ours. Getting flattened by a horny elephant is not the way I'm planning on dying."

"Do what the professor says," Gray warned. "Move out, but set a cautious pace."

Kowalski grumbled under his breath as he put the cruiser into gear. They headed through the shallows, making a wide circling arc to stay clear of the deeper pools of the flooded terrain. The *Pachyceri* meandered out of their path, a few snorting at them, as if rebuking them for the rude intrusion. They rolled past one tall enough to peer into the side of the cab, eyeballing the strangers inside.

"Nosy guy," Kowalski said, glancing back for approval. "Get it . . . *nosy.*"

Stella and Jason both groaned.

Gray kept a watch on the rearview mirrors, making sure none of the beasts decided to challenge them, worried that even the stout cruiser might not survive a full-on assault by one or more of these giant creatures.

As he kept guard, a flash of light caught his attention in the mirror, much brighter than the herd's glow. It came from farther back, where the petrified forest grew thicker. Then he spotted another set of lights to the left, like a pair of xenon-glowing eyes. And a moment later, a third pair joined the other two.

Gray's fingers tightened on the seatback in front of him.

"We've got company."

4:32 P.M.

No wonder it took us so long to run these bastards down . . .

Dylan Wright stood behind the driver of the largest CAAT, staring out at the expanse of swampland and the lumbering herd of *Pachyceri*. Far to his right, a vehicle blazed a bright trail across the periphery of the glowing herd, a comet arcing along the floor of the dark cavern.

So they got Byrd's old snow cruiser moving again.

It must have happened after Dylan and his team fled Hell's Cape a year and a half ago. But it was no great matter. Land-bound, the cruiser could not match the speed and amphibious dexterity of a CAAT, especially the smaller ones.

Plus the odds were stacked in Dylan's favor: three against one.

Not to mention, his team already outmanned and outgunned their opponents, likely by the same uneven ratio.

Dylan touched his radio's earpiece. He spoke to the smaller CAATs to either side. "McKinnon, flank right. Seward, head left. Keep them pinned down. I'll take the big CAAT and run it right up their arses."

He got affirmations from both men.

"Go!" he ordered, tasting the familiar lust of the hunt in the back of his throat.

Now to end this.

4:33 P.M.

Jason rode shotgun next to Kowalski as the snow cruiser raced across the swamplands, crushing through the reeds, scattering wildlife, while avoiding the larger obstacles in their path, namely the lumbering *Pachyceri.* The big beasts trumpeted their complaint, trotting out of the way as best they could. Kowalski jackknifed the big rig back and forth to avoid hitting any stragglers—not necessarily out of concern for the animals, but out of fear that a collision would do more harm to their vehicle than to the thick-hided creatures.

The snow cruiser struck a ridge and jolted up, going impossibly airborne for a moment, then crashing back down on its giant wheels.

Jason clutched the arm of his chair, while keeping watch out his window. Across the cab, Stella crouched in a jump seat behind Kowalski, keeping her eyes glued to the left side of the cruiser.

Lights flared out in the darkness to the right.

"Here they come on our starboard side!" Jason yelled, loud enough for Gray to hear down in the lower cabin.

"Over here, too!" Stella echoed.

On both sides, twin spears of headlamps flanked the barreling cruiser, racing about thirty yards out, running faster and more nimbly than their cumbersome rig. The smaller CAATs were plainly trying to get ahead, to slow them down. A larger CAAT trailed, but it was closing fast, its buoyant treads allowing it to skim across this watery landscape.

"We need to go faster," Jason mumbled under his breath.

Kowalski heard him. "Got it floored, kid. Unless you want to go out and push, this is it."

Jason shared a worried glance with Stella.

They'd never outrun these hunters.

The flanking CAATs began to squeeze closer, drawing tighter in a pincer move, attempting to cut them off. Gunfire erupted. Rounds pelted the side of the cruiser and chipped the front windshield. The thick glass held—for now. The cruiser had been built for the harsh terrain of Antarctica, to withstand avalanches and icy crashes, but there were limits to its World War II–era technology.

They needed to break free of this snare. It was now or never. The hunters were as close as they dared let them get to the cruiser.

"Get ready!" Jason yelled down to Gray.

Stella pointed ahead and to the left. "Over there . . . that one!"

Jason nodded and hollered. "Port side! Got a big bull on the port side!"

"Do it!" Gray called back.

Kowalski leaned over the rig's wheel. "Hold on to your asses."

4:35 P.M.

Gray had belted himself into the last seat in the cabin, facing the back of the cruiser. Harrington sat on the opposite side, equally secure in place.

The snow cruiser suddenly swung to the side, making a sharp right turn. It lifted up on two tires, rubber squealing across wet rock, teetering precariously as it still spun to the right, swinging its tail end around to the port side.

Gray held his breath, sure they would topple over— but the cruiser finally righted itself and crashed back down to all four tires.

"Now!" he yelled to Harrington.

The professor hit a large black button above his seat.

Bolts blew near the top of the back wall—and the rear door fell open, dropping away to form an exit ramp. The far edge struck the ground, and the ramp got dragged along behind the cruiser, rattling and bouncing across the cavern floor, plowing through shallow puddles or streams.

Harrington bellowed to be heard above the racket of steel on stone and the bugling of the frightened herd outside. "That must be the one!"

The professor pointed to where an exceptionally large *Pachycerex* came into view out the back door, thundering along, trumpeting its anger. The bull stood a third taller in the haunches than the others. Beyond its bulk, one of the small CAATs raced, still trying to compensate for the sudden maneuver by the large rig.

Gray raised his DSR rifle aiming for the rear quarter of the massive bull *Pachycerex*. He waited until the pursuing CAAT drew abreast of the beast—then fired.

The recoil of the electric rifle slammed his shoulder. He got enough of a backwash from the pulse to set his teeth on edge. The sonic bullet struck the flank of the bull. He could tell because its hide had been glowing a dark crimson—then suddenly flared in a splatter of blue, as if Gray had fired a paint gun into its side.

The bull roared and reared up on its hind legs, twisting away from the noise and pain. It dropped back to all fours and charged in the opposite direction—straight toward the CAAT racing along that side.

The bull took its wrath out upon this intruder in the herd. It lowered its head and struck the vehicle broadside with a ringing crash of bone on steel. The smaller CAAT got knocked off its treads, going airborne, flipping sideways. It struck the pond's far bank, landed on its side, and skidded away in a grinding flurry of sparks.

One down.

Knowing they were outnumbered, Gray had come up with this plan to use this harsh world as a weapon, to turn it against these hunters.

Kowalski threw the rig in the direction of that crash, sending the rear end swinging around again. Gray got tossed hard against his seat's straps, almost losing his grip on the rifle. The cruiser aimed for this new break in the closing snare, intending to burst free.

The lumbering vehicle roared past the crash site. In the distance, the larger CAAT fell back. Gray stared toward those fading headlamps, sensing his nemesis was aboard there.

Bring it on . . .

4:36 P.M.

Dylan caught a glimpse of a shadowy shape through the dropped rear gate of the snow cruiser. The flare of his headlamps revealed a figure belted inside, holding a long rifle. Though it was too far and too brief a look, Dylan remembered the man from twenty-four hours earlier, seated atop a Sno-Cat, firing up at his Twin Otter, almost taking out the plane.

It had to be that same American.

So the bastard survived . . . made it to the station anyway.

A trickle of respect flared through him. He now understood why Harrington kept eluding him. The old man had help, someone skilled and competent.

Dylan's fingers found the butt of his Howdah pistol and tightened on the antique wooden grip, readying for the challenge to come.

The CAAT's driver slowed as they neared the crash site. The smaller vehicle lay on its side in an island of light, treads still spinning uselessly at the air. The exit ramp had torn open with the impact. Gunfire flashed from inside the cabin.

Someone was still alive, still fighting.

And with good reason.

Through that open hatch, the world of Hell's Cape—riled and angered by the chaos—pushed into the upended cabin in a riot of flesh and acid. Shadows lurched and crawled and slithered, piling one atop the other, likely drawn by the blood of the injured inside. One man burst out against that deadly tide, stumbling and struggling. Something scabrous and spidery clung to his shoulder and neck. Long legs pierced his flesh, digging a firm hold.

It was Seward, the team leader of that squad. The man fought through the reeds toward the approaching headlights, an arm raised in a silent plea.

"Sir?" the driver asked, still slowing.

Then a huge dark shadow swept across the glowing tops of the reeds and speared the man through the ribs, lifting him off his feet and carrying him away.

Three other men had been aboard the crashed CAAT.

But by now all gunfire had ceased inside.

Nothing to be done.

Dylan turned his attention forward and pointed his arm at the retreating rear end of the cruiser. He still had a mission to complete.

"Keep going."

4:39 P.M.

Gray guarded the open rear door with his rifle. The back gate was too damaged to close. The end of the ramp bounced and sparked as it was dragged along the cavern floor behind the cruiser. Exposed to the elements, the cabin was at great risk. He fired his DSR at any shadows that came too near, but the rig's knee-rattling pace, along with its belching fumes and roaring engines, continued to be their best defense.

Then a sharp whistle blast cut through the cacophony.

It was Kowalski, laying hard on the cruiser's horn.

Now what?

Gray glanced over a shoulder to see Jason and Stella come flying down the ladder from the rig's cab.

"Kowalski needs you!" Jason called out, then nodded to Stella. "We'll guard the cabin."

The young woman reached Harrington's side. "You should go, too, father."

"Wait." The professor had found an old pair of World War II–era binoculars and stared out into the darkness. He lowered them and pointed. "Looks like Wright's heading away from us."

Gray turned and saw Harrington was right.

The CAAT's headlights swung away from the rig, angling to the left, taking the vehicle farther out into the swamplands, toward the darkness at the back of the cavernous Coliseum.

Where's he going?

Harrington motioned with his binoculars. "I saw something lashed down atop that CAAT. It looked like—"

A tremendous *boom* blasted away his last words, echoing throughout the cavern, momentarily silencing the screams and cries of the maddening life outside. It sounded far off.

As the thunder rolled away, Gray turned to Harrington. "Was that your bunker busters?"

Dread clutched Gray's throat.

Had Wright just collapsed the far end of these tunnels?

Harrington's eyes had gotten huge—but from a different fear. "No. If those big bombs had blown, the blast would've been *much* louder. Would've shaken this entire system."

Then what was it?

The professor answered his unspoken question. "I think Wright set smaller charges, enough to blow a hole through the Hell's Cape station."

"Why would he do that?"

Harrington pointed toward the vanished CAAT. "I was trying to tell you . . . Atop his vehicle, he had a large disk strapped down, partially covered by a tarp. I think it was an LRAD dish. Had to be four times the size of the ones guarding the station."

Gray stared in the direction of Wright's trajectory across the cavern, aiming for the deeper sections of this lost world.

He suddenly understood Wright's plan.

He pictured a hole blasted through the superstructure of Hell's Cape, exposing this biosphere to the larger world above. *If Wright got far enough into this system and swung that large LRAD dish back toward the mouth of these tunnels . . .*

"He intends to flush this world out into the open," Gray realized aloud, picturing that sonic device driving the creatures of this land toward his newly blasted exit.

Harrington looked sick. "The damage wrought by these aggressive XNA species being set loose upon our established ecosystems would be incalculable." He shook his head. "Why would anyone do that?"

"The question of why can wait," Gray said. "For now, we've got to stop that from ever happening."

Stella nodded. "If we could reach the Back Door, set off those bunker busters, and collapse the tunnels at the far end, we could still keep everything bottled up. Regardless if Wright turns on that massive LRAD dish."

It was their best hope.

The rig's horn blasted again, now a continuous wail for attention.

Gray pointed to the bouncing ramp, yelling to be heard. "Jason, Stella! Don't let anything in!"

If Harrington was right, they couldn't let anything slow them down.

After he got nods from Jason and Stella, Gray rushed toward the front of the rig, drawing the professor in his wake. He vaulted up the ladder and helped Harrington into the upper cab.

Kowalski scowled back at them, letting go of the chain that led to the blaring horn. The wail finally cut off. "'Bout time." A thick arm pointed forward. "Doc, is that your Back Door?"

The rig's massive headlamps cut a swath through the darkness, revealing an installation encrusted like a steel barnacle high up the far wall. The gondola cables along the roof dove down to meet this small base, which from its interconnected series of boxy rooms and sealed tunnels could be mistaken for a grounded space station.

"That's the substation," Harrington agreed. "We wedged it into a natural crack, a fissure that led almost to the surface. We drilled a tunnel the rest of the way up."

Creating this rear exit.

"Then we have a problem," Kowalski said, lowering his arm and drawing their attention to the terrain directly ahead.

Between the rig and the Back Door, a wide tributary cut across their path. The flow churned swiftly, frothing its path through jagged rocks and sharp stalagmites. It looked too deep for the snow cruiser to cross on its own.

But all was not hopeless—or at least not *completely* hopeless.

"What do you think?" Kowalski asked.

Off to the left, an old wood-and-steel bridge arched over the river. During their passage through the Coliseum, the remains of other spans dotted this watery landscape, likely built by the Americans who first explored through here. It must have been a daunting undertaking.

Gray remembered Harrington's story of Operation Highjump. No wonder Byrd needed so many ships, aircraft, and manpower. Venturing down here would've been like exploring the surface of Mars.

As the cruiser barreled toward the bridge, Gray noticed several of the railroad ties that formed the span ahead had rotted or fallen away long ago. He pictured the ruins of the other bridges.

"Think it'll hold us?" Kowalski asked.

Harrington chewed his lower lip, plainly searching for some reason to be optimistic. "These old trestles must have been originally engineered to handle the weight and size of Byrd's cruiser."

But that was seventy years ago.

Still, Gray didn't see any other choice. The Back Door still lay three hundred yards off. To reach the station in time to stop Wright, they needed the rig's speed—along with the relative safety of its refuge.

"We'll have to risk it," Gray said. "With enough momentum, we might be able to fly over it before it collapses under us."

"You're the boss," Kowalski said.

The big man got the cruiser moving faster again, using the last of the diesel fumes to eke out more speed.

Gray called to the two below. "Grab something and hold on!"

He considered kicking Jason, Stella, and Harrington off this bus before they risked this dangerous crossing. But to do so would cost them too much time, momentum, and fuel. Besides, if all went to hell, leaving the three of them alone would be no safer than what they were about to attempt here.

Maybe even less so.

"Hold tight!" Gray yelled as the cruiser reached the river and raced for the bridge.

Gray cringed as the front tires hit the first set of wooden ties, but the stout beams held. He let out a slow breath, still bracing himself for the worst. The rig shot out along the span, which stretched fifty *long* yards ahead.

In the rearview mirror, he watched a couple of planks shatter under their passing weight and fall into the churning maw below. But the massive tires rolled their way across any smaller gaps. It was nothing the rig couldn't handle. So far speed and momentum were on their side.

Just not luck.

Something fiery shot low over the river, cruising toward them.

Gray caught a glimpse of its source. A pool of light revealed the distant presence of the second of the small CAATs. Apparently it had not followed its bigger brother, but instead had been sent to ambush them.

A figure stood atop that vehicle's cabin, risking the dangers here, balancing the smoking length of an RPG launcher in his arms.

The fired rocket struck the bridge ahead of them, exploding old ties and rending apart steel.

Unable to stop in time, the snow cruiser hit the blasted gap—and plunged headlong toward the river.

FOURTH

Uncivilization

25

Who knew so much trouble could come in such a small package?

Standing in the shadows at the edge of his estate, Cutter Elwes watched the young woman step tentatively from the helicopter to the summit of the tepui. She held a hand up against the sun's glare, pulling the brim of her baseball cap lower. She wore a loose blouse and vest, her hair in a ponytail in back.

Not unattractive.

But nothing like the beauty that followed out at her heels and grabbed her elbow. Cutter smiled, seeing the twin of his wife, a match to Ashuu's every feature, except Rahei had a heart of stone compared to her sister's gentle soul. Even now Rahei showed no emotion at seeing Cutter, only turning those obsidian eyes upon him and drawing her captive in his direction.

Earlier, Cutter had received a fax of the newcomer's passport, found while searching her belongings after she'd been captured. A brief background check had revealed many interesting details about his new guest, a woman named Jenna Beck. Apparently she was with the California Park Rangers, stationed at Mono Lake, where Kendall Hess had established his research facility.

It couldn't be a coincidence.

Mateo had reported a persistent ranger who had possibly witnessed the kidnapping of the good doctor. The man had also related the details of a hilltop firefight with that same ranger.

Could this be that person?

Interesting.

Curious to know more, Cutter stepped out of the shade of the cave that sheltered his home. The sun blazed above, but still failed to burn off the mists that shrouded the flanks of his mountaintop home.

He noted several emotions flash across the woman's face as she spotted him. From the slight widening of her eyes, one expression was plain and easy to read.

Recognition.

So she knows me.

Had her ill-timed visit to that base at Mono Lake triggered events that led to the American team arriving in Boa Vista, inquiring about a dead man? This one question raised others, but there would be time for that in a moment.

He stepped forward and offered his hand to shake.

She ignored it. "You're Cutter Elwes."

He gave a slight bow of his head in acknowledgment, seeing no reason for subterfuge at this stage.

"And you're Jenna Beck," he answered. "The park ranger who has caused us so much grief."

He found a certain amount of pleasure in her crinkled look of surprise. Still, the woman recovered smoothly.

"Where is Dr. Hess?" she asked, glancing around, her gaze lingering on the house behind his shoulders.

"He's safe and sound. Doing some work for me."

Doubt shone in her face.

Cutter had a question of his own. "How did you find me, Ms. Beck? I've gone to great lengths to stay among the deceased."

The woman weighed her answer before speaking. A defiant lift of her chin suggested she opted for the truth, devil be damned.

"It was Amy Serpry," she said. "The mole you planted in Dr. Hess's lab."

Cutter had already suspected as much, as his prior attempts to contact his young Dark Eden acolyte had failed. Initially he had assumed she had died during the containment breach, but plainly she must have been captured.

"And where is Amy now?" Cutter wondered how much the woman had told the authorities. Not that he was overly worried. Amy had never visited his tepui and knew nothing about the true extent of his plans.

"Dead," Beck said. "From the same organism she unleashed in California."

Cutter searched inwardly to judge how he felt about this loss, but he discovered no strong emotional response. "Amy knew the risks. She was a dedicated soldier for Dark Eden, happy to advance the cause."

"She didn't look *happy* at the end."

He shrugged. "Hard sacrifices have to be made."

As will many more, which this young woman will soon learn.

He motioned for Rahei to bring the prisoner along as he turned away. He headed toward his home's front door. He caught a small face peering from around the edge. His son, Jori, was always curious about strangers. It was his own fault, for keeping the boy so isolated.

He waved his son back inside.

Here was one visitor Jori didn't need to meet.

"I want to see Dr. Hess," the woman persisted. "Before I say another word."

Despite the woman's bluster, he knew Rahei had the skills to get her talking within the hour, but that wouldn't be necessary.

He glanced back. "Where do you think I'm taking you?"

12:48 P.M.

It can't be . . .

Kendall stared at the computer screen in the main lab as Mateo loomed in the background.

After completing his analysis of the genetic code that Cutter designed—the code meant for Kendall's viral shell—he had shed his biosafety suit and returned to a workstation in the outer room.

He had used the CRISPR-Cas9 technique to break down Cutter's code, gene by gene, nucleotide by nucleotide. He discovered the code was a simple one: a single strand of RNA, a common presentation for a whole family of viruses.

This minimalist approach suggested that Cutter had likely picked an ordinary virus, then engineered new code into it, using the same hybridization technique that he employed to create the chimeric species populating that sinkhole.

But what was the original viral source?

It was a simple puzzle to solve. He ran the code through an identification program and found a 94 percent match with the common norovirus. This particular bug was the plague of cruise ships or anywhere people gathered in great numbers. It was one of the most highly contagious viruses in nature, requiring only twenty or so particles to infect a person. It could be transmitted through bodily fluid, through the air, or simply by coming in contact with a contaminated surface.

If you wanted to create a universally contagious organism, the norovirus would be a good choice. The disadvantage was that it was highly sensitive to common disinfectants, bleaches, and detergents, so could be readily thwarted.

But if that virus were armored inside my engineered shell, nothing would stop it.

Still, the norovirus was not generally fatal, especially in healthy individuals. It only triggered flu-like symptoms. So that raised a larger concern.

What did Cutter add to the mix?

What made up that other 6 percent of the code?

The remaining material appeared to be the same repeated sequences for a specific protein-coding gene. To figure out *what* protein that was, he ran his findings through a modeling program that converted the code into a string of amino acids, then from that chain, the computer built a three-dimensional model of that final protein.

He stared at the model of it now, watching it slowly spin on the screen.

Though it had been slightly altered, he still recognized this unique foldable protein. He confirmed it with that same matching program.

My God, Cutter, what are you planning to do?

As if summoned by this thought, the door to the lab opened and Cutter arrived. Two women accompanied him. One was his wife—or at least she appeared to be, but something felt off about her. She had none of the sultry allure of Cutter's wife, nor was there the unspoken affection he'd formerly witnessed between husband and wife.

Then it dawned on him, remembering the unusual tribal heritage.

This must be his wife's twin—Mateo's other sister.

Supporting this assessment, the scarred man's reaction to the woman was very different from the way he had greeted Ashuu. Mateo would barely meet this sister's eyes, looking strangely fearful and nervous.

Before he could discern why, the second woman stepped into view. From her clothes and manner, she must be American. Still, there was something oddly familiar about her, like they had met before. But he could not place when or where.

Cutter made introductions. "Kendall, this is my sister-in-law, Rahei. And this lovely young woman at my side is from your own neck of the woods. A California park ranger. Ms. Jenna Beck."

Kendall blinked in surprise, suddenly remembering. He *had* met this young woman briefly in Lee Vining, over a cup of coffee at Bodie Mike's. She had been inquiring about his research at the lake. He struggled through his confusion.

What was she doing here now?

From the anger in her face and her stiff stance, she was no accomplice in all of this.

Jenna crossed to his side, touching his elbow in concern. "Are you okay, Dr. Hess?"

He licked his lips, too shocked to know how to even answer that question.

Cutter's gaze fell upon the computer screen. "Ah, Kendall, I see you've accomplished much while I was gone."

He glanced back to the slowly revolving protein. "That's some type of *prion*, isn't it?"

"Very good. It is indeed. In fact, it's a modified version of the infectious protein that causes Creutzfeldt–Jakob disease, an illness that presents with rapidly progressive dementia in humans."

Jenna looked between the two men. "What are you talking about?"

Kendall didn't have time to fully explain—not that he understood it all himself. Prions were mere slivers of protein with no genetic code of their own. Once a victim was infected, those proteins damaged other proteins—usually in the brain. As a consequence, prion diseases were usually slow, more difficult to spread.

But not any longer.

Kendall faced Cutter. "You engineered a contagious norovirus, one that could spread rapidly and churn out this deadly prion in great volumes."

"First of all, it's not exactly *deadly*," Cutter corrected. "I modified the prion's genetic structure so it would not be fatal. Like I promised you from the start, no human or animal would be killed as a direct result of my bioorganism."

"Then what is your goal? Clearly you want to insert your creation into my armored shell, to make your code almost impossible to eradicate. Once encapsulated, it could spread swiftly with no way of stopping it."

"True. But it was also the *small* size of your shell that intrigued me, a genetic delivery system tiny enough to pass easily through the blood-brain barrier. To allow these little prion factories ready access to the neurological systems of the infected."

Kendall could not hide his horror, and even the ranger understood enough to go pale. Prion diseases were already incurable, the damage they wrought permanent. The typical clinical symptoms were generalized dementia and the progressive loss of higher cognitive functions, turning an intelligent person into a vegetable.

He pictured Cutter's engineered disease spreading throughout the population, as unstoppable as the organism that escaped his lab, leaving a path of neurological destruction in its wake.

Cutter must have read the dismay in his eyes. "Fear not, my friend. Not only did I engineer the prion to be *nonfatal,* but I also designed it to *self-destruct* after a certain number of iterations. Thus avoiding complete annihilation of the victim's brain."

"Then what's its purpose?"

"It's a gift," Cutter smiled. "It will leave the infected living in a more simple state, one harmonious with nature, permanently free of higher cognitive functions."

"In other words, reducing us to animals."

"And the earth will be the better for it," Cutter said.

"That's inhuman," Jenna gasped out, equally horrified.

Cutter turned to her. "You're a park ranger, Ms. Beck. You should surely understand better than anyone. Being *inhuman* is human. We are already beasts who feign morality. We need religion, government, and laws to force a level of control over our baser natures. I intend to strip away the disease that is *intelligence,* to rip away the deception that allows humanity to believe itself mightier and more deserving of this planet."

Cutter waved an arm to encompass everything. "We burn the forests, we pollute the oceans, we melt the ice caps, we dump carbon dioxide into the air . . . we are the main driving force behind one of the greatest extinctions on this planet. It is a path that will inevitably lead to our *own* end."

Kendall tried to argue, but Cutter cut him off.

"Ralph Waldo Emerson said it best. *The end of the human race will be that it will eventually die of civilization.* We're already at that cusp, but what will we leave in the wake of our death throes? A planet polluted to the point where nothing survives?"

The ranger stood up against that rant. "But it's *civilization* . . . it's our innate *intelligence* that holds the possibility to save ourselves, too, and along with it the planet. While the dinosaurs failed to see that asteroid heading toward them, many of us do *see* what's happening and are fighting for change."

"You share a narrow perspective about civilization, my dear. The dinosaurs reigned for a hundred and eighty-five million years, while modern man has only been around for the past two hundred thousand years. And civilization a mere ten thousand."

Cutter shook his head for emphasis. "Society is a destructive illusion of control, nothing more. And look what it's wrought. During this short experiment with *civilization*, we as a species are already at the precipice of total ecological collapse, one driven by our own hands. Do you truly think in this industrial world of warring nations, of greed-driven politics, that anything will change?"

Jenna sighed loudly. "We must try."

Cutter snorted. "It will never happen, certainly not in time. The better path? It's time to *uncivilize* this world, to halt this ridiculous experiment before nothing of this planet is left."

"And that's your plan?" Kendall asked. "To let loose this contagion and strip humanity of its intelligence."

"I prefer to think of it as *curing* humankind of the disease called civilization, to leave only the natural animal, leveling the playing field for all. To let the only law of the land be *survival of the fittest*. The world will be stronger and healthier for it."

Jenna stared at Cutter, her face full of suspicion. "And what about you?" she asked. "Will you also take this *cure?*"

Cutter shrugged, but he looked irritated by her question—which made Kendall like her all the more. "Some few must be spared, to oversee this transition."

"I see," Jenna said, clearly calling him out on his hypocrisy. "That's very convenient."

With his feathers duly ruffled, Cutter faced Kendall. "It's high time, my friend, that you show me your method for arming your viral shell."

Kendall took strength from the young woman's demeanor. "I can't," he said honestly.

"Can't or won't?" Cutter asked. "I've been very patient with you, Kendall, because we were once friends, but there are ways to convince you to cooperate fully."

Cutter glanced to his wife's sister. A glint in Rahei's dark eyes suggested she would invite such a challenge.

"It's not a matter of refusing you, Cutter—which I would still do if it made any difference, but it doesn't. It's a simple matter that the key you want is beyond both of our grasps. I can't synthesize it. Not here. The XNA sequence necessary to unlock my engineered shell can be found only in nature."

That nature you love so well.

"Where?"

"You know where, Cutter."

He nodded, closing his eyes. "Of course . . . Antarctica," he mumbled. "There must be a particular species from that shadow biosphere, something with a unique genetic code that acts as that key."

It still disturbed Kendall how quickly this monster's mind worked.

Cutter opened his eyes. "Which species is it?"

Kendall met that stolid gaze, ready to draw a line in the sand. If Cutter put a mole in his lab, he surely had a person or a team inserted at Harrington's station. Cutter certainly knew enough details about Hell's Cape. If that bastard learned the truth, he could obtain the last piece to his horrifying genetic puzzle.

That must never happen.

Cutter read the resolution in his face and gave a sad shake of his head. "So be it. Then we'll have to do it the hard way."

Kendall felt his knees shake. He would do his best to hold out against whatever torture would follow.

Cutter turned to Jenna while waving a hand to Rahei. "We'll start with her and make Kendall watch, so he'll better understand what's to come."

1:00 P.M.

"One hour out!" Suarez called from up front, seated next to the Valor's pilot.

Painter looked out the window behind his bandaged shoulder. Before lift-off, he had popped a handful of ibuprofen and abandoned his sling, but even this small movement triggered a dagger-stab of pain. He studied the passing terrain, seeing only the green sea below the droning nacelles of the tiltrotor. Somewhere ahead lay their destination, the tepui where the dead man, Cutter Elwes, might have made his home.

And hopefully where we'll find Jenna and Dr. Hess.

Time was rapidly running out.

He still had the satellite phone pressed to his ear. "There's no way to hold Lindahl off?" he asked.

Lisa answered, "The weather patterns have changed in the last hour. And not for the better. The next storm front is moving in faster than originally projected, expected to hit the mountains by midafternoon. The wind speeds and rainfall estimates suggest this storm will be three to four times as fierce as the prior one. Because of that threat, the timetable for the nuclear option has shifted from sundown to noon."

Noon . . .

He checked his watch and calculated the time difference. That was only two hours from now. And they were still sixty minutes out from reaching the tepui, leaving them almost no time to find Kendall Hess and discover if a non-nuclear option for dealing with the threat existed.

Painter recognized the impossible task before him. He stared at the Marines around him. He was flanked by Sergeant Suarez's two men: Abramson and Henckel. Across the cabin, Drake conversed in low tones with Malcolm and Schmitt. He took strength from the rugged team accompanying him.

Still . . .

"When are they evacuating the base?" he asked.

"It's already under way. The National Guard combed the countryside at daybreak, clearing any recalcitrant locals who hadn't obeyed the mandatory evacuation order. Base personnel are breaking down the labs, moving Josh as I speak."

"And you and Nikko?"

"I don't trust Lindahl. I'm going to wait for the last bus out. Sarah . . . Corporal Jessup has prepped a small helicopter to ferry us out of harm's way."

"Don't wait too long," he warned, fear for her drying out his mouth.

"I won't. Edmund updates me regularly on the status of the nuclear team who are prepping the device. They're still doing final calculations. The plan is to lift the bomb via a drone helicopter to a specific altitude for maximum effect across the local mountaintops and valleys. The team is still working on those last details." Lisa's voice hardened. "So, Painter, you need to find something . . . if not a cure, at least some hope to delay the inevitable."

Painter sighed heavily. It was a tall order. Even if he could discover some solution to this threat—some unknown biological counteragent—could it be engineered or employed fast enough to discourage this pending nuclear response?

"I'll do all I can," Painter promised.

He said his good-byes and ended the call, resting the phone on his lap.

Drake must have read his face. "Let me guess. The news from home isn't good."

He slowly shook his head.

Not good at all.

With a twinge from his shoulder, he turned to the window, finally noting a distant dark mountain rising near the horizon.

I doubt the situation is any better over there.

1:05 P.M.

"This may sting," Cutter Elwes said.

Jenna sat on a chair in the lab, pinned in place by the hulking native, Mateo. It was the same man who had ambushed her at that hilltop ghost town. She recognized him from the purplish scar running down his cheek to his chin. It seemed everything had come full circle.

"Don't do this," Kendall said. "Please."

Cutter straightened, holding a pistol-shaped tool in his hand. She recognized a modified jet injector used for delivering vaccines. Sticking out the top was an inverted vial, holding an amber liquid.

She suspected she wasn't being threatened by a flu shot.

"Simply tell me the name of the XNA species that is the biological key," Cutter told Kendall. "And none of this nastiness needs to continue."

"Don't do it," Jenna said. Fingers dug painfully into her shoulders, warning her to stay silent, but she ignored the threat. "Don't give him what he wants."

Kendall clearly vacillated, but finally he crossed his arms.

"Very well," Cutter said.

The dark woman, Rahei, tugged Jenna's sleeve higher up her arm.

Cutter pressed the muzzle of the injector against her shoulder. "Last chance, Kendall."

The researcher's gaze shifted guiltily away from her.

Cutter gave a small shrug and pulled the trigger. Compressed gas whistled, and a sharp bite penetrated her skin, felt all the way down to the bone.

She swore under her breath as Mateo released her. She rubbed her arm and gained her feet. "What was that?"

Cutter lifted the injector, sloshing around the remainder of the vial's contents. "Non-enveloped viral RNA."

Jenna recalled the discussion from earlier. "It's that genetic code you engineered. The one that affects the brain."

"Correct. But in its current form, it's only mildly infectious and very fragile to environmental stresses. It's why I need Kendall's viral shell."

She understood. He wanted to engineer a superbug that could knock the human race back to the Stone Age—or even *before* the Stone Age.

"But in its raw state," he added, "the neurological damage will be the same."

She took a deep breath, fearful of the answer to her next question. "How long do I have?"

"You should start feeling the effects within the next thirty minutes. Mild fever, slight headache, neck stiffness . . . then over the following few hours, the degenerative changes will progress at an exponential pace. Language is usually affected first, then complex thoughts, finally the sense of self wears away, leaving only base desires and survival instinct."

Horror settled into the pit of her stomach.

"So . . . so you've tested this on people before?" Jenna asked, expecting him to try to justify his heinous acts.

Instead he answered calmly, "Thoroughly, my dear. Most thoroughly."

Kendall touched Jenna's hand. "I'm sorry."

Cutter turned to Rahei. "Take Ms. Beck to one of our test cages. Down on Level Black."

Upon hearing this, the native woman's lips pulled into a smile of dark delight. It was the first strong emotion Rahei had shown.

That scared Jenna more than anything else.

Rahei grabbed her upper arm and led her off, collecting another native near the door, who carried a rifle over one shoulder. Jenna noted the weapon was fitted with a U-shaped yellow rod sticking past the muzzle like a bayonet, with exposed copper contact points at the tips.

She recognized the design.

Electric cattle prod.

She kept well away from that weapon as Rahei led her out of the lab. She was marched down a long tunnel that seemed to cross through the stone heart of the mountain. After stepping through a heavily bolted door at the end, she found herself outside again.

She shaded her eyes against the sun, which blazed directly overhead, shining brightly down the throat of what appeared to be a sinkhole. Someone had converted it into a series of tiered gardens, festooned all around with orchids, bromeliads, and flowering vines. Down at the bottom, the green canopy of a forest reflected the sunlight. Each level from there to here appeared to be broken into fenced-off tiers, connected by a corkscrewing stone ramp carved from the walls.

Rahei pushed her toward a ladder that led off the steel apron and down to that winding road. An enclosed golf cart waited below. She was forced to sit in the back with Rahei while her armed guard joined the driver up front.

Once everyone was seated, the golf cart rolled down the ramp, its electric motor purring. It passed through a series of gates, which magically opened in front of them, possibly responding to some RFID chip embedded in the cart.

At first nothing seemed out of the ordinary about these gardens, but after passing through a few levels, she started to notice oddities. While she wasn't intimately familiar with all rain forest life, some of the plants and animals appeared otherworldly. At first the signs were subtle: bees the size of walnuts, a wall of black orchids whose petals opened and closed on their own, a dwarf boa that slithered into a clear pond, revealing a series of gills along its flanks.

But the deeper they traversed, larger creatures appeared, more boldly abnormal. From a slim branch over the road, a row of zebra-striped rats hung from prehensile tails, similar to those found on an opossum. While they waited for a gate to fully open, a thick vine shot thorns at them, peppering the sides of the cart. Around another turn, a flock of oversized Amazon parrots took flight at their passage, revealing a riot of plumage in every shade, a kaleidoscope of feathers that dazzled the eye.

One of these last flew too high—then suddenly seized up and tumbled several yards before regaining its senses and winging away to join its flock.

Jenna stared upward. Was Cutter utilizing electronic tags or chips to keep each creature restricted to its own tier? She pondered this possibility—anything to occupy her mind and stave off the terror inside her.

All the while, the cart continued to wind down through the levels, the air growing ever warmer and more humid. Sweat beaded on her forehead and rolled down the small of her back.

She searched longingly up at the distant mouth of the sinkhole, estimating they were a mile down by now.

I'll never get out of here.

Despair dampened her attention—until finally they reached forest growing at the bottom of the sinkhole. She estimated it was over twenty acres in size.

Crossing a final gate, they dropped through the canopy.

Welcome to Level Black, she thought grimly.

But what was down here?

Their descent along the ramp grew progressively darker. The blaze of sunlight filtered down to a dull green glow. As her eyes adjusted, she spotted shelves of fungi, softly aglow, sprouting along the trunks of trees. Across the floor, tiny ponds and thin streams reflected that meager light, while stands of heavy-leafed ferns towered all around, densely packed along the lone gravel road into the forest.

The cart reached that road and headed off into the jungle.

Their head lamps finally clicked on.

Using that brighter light, Jenna tried to peer through the thick walls of undergrowth, but she could not see very far. Occasionally the cart's bumper would brush a fern and its leaves and rubbery stems would retract and curl up, opening a wider view into the jungle.

But it was only more of the same.

Giving up, she turned her attention forward, wondering where she was being taken. Gnats buzzed thickly in the beams of their headlamps. Everywhere, water dripped from leaves, and flower petals gently drifted down.

The chatter between the driver and guard had died away upon reaching this level. Their fear was palpable, which set her heart to pounding harder.

Then thirty yards ahead, something large dropped from above and splattered onto the road. When they reached the site, the cart edged past what lay broken in the gravel.

Jenna stared down at the bloody skeleton of a goat or deer. Some flesh still clung to the carcass, including one eye that stared forlornly back at her as the cart passed by.

Leaning against the window, she searched the tangle of thick branches overhead and the leafy bower of the dark canopy.

She spotted nothing.

Who or what had—

A tremendous roar shattered the heavy silence, full of territorial anger and hunger. It was answered by cries deeper in the forest, echoing all around.

Horrified, Jenna turned toward Rahei.

The woman was smiling again.

26

"Is everyone okay?" Gray hollered. "Call out!"

He climbed off the floor of the snow cruiser's cab and took personal inventory, fingering a scalp wound where his head had clipped a stanchion. A glance forward showed the river flowing past the vehicle's cracked windshield. A moment ago, the cruiser had toppled off the blasted bridge, crashed through the trestles below, and struck the river flat-bellied.

So why hadn't they plunged fully underwater?

Kowalski helped Harrington out of the footwell in front of the passenger seat. The professor had a wicked knot on his forehead, and his eyes looked glassy and dazed.

Jason called up from the main cabin in back. "Need help down here!"

Gray responded to the panic in his voice and shoved over to the ladder that led down from the cab. He found the lower level roiling with water, the river flowing in through the open back hatch. A huge black spike pierced up from the floor to the roof. Gray remembered spotting the fang-like stalagmites rising from the river. The cruiser must have impaled itself onto one of them as it fell, piercing its underbelly.

The stone stake was likely all that was holding them from being dragged away by the strong currents and rolled into the depths.

Jason struggled with Stella. He clung white-knuckled to a pipe near the roof; his other arm clutched Stella to his chest. Her head lolled drunkenly, half her face bloody. The riptide inside the cabin threatened to tear Jason away at any moment.

And it wasn't only the kid at risk.

The entire cruiser lurched under the pressure of the current, spinning a few degrees upon that spike. Neighboring wooden trestles snapped free, bringing more of the bridge raining down into the river. Their precarious perch would not hold out much longer.

He prepared to dive into that black maelstrom—until Jason yelled.

"Something's in the water with us!"

Gray pulled his night-vision goggles back into place and swung his DSR rifle from his shoulder and flicked on its IR illuminator. The beam penetrated the water enough for him to search its depths, reflecting off the steel bottom of the cruiser. He scanned the cabin until he discovered a clutch of tentacles reaching through the back hatch and probing into the cruiser. Unlike an octopus, these appendages bore sharp pincers in place of suckers. An unwary fish brushed too close and was sliced in half in a lightning-fast attack. Smaller limbs snatched up the pieces and reeled them away.

Gray didn't want to know what creature belonged to those tentacles.

"Try not to move!" he called to Jason.

Unfortunately, Stella began to regain her senses, flailing in surprise in Jason's grip. A few of the black tentacles snaked toward them.

Gray considered firing a sonic bullet, but he doubted the weapon would have much effect against the tentacles, when the main adversary still hid outside. But that thought gave him an idea. For the most part, life down here was sensitive to vibrations and sounds. A single bullet might not do much to discourage the hidden predator, but if he could *amplify* the effect, he could turn the entire rig into the equivalent of a hot foot.

"Jason, on my signal, you haul ass toward me."

He looked terrified, but he gave a firm nod.

Gray shifted his rifle away from the water and pointed it at the roof. He hoped the noise in the confined space didn't knock Jason out, but he had to take the chance. He pulled the trigger. The sonic pulse struck the steel roof and reverberated through the entire carriage of the cruiser, setting it to ringing like a bell.

Jason flinched under the assault, losing his grip and plunging into the water. Gray dove in after the pair, noting the tentacles spasm and flail back out of the cabin. The current carried Jason partly in Gray's direction. Thankfully the kid kept hold of Stella.

Gray caught them both, and together he and Jason swam with Stella back to the ladder. The plunge had woken her enough so she was able to climb the rungs. Kowalski pulled her the rest of the way up, where Harrington hugged his daughter tightly.

"I'm okay," she mumbled into her father's chest.

But none of them would be for long.

Gray followed Jason back into the front cab and pointed to a hatch in the roof. "Everyone topside!"

The cruiser's bulk lurched again in the current.

"We're still wedged in the remains of the bridge," he explained. "We can try to climb up what's left of the trestles to reach the top, then cross back to shore."

Kowalski went first, hardly needing the ladder to pop the hatch and haul himself out, even while burdened with his machine gun. Once topside, he helped Harrington and his daughter up. Jason and Gray hurried behind them.

Gray straightened, relieved to see that the broken trestles should be easy enough to climb to reach the top of the bridge.

"Company's coming," Kowalski intoned grimly.

Gray swung around to see headlights racing along the river toward them. It was the CAAT that had ambushed them, likely coming to make sure they were all dead.

Gray pointed to the opposite bank, in the direction of the Back Door. "Jason, you get Stella and her father up into that substation, blow those bunker busters, and seal this place up tightly. Kowalski and I'll deal with the others."

"What're you going to do?" Jason asked.

"They ambushed us . . . only polite for us to return the favor. With luck, we'll commandeer their vehicle."

Jason eyed him, his brows pinched. "You're planning on going after Wright, aren't you?"

"If something goes wrong with those bunker busters, we can't let that bastard use that LRAD to cause a stampede, to flush this cavern system out into the world."

Jason nodded and headed toward the supports near the front of the cruiser. Gray moved out with Kowalski toward the tangle of steel and wooden trestles at the back end.

Kowalski glanced back at the other three. "Since when is splitting up ever a good idea?"

5:07 P.M.

Free of the bridge, Jason slogged with Stella and Harrington toward the substation high up the back wall. They had only the one DSR between the three of them. Stella lost her weapon during the crash. Still, after so long in the dark, the single IR illuminator cast enough light to let them see with their night-vision gear.

Like hiking under a full moon.

Jason studied his goal ahead. The Back Door was a collection of boxy workstations jammed into a high crack. A few units spilled out and were stuck to the wall, like toy blocks glued to the side of a building.

"How do we get up there?" Jason asked.

From the cables running along the roof, the aerial gondola must be the normal way of reaching that steel penthouse in the sky.

Stella marched with her father, holding his hand. Both of them were bruised, battered, and bloodied, but they forged on through the knee-high tufts of moss and boot-sucking expanses of thick algal mats.

Stella pointed her free arm toward the substation. "There's a ladder. Steel rungs pounded into the wall that climbed from the cavern floor to the station."

They had crossed only thirty yards when a loud grinding crash drew Jason's attention over his shoulder. The war between the river's current and the jammed cruiser ended. Byrd's old machine tore free of the bridge and rolled into the depths.

Farther out, a flare of bright lights closed toward the far end of the bridge. Jason prayed Gray's ambush was successful. Otherwise, the CAAT could probably ford that river atop its floating treads and quickly run them down.

Knowing that, Jason urged the others faster.

"On the left," Stella warned.

Jason swung his rifle, casting his IR beam in that direction. Dark shapes came loping across the plain toward them, looking like a pack of wolves, each about the same size as a large dog.

He counted at least a dozen.

"What are they?" Jason asked.

Harrington answered. "Trouble."

5:09 P.M.

Gray lay on his stomach in pitch-darkness, an unnerving experience considering the harsh life found in this hellish landscape. A few yards off, Kowalski breathed heavily, plainly not any happier.

After climbing the trestles to the bridge, Gray had insisted they go dark, clicking off his IR illuminator. He didn't want to alert the approaching CAAT of their presence on this side of the river. The two of them crawled blindly on their hands and knees until they found a cluster of rocks twenty yards from the bridge, then went into hiding. They also coated their bodies with algal muck to reduce their body heat signatures.

In the darkness, creatures skittered across his skin or buzzed around his face, likely drawn by the smell of his sweat and the blood dripping from his scalp. Some bit; others stung. He did his best to swipe them away.

Luckily they didn't have long to wait.

The CAAT came blazing forward, brightly enough that Gray shifted his night-vision goggles off his eyes.

The treads tore across the terrain, skidding slightly as the vehicle made a sharp turn at the bridge, stopping at the river's edge.

After a moment, the cabin door on the passenger side popped open. A figure climbed out and rolled expertly over the treads, dropping lightly to the ground. He lifted a set of night-vision goggles and stared down at the river, then across to the other side.

"Got three targets!" the man shouted in a British accent. "On the move . . . headed toward the Back Door."

The driver swore. "Bloody bastards got nine lives."

The commando outside studied the river. "Sir, the current looks too treacherous to risk the CAAT. Could pull us under."

"Understood." The driver sounded like the squad leader, his words flavored with a distinct Scottish brogue. He called to another teammate. "Cooper, grab the AWM. Clean this mess up."

Gray tensed. AWM likely stood for Arctic Warfare Magnum, a cold-weather version of a common British sniper rifle. They were planning on picking the others off.

Gray waited until a second man exited the same door. Once on the ground, the commando slapped a box magazine into his rifle and lifted the rifle to his shoulder, adjusting the sight.

"No worries, sir," he announced. "They're all out in the open. Easy shots all around."

Same here.

"Now," Gray whispered, leaping forward.

Kowalski fired from his right side. His machine gun chattered and rounds ripped through the sniper's chest. Even before his body fell, Kowalski swung his gun and took out the commando at the bridge, blasting him into the river.

Gray sprinted to the CAAT and lunged at the open door. He fired his DSR point-blank into the confined space of the vehicle's cabin, a deafening barrage of sonic bullets.

As cries erupted inside, he rolled into the interior.

Before Gray could stop him, the driver bailed out the far side, plainly dazed, but with enough wits about him to expect such a follow-up attack. Another wasn't so quick. Gray planted a dagger through the man's throat and twisted. As he yanked the blade free, the man choked, clawing at his neck, then collapsed.

Gray searched the remainder of the cabin.

Empty.

So only the four.

Through the windshield, he saw the squad leader sprinting along the riverbank, smartly keeping the CAAT's bulk between him and where Kowalski was firing. While running, the commando struggled to free a radio.

If he reached his superior, alerted him of the attack, any hope of using the CAAT as a Trojan horse to get close to Wright would be gone.

Gray jumped out the driver's door and lifted his rifle, but he knew the distance was too great to do much good. Likewise, Kowalski came charging around the back of the CAAT, machine gun in his arms, dragging a belt of rounds.

The squad leader already had the radio to his lips.

Too late.

Then something dark snapped out of the river, wrapped around the man's waist, and yanked him off the bank. He vanished into the water with a thrashing splash.

Gray had recognized that pincer-lined tentacle. The gunfire—both sonic and regular—must have drawn the beast to the shoreline here. Apparently giving that monster a hot foot earlier had not only shocked it but also pissed it off.

Even in Hell, revenge is sweet.

5:11 P.M.

Jason ran alongside Stella and her father. He had heard the firefight break out across the river, but he dared not take his focus off the closing pack of predators in order to check on Gray and Kowalski.

With the DSR locked to his shoulder, he shielded Stella and her father. He took potshots at the beasts, but the sonic rounds only seemed to scatter the pack temporarily, buying them an extra few seconds. Worst of all, the power meter on the side of his rifle had flickered into the red as he fired repeatedly.

Almost out of juice.

"I'll lead them off," Jason gasped, his boots heavy with mud and algae. "You two make for the Back Door."

He slowed, waving them toward the far wall.

"Go, father." Stella pushed the professor forward, while slipping out a knife from her belt. "I'll help Jason."

"We stay together," Harrington said, stopping with them, breathing heavily. "*Leox depilis* are like their African lion counterparts. They try to split off the weak. And besides, I don't think I could run the rest of the way. We'll make our stand here."

Jason fired another shot, hitting the lead *Leox*, which reacted as if struck in the snout with a baseball bat. The others jerked to the left and right, slowing until their assaulted pack member could recover his senses.

Must be the leader.

By now, Jason had gotten a good look at them. Their muscular shoulders stood waist-high, their hairless skin oiled in black, almost iridescent under the IR beam's glow. Their heads were wolfishly long, with jaws hinged near the back of their skulls, allowing them to open their dagger-lined maws disturbingly wide, reminding him of photos of the now-extinct thylacine, the Tasmanian tiger.

A hair-raising howl burst from the throat of the pack leader, plainly a challenge. Apparently, in this dark world, the louder you shouted, the bigger your balls.

The pack closed ranks to either side, stalking more cautiously forward now, preparing to close the last of the distance.

Jason lifted his rifle, which slowed the leader.

Smart . . . he recognizes the threat.

Jason's only hope was that at closer range the sonic weapon would do more harm, encourage the pack to go after easier prey. A glance to his rifle's power meter suggested he had only one shot left, so he had better make it count, which meant letting the pack get as close as possible before firing.

He fixed his aim upon the pack leader, knowing that was his true adversary.

Stella shifted to his side, ready to defend her father.

"Give me the gun," she whispered.

Jason hesitated.

"I have an idea," she pressed.

He relented and passed her his rifle, taking her dagger in trade. "I think we only have a single pulse left."

"Then let's hope I'm right about the dominance patterns of this species."

She extracted what looked like a small microphone from where the rifle's stock joined the gun. Jason suddenly remembered Harrington's prior instructions about the DSR: how it could not only fire a sonic bullet, but it could also be used to amplify voices like a megaphone, or in reverse mode, to eavesdrop from a distance.

Stella settled the butt of the rifle to her shoulder, bringing the microphone to her lips. Instead of pointing the muzzle toward the pack as it silently stalked toward them, she lifted the gun toward the roof.

And howled.

It was a fair mimic of the pack leader's cry, only magnified a hundredfold as she pulled the trigger, pulsing that scream of challenge up to the rooftop.

The blast echoed across the cavern.

The savage wail stopped the leader in his tracks, driving the beast into a wary crouch. It was plainly intimidated by the volume of that echoing scream.

Jason recalled his own thought from a moment ago.

In this dark world, the louder you shout, the bigger your balls.

The leader pushed away from them, one step, then another, never turning his back. The pack followed his example, shifting and darting to either side nervously, all the while slowly retreating.

Then upon some unknown signal, the pack turned and fled back into the darkness, yipping as they ran, ready to pursue less noisy prey.

Jason stared over at Stella. "You're amazing."

She shrugged and returned his rifle, now out of charge. Still, she tried to hide a smile of pride as she turned away. They continued on toward the far wall. At least there was enough trickling juice to keep the IR illuminator lit, but for how much longer?

He set a hard pace and crossed the last hundred yards in a matter of minutes. Far overhead, the substation shone dimly, lit by a couple of standby emergency lights.

Closer at hand, Jason stared at the steel rungs bolted into the wall. They formed a ladder that climbed the dozen or so stories to reach the Back Door.

It would be a tough haul.

Stella pointed out into the cavern. "Over there!"

Jason tensed, swinging around, expecting another attack. But she was pointing to a pool of light on the far side of the river. It was the CAAT. As they watched, it began to roll along the waterway, heading off.

Jason held his breath, then a distant triple beep of a horn sounded.

It was the prearranged signal.

Gray and Kowalski were okay. They had successfully commandeered the enemy's CAAT, ready to pursue Dylan Wright.

Must've held off departing until our own lights reached the back wall.

Jason didn't know if the others could see him, but he lifted his arm.

Good luck.

In retrospect, he should've saved some of that *luck* for himself.

As he lowered his arm, the IR illuminator flickered and died, plunging them into darkness.

27

Roraima, Brazil

What have I done?

Kendall sat at a workstation in the main lab. He had
no choice but to stare at a large LCD monitor. It dis-
played live video feed from a tree-mounted camera.
From the stark shades of grays, it must be recording
through a low-light sensor. The view revealed a thick
forest, draped in vines, shaded by a dense canopy. The
lens pointed down into a clearing lined by gravel.

A series of three tall cages stood in the middle of the
glade. Hazard signs warned the pens were electrified,
like the fences between the tiers of Cutter's macabre
garden.

This must be the lowest level.

Kendall remembered catching a glimpse of that isolated piece of rain forest. But what else was down there?

On the screen, he watched Jenna being manhandled into the centermost cage. From the way she hugged her arms around her chest, keeping clear of the bars, she must know about the danger.

Rahei slammed the pen closed.

"Our Ms. Beck should be feeling the first signs of infection," Cutter said, pacing behind him, shadowed by Mateo in the background. "Headaches, maybe neck pain."

"Please don't do this," Kendall said.

On the screen, Rahei retreated with the two other men. The pair kept a close watch on the jungle, guarding with electrified cattle prods and rifles. They all quickly piled back into the cart, swung the vehicle around the clearing, then headed out the way they'd come in.

"Why did you take her down there?" Kendall asked, glancing back at Cutter. "Why leave her alone?"

"Oh, she's not alone."

Proving this, something massive moved past the camera, too fast to catch more than the briefest glimpse of huge hooked claws and a shaggy coat. Still, Kendall recognized the species, falling back into his seat in horror.

"You didn't . . ." he moaned.

Cutter shrugged. "It was an early experiment, taking a page from your preservationist playbook. *De-extinction* was the word you used in that paper, as I recall. It was a simple matter of using the MAGE and CAGE techniques to take a species already found in this rain forest, alter its genetic code, and resurrect its ancient ancestor."

Kendall knew it was theoretically possible, that labs around the world sought to accomplish this very goal, and would likely succeed in the next few years. Already multiple facilities searched for ways to resurrect the woolly mammoth from elephant DNA, another sought to revive extinct passenger pigeons from its common relative, yet another worked to pull the long-deceased wild aurochs from the genetic heritage of present-day cattle. These ventures went by many names: Revive & Restore, the Uruz Project, even one appropriately called the Lazarus Project, which sought to de-extinct an Australian frog that gave birth through its mouth.

But what Cutter accomplished here . . .

"You can't leave her down there," he insisted.

"She's safe enough for now, behind those electrified bars. We'll give her another half hour, when the infection reduces her to something simpler. Then you'll get a glimpse of what this new world will be like for humankind, when our species is stripped of its cancerous intelligence."

Kendall felt tears threaten, knowing this monster would force him to watch what happened to Jenna.

"But you can stop all of this," Cutter insisted. "Just tell me the name of the XNA species that holds the genetic key to unlocking your armored viral shell. One name . . . and this all ends. I will take matters over from there."

If Cutter ever got hold of this last critical piece of information, Kendall knew he could figure out the rest of his biological puzzle.

"Do not take long." Cutter waved to the screen. "There is a counteragent to what plagues Ms. Beck, but it must be administered within the hour or the neurological effects will be permanent."

"There's a cure?" Kendall swallowed.

"Indeed." He glanced toward the large refrigerator at the back of the BSL4 lab. "A protein that's a mirror image of what I engineered. It's capable of repairing the neuronal damage wrought by my prion, but like I said, there is a time limit. A point of no return for Ms. Beck."

Kendall had a larger worry beyond the young park ranger. "And if I give you that name, you'll tell me how to stop what's spreading in California."

Cutter rubbed his chin, plainly feigning concentration. "I am a man of my word. That was my *original* offer. But that was before Ms. Beck arrived."

"What do you mean?"

"Tell me what I want to know, and I'll let you choose. I can either teach you how to eradicate the horror unleashed from your lab . . . or I can save Ms. Beck. But not *both*."

Kendall stared at the screen, knowing he would have to tell Cutter the truth eventually. With time, the bastard would get the information out of him anyway.

He turned to Cutter, his voice low with defeat. "You'll need the *blood* from one of the Antarctic species."

"Which one?"

"*Volitox ignis*."

Cutter looked truly thoughtful now. "Those fiery eels. A daunting task indeed. I'll have to make a call before it's too late. Seems I might have gotten ahead of myself with my plans. *Jumping the gun*, as you Americans say."

The man began to turn away.

"Cutter, you promised."

He turned back. "Of course, sorry. Which cure do you want? The one for Ms. Beck . . . or for the world?"

Kendall stared back at the screen, at the small woman huddled in the cage. At the same time, he pictured the wrath of destruction spreading over the mountains of California.

I'm sorry, Jenna.

Kendall turned to Cutter. "How do I kill what I created?"

"It's the simplest of all solutions. Have you never wondered why that biosphere under Antarctica never spread to the greater world? Surely there have been breaches in the past, small escapes that have leaked out. But it's never fully broken loose. I suspect it would take great numbers to do that."

Kendall struggled for an answer. What was so unique about Antarctica? What kept that world trapped below? Was it the salty seas, the ice, the cold? He had already experimented with such variables in the past at his lab.

"We've tried subzero temperatures, various salinities, heavy metal toxins, like those found in the surrounding oceans," Kendall admitted. "Nothing's killed it."

"Because you were thinking too small, my friend . . . that's always been your problem. You look at the trees and miss the forest. You think locally versus *globally.*"

Cutter lifted an eyebrow, as if testing Kendall.

He pondered the significance.

Globally.

What was Cutter driving at?

Then he suddenly knew.

1:24 P.M.

Jenna rubbed the nape of her neck, careful not to shift too close to the bars of the cage. The dull ache in her cervical vertebrae had become a tight muscular spasm, shooting fiery lances of agony throughout her skull. Even her eyes hurt, making the dull green glow of the forest seem too bright.

She knew the significance of these symptoms.

It's already starting.

She began to repeat a mantra, fearing what was coming.

I am Jenna Beck, daughter of Gayle and Charles. I live at the corner of D Street and Lee Vining Avenue. My dog's name is Nikko, his birthday is . . .

She fought through the pain to hold on to every scrap of her identity, testing her memory for any sign of deterioration.

But will I even know when it's happening?

She breathed deeply, taking in the rich perfume of the jungle, trying to find her center, to keep panic at bay. All around, she heard water dripping, the thrush of bird's wings, the creak of branches, the whisper of leaves.

One detail struck her as wrong, nagging at the edges of her consciousness. It was still *too* quiet here. She detected no birdsong, no chatter of monkeys, no scurried passage of something small through the underbrush.

Then, as if something sensed her awareness, a branch snapped to her left. Her gaze flicked in that direction, but all she saw was a shift of shadows. Her eyes strained to pierce the walls of ferns surrounding the clearing.

Nothing.

But she knew the truth, remembering the angry roaring from earlier, along with the extreme caution of the guards when delivering her to this prison.

I'm not alone.

1:25 P.M.

Think globally . . .

Was that the answer all along?

Kendall closed his eyes, picturing the planet spinning, the crust riding atop a molten sea, all surrounding a sold iron core that was two-thirds the size of the moon. Convection currents in that molten iron, along with the Coriolis forces from the earth's rotation, generated an electrical geodynamo that engulfed the earth in a vast magnetic field.

"*Magnetism,*" Kendall said. "That's what keeps that shadow biosphere trapped under Antarctica."

"And where on the planet is the earth's magnetic field the *strongest?*"

"The poles." He imagined that field blasting strongly out from either end of the earth, encircling the globe. "And it's weakest near the equators."

"But where *else* is it weakest?"

Kendall knew the answer had to be tied to the location of the Hell's Cape. He pictured that hot world far beneath the ice, the perfect incubator for strange life. He remembered the sulfur, the bubbling pools.

He looked up at Cutter. "Geothermal zones," he said. "The earth's magnetic field is weaker in regions of volcanic activity."

"Correct. The molten magma underlying those regions cannot hold its ferromagnetism, creating a local dip in the earth's field, an island if you will in a sea of stronger magnetic currents."

Kendall imagined Hell's Cape as that island, trapped within Antarctica's stronger field. It still seemed a far stretch to assume that magnetic differential was enough to keep life trapped in place. Something had to make life down there especially sensitive to magnetic fields, something basic to its nature.

"XNA," he said aloud, sitting straighter in his chair. "All life down there is based on a genetic helix that doesn't use the sugar deoxyribose as its backbone. It's unique, unlike any other life. That sugar backbone is replaced by a combination of arsenic and iron phosphate." Kendall stared at Cutter. "It's the *iron*, isn't it? That's what makes the XNA life so sensitive to magnetic fields."

"I studied that iron structure using X-ray diffraction and photoelectron spectroscopy. It forms ferrous nanorings throughout the XNA helix, somewhat like vertebrae that make up a spine."

"And with exposure to the right magnetic signature, it should be possible to shatter that spine." He looked hopefully upon Cutter. "Have you calculated out what that signature is?"

"I did . . . and tested it. It's not all that groundbreaking. Your own FDA has already been testing oscillating magnetic fields to kill bacteria, viruses, and fungi in water and food supplies. I simply modified that study's finding and discovered the signature that works best in this case."

Kendall pictured the organism he created in his lab, shriveling up inside his synthetically created capsids, leaving behind those shells like so many discarded snakeskins.

"Without this cure," Cutter said, "I would never have unleashed your organism. Like you, I don't want the world destroyed by what you created. In fact, if you had chosen to cure Ms. Beck instead of seeking this answer, I would've told you anyway. I can't have the world dying before I can save it, now can I?"

Kendall glanced to the video feed. A flicker of dismay rattled through him, but he had to force it down. There was still too much at risk. "So you'll allow me tell the authorities in California about the magnetic cure."

"In time."

"What do you mean, *in time*?"

"From what I hear, your illustrious colleagues are about to ignite a nuclear device in those mountains. Foolish as that may be. As we both know it will do little good, beyond casting your organism over an even wider field, while irradiating much of that area for decades to come. But that is humanity's penchant: to destroy before thinking. It is why we are doomed as a species."

"But you said you didn't want my organism to destroy the world."

"I don't. Once you give them the solution, it'll simply take longer to clean their mess up. It'll keep them busy for a much longer time."

"And the radiation? All that damage?"

"The earth has survived such flesh wounds from mankind before, and it will abide this one, too." Cutter sighed. "Besides, this distraction will serve me well. To keep humanity looking one way while their doom comes from another direction entirely."

From your work here.

"And if you'll excuse me, I do have to make that call. See about getting a sample of blood from a *Volitox* before it's too late."

"Too late?"

Cutter paused. "You've been hiding that subterranean world for too long, Kendall, keeping it trapped, stunted from its full potential."

He thought he could feel no deeper level of dismay and shock. "What . . . what are you planning?"

"I'm going to flush that darkly beautiful and wonderfully aggressive biosphere into our world. I believe it's time they left their tiny island of isolation. Some will perish during this transition, of course, victims of the very magnetic flux we talked about, but as you know Nature is the greatest innovator. In such volumes and varieties, some species will survive by adapting, bringing forth to our world that XNA hardiness and mutability, perfect traits to survive the harsh times to come."

Kendall pictured the environmental damage from the sudden onslaught of so many alien species. An entire aggressive biosphere set loose upon the world. The ecological repercussions would be devastating.

"I plan to pit your ancient world below against the modern above. During that war, I'll unleash my species from here, casting them wide and far, bringing new and innovative genetic permutations, speeding up the evolutionary process by gifting these traits with the ability to jump between species. It will be the ultimate evolutionary crucible, where survival of the fittest will be the law of the land. To paraphrase the ancient Chinese strategist, Sun Tzu, within such *chaos* lies *opportunity*."

Kendall must have looked aghast.

"You can be at my side, Kendall. To witness this transformation, the genesis of a new Eden, free from the degradations of man."

Kendall pictured that prion-induced wildfire, knocking humankind back to a primitive state.

His eyes exultant, Cutter stepped back to the workstation. "Watch a small glimpse of that war to come, where the plague of man's intelligence is stripped away, leaving humanity bound at last to natural law."

Kendal knew which *law* Cutter adhered to with a religious conviction.

The Law of the Jungle.

Cutter tapped a key.

On the screen, the door to Jenna's cage swung open.

1:29 P.M.

"How much longer?" Painter called up to Sergeant Suarez.

"Another thirty minutes, sir!"

Too long.

Painter shifted in his seat, impatient, his upper arm burning, the pain stoking his anxiety. He was all too conscious of the deadline. The nuclear device was set to detonate in California in another ninety minutes.

And here I am sitting on my ass.

After another minute, Suarez shouted. "Sir, you might want to come up front and see this."

Glad for any distraction, any reason to move, Painter undid his seat harness and ducked forward. Drake snapped free and followed him up to the cockpit of the Valor.

"What is it?" Painter asked.

Suarez passed him a set of binoculars and pointed toward the distant tepui. It was still too far to make out any details, but Painter obeyed.

Suarez found a second pair of scopes and tossed them to Drake.

Painter took a moment to focus upon that distant mountain, its flanks shrouded in clouds.

"Look toward the south end," the sergeant instructed. He also motioned to the pilot. "Give us a little waggle."

Painter concentrated, leaning his bad shoulder against a bulkhead to keep his balance as the pilot shimmied the tiltrotor back and forth.

At first he didn't see anything, just wind-sculpted rocks and a scraggly forest at the north end. Then as the plane shifted again, something flashed brightly, reflecting the sunlight, sparking out from the forest of stones along the southern rim.

Drake whistled. "To get that much flare, that's got to be something metallic."

"I've been studying it for the past couple of minutes," Suarez said. "I think it might be a wind turbine."

Turbine?

Painter squinted, but he still failed to discern enough details to come to that same assessment. But the sergeant had the eyes of a younger man and had logged countless hours of aerial surveillance aboard the Valor.

Painter took him at his word. And if there were wind turbines up there, then somebody must have set up an encampment atop that mountain.

That could only be one person.

Cutter Elwes.

"Can you make this bird go any faster?" Painter asked.

This news made him all the more anxious to make landfall.

"Going top speed already," the pilot said.

Suarez checked his watch. "Twenty-seven minutes still to go."

1:33 P.M.

The click from her cage door drew Jenna's attention out of the fog of pain. Agony stabbed through her skull as she looked up. The persistent red light at the top of the gate had turned green.

The door fell open a few inches.

She remained standing, fearful it might be a trick. She used the rubber sole of her boot to touch the bars. There was no discharge, so she pushed the gate the rest of the way open and stepped free of the cage. Her boots crunched onto the gravel outside.

She froze at this small noise, the hairs quivering at the back of her sore neck. She sensed eyes observing her. She studied the road leading through the forest, picturing the gate and the electrified fence that closed off this level.

Even if I made it there, I'd still be trapped.

She faced to the cage again. The safest place might be back inside, locked tightly up, but there must be a reason the pens were electrified. It suggested steel bars alone were not strong enough to resist what haunted this forest.

Still, steel was better than nothing.

She edged back toward the cage—only to see the door swing and clamp magnetically closed in front of her. The light flashed to red again.

Locked out . . .

She struggled to think, to plan, but her mind had turned slippery, unable to concentrate on one thought for very long. She wanted to blame this lack of focus on pain and terror, but she feared this difficulty was a symptom of a more serious condition.

She whispered to the silent forest. "I am Jenna Beck, daughter of Gayle and Charles. I live at the corner of D Street and Lee Vine Road . . ."

Wait. Was that right?

She pictured the small Victorian with green gables.

That's where I live.

She took strength from this memory. "My dog's name is Nikko, and his birthday is . . ."

With each whispered word, she took another step across the clearing, choosing to avoid the road. Though, the decision might not have been a conscious one. Instinct drove her to hide, to get out of the open. She decided to trust that instinct. Her mantra dissolved to a silent internal monologue as she reached the forest's edge and pushed into the shadowy bower.

My best friends are Bill and Hattie. She let the image of the older Paiute woman grow more vivid in her mind's eye. *Hattie belonged to the Kutza . . .* She struggled for a breath, trying to remember her friend's specific tribe, her feet stumbling with her frustration; then she found the name.

Kutzadika'a . . . that was it.

She reached forward to move the frond of a fern out of her way—but she had forgotten about the unusual nature of the botany here. The plant flinched from her touch, curling its leaves and rolling all its stems into a tight ball.

Beyond that contracted fern, a massive creature appeared in plain view, only yards away. It stood on all fours, the size of a rhinoceros but as furry as a brown bear with a long thick tail. Its front legs curled atop savagely hooked claws, five to a side. Its muzzle and neck were massive, thick with muscle. Large brown-black eyes stared at her.

She froze, recognizing enough of the physiology to know that what stood before her belonged to the sloth family, those slow-moving arboreal herbivores that lived in the Brazilian forests. But this example was monstrous in size, a throwback to a great ancestor of the modern sloth. Though it looked like something out of the prehistoric past, in reality this species had gone extinct only ten thousand years ago.

Megatherium, she remembered. *The giant ground sloth.*

But Jenna sensed this creature was no more natural in form than what she had witnessed during her trip down here. Proving this, lips rippled back to reveal thick, sharp teeth, built for rending flesh from bones.

This was no herbivore—but a new carnivore born to this world.

With a roar, it reared up on its hind legs, rising to a height of twelve feet. A short arm lashed out, lightning fast, cleaving a sapling in half.

Jenna fell back, stumbling away.

More throaty cries burst from the jungle all around her, echoing off the stone walls, making it harder to think.

Still, she remembered the goat carcass getting tossed down to the road from above, possibly meant as a warning.

Heeding that warning now, she glanced up—and screamed as a shadow fell out of the canopy toward her.

28

April 30, 5:33 P.M. GMT
Queen Maud Land, Antarctica

"How long until this bloody thing is set up?" Dylan asked, pointing the radio clutched in his fist at the partially assembled LRAD dish.

The lights of the large CAAT shone upon the three-man team working at getting the six giant panels, each weighing eighty pounds, secured in a standing frame. Another two men connected cables from the portable diesel generator. Dylan had chosen a spot as far back into the Coliseum as he could get, facing the dish toward the mouth of this tunnel system, toward Hell's Cape station.

So far so good.

Dylan had left a small contingent of men back at that station. They had successfully blasted and blowtorched a tunnel through the station, opening a gateway to the world at large. Their efforts took longer than expected due to the additional caution necessary not to trigger the bunker buster bombs, which had been booby-trapped to explode if interfered with.

But everything went well.

All that was left now was to get this lost world stampeding for the new exit. The LRAD 4000X that was under assembly could blast an ear-aching 162 decibels and had a range of three miles, even farther with the echo-chamber acoustics of these caverns.

"How long?" Dylan asked again.

"Need another ten minutes!" a teammate answered, yanking on a cord to start the generator chugging.

Dylan shouted to be heard over that racket. "Christchurch and Riley, you're with me! I need the smaller LRAD atop that CAAT unhooked and brought down. Grab its portable battery and the remote activator for the 4000X."

His orders were immediately obeyed without question, even though what he requested had not been a part of the original plan. Dylan and his men knew the ramifications of what they were about to do, understood the ecological damage that would be inflicted from releasing this isolated and aggressive biosphere into the larger world, but considering how much they were getting paid, it didn't matter. Fixing the environmental damage would be someone else's problem.

Still, it nagged at him that he didn't know the entire picture. Especially after this call. He stared down at the radio in his hand. A connection had been patched through to him from Hell's Cape station, relayed from South America. It seemed Cutter Elwes had decided to alter the mission parameters at the last minute. After negotiating for a hefty hazard pay bonus, Dylan had eventually agreed, pushing aside his worries.

An extra two hundred thousand quid bought a lot of peace of mind.

Christchurch hopped off the CAAT, carrying the heavy two-foot dish under his arms as easily as if lugging a rugby ball. In fact, the man was built like a fullback, with his stout limbs and huge hands. Riley, a head taller and ten stones lighter, followed with the battery pack, winding the cables around his forearm.

When they joined him, Dylan pointed deeper down the tunnel behind the parked CAAT, to parts unknown. "Looks like we've got some hunting to do."

"For what?" Riley asked.

"*Volitox.*"

His two teammates exchanged glances, looking none too happy. He didn't blame them, but orders were orders. Plus, he was up to the challenge. He let his palm rest atop the butt of his holstered Howdah pistol. He looked forward to testing his skill against one of the most aggressive species down here—and the most dangerous.

Still, when it came to this hellish place—he glanced to the portable LRAD—*you couldn't be too careful.*

"Sir!" a man shouted to him and pointed to a pair of lights in the distance, coming their way.

It was McKinnon's team returning.

Finally.

"Once his team gets here," Dylan said, "start getting everything packed up. Keep this channel open in case I need to reach you."

With everything locked down here, he set off. Still, something nagged at him, kept him more on edge than usual. After following the river that flowed out of the Coliseum for fifty yards, he glanced back toward the pool of light around the work site—then off to the pair of lights still crossing the cavern.

McKinnon had reported in earlier, detailing the successful ambush of Harrington's snow cruiser. Ever the thorough soldier, the Scotsman had gone to make sure there were no survivors. But Dylan had heard no further updates from his second-in-command.

Distracted by the unexpected call from South America, Dylan hadn't given it much thought. But now . . .

He pictured that resourceful American firing from the back of that cruiser.

"Hold up," Dylan said. He pulled out his radio and dialed McKinnon's channel. "Wright here. McKinnon, what's your status?"

He waited thirty seconds and repeated the inquiry.

Still nothing.

Sighing heavily, he dialed up the work site and got an immediate answer.

"Sir?"

"Is the LRAD assembly complete?"

"All done."

"Keep hailing McKinnon. If there's no response by the time his vehicle reaches thirty yards out, activate the LRAD."

"But that'll knock his team—?"

"Do it. Once they're stopped, switch it back off, and go in fully armed. Secure that CAAT."

"Yes, sir."

Dylan lowered his radio.

No more surprises.

He pointed ahead. "Let's bag us a *Volitox*."

5:43 P.M.

Through a set of night-vision binoculars, Gray stared at the men working around the massive LRAD dish. He counted nine men. Earlier, Dylan had left with two others, heading deeper into the cavern system.

Bad odds . . . even with the element of surprise on their side.

"Ready?" Gray asked, yelling a bit to be heard.

Kowalski drove the rumbling CAAT, expertly learning to maneuver the treaded vehicle in the short time it had taken to cross the remainder of this massive cavern.

"As I'll ever be." The big man patted the machine gun across his lap, as if making sure it was still there.

Gray gripped his DSR rifle, its battery almost drained from so much recent use.

The radio on the dash squawked again. "Respond, McKinnon. If your comms are down, flash your lights if you hear this!"

Kowalski glanced to him.

It was the third call in as many minutes.

"Don't do it," Gray said. "That'll only make them more suspicious, not less."

The former British X-Squadron ahead might believe the CAAT had lost communications—antennas did get damaged in battle—but Gray suspected this last call was the equivalent of the enemy casting out a fishing lure. It would take extraordinary circumstances to allow their equipment to receive calls but not transmit a response.

For now, better to play deaf and dumb.

"They're getting antsy," Kowalski said.

With no other choice, they continued in silence, holding their breath, waiting for the inevitable. Then it happened.

The world exploded, screaming at them, vibrating the windshield. Gray's ears felt as if they'd been stabbed with ice picks. His vision closed in at the edges. Bile rose in his throat as vertigo spun his senses around.

Beyond the shaking windows, the world exploded around the CAAT. Creatures burst into flight, fleeing the cacophony. Others bound out of hiding, leaping, crawling. A towering *Pachycerex* thundered past, a blurry sight as Gray's eyes started tearing up. Soon it was hard to make out any details, just a tide of movement, retreating from that sonic assault.

Can't hold out much longer . . .

To the side, he watched Kowalski finally slump over the wheel.

Without its pilot, the CAAT slowed and stopped.

Then Gray fell to his side, sagging along the passenger window, but not before one last worry.

Not for himself, but for the others.

Jason, you'd better have reached that Back Door.

5:44 P.M.

Make it stop . . .

Jason hung halfway up the cavern wall, an elbow hooked around a rung bolted into the stone face, his toes jammed into the step. He hugged his other arm around his head, trying to block the sound and keep his skull from splitting in half. Snot ran down his face, mixed with tears.

Far off, a distant star glinted near the far end of the Coliseum, marking Dylan Wright's encampment. While climbing up the ladder, Jason had glanced frequently in that direction, worried that the British team would finish their work and activate the LRAD before Jason's group could reach the well-insulated substation.

His worst fears were realized a moment ago.

He also noted a tinier star on the cavern floor. It was the CAAT that Gray had commandeered. While scaling the wall, Jason had monitored its slow progress, but now he saw it had ground to a halt. Jason could only imagine the intensity of that sonic barrage when so near to its source.

It took all of his effort to crane his neck and stare up. Stella and her father were yards ahead of him. A small flashlight hung from the professor's belt. After the DSR died, it was their group's only remaining light source, found in Stella's backpack. She had given it to her father to help him see the rungs better as they ascended the ladder.

It was a mistake.

The noise suddenly ended, as abruptly as it had started. Caught off guard, Jason's toes slipped from the rungs for a hair-raising second. He scrabbled back to his perch, gasping, grabbing again with both hands. It was as if the strength of the sound had pinned him to the wall, and when it suddenly ended, his body rebounded outward.

He knew it was only an illusion from his assaulted senses. Still, he clung tightly for two more breaths before lifting his face.

Stella stared down at him, back lit by the glow of her father's flashlight.

"I'm okay," he said, his ears still ringing, responding only to the concern in her face.

Past her shoulder, something swept along the wall.

A *Hastax*.

It was plainly still panicked from the noise and lashed out at the nearest target, that irritating bright light invading its lofty territory. It dove and struck her father a glancing blow—hard enough to knock Harrington off the rungs.

In slow motion, Jason watched the professor go cart-wheeling past him, tumbling silently, vanishing into the darkness, nothing but a falling star now.

Stella cried out, a wail of anguish, one arm reaching, as if ready to follow her father's plunge.

"Stay! I'll go down!" He descended rapidly, though he didn't hold out much hope. "I'm sorry, Stella, but you must get to the station. Blow those bombs."

But was it too late?

A glance below showed a shadowy migration already under way, lit by patches of bioluminescence, flowing away from the source of that sonic assault. Even that short blast could have dire consequences. The panic here would inevitably spread and amplify down the long tunnel toward the exit, like a snowball rolling downhill.

Jason glanced to the distant lights of Wright's camp, knowing one other certainty: *That blast won't be the last.* With each toot of that horn, the panic would worsen. Unless that far exit was sealed, the world above was doomed.

"Wait!" Stella called down to him, tears in her voice. "I can't—"

He didn't have time to argue. "You have to!"

"Listen, damn it!"

He paused and glanced up at her.

"I . . . I don't know the code," she said, choking down a sob. "Only my father knows it."

Jason hadn't considered that possibility. He had assumed she knew the password, too. He looked down between his toes, to a small dot of light near the foot of the ladder. He closed his eyes for a steadying breath, then opened them.

"Continue up anyway," he said. "Prep whatever needs to be done. I'll follow as soon as I can."

"Okay," she answered, her voice small and fragile.

Good.

Even if there was nothing she could do above, he didn't want her to see her father below, not in the state he expected to find the old man.

Jason hurried, praying her father was still alive.

29

Jenna stumbled back from the shadow falling out of the canopy. Her scream stifled away as she struggled to make sense of what landed before her. It was a gangly boy of ten or eleven, with black hair and bright blue eyes. He was barefooted, wearing shorts, with a safari vest over a T-shirt.

He rushed to her, grabbed her hand, tugging a bit for her to follow.

"Come . . ."

In his other hand, he carried a long yellow cattle prod.

He pointed it toward the giant fern that had begun to unfurl its fronds again, starting to hide the massive beast on the far side.

The *Megatherium* dropped from two legs down to four. It hunched its shoulders, hackles raising high, the dark fur striped in blacks and browns, perfectly shaded for camouflage in this shadowy primeval forest.

It bared its thick, sharp teeth.

The boy pressed the button on the prod. Electricity danced in bright blue sparks across the U-shaped contacts. From the fierce display, the tool must be much stronger than any standard model.

The *Megatherium*'s eyes narrowed. Its massive razor-sharp claws dug deep into the soft forest loam.

The boy tugged on her arm again.

She retreated with him.

The beast stalked after them, moving deliberately, keeping its distance. At least so far. She glanced right and left, hearing branches snap and leaves rustle, paralleling their path.

This beast was not the only one of its kind here.

Moving more quickly, they backed their way to the gravel-floored clearing. The three conjoined cages stood in the center, still locked and electrified. There was no hiding inside there.

Still, the boy retreated until their backs were against that electrified pen. The cages at least protected against any attack from behind.

And maybe it wasn't just the cages that offered protection.

The *Megatherium* reached the clearing's edge and stopped. One clawed foot retracted back from the gravel, plainly wary of this place. Was this arboreal predator just uncomfortable stepping fully out in the open, or was it some memory, a warning of old pain? It clearly recognized the cattle prod.

The boy leaned his head a bit, checking the status of the pens.

The red light glowed from all three cages.

From the frown, he clearly had not expected that. He stared up at the canopy overhead. Branches hung low, easily reachable if you could mount those cages.

"Was that the way you wanted to go?" Jenna asked, not sure how well the boy spoke English. "Up into the trees?"

He nodded, showing he understood, but his eyes looked scared.

He must have done this before, learning to explore this forest from a safe distance. If he stayed up high, scaling among the thinner branches, the large predators couldn't reach him. Anything smaller he encountered could be discouraged with that cattle prod.

It was a good exit strategy, but surely they didn't need the cages to take advantage of it.

She pointed to a neighboring tangle of vines, one among many that draped down from the branches. "We could climb those."

"No," he said.

He bent down, picked up a larger stone from the gravel bed, and tossed it toward the vine. Where the rock struck, the leafy cord gave a muscular twitch, and hooked barbs sprang out, glistening with sap.

"Poisonous," the boy said. "Stings very bad, then you die."

She flinched, thinking about how blithely she had entered this bower earlier. She watched those hooks retract again, reminded of an Australian rain forest vine that was armed with similar barbed hooks. She tried to remember the name, but the growing fog in her mind made it harder and harder to think.

Off at the clearing's edge, the *Megatherium* returned a paw to the gravel, its claws digging furrows. Whatever fear held it back was waning.

The boy found her hand and squeezed tightly.

More shadows shifted around the edges of the glade, closing in around them.

Jenna pulled the boy closer and slightly behind her, ready to protect him. She whispered to him.

"What's your name?"

1:48 P.M.

A concerned voice drew Kendall's nose out of the stack of Cutter's research notes. He glanced over to see Cutter's wife enter the lab. She looked distraught, lifting an arm upon seeing her husband.

"*As-tu vu Jori?*"

"Jori?" Cutter asked, crossing from a workstation toward his wife, speaking French. "I thought he was with you."

Ashuu shook her head.

Kendall placed a finger down on the paper to mark his place. He had been reading rapidly for the past few minutes, not sure how long Cutter would allow him access to these files. They concerned his experiments with magnetism to shatter XNA strands, ripping those iron backbones under just the right pulse. He had scribbled down the man's findings on a notepad: *must generate a field strength of at least 0.465 Tesla using a static magnetic field.*

"We'll check the cameras," Cutter said, touching his wife's shoulder reassuringly. "You know the boy. He's always exploring. He's at that age, full of curiosity, his hormones beginning to surge, struggling to find his place in that world between a boy and a man."

Cutter crossed to Kendall and shooed him out of the way. "You can read those later."

Kendall rolled his chair aside, taking the papers with him. He had dimmed the monitor after seeing Jenna leave her cage and wander into the forest. He hadn't wanted to see what happened from there. Cutter woke the screen back up, returning the view into that forest clearing.

Kendall had been about to return to the notes when movement caught his eye on the screen. Jenna had returned, her back against those cages—but she wasn't alone any longer.

A young boy had her by the hand, holding a cattle prod.

Cutter leaned closer. "Jori . . ."

Ashuu hurried forward, saw the screen, and let out a small gasp of fear, clutching her throat.

Cutter turned, grabbed her by the shoulders, and gently but firmly shifted her toward Mateo. "Stay here, *mon amour*. I'll get our boy."

Kendall kept staring at the screen. He saw a dark, hulking shadow move into the clearing. Whatever it was, it remained at the periphery, but he imagined it was what he had briefly spotted earlier. He pictured those claws, that shaggy dark coat.

Megatherium.

A creature out of the last Ice Age.

"Look!" Kendall called out, drawing the other's attention back to the screen.

Cutter stepped over, glanced at the monitor, and swore.

By now more shadows shifted at the edges.

"You'll never make it down there in time," Kendall said. "But look at Jenna. Look at what she's doing."

1:49 P.M.

C'mon . . .

Jenna faced the camera. It was strapped high up a tree, pointed down into this glade. Earlier, she knew she must have been under surveillance. Luckily the boy had known where the camera was located.

She craned up to the lens and pointed an arm toward the cages, while making a cutting motion across her own throat.

Turn the damned electricity off.

The boy called to her. "Light is green!"

Finally.

She swung back to the cage. They had two options: hide inside and hope someone reelectrified the bars again . . . or travel the boy's path up into the canopy.

It was not a hard choice.

She glanced over to the *Megatherium*. The beast stood half in the clearing, half in the forest, balancing at that edge. She remembered it rising up to its full twelve-foot-height, each claw eighteen inches long. She didn't feel like trusting her life—or the boy's—to those thin steel bars, electrified or not.

And it wasn't just this one sloth they needed to fear.

She had caught glimpses of at least another four.

Pointing to the top of the cage, she said, "Up you go."

Jori passed her his cattle prod and clambered like a monkey up the bars. Once he reached the top, she passed the prod up to him. He crouched above, covering her, snapping sparks of electricity toward the *Megatherium* in the clearing.

She grabbed the cage, set a foot in the first crossbar—and watched as a sloth crashed out of the forest on the far side of the pens and came charging toward her.

She realized her mistake.

It hadn't been *fear* that held off the pack.

The beasts had waited until they knew the electricity was off, and not likely to be turned on again, using the boy like a test balloon. As long as he was up there, they knew they could attack without fear of getting shocked.

"Jori! Jump!"

She got the door open a second before the sloth struck the far side. She rolled inside the pen and slammed the door. Overhead, Jori leaped from the top, caught hold of a branch, and flipped expertly over it.

Under his heels, the sloth hit the triple pen, rocking the entire unit up on one edge. As the beast reared, claws grabbed the top edge, ready to topple the cages the rest of the way over. She would be trapped inside if it landed door side down.

"Jenna!"

Jori hung upside down and dropped the cattle prod toward her. Rather than falling cleanly through the bars, it struck askew, and began to roll down the slanted side of the pen, right between the paws of the giant. She scrabbled for it, grabbed the handle, and flipped its business end toward the towering sloth. She stabbed at the tender armpit, where it was less furred, and the contact points exploded against its skin, looking hot enough to sear.

The *Megatherium* bellowed and fell away, letting the cage settle back into place. Twisting to the side, the creature dropped down, licking at the sting under its arm, and retreated.

Jenna popped back out of the cage, waving the prod broadly, trying to encompass the entire clearing.

The *Megatherium* who was still in the clearing eyeballed her, one lip curling. But after a moment it also slipped backward into the shadows. In those eyes was a fury, a promise that this was not over.

She took advantage of the momentary lull to climb the cage door, roll onto the top of the pen, then leap to join Jori in the trees.

"Follow me," the boy said. "Very careful."

He led the way higher into the canopy, moving from stout branches to limbs that swayed under her weight. Once seemingly satisfied with their height, Jori set off on a trek that led toward the distant gates of this level.

She imagined he must have some way of getting past that barrier.

Then what? she wondered. *I'll still be trapped on this island in the sky . . . while a virus ravages a path through my higher consciousness.*

She pushed those worries aside for now. One problem at a time. That's all her mind could handle.

Jori followed a path with which he seemed familiar, knowing where branches between trees were close enough to leap or a bridge of vines could be crossed by hanging from hands and feet. Together they worked their way across the canopy.

"No!" Jori warned, moving her away from what appeared to be a simple jump to the next mahogany tree. He pointed to a hive growing on the far side of that trunk. "Hornets."

She nodded, not in the mood to get stung.

He led her to another, more difficult path, but she kept watch on that hive. A small sparrow darted among the branches and came too close to that buzzing mud-and-daub nest. A flurry of hornets burst forth, swarming the little bird. With each sting, its flight grew more erratic. Then it tumbled away toward the forest floor, still coated in hornets.

"Are they poisonous?" she asked Jori, who had noted her attention.

"No." He continued across a dense net of vines, balancing with his arms out. He reached the far side. "Sting with . . ." He plainly struggled with the word and rubbed his belly. "Juices that melt food."

She glanced more warily at that hive.

Digestive juices.

So their stingers must produce chemicals similar to spider venom.

"Eat you from inside out," Jori warned, as if this were the most normal thing in the world to state.

They continued for another twenty yards in silence, accompanied by nothing but birdsong and the squawk of parrots from a higher level of this garden. Then a softer mewling reached her, rising from the left. The plaintive cry drew her closer.

"No," Jori warned again. "Too dangerous."

She wanted to obey, but the noise sounded close, just in the next tree. She shifted around the bole of the mahogany and pushed leafy branches out of her face.

It took her a long moment to identify the source of the soft crying. A nest of vines hung from the branches across a short gap. A small movement caught her eye, a furred limb, about the size of a small child's, seemed to beckon, to plead. A set of hooked claws opened and closed, more in pain than any conscious will. She followed the arm down to a body the size of a bear cub, encased in loops of vines. Even from here she could see the barbed hooks, the dribbles of crimson blood. The body shifted, and the vines tightened, squeezing another cry out of the small creature.

Her heart ached at the sight.

Jori pushed her arm down and the branches she had been holding down snapped back up. "Law of the Jungle," he said.

She could tell he tried to say this bravely, as if it were a lesson he wanted to show her that he learned, but he looked mournful nonetheless.

He continued across the canopy, trying to draw her with him.

"Why did you help me?" she called out. "Why break the Law of the Jungle for me?"

He stopped and turned. He glanced to her face, then down to his hands, then away again. "You're pretty. Law of the Jungle." He shook his head. "Not for you."

With those sage words, he set out again.

1:55 P.M.

Cutter slammed through the hatch into the sinkhole, trailed by a pair of armed men. He had radioed for two carts to meet him. One held four more armed Macuxi. His sister-in-law stood before the second.

Rahei glowered at him, as if this were all his fault. Though the woman had the cold-bloodedness of a snake, she loved Jori. Only the boy could bring out a measure of warmth in the woman, but that love could also turn savage, transforming her into a lioness defending a cub.

Still, he welcomed that now.

They piled into the electric carts and raced around and around, barely waiting for the gates at each level to fully open, before scraping through to continue onward.

Cutter could not erase the image of his son vanishing into those dark trees, a habitat as dangerous as they could come. *What was I thinking stoking his curiosity for the life I'd created?*

He knew a part of it was pride, to see the respect and awe in Jori's young face. It was all the accolades he needed for his hard work and ambition. He had an audience of one and that was enough, especially if it was Jori.

He found his breath growing labored as tension and fear mounted. Rahei must have sensed it and grabbed his knee, fingers digging like daggers, telling him silently to hold it together.

For Jori.

At last they reached the final gate, and the two carts parked on the far side. "Leave the gate open," Cutter said as he climbed out. "If Jori is hurt, I don't want to lose a second."

He left one driver guarding the carts and the gateway. He headed down the ramp with the others, descending deeper into the forest's depths.

Cupping his mouth, he bellowed his challenge to this harsh world. "Jori! Where are you?"

1:56 P.M.

Kendall sealed the last zipper on his biosafety suit and entered the BSL4 lab. Before Cutter had stormed out, he had warned Kendall to begin his preparations for inserting that destructive code into his engineered shell. More worrisome, Kendall was instructed to expect a sample of *Volitox* blood before nightfall.

Kendall hadn't argued. He wanted access again to this quarantined space anyway. He glanced out the window to where Mateo and Ashuu spoke in low voices, their heads bowed together, a brother and a sister consoling each other. The giant loomed over the fragile form of his sister. She sheltered under his strength and support.

Kendall felt bad that he would have to kill them, but he had to reach a phone, some way of sharing with the outside world about the cure to what plagued California, a magnetic frequency that could rip apart his bioengineered organism at the genetic level.

The current chaos with the boy offered him his best chance.

Even Cutter had slipped up, a rarity for the genius.

Kendall patted his pocket, where he had hidden the object he had stolen from a tabletop while everyone was distracted. He crossed to the large refrigerators at the back, opened the doors, and searched the racks of vials. He thanked Cutter for his thorough cataloging and indexing. He quickly found what he needed and grabbed a dozen vials, shoving them into a pocket.

He glanced over his shoulder, making sure Mateo stayed occupied.

Only for another minute or two.

He strode over to one of the medical exam rooms at the rear, the spaces used for studying tissues and gross anatomies of Cutter's creations. Kendall stepped past the X-ray machine and the PET scanner and entered the copper-lined MRI room.

Magnetic resonance imaging.

The irony did not escape him. *Magnetism* was the key to saving the world, but it could also lead to Cutter's downfall.

He stared at the table surrounded by the enclosed ring of giant magnets. They were powerful enough to do great damage when operated by someone improperly trained or careless. Injuries, even deaths, had occurred due to mismanagement of these massive magnets, but they were dangerous for another reason.

He moved over to the quench box on the wall near the door and lifted the spring-loaded cover. The magnets of an MRI were cooled by liquid helium. In case of emergency, the helium could be rapidly vented to power down a magnet, but it was a dangerous proposition in an enclosed space, as in a sealed-up BSL4 lab, especially one buried in the heart of a tepui.

Most hospitals vented this pipe to the outside, but Kendall had already investigated and found that Cutter in his hubris had not bothered to do so.

Kendall leaned out the MRI room and checked on the situation in the main lab. Mateo was alone now, staring straight back at him. It looked like Ashuu had already left.

Kendall met the native's gaze, then pounded the button.

He dove out the door and flew headlong, sliding across the floor on his belly.

Behind him, a frigid blast exploded with tremendous force as the helium liquid expanded eight-hundred-fold, pushing oxygen ahead of that wave. Windows blew out into the main lab, smashing into Mateo's face. A chunk of magnet whistled past and struck a row of oxygen tanks in the next room. They exploded, ignited from a spark, and rolled into a fireball, challenging the freezing white cloud of helium erupting out that shattered window.

It was more of a detonation than he had been expecting.

He pushed to his knees, then gained his footing. He stumbled for the exit, choosing to climb out the observation window versus using the air lock.

I think I already broke containment here.

He saw Mateo crumpled on the floor, his face burned by the fireball, his hair singed away. Kendall had to step over him to get past the window, prepared to climb to the main villa above, to find a phone.

Something snagged his leg.

He glanced down to find fingers clamped to his ankle.

Mateo lunged up, his eyes shining out of his blackened flesh.

Kendall tried to escape, but Mateo lifted a broken glass cylinder and plunged it into his side.

30

April 30, 5:47 P.M. GMT
Queen Maud Land, Antarctica

"Nymph nest ahead," Christchurch announced, swinging his DSR rifle and pointing its IR beam along the riverbank.

Dylan called a halt and examined the site with a pair of night-vision binoculars. Twenty yards ahead, a small pool jutted from the main waterway, formed by a dam, not unlike what a pack of beavers might build.

Only this dam was made of bones.

The mud-packed mound of broken skulls, ribs, and other decaying remains rose waist-high, spreading in a curve, dividing the shallow pool from the river. Squirming in that pool and scrabbling over that abattoir were hundreds of gray muscular slugs that ranged from the size of fat thumbs to as long as his forearm. A few scrabbled on the neighboring bank, rooting through the mosses and algal beds.

He watched one of the older nymphs—as they were euphemistically called—bunch itself and leap from the rocky bank, fly across the pool, and dive into an opening in its foul dike, vanishing into its depths.

Dylan shuddered.

The nest was clearly still agitated from the sonic blast that had ended a minute or so ago. Though this tunnel was behind the LRAD, the backwash and echoing acoustics still extended somewhat in this direction. The low-frequency infrasonics had set Dylan's teeth on edge, like fingernails on a chalkboard.

"We'll move up another ten yards and set up the LRAD," Dylan ordered.

"So close?" Riley asked.

Normally Dylan wouldn't tolerate anyone questioning an order, but in this case, he didn't blame his young teammate. Dylan hated these vile little hunters with a passion. They were an abomination.

But right now he needed one.

"Move up," he said.

They crept slowly, careful with each step. Nymphs were known to attack en masse. To rile one of these nests was like stirring up an anthill. The term used by the researchers was a *boil-out*—when the entire lair burst forth in response to a threat. It was one of the most terrifying sights he'd ever seen, a carnivorous explosion that could reach tens of yards through the air.

So he understood Riley's concern.

Still, Dylan was a skilled hunter. He led the way himself, picking a silent path. Finally he lifted a fist and motioned for Christchurch and Riley to move to his right side and prepare the portable LRAD.

They worked as an experienced team. Christchurch lifted the dish high, letting Riley hook up the power cables. Once this was done, Riley took a step behind his teammate's shoulder, cradling the battery pack.

Dylan pointed to the nest, then gave a thumbs-up.

Riley hit the switch. The LRAD hummed for a second, then screamed at the nest like a banshee in heat. The reaction was instantaneous. While not as dramatic as a full boil-out, it was still a sight to behold, something out of the deepest circle of hell. Hundreds of gray bodies squirmed, bounded, and flew out of their nest, pouring into the main river. Those in the pools or along the banks followed their foul brothers, fleeing from the noise as if blasted by a leaf blower.

Dylan waited for a count of three, then made a cutting motion across his neck.

Riley flipped the battery off and Christchurch lowered the dish.

Dylan rushed forward toward the pond, his scrotum still tightening at the thought of getting near that rotting nest. He searched the pool, but he found what he wanted near the edge of the bone pile.

A single slug squirmed leadenly, stunned by the assault.

Dylan snatched it up in a gloved hand, careful of its circular maw of needle-sharp teeth. He hung it upside down, knowing that the glands rimming its mouth were full of flesh-burning acids, capable of dissolving through his glove to his skin.

With his bait in hand, he hurried to the river's edge. The nymph was already reviving, pushing out little appendages from its muscular segments, like legs on a centipede.

As it began to squirm more violently, he slipped out his dagger, slit the creature's belly open, and held out the gutted carcass.

Black blood flowed into the river.

He waited until the nymph stopped writhing, then draped the body on the bank near the water's edge. He bent down and tied a length of fishing line around its midsection—then took ten fast steps backward.

Once in position, Dylan signaled his teammates to move to his right side and switch the LRAD back on, to keep it pointed at the bone pile. While he lay in wait, he didn't want those other nymphs to come flooding back to the nest. Unlike the nymphs, what he sought to lure here was deaf to these sonic discharges.

He crouched to one knee, slipped the assault rifle from his shoulder, and placed it at his toes. To hunt this prey, he preferred another weapon.

He pulled out the Howdah pistol from its holster. He'd already chambered the .557 cartridges, one in each of the double barrels. Though the gun was over a century old—used to hunt rhinos and tigers by his ancestors—he maintained it in perfectly good working condition, expecting it still to be firing another century from now when his great-grandson eventually wielded it.

But he wasn't hunting something as meek as a lion here.

Faster than he expected, his prey arrived. The only warning was a V-shaped eddy in the water, sweeping toward the shore. Then from the river, a scintillating globe rose to the surface, borne aloft on a muscular tentacle. The toxic orb swirled in bioluminescent shades: brilliant blues, electric greens, blood reds.

It was easy to see how these deadly lures might dazzle and attract the denizens of this dark world, but Dylan ignored the display and used a thumb to draw back the hammer of one barrel.

The sphere lowered to the rocky bank, searching the shoreline blindly until discovering the slug's body. Nymphs were the offspring of *Volitox ignis*, an immature stage of this monstrous adult hunter.

The orb rolled the limp body around. Its oddly gentle touch did not burn the nymph's flesh, as if this *Volitox* queen could control her acidic fire. Little was truly known about the life stages of these creatures. They were too violent, too dangerous to truly study. But the researchers here had already recognized the strong maternal instinct of these queens.

Dylan took advantage of that now.

Lowering one hand, he pulled on the fishing line and drew the carcass farther up the bank and away from its mother. He teased the *Volitox* closer, letting it believe its offspring might still be alive and trying to crawl away.

The orb probed along its retreating path, stretching to reach the fleeing nymph's body. Finally the queen had to arc its bulk out of the water to continue her pursuit.

About time.

Her head beached up onto the riverbank, revealing its torpedo-shaped bulk, the size of an orca whale, but tipped by a circular mouth, like that of a lamprey eel. Inside that puckering maw lay a bottomless well of spiraling hooked teeth.

Dylan let go of the fishing line and steadied his aim, cupping one hand under the other. He centered his shot on the exposed base of the stalk, where he knew a huge ganglion lay, leading straight to the brain.

One shot there should drop this beast.

And if he missed, he still had a round chambered in the other barrel.

I never need more than two shots.

His finger firmed on the trigger and began to pull—

—when gunfire erupted down the tunnel.

Surprised, he twitched and his Howdah exploded. The wild round sparked off the rocky bank and ricocheted harmlessly into the darkness.

The firefight continued at the far end of the tunnel, accompanied by the distinct chatter of a machine gun.

What the hell?

5:52 P.M.

Huddled in the cab of the CAAT, Gray took out another man with a shotgun blast to the chest. The soldier's body went flying back. Out of shells, he tossed the weapon aside and lifted the Heckler & Koch assault rifle from beside his seat.

Nothing like commandeering a vehicle full of your enemy's weapons.

Not that he and his partner hadn't come without some firepower of their own.

Across the way, Kowalski stood outside the cab, crouched on the belted tread of the CAAT, shielded behind the open armored driver's door. He balanced his machine gun on the door's edge, creating his own makeshift gunner's nest.

Bodies littered the ground around the vehicle.

Seven total.

The two remaining soldiers teamed up and strafed the CAAT, giving up their attempt to reach the tunnel leading out of here. They turned tail and ran into the depths of the Coliseum, fleeing the lights and disappearing into the cover of darkness.

Gray took a few potshots at them, but they were gone.

"What now?" Kowalski asked.

Gray stared off into that cavern. "Guard the fort," he said, not trusting that the vanished pair might not try to retake this base. "I'm going after Wright."

Kowalski hauled his machine gun up and hopped down to the ground. He pointed his weapon at the bigger CAAT. "Time to switch rides. We have a river to cross if we still want to reach that Back Door."

It was a smart choice. Back at the bridge, he remembered overhearing a commando express concern about taking a smaller CAAT across those treacherous currents. The bigger vehicle would have a better chance.

"Keep a watch out there," Gray said.

"You watch yourself." Kowalski glanced back to the tunnel leading out from the Coliseum. "You're not going to catch these bastards with their pants down. Not a second time. Especially Wright."

Gray silently agreed, reaching to his ears and tugging out the plugs.

Their ruse had worked perfectly. Earlier, when he had first caught sight of the camp here, he had used the directional microphone built into his DSR rifle to eavesdrop on the soldiers' conversations. He heard Wright talking to someone on the radio. He could only pick up the commando's side of the call, but it was clear Wright had new orders, something important he needed to get before evacuating with his men.

Whatever that was, Gray intended to stop him.

Also, while en route, he had overheard the enemy's plans to use the LRAD against the approaching CAAT, to knock the occupants out and take the vehicle by force. Knowing that, he and Kowalski had found protective gear in their ride: plugs and noise-dampening earphones. Down here, where many of the CAATs came equipped with portable LRADs, such emergency gear was likely standard equipment.

So it was a simple matter of feigning incapacitation, slumping in their seats, which wasn't a hard act since that sonic assault was agonizing, even with the noise-suppression gear. Still, the trick got the enemy to successfully lower their guard. Once the ex-British soldiers were near enough—laughing at their supposed victory—Gray and Kowalski had let loose with both barrels, firing from either side of the CAAT, catching the entire crew by surprise.

But that's where their ruse ended.

Surely Wright had heard the brief firefight—and would be waiting for him.

So be it.

As he headed into the tunnel, he glanced to the far right, to where a twinkle of a star glowed high up the wall on that side. Jason and the others should have reached the Back Door by now. Gray had expected to hear that earth-shattering blast of those bunker busters by now.

But so far nothing.

What's taking them so long?

5:53 P.M.

Jason leaped off the last rung and rushed toward the small glow in the darkness. He had made the descent as fast as he could in the darkness, coming close to falling twice. But he knew now was not the time for caution.

He hurried through the muck and moss and reached Professor Harrington's body. The man lay on his back, his eyes open and glassy. Blood ran from the corner of his lips, one arm broken and twisted under him.

Oh, God . . .

Jason fell to his knees in the ankle-deep algal sludge. He touched the professor's shoulder, reaching with his other hand to close his eyes.

I'm sorry.

Then those eyes twitched, following his fingers. A small bloody bubble escaped from a left nostril.

He's still alive!

But Jason knew it would not be for long. A bony kink in his thin neck looked like a cervical fracture.

"Professor . . ."

His pale lips moved, but no words came out.

Jason hated to disturb the last moments of his life, but the situation here was too dire, the need too great. He reached to Harrington's cheek and held it.

"Professor, we need the code. Can you speak?"

Harrington's gaze found Jason's face. Fear shone there—but not for himself. Those eyes flickered up toward the distant substation, toward his daughter.

"I understand," he said. "Don't worry. Stella made it safely up top."

He wasn't certain of that, but a lie that brought comfort couldn't be a sin.

With his words, some of that anxiety dimmed from the professor. His entire body sagged into the soft bed beneath him. He likely only lived because of the thick, damp growth covering the stone floor.

"The code, professor," Jason pleaded.

The only acknowledgment was the slightest nod, only detectable because of his palm resting on the man's cheek. Jason tried to get him to speak, but the professor's gaze never left the glow of that distant station, to where he believed his daughter was safe.

Finally the old man gave one last breath that sounded like a sigh, dying with a measure of peace, taking his secrets with him.

Jason rose to his feet, defeated and grief-stricken.

There's nothing else I can do . . .

31

"Picking up a smoke column ahead," Sergeant Suarez said from the cockpit of the Valor. "It's rising from that summit."

Painter leaned to the window as the tiltrotor swept toward the lofty plateau of the summit. The engine nacelles turned, slowing their forward momentum. The pilot expertly shot the Valor over the tepui, banking slightly, then came to a perfect hover. Its blades chopped through a stream of smoke flowing out the open doors of a rustic French Normandy–style home, hidden within the mouth of a cave.

Had to be Cutter Elwes's abode.

Elsewhere, Painter noted a still pond and a sinkhole in the middle of a stunted forest. As they hovered, a handful of men ran into view on the ground, taking potshots at the intruder.

"Abramson! Henckel!" Suarez called out. "How about we show them how the Marines say hello?"

The Valor swooped lower, lifting Painter slightly out of his seat. The hatch opened on one side, bringing in the roar of those engines and the bluster of the props. The two lance corporals already had their lines hooked. The ropes were thrown down and the men rolled out just as quickly. They fired as they spun along those lines, dropping several assailants, scattering the rest.

The Valor's wheels touched down a moment later.

"Let's join the party," Drake said to Malcolm and Schmitt.

Painter followed, a SIG Sauer in his fist, as the Marines bailed out.

Suarez came behind them. "My men and I'll hold the summit." He tapped his ear. "Comms are open. Call if you need help."

Painter looked to the haze-shrouded home, knowing where they needed to search first.

Where there's smoke, there's fire.

Painter led the team at a low run toward those open doors. The Marines had rifles at their shoulders, their beard-rusted cheeks fixed to their stocks. Painter kept his pistol ready, gripping the weapon two-handed.

A lone assailant shot from an upper-story window.

Drake shifted faster than Painter could react—and fired. Glass shattered, and a body fell through and toppled to the stone. They rushed past and entered a huge reception hall.

Empty.

"Elevator!" Painter said, pointing his pistol toward the wrought-iron cage.

They hurried forward and found a handsome woman huddled on the floor in a neighboring alcove. She appeared unarmed, distraught. She offered no sign of resistance. From her puffy eyes and tear-stained face, whatever distressed her had little to do with their arrival.

Painter pulled out a pair of laminated photos: one of Kendall Hess, one of Jenna Beck. He held them in front of her face. "Are these two people here?"

She looked up, pointed to Hess, then the elevator.

Painter had no time for niceties, not with a nuclear device set to detonate in California in under an hour. He pulled the woman to her feet. "Show me."

She stumbled to the elevator and pointed to a lower-level button, somewhere beneath this home.

Painter let her go and piled into the cage with Drake. "Malcolm, Schmitt, search this place floor by floor. Look for Jenna. For Cutter Elwes."

He got confirmatory nods.

Drake yanked the cage gate, and Painter pressed the button. The elevator sank away, passing through solid rock, dropping for longer than Painter had expected. Finally, the smoke grew thicker, and the cage dropped into a huge lab.

Fires burned in spots, soot hung in the air, and a wall of glass looked like it had been shattered into this room from a neighboring lab.

A pair of struggling men rolled into view from behind a workstation.

The one on the bottom was clearly losing, his belly bloody, his neck throttled by a huge hand. His attacker lifted his other arm, baring a shattered piece of bloody glass. The aggressor's face was a blackened ruin—but Painter still noted the trace of a familiar scar.

He aimed his SIG Sauer and shot twice, both rounds piercing the man's forehead. The giant toppled backward to the floor.

Painter hurried forward, going to the aid of the injured man. He wore a biosafety suit with the hood torn away. It was Kendall Hess.

"Dr. Hess, I'm Painter Crowe. We've come to—"

Hess didn't need any more encouragement. Maybe the Marine in full battle gear behind him was enlightenment enough. Gloved fingers clutched Painter's arm.

"I need to get word to California. I know how to stop what was unleashed from my lab."

It was the first good news in days.

"What about Jenna Beck?" Drake asked.

Hess glanced to him, likely hearing the distress in the Marine's voice. "She's here . . . but she's in grave danger."

"Where is she? What danger?"

Hess's gaze flicked to a wall clock. "Even if she lives, she'll be gone in another thirty minutes."

Drake's face paled. "What do you mean, *gone*?"

2:04 P.M.

Jenna struggled through the fog filling her head. It took an extra thought for every movement:

. . . *grab vine.*

. . . *hook leg.*

. . . *shimmy to the next branch.*

Jori kept glancing back at her, his brow wrinkling in concern, not understanding why she was slowing so much.

"Go on," she said, waving him forward. Even her tongue felt sluggish and leaden, refusing to form words without that same extra bit of attention.

She tried her mantra to keep her moving like before.

I am Jenna Beck, daughter . . . daughter of . . . She shook her head, trying to dislodge that haze. *I have a dog.*

She pictured his black nose, always cold, poking her.

Nikko . . .

Those sharp ears.

Nikko . . .

His eyes—one white-blue, the other brown.

Nikko . . .

That was good enough for now.

She focused on the boy, following his actions, mimicking instead of having to think. He slowly got farther ahead. She lifted an arm to call him, but no name came out. She blinked—then remembered, the name rising through the fog, but she feared if that haze got any thicker soon nothing would come through.

She opened her mouth again to call him, but another beat her to it, shouting from somewhere ahead.

"JORI!"

2:06 P.M.

Cutter called again, growing hoarse. "Jori!"

Earlier he had heard an explosion, saw a strange aircraft thunder past the sinkhole, followed by an echoing spatter of gunfire. He felt his world collapsing around him, but nothing else mattered at this moment.

"Jori! Where are you?"

His group had reached the base of the corkscrewing ramp and started along the long gravel road through the forest. Rahei had the lead, shouldering a rifle equipped with a stun attachment. Five more men flanked and trailed him, all heavily armed. Cutter also had a triggering device for the munitions buried below the floor of this sinkhole. It was a contingency plan if he ever needed to cleanse this place, but at the moment, he contemplated it more as an act of revenge.

If these beasts harmed my son . . .

"Jori!"

Then to the left of the road, a faint call pierced the forest. "PAPA!"

"It's him! He's alive."

A joy filled him like no other—accompanied by a measure of dread. He could not let anything happen to his son.

Rahei fell back and pointed into the forest in the direction of his son's voice. If anyone could find him, it was his sister-in-law. She was one of the best hunters he knew. She set off, dragging them all with her. She did not curb her pace to compensate for any deficiency in those that followed, and Cutter would have it no other way.

"Papa!"

Closer now.

After another minute, Rahei rushed forward as a figure that was all gangly limbs dropped out of the trees into her arms. She swung Jori in a full circle, then placed him on his feet, giving him one hard hug.

Cutter dropped to one knee, his arms wide.

Jori ran up to him and leaped into his embrace.

"I'm very angry with you, my dear boy." But he hugged his son even tighter and kissed the top of his head.

From that same tree, another figure climbed down, falling the last two yards, but still landing on her feet.

Rahei looked ready to stun her into submission, but Cutter knew Jenna had not caused any of this. In fact, she likely saved Jori's life. He crossed to her and embraced her, too, feeling her stiffen in his grip.

"Thank you," he said.

Once loose, she swallowed visibly, looking like she was trying to say something. Her eyes were stitched with thick blood vessels, as they flicked around the forest.

She was nearly gone.

I'm sorry . . .

"Take her with us," he said. She didn't deserve to die down here, not any longer, not after saving his son. "Let's hurry. We'll take the secret tunnels down to the forest. I don't know what's happening topside, but I think we're compromised."

Rahei led the way again, setting a hard pace.

The road appeared ahead, but before they could reach it, the man to Cutter's left dropped, his head falling backward, his neck cleaved to the bone. Blood spayed the branches as he toppled.

Something struck Cutter from behind, lifting him off his feet and throwing him several yards. He crashed and rolled through a thornbush. He caught sight of a massive furred flank barreling past him. He rolled to his side, staying low as gunfire erupted all around, shredding through ferns, ripping away bark, but there was no longer any sign of the attackers.

Cutter sat up, searching around.

What the hell happened?

"Jori . . ." Jenna said, her voice strained. "They took him."

Cutter spun around, rising like a whirlwind, searching everywhere.

His son *was* gone.

Rahei stalked to his side, her face cold with fury.

"Where?" Cutter turned to Jenna. "Where did they go?"

Jenna pointed toward the darkest part of the forest, where the ancient jungle washed up against the walls of the sinkhole.

"Their caves . . ." he realized.

Megatherium were cave dwellers, using their thick claws to dig out burrows and dens.

Without a word, Rahei ran off, heading in that direction. Her disdain for all of them was plain. She intended to take matters into her own skilled hands.

Even if it meant wiping the entire species back into extinction.

"Let's go," Cutter said, preparing to follow.

Jenna stepped in front of him, placing a palm on his chest. "No. That's not . . . the way."

She struggled, shaking her head as if to knock her words loose.

He tried to move past her, but she blocked him, her eyes pleading.

"They didn't kill him," she tried again, pointing to the dead man. "*Took* him. Rahei. Her way—survival of the fittest—will get him killed."

"Then what do we do?"

She stared at Cutter, showing on her face all the sincerity and earnestness that she struggled to find in her words.

"We must go another way."

11:14 A.M. PDT
Sierra Nevada Mountains, CA

Lisa stood at the chapel window and stared across to the neighboring airfield. A drone helicopter the size of a tank sat on the tarmac. It was boxy in shape with four propellers, one at each corner. It looked like a giant version of those toy quadcopters sold in hobby shops, but this was no plaything.

In its cargo hold was a nuclear device strapped by thick belts to a metal pallet. A group of technicians still labored alongside it. Others stood on the tarmac clearly debating. She knew one of those men was Dr. Raymond Lindahl. As director of the U.S. Army Developmental Test Command, it was appropriate he was out there, but Lisa wished it was Painter instead, someone less reactionary, more able to think outside the box.

A voice cleared behind her. "You did hear that it's time to evacuate," Corporal Sarah Jessup said. "Detonation is set for forty-five minutes from now. We're already cutting matters close, especially as I heard that they might move that time frame up due to the crosswinds kicking up."

"Just a few minutes longer," Lisa said.

Painter has never let me down.

As if summoned by this thought, the phone rang. Only a handful of people had this number. Lisa spun to the receiver and yanked it up. She didn't bother getting confirmation that it was Painter.

"Tell me good news," she said.

His voice was full of static, but it was oh-so-welcome. "It's magnetism."

She was sure she hadn't heard that correctly. "Magnetism?"

She listened as Painter explained how he had found Kendall and that the man did have a solution, an answer as strange as the disease itself.

"Any strong magnetic force would likely do," Painter ended, "but according to some real-world testing, you want—and I'm quoting—to generate a field strength of at least 0.465 Tesla using a static magnetic field."

She jotted the information down on a sheet of paper.

"The effect should be almost instantaneous as that field shreds the organism at the genetic level, while not harming anything else."

Oh, my God . . .

She stared out the window, knowing the destructive force about to be unleashed needlessly here.

Painter had additional information. "Hess says that the nuclear blast will have no effect on this organism. It will only succeed in spreading it farther and wider."

"I have to stop them."

"Do what you can. Kat is already working up the chains of command to stop this, but you know Washington. We have less than forty-five minutes to move a stone that seldom budges."

"I'm already gone." She hung up, not even sparing a good-bye. She turned to Jessup. "We need to move Nikko. He's our only hope."

32

April 30, 6:15 P.M. GMT
Queen Maud Land, Antarctica

Dylan Wright cursed his failed shot.

He thumbed the second barrel's hammer back, wary of the beast before him. The *Volitox* queen still quested for the body of its offspring, hunching higher out of the water, its glowing lure rolling along the rocky bank.

Whatever that recent volley of gunfire was, it had ended as quickly as it had started. He pushed it out of his mind for the moment, concentrating on the immediate task at hand, at the looming danger before him.

A hunter let nothing distract him from the kill.

He pushed aside the humming backwash coming from the portable LRAD to his right, the dish still pointed toward the neighboring nest. He ignored the brilliantly hypnotic glow of the *Volitox*'s lure before him. He even dismissed the primitive terror at the base of his brain in the face of this huge monster.

Instead, he lifted his pistol and fixed his aim at the base of that tentacle, to where the buried ganglion offered a kill shot.

And fired.

The large-caliber round blasted slightly to the left of the thick stalk. While it wasn't a perfect kill shot, it was good enough.

The *Volitox* queen reared out of the water in a spasm, her flanks jolting with bioluminescent energy. Her mouth peeled open to splay thousands of hooked teeth.

To his left, Riley stumbled back a couple of steps, bumping into Christchurch, who dropped the LRAD dish. It clattered with a spark of electricity against the stone floor.

While the *Volitox* species might be deaf and blind, they were keenly attuned to electric fields or currents— *any currents.*

The spatter of sparks triggered a reflexive attack. The tentacle lashed out, finding Christchurch's neck. It wrapped once around his throat, burning that flaming gelatinous sphere into the side of his face. Flesh smoked as the soldier screamed, choking on a flow of acid down his lungs.

Christchurch was yanked off his feet, his neck snapping, and thrown far into the river.

Riley fled past Dylan and out into the darkness, back toward the distant camp.

Coward.

Dylan held his ground, remaining still, trusting his shot. He waited for death to take its course.

The *Volitox* queen—her last energies spent on this attack—slumped to the ground, her huge head cracking hard against the rock.

He waited a full minute, then approached cautiously with his dagger. He slipped a screw-top metal water bottle out of his pack.

Cutter Elwes had said he only needed the creature's blood.

Easy enough.

He stabbed the beast in the side and collected the black flow into the aluminum container. Once filled up, he secured the cap.

Mission accomplished.

Now to get out of here.

The pound of running boots reached him, growing louder. He leaned around the dead bulk of the *Volitox* to see Riley returning toward him.

Apparently the young soldier had found his spine after all.

Unfortunately he quickly lost his head.

A rifle shot blasted loudly, and the side of Riley's face exploded into a mist of blood. His body flew forward, crashing headlong across the cavern floor.

Dylan dropped back behind the carcass of the *Volitox*. His hand found his holstered Howdah, but he had shot his load. He looked across the cavern to where he had set down his assault rifle. If he attempted to reach it, he knew he'd suffer the same fate as Riley.

Whoever was out there was a keen shot.

He could guess who it was, picturing that American, knowing it had to be him.

Not dead yet, are you?

Maybe it was time to change that. He knew his adversary wasn't as knowledgeable about fighting in the dark as Dylan was. He planned to take advantage of that.

He called out. "It's high time we talked, mate!"

6:17 P.M.

"About what?" Gray yelled back.

He crouched behind a rocky outcropping about thirty yards from where Dylan Wright hid. He studied the terrain through his night-vision goggles. The body of the soldier lay sprawled on the rock between them. Earlier, he had heard another man scream, followed by a loud splash—then the commando he'd just shot had come running in terror.

By Gray's count, only one man should be left, the X-Squadron leader.

He kept his rifle fixed on the bulk of the dead beast beached on the riverbank. From the slack tentacle draped over its side, it had to be one of those predatory eels with the bioluminescent lures.

"About a deal," Wright answered. "The bloke I work for can be very generous."

"Not interested."

"Can't say I didn't try then."

Suddenly the world exploded in front of Gray, blinding him. He ripped off his night-vision goggles—just in time to see Dylan click off a flashlight and dash out of hiding. The sudden flare of bright light in the darkness, amplified by the goggles, still left a burn on his retina.

Gunfire erupted from Dylan's new hiding place.

Gray fell back, realizing his mistake. The bastard had used the darkness against him in order to reach a weapon. But it wasn't just the gun. A pop of electricity and a short hum erupted into a screaming wail.

An LRAD.

The noise stabbed into his ears, shaking the sutures of his skull. He had no protection against it this time.

Vertigo quickly set in. He lifted his rifle and blindly shot in the direction of the sound, but it didn't stop.

His vision squeezed tighter from the sensory overload.

He was moments from passing out.

6:18 P.M.

Positioning the LRAD dish atop a boulder, Dylan kept it pointed toward the location of the American. He then shouldered his assault rifle and shifted sideways, staying clear of the sonic cannon's blast. Still, some of the infrasound backwash crawled over his skin, raising the hairs on his arms.

He smiled, imagining what the American must be experiencing.

Ready to put an end to this standoff, he took another two steps to the side, almost back to where he hid beside the bulk of the *Volitox*. He sought a clear shot to take out his target.

Another step—and something bit deep into the back of his leg.

He reached to his thigh and yanked off a sausage-sized slug, taking a chunk of skin with it. Teeth gnashed at his fingers, burning his palm with acids. Disgusted and horrified, he tossed the nymph into the river.

He glanced back to the nest. With the LRAD diverted away, the builders of that bone pile must be returning. But for the moment, he saw no movement, no evidence of that missing horde. The nest looked as empty as before.

So where were they?

In his fear, his shoulder brushed against the *Volitox*'s body. He felt a tremor in that dead flesh, as if the beast were suddenly reanimating.

No . . .

He stumbled away, suddenly realizing the truth.

It wasn't the queen that was stirring.

It was something *inside* her.

Proving this, a fat gray grub squirmed out of a gill slit and dropped heavily to the shore.

Choking on horror, he backpedaled away from the carcass as more nymphs squirmed out of other gills, poured from that gaping maw, or corkscrewed out of nasal folds.

After fleeing the nest earlier, the nymphs must have sought their mother, hiding inside her, fleeing from the sonic assault to a refuge that was safe. The adults were immune to such attacks, likely protected by the bioenergies surging through them, which in turn protected their offspring in times of danger. He knew some species of fish and frogs could carry their young—but no one suspected this trait in the *Volitox*.

Dylan could also guess what had just stirred them up.

I did . . .

He glanced over his shoulder to the LRAD unit. He remembered how agitated the nest had been when his team had first arrived, still disturbed by the infrasonic backwash of the larger dish. When he activated the smaller weapon a moment ago, its echoing infrasound must have agitated the horde hiding inside that lifeless body, angering them.

He knew what was coming, what this activity was building toward.

By now nymphs poured into the river, onto the bank, several bounding with muscular leaps toward him. He dodged and batted at them with his rifle butt until he reached the LRAD.

He snatched the dish off the boulder and swung it to his chest like a shield, turning the sonic cannon toward the horde—and just in time. From river, rock, and flesh, the nymphs boiled toward him, a carnivorous wave of vengeance.

He held his ground, sweeping the sonic cannon before him like a fire hose. The nymphs cringed and squirmed away. Some sought to regain their mother's refuge, drilling through her dead flesh. Others dove back into the river, splashing heavily to escape the onslaught.

He let out a sigh of relief—until two blasts of a rifle exploded in the tunnel.

The *first* round severed the power cord to the LRAD.

The *second* took out his right knee.

As the cannon died in his arms, he toppled to his side, landing hard. He twisted to see the American standing near a rock pile, his smoking rifle at his shoulder.

Dylan faced his adversary for the first time.

No, not the first time, he suddenly realized, remembering that same face staring at him through a window at DARPA headquarters.

"That's for Dr. Lucius Raffee," the man said.

6:19 P.M.

Enough . . .

Still dazed and partially deafened from the sonic assault, Gray turned away, leaving Wright bleeding on the cavern floor—but not before he watched several of those carnivorous slugs leap across the rock and strike the man's chest and belly.

Wright swatted a few from his rib cage, but when he tried to grab the one on his abdomen, his hands were too bloody, his skin smoking from acids. He failed to get a grip in time and the creature drilled inside him, snaking away, like a worm into a diseased apple.

Wright cried out, writhing on the rock.

Satisfied, Gray swung around and hurried back down the tunnel to the entrance of the Coliseum, chased by the man's screams until they finally went silent. He found Kowalski waiting inside the cab of the larger CAAT. He clambered up the opposite tread and hauled through the passenger door.

"All done?" Kowalski asked, putting the vehicle into gear, the engines growling.

"For now."

"Been all quiet here . . . except for some cries out there in the dark. I think this place took care of those two deserters for us."

And Wright, too.

Gray pointed to the lights glowing up the wall, worried about Jason and the others. He didn't want to wait a moment longer. "Let's get to that Back Door."

6:22 P.M.

Jason crouched over the control console of the substation. Stella stood behind him, her arms hugging her chest, her eyes glassy with tears. She would glance often to the window that overlooked the Coliseum.

After Jason had climbed up here, he had told her about her father, about what had happened. She had merely nodded, the news expected but not welcome. She had barely said a word since then.

"Tell me about this code," he said, trying to get her talking, needing her help for any chance to solve this riddle. "Do you know if the password must be a certain length? Is it case sensitive?"

Jason stared at the access screen to the detonation controls. He had tried hacking his way past this level, but he kept hitting sophisticated firewalls. The security was rock solid. Without Sigma's decryption software, this was a lost cause.

He needed that code.

Stella finally spoke. "If this system is like the others at the station, the password could be any length. But the sequence must have both upper and lowercase letters and at least one number and symbol."

That was common protocol.

"Do you know any of your father's old codes?" he asked. Many people reused the same password for convenience sake.

"No." Stella moved closer to him. "And my father gave you no clue at all to his password?"

Jason stared into her wounded face. "He was more concerned with *you*. I think he only held out for as long as he did to make sure you were safe."

A single tear finally fell, rolling down her cheek. It was quickly wiped away. "What if it wasn't all about *me*, about my safety?"

"What do you mean?"

"What if the password has something to do with me? Maybe that was what my father was trying to communicate to you."

Jason considered this. Many people picked meaningful people in their lives to base their passwords upon. The professor certainly loved his daughter. "Let's give it a try."

Jason typed in *Stella* and tried various common iterations, but with both a number and a symbol required, the possibilities were too broad, too variable. It still could be anything.

He closed his eyes, trying to concentrate.

"Tell me about your father," he said. "What sort of man was he?"

A small trickle of confusion entered her voice at this odd question. "He . . . he was smart, loved dogs, was a stickler for details. He believed in order, structure, everything in its place. But when he loved something . . . or someone . . . he did it with all his heart. Never forgetting birthdays or anniversaries, always sending presents."

These memories slowly warmed the cold grief from her words.

Jason rubbed the scruff on his chin. "If he was that structured, then your father likely wouldn't have picked something whimsical as his code. It would be something practical, yet personal, to him." Jason turned to Stella. "Like your birthday."

"Maybe . . ."

Jason leaned over the keyboard, glancing back at her. He typed as she told him her birthday, using the British order for denoting dates.

17 JANUARY, 1993

He held a finger over the enter button. "This password *does* have an upper and lowercase letter, along with numbers and one symbol."

Stella's hand found his, squeezing hopefully.

He hit the button.

The same error message came up.

"That's not it," he said.

He had been so sure. It had felt right.

He tried the Americanized version.

JANUARY 17, 1993

Another failure.

A defeated tone returned to Stella's demeanor. "Maybe we should just give up."

Jason considered this option. He pictured that tide he had witnessed below, flowing away from that the earlier blast from Wright's camp. That tidal wave of panic was surely rolling inevitably toward the station.

But maybe I'm wrong . . . maybe one blast wasn't enough.

Plus so far, that sonic cannon continued to remain silent.

Surely that was a good sign.

6:23 P.M.

Dylan Wright lay in a bloody pool, racked in pain, barely able to move. He felt the nymphs squirming inside him.

I've become their nest.

Others fed upon his flesh, latched on to his legs, his arms, his face. They wormed under his clothes, burrowed beneath his skin, and explored every orifice.

In his right hand, his three remaining fingers clutched a small device. Shortly after being abandoned, he had pulled it from his belt. He must have passed out for a few minutes, but death would not take him.

Not yet.

Not until I do what I must.

He moved his thumb to the button of the remote activator for the LRAD 4000X—and pressed it.

Distantly, the world wailed, mourning its own doom.

If I must die this way, then let Hell take the rest of the earth, too.

6:25 P.M.

Gray covered his ears against the sonic assault, staring back the way they had come.

"Turn us around!" he hollered.

Kowalski had stopped the CAAT at the edge of the river, not far from the blasted-out bridge. They had almost made it back to the substation when the LRAD ignited once again.

What the hell?

Even at this distance, the barrage rattled everything on the vehicle and everyone inside it.

A moment ago, they had both searched for noise-suppression gear aboard this CAAT, but all they found were moldable earplugs, which they quickly donned. The crew working on the LRAD must have nabbed those more powerful sound-muffling headphones.

"Never make it to that camp without better protection," Kowalski warned. "By the time we got there, our eyes would be bleeding, probably our brains, too."

Gray knew his partner was right. He stared across the river toward the glow of the Back Door.

Then, Jason, it's up to you. You need to bottle this place up tight.

"What do we do?" Kowalski asked.

Gray considered his options. "I know one piece of noise-suppression gear we overlooked."

"What's that?"

Gray shifted out of his seat and retrieved something from below. He returned with it in his arms.

Kowalski nodded when he saw it. "That oughta do the trick."

Let's hope Jason is just as resourceful.

6:26 P.M.

Up in the substation, the wail of the LRAD rattled the glass in the frames and vibrated the floor underfoot. Stella and Jason stood at the window, staring across the Coliseum toward the pool of light near the back wall.

Had Gray failed to stop Wright?

Someone had plainly reactivated the large dish.

"Look down there," Stella said. "There's a CAAT stopped on the far side of the river."

Jason had already noted the twin spears of light glowing along the floor.

But are they friend or foe?

The answer wasn't as important as stopping that blaring train whistle that was driving all life down here toward the surface—or better yet, sealing that far exit permanently.

Jason returned to the control console. His last entry—Stella's birthday—was still entered with the red error message overwriting it. He hadn't tried anything else, stuck with a vague certainty that he was right about the password being Stella's birthday.

What am I missing?

Working swiftly, he tried other variations, abbreviating JANUARY to JAN. He changed 17 to 17TH. He tried writing the Latin and Greek equivalents, the ancient languages her father preferred.

Nothing, nothing, and more nothing.

Jason pounded his fist on the console. "Is there something else we're missing about your birthday?"

Stella shook her head. "Not that I know of."

Jason fought to concentrate, which was made especially hard by the muffled screaming of the LRAD.

"From your description," he said, "your father was a stickler for details, not prone to flights of fancy."

"Right," she said. "Maybe with the exception of this place. Antarctica. To him, the bottom of the world was always a magical place."

As magical as his daughter . . .

Then the answer dawned on him.

Of course.

People often employed a simple trick to make obvious codes seem more complicated, yet still maintain their simplicity or significance. That solution would have been especially amusing to someone whose only fancy was Antarctica, the land at the bottom of the world.

Jason typed in the new password and hit enter.

A green acceptance window opened.

"You did it!" Stella said.

Jason stared down at the accepted code.

3991 ,YRAUNAJ 71

It was Stella's birthday, simply written backward, a flipped-around version, like how one would have to reverse the globe in order to view this continent properly.

Jason clicked on the acceptance window to reach the detonation controls. A new screen opened with simple instructions. Jason followed them to the letter until at last a red warning blinked with a button that read *Detonate.*

Jason shoved back and motioned Stella to take his place.

"You should do this."

She nodded, reached forward, and touched that button.

6:28 P.M.

Gray stood atop the CAAT when the world jolted underfoot, bouncing the vehicle on its treads. A thunderous boom accompanied it. He glanced back toward the distant station—then up to the Back Door.

Good job, kid.

But in case those bunker busters failed to fully collapse the mouth of the cavern system, Gray lifted his own improvised noise suppressor and rested it atop his shoulder. Considering it had been Dylan Wright's weapon of choice up top, it was no surprise Gray had discovered it below in the man's CAAT.

He aimed the long tube of the rocket launcher and fixed its sights on the distant glow of the LRAD workstation—then pulled the trigger.

The rocket-propelled grenade blasted out of the tube and tore across the near-empty Coliseum. It exploded with a flash of fire at the back wall, striking true. The blast quickly echoed away.

He closed his eyes, enjoying this moment.

At long last, silence had returned to Hell.

33

April 30, 2:29 P.M. AMT
Roraima, Brazil

Jenna stood at the base of a Brazilian mahogany tree, her arms crossed. It had taken too long to retrace her path, the one she and Jori had followed through the canopy. Instead, it was the familiar buzz of the hornet's nest—the same hive that had killed that poor sparrow—that finally helped her find her way back to this spot.

Cutter touched her shoulder and drew her aside. "Stand clear."

From the canopy overhead, a pair of natives dropped to the forest floor. One carried a machete; the other bore a blanket-wrapped object under one arm.

"Hurry," she said.

The blanket was placed on the ground and folded back. Inside was the sloth cub, still painfully tangled in the barbed vine.

Was it still alive?

Jenna reached to pull the vine away, but Cutter pushed her arm back.

"Watch," he said.

He took a cattle prod and shocked the severed end of the vine, sending a charge down its length. It contracted once, then relaxed, withdrawing the hooked barbs back into its green flesh. Cutter used the tip of the prod to tease the loops off the cub.

Once it was free, Jenna bent down next to it, placing a palm on its chest. She felt a heartbeat. The ribs swelled and contracted with shallow breaths. Multiple small punctures covered its body, seeping blood.

"Jori . . . said poison," she struggled out through the haze and thick tongue.

"*Megatherium* are tough. I engineered them that way. It's why I made them omnivores, instead of herbivores. Gives them a wider range of nutritional options." He nodded to the cub. "They're also more resistant to this vine's toxin. Slowly adapting to it due to the vine's presence in their immediate environment."

She leaned down and scooped the cub into her arms. He was heavier than she suspected from his compact size, at least forty-five pounds. She carried him over one shoulder. She heard that soft mewling again, and his snout moved closer to her neck, leaning against her with a sigh.

"Caves," she said.

"Over this way," Cutter set off with his remaining four men.

Jenna kept among them, letting them lead, placing her boots where they did, wary of this dangerous forest. She held the cub close, shifting it from one shoulder to the other.

"Do you want me to carry it?" Cutter asked.

"No."

She couldn't explain why, but she knew she had to be the one carrying this burden. The creatures they sought were not dumb animals. Back at the electrified pens, they had waited until Jori climbed the cages before attacking. And now they had kidnapped the boy, possibly hoping the unspoken threat would drive these trespassers off their lands. For Jori to have any chance, she had to respect their intelligence.

Slowly the forest grew taller, the canopy thicker. The sunlight waned down to a persistent emerald twilight, while the fungi growing along the trunks seemed brighter. As they hiked, the undergrowth also thinned out, starved of the sunlight by the taller trees.

At last the darker shadows ahead became discernible as cliffs of black rock, draped with vines and orchids. The air grew muskier with the reek of damp pelts and the rot of spoiled meat. Multiple cave openings appeared. Some looked entirely natural; others looked widened by the scratching and sharpening of claws.

Cutter slowed their pace.

The denizens of these caves were nowhere in sight.

"What now?" Cutter asked.

"I should go," Jenna mumbled out. "Alone. Stay here."

She passed Cutter and headed forward on her own. She crossed until she could see the darker shadows shifting in those black caves.

Watching me . . .

She lifted the cub, crossed her legs, and sank to her backside, cradling the small sloth in her lap. He mewled a soft complaint, batted her with a hooked claw, but then settled.

She sat there, waiting.

At some point she started to hum a lullaby, not remembering the words, but the melody remained inside her.

Finally a lone sloth appeared, knuckling on her claws, and it was plainly a female from her stained teats on her chest. The female bobbed her head up, letting out a soft chuffing noise.

The cub stirred, rolling his head toward the sound, and gave off a couple of answering bleats.

Clearly mother and child.

Very slowly Jenna lowered the cub to the ground and retreated away, staying hunched, her head bowed submissively.

The female crept forward, scooped the body up one-armed, using those claws like gentle hooks to pull the cub to her chest. Then she turned and lumbered back into her den.

Jenna sat again, waiting. Occasionally she would nudge her chin up and imitate that chuffing noise. The pack here had seen her traveling through the canopy with Jori. They would believe he was her child. It was why she had to carry that cub herself. Getting its scent all over her. To intensify the sense of maternity and nurturing.

After another ten minutes passed, she found it harder to think. For a brief moment, she forgot why she was here. She started even to rise. Then movement again. A small figure came running out of a cave to the left.

Jori ran up to her and hugged her, flying hard enough to roll her to her back.

"Careful," she said hoarsely.

He helped her up. She did so with great care.

Then a massive bull sloth charged out of a cave and barreled toward her. She pushed Jori behind her, knowing if she ran they'd both be killed. She stood her ground, arms out, sheltering the boy. She kept her face turned, not wanting to challenge him.

The *Megatherium* bull skidded to a stop, its nose right at her face. Its breath blew the small hairs from her damp face, reeking of blood and meat and savageness. She knew it was the same creature from earlier, the same one who had followed her to the edge of the clearing.

It sniffed her in turn, moving from face to crotch— then bumped her with that nose, not to dismiss her, but as some manner of acknowledgment, as if to say *I know you, too.*

It began to turn away, and she took a step backward.

A gunshot cracked across the silent jungle.

The bull's ear exploded into a pulp of blood and fur. It roared, swinging around and clubbing her in the side, knocking her flying.

Another shot struck its flank, flinching the limb on that side.

"Run, Jori," she said, struggling for breath after the blow.

The boy refused, coming instead to help her. Cutter saw this and came rushing low toward them, ready to protect his son.

Another shot struck the beast in the head, but it glanced off the thick skull. Jenna spotted Rahei flat on her belly near a rock fall by the cliff's edge. She must have crept into that position very slowly, keeping her presence from the pack.

Cutter reached them, grabbed Jori by the arm, and pulled the boy back with him.

The bull noted this movement and charged.

Jenna managed to pull Jori to the ground, rolling on top of the boy. Cutter took the full brunt of that fury as he was bowled onto his back and a claw ripped through his vest and shirt, scouring a bloody track down his chest.

The other men behind Cutter opened fire, a fierce barrage.

The poor beast hunched itself against that onslaught, as if leaning into a stiff breeze. But even its majestic bulk could not sustain such damage for long. It trembled, took a step backward, and fell heavily to the ground, almost crushing Cutter.

Jenna hurried with Jori in tow, both of them collecting Cutter from the ground.

Rahei came bounding as light as a gazelle from out of hiding, plainly triumphant for her part in slaying the beast. Still, she kept wary watch on the cave openings, never turning her back.

From one of the tunnels, a smaller *Megatherium* charged out of a den, maybe the mate to the slain bull. Rahei swung her rifle and fired, but the first shot only grazed the beast's shoulder. The creature's other forelimb cast out toward Rahei, claws unfolding, as the beast braked hard in the loam. From its grasp, the *Megatherium* launched something wrapped in a leaf. As it flew, the leaf fluttered open and fell away. What it had held—something small and black—spun through the air and struck Rahei in the cheek.

She stumbled back as if hit by a bullet. Her face turned, revealing a small ebony-skinned frog glistening on her cheek. Rahei screamed, dropping her rifle and pawing at her face. She knocked the amphibian off, but emblazoned on her skin remained a bloodred burn in the shape of that frog. Rahei fell to her knees, her spine arching backward, her mouth open, her limbs quaking in a grand mal seizure.

Then finally she collapsed to her side, unmoving, dead, the mighty hunter brought down by a lowly frog.

Must have been one of Cutter's toxic creations.

As if the violent death were a cue, more of the sloths charged out, drawn by the scream, the bloodshed, the death of one of their own.

Jenna retreated with the others, pursued through the jungle, chased by the roaring from many throats.

They all simply ran, forgoing any attempt to even fire at the beasts.

Never make it . . .

Then the canopy ripped apart over them, letting in the blinding sun shattering the darkness. Winds whipped and tore at the forest. The craft overhead roared far louder than any *Megatherium*.

The pack fell back, intimidated and confused. Then as one, the beasts slunk back into the deeper shadows and retreated.

Lines fell from the aircraft, and men traveled smoothly down them to land in the forest, carrying heavy automatic weapons and wearing body armor.

Cutter's group was quickly subdued, stripped of their weapons.

One of the soldiers came forward to her. "You're a hard lady to find."

He tipped his helmet back, revealing a familiar face. Even through the fog, she knew him—and smiled. Relief flooded through her, accompanied by a surge of warmth from deeper inside, an emotion still new and unexplored with this brave man.

"Drake . . ."

"At least you remember me. That's gotta be a good sign." He reached forward, jabbed a syringe into her neck, and pushed the plunger. "A small gift from Dr. Hess."

2:39 P.M.

Cutter rose through the air on a stretcher, lifting free of the dark canopy and out into the blaze of the day. He surveyed his handiwork, the many-tiered gardens, his Galapagos in the sky. He took a moment to appreciate his triumphs and defeats.

Around him was a crucible of evolution, one driven by a simple edict.

Survival of the fittest.

The Law of the Jungle.

But doubt had settled into that perfect garden of his soul, a bright seed of new possibility, shown to him by the small figure of a woman, an Eve in the guise of a park ranger. She had pointed to a new Eden, maybe one that need not be so *dark*.

He had witnessed today something new.

The Law of the Jungle was not all there was to life, to evolution, but that in equal parts altruism, even morality, could be as strong an environmental factor as any, a wind for change to drive the world to a more vital, healthier existence.

Yes . . .

It was time to start anew, to plant a fresh garden.

But to do that, the old one must die and be tilled over.

Besides, it is my work. Why should I share it with a world that was far from ready, too myopic to see as clearly as myself?

He slipped a hand to his pocket, picturing the munitions buried in the oldest tunnels underneath the sinkhole.

He pressed the button, activating the countdown.

God created the heavens and the earth in seven *days*.

He would destroy his in seven *minutes*.

11:40 A.M. PDT
Sierra Nevada Mountains, CA

Lisa rode in the back of a Dodge Ram 2500 fitted with a camper shell as it raced across the Marine base. She kept a hand on Nikko's sealed gurney to steady it. Up front, Corporal Jessup sat beside her boyfriend, an apple-cheeked young chaplain with a big heart named Dennis Young.

As she requested, he had the pedal firmly pressed to the floor, flying across the deserted base. They had no time to spare with trivialities like stop signs or traffic lights. She stared down at Nikko. The dog would not likely last past the next couple of hours. He was show-ing evidence of major organ failure.

Hang in there, Nikko.

They sped into the empty parking lot of the small base hospital. The medical facility had just upgraded their radiological suite to include an MRI machine. Edmund Dent already waited at the entrance. Lisa had used the time preparing Nikko for transport to gather all key players to this one spot.

The Ram truck blasted into the emergency bay and braked hard in front of Edmund. The virologist waved to some of his colleagues who were also scheduled to leave on the last chopper. Together, they all got Nikko out and rolling toward the radiology unit.

Edmund panted beside her. "Already got the scanner warmed up. A technician attuned the magnets to"—he checked what was written on the back of his hand—"0.456 Tesla. Static field."

"What about a sample of the engineered organism?"

"Oh, right here." He reached to a pocket and pulled out a test tube that was tightly plugged and duct-taped.

Nothing like improvisation.

They reached the radiology unit to find two members of the nuclear team, along with Dr. Lindahl.

"This had better not be a waste of everyone's time," Lindahl greeted her. "Plus after this is all over, I'm going to initiate a formal inquiry into your behavior. Absconding with a test patient."

"Nikko is not a *test* patient. He's a decorated search-and-rescue dog who just happened to get sick assisting all of us."

"Whatever," Lindahl said. "Let's get this over with."

It took four of them to lift Nikko's sealed patient containment unit from the gurney and place it on the MRI table.

The technician pounded on the glass. "No metal!"

Lisa swore under her breath. In all her haste, she hadn't considered this detail. Nothing metallic could go through an MRI machine; that included the components of Nikko's patient containment unit.

Edmund looked at her.

Got to do this the hard way.

She pointed to the door. "Everyone out."

"Lisa . . ." Edmund warned. From his tone, he knew what she was planning. "What if the data is false? Or simply wrong?"

"I'll take that chance versus nuking these mountains. Besides, the science sounds right." She shooed him toward the door, taking his test tube first. "Out."

Once clear, she crossed to Nikko's PCU, took a deep breath, and cracked it open.

Painter, you'd better be right.

With great care, she gently lifted Nikko over to the table. His limp form seemed much lighter, as if something vital had already left him. She placed him down and rested a hand on his side. It felt good to be able to touch him with her bare hands rather than with a glove. She combed her fingers through his fur.

Good boy.

She placed the tube of virus next to the dog and gave the technician a thumbs-up.

After a few seconds, the machine erupted with a noisy clacking, and the table holding Nikko slowly slid through the ring of those magnets. They did a double pass to make sure.

All the while, she paced the room nervously, chewing a thumbnail.

Gonna need a manicure before the wedding.

"That's it," the technician announced over the intercom.

Lisa quickly took a syringe from a rolling plastic cart and drew a blood sample from Nikko's catheter. She injected the syringe into a Vacutainer tube. Then sealed both it and Edmund's tube into a hazardous waste bag, which she handled only with sterile gloves. She left it near the door and stepped back.

Edmund risked collecting it himself.

"Hurry," she said.

He nodded and raced off, heading to his lab at the hangar.

It was the longest ten minutes of her life. She used the time to pass her own body through the scanner to kill any contamination from handling Nikko. She then sat on the table with him, cradling his head on her lap.

Finally a call came through, patched through the intercom.

She heard the triumph in his voice. "Dead. It's all genetic mush. Both the raw sample and the viral load in Nikko's blood."

She closed her eyes and bent over Nikko.

"See what a good boy you are," she whispered to him.

She took another moment to collect herself, then picked up the phone and spoke to Edmund. "What's the plan from here?"

She heard arguing in the background, raised voices, most of it coming from Raymond Lindahl.

"Still trouble," Edmund said. "And you can guess from who."

She hung up and stared at the door, wondering what she should do.

Before she could decide, the door shoved open, and Sarah flew in, pointing a finger at her. "I heard. You'd better get over there. I'll dog-sit. Dennis will drive you."

She smiled, hugged the corporal, and flew out the door.

Dennis drove his Ram truck at top speed over the quarter of a mile to the hangar. She was out the door before it had even stopped moving. She ran into the hangar to find Lindahl with his back to her, nose to nose with the head nuclear technician.

"We stick to the original plan until I hear otherwise from D.C.," Lindahl said. "All these new results are . . . are at best preliminary. And in my opinion, still disputable."

"But, sir, I can readily modify—"

"Nothing changes. We stay the course."

Lisa strode up behind Lindahl and tapped him on the shoulder. When he turned with a look of stunned surprise to find her there, she drew back her arm and punched him hard in the face. His head snapped back, and he slumped leadenly to the floor.

Wincing, she shook her hand and nodded to the head tech. "You were saying?"

"From what we just learned, I should be able to lower the yield of our nuke to as little as a single kiloton. If we can get that bomb to blow four miles up—which that drone chopper can reach—it should produce an electromagnetic pulse of at least 0.5 Tesla. It'll cover more than enough territory to sweep the hot zone with negligible radiation. Nothing worse than what you'd get from a dental X-ray."

"How long will it take?"

"I can still make that noon deadline."

She nodded. "Do it."

"What about D.C.?"

"Let me worry about D.C. You get that nuke in the air."

As he hurried off, she looked at her bruised knuckles. *Definitely will need a manicure.*

2:45 P.M.
Roraima, Brazil

Kendall watched the tepui drop below as the V-280 Valor fled from the summit. They had only a minute to spare before Cutter's charges exploded, destroying his macabre experiment in synthetic biology and genetic engineering.

Good riddance.

He returned his attention to the cabin. The space was packed with people. Cutter's private helicopter had already left with Ashuu and Jori, but only after ferrying two flights of native workers out into the surrounding rain forest, getting them clear of any danger.

He presently shared the back of the cabin with Cutter, who was strapped down in his stretcher, one wrist handcuffed to a railing. An IV line ran to a catheter in the back of his hand. His deep wounds still needed surgical attention, but a thick compression wrap around his chest should last until the aircraft reached Boa Vista in a couple of hours to refuel.

Cutter stared out the window near his head. "Ten seconds."

Kendall followed the other's gaze toward that cloud-wrapped summit. He silently counted down. When he reached zero—a towering blast of smoke and rock shot from the summit, occluding the sun, turning it bloodred. Thunder rolled over that shattered mountaintop, as if mourning the deaths of so much strange life. Then slowly the plateau cracked, shedding a shoulder of rock, like a calving glacier. The pond on top spilled over that fracture, reflecting that bloody sunlight, becoming a flow of fire down that broken rock.

"Beautiful," Cutter whispered.

"A fitting end to Dark Eden," Kendall added.

Cutter glanced over to Jenna. "But you saved a sliver of it. For her."

"And maybe for the world." He pictured his frantic search for those vials before destroying the lab. "That counteragent may hold some promise of treatments for other mental disabilities. It will certainly bear more study. Some good may yet come from your work."

"And you saved nothing else? Nothing from my genetic library?"

"No. It's better off lost forever."

"Nothing's lost forever. Especially when it's all up here." Cutter tapped a finger against his skull.

"It won't be there for long," Kendall said.

The man was simply too dangerous.

With everyone distracted by the show beyond the window, Kendall lifted what he had secretly pocketed back at the lab, what Cutter himself had foolishly left on a tabletop in his panic over his son. He leaned forward and pressed the jet-injector pistol against the side of the man's throat. It was the same tool used on Jenna. The intact vial still held one last dose of Cutter's engineered code.

Cutter's eyes widened with horror as Kendall pulled the device's trigger. Compressed gas shot the dose into the man's neck.

With his other hand, Kendall injected a sedative into Cutter's IV.

"By the time you wake, my friend, it'll all be over."

Cutter looked on in dismay.

"This time Cutter Elwes will die," Kendall promised. "Maybe not the body, but the man."

34

"Wasn't exactly your beachside wedding," Painter said, swirling a glass of single malt in one hand, the love of his life snuggled under his other arm.

"It was perfect." Lisa pulled tighter against him.

They had both changed out of formal attire and found this deep-cushioned love seat before the massive stone fireplace of the Great Lounge of the Ahwahnee Hotel. The reception party was winding down behind them as guests either filtered to rooms or headed home.

The wedding had been at sunset on a great swath of lawn, beautifully lit, flowers bountiful, including his wife's favorite chrysanthemums, each petal a deep burgundy trimmed in gold. The hotel had even picked up the tab, a small thank-you for all the pair had done to save the valley and surrounding area. The generous offer was made possible because tourism was still slow to return.

Bioterrorism and nuclear bombs . . .

It would take a little more time to shake that reputation, but it made it easier to arrange these last-minute wedding plans. They had held off until Josh was recovered enough to attend, sporting the latest in DARPA prosthetics. He and Monk had plenty to talk over at the dinner table. Lisa's kid brother was remarkably resilient considering the circumstances, even amped to get back out on the mountains and face new challenges.

The final reason they'd chosen this venue was its proximity to the cleanup and monitoring of the neighboring Mono Lake area. Lisa was still working with Dr. Edmund Dent, the virologist, and his team. In turn, Painter used the opportunity to spend some time away from the office with Lisa. Kat was able to handle the day-to-day, with the exception of this weekend.

She and Monk had left shortly after dinner with the two girls propped up in their arms, returning to their rooms before an early morning flight home. During their absence, Gray had been holding down the fort out in D.C., having to stick close to home for personal reasons.

Some other guests, well . . .

Kowalski sidled up to them, his jacket over one arm, the top two buttons of his shirt undone. He puffed on a cigar.

"I don't think you're supposed to smoke in here," Lisa warned.

Kowalski took the stogie out and stared at it. "C'mon, it's a Cuban. Can't get any more formal than that."

Jenna passed behind him with Nikko on a leash. "Gotta see a man about a horse!" she said, heading for the parking lot. "Or at least Nikko does."

Like Josh, the Siberian husky had fully recovered, even earning a medal for his actions.

Kowalski scowled after the pair and shook his head. "First Kane, now that dog. Before long, Sigma will have to build its own kennel." He pointed his cigar at Painter. "And don't get any ideas—I'm not cleaning up after them."

"Deal."

Kowalski nodded and headed away in a cloud of cigar smoke.

Painter sighed and held out his hand. "Shall we retire ourselves?"

"Certainly." She placed her palm atop his. "But you weren't expecting to sleep?"

With a gentle tug, Painter pulled her to him, slid his hand behind her head, and kissed her, breaking away only long enough to say, "Who can sleep? We've got a family to start."

May 30, 6:36 A.M.
Lee Vining, California

Jenna headed down 395 through the center of town in her new Ford F-150 pickup, freshly decaled with the star of the California State Park Rangers. It was courtesy of the department after everything that had happened. Even the interior still had that new-car smell.

Not that it'll stay that way for long.

Nikko panted in her ear from the backseat. She would normally scold him, but instead she reached back and scuffled his muzzle. Though he had recovered physically, she could read the smaller signs of post-traumatic stress. He clung more to her and was incrementally less apt to charge into situations, but he was slowly recovering even from that.

Like me.

She still remembered the sense of feeling herself slipping away, the fog flowing thicker, filling her up and pushing all else out.

Even now she shuddered. She found herself constantly doing personal inventory. If she forgot her keys, was that a sign of residual damage? What if she fumbled for a word or couldn't recall an address or phone number? That alone was disconcerting.

So she had taken to getting up at daybreak. She had always loved the mornings on the lake. The sun turned the mirrored waters into myriad shades, changing with each season. The streets stayed mostly deserted. Or if it was high season, then the city would just be beginning to wake, yawning and stretching its legs.

The quiet of the mornings had always given her time to think, to collect herself. And right now she needed that more than anything.

But mornings meant one other thing to her now.

She picked up the radio and called into dispatch. "Bill, I'm going to stop and fuel up."

"Got it."

She parked under the yellow sign of Nicely's Restaurant and hopped out, followed by Nikko. She headed inside, the bell tinkling. Behind the counter, Barbara lifted the to-go cup already full of hot black coffee, the best in town, and tossed Nikko a dog biscuit, which he caught midair, a skill learned from years of experience.

But she now had a new routine.

A figure called to her from a booth, not even bothering to look up from his paper. "Morning, dear."

She crossed and slid into the booth with her coffee. "So what's your day look like?" she asked Drake. He had accepted a permanent position as a Marine trainer at the mountain base.

"You know," he said, "probably have to save the planet again."

She nodded, sipped her coffee, winced at the heat. "SSDD."

Same shit, different day.

He passed her the sports page, which she accepted.

Nothing like keeping it simple.

2:07 P.M., GMT
Queen Maud Land, Antarctica

"Mate, if you keep coming back here, you might want to sign up for my frequent flier program."

Jason clapped the UK airman on the shoulder and zippered more snugly into his parka, pulling up the hood. "I just might have to do that, Barstow."

Jason hopped out of the Twin Otter and onto the ice. He stared at the cluster of buildings that had spread like a tumble of toy blocks in the shadow of the black crags of the Fenriskjeften mountains. It was as if the Back Door substation had been a seed that had germinated out of the warmth below and sprouted into this ever-growing international research complex on the frozen surface.

They'd made a lot of progress.

Still, he remembered that journey a month ago, rising out of Hell's Cape through that Back Door with Gray, Kowalski, and Stella. As Stella had promised, they found an emergency CAAT garaged on the surface and used it to venture back to the coast, joining up with Dr. Von Der Bruegge and the remaining researchers from the Haley VI station. With the solar storm ended, they were able to contact McMurdo Station for help.

Now I'm back again.

But he had a good reason. She came out of one of the tallest of the new structures, which was painted in the red-and-black of the British Antarctic Survey, a match to the Otter's coloring. Even her parka had the letters BAS emblazoned on the chest.

She strode toward him, her hood down, as if strolling across a park versus forging through an Antarctic winter. This time of year the continent was sunk into a perpetual midnight, but the sweep of bright stars and a silvery full moon offered plenty of light, especially when accompanied by the swirling electric tides of the aurora australis.

"Jason, it's so great to see you." Stella hugged him, her embrace lingering a little longer than expected—but he wasn't complaining.

"I've got so much to show you, to tell you." She started to lead him toward the station, but he kept his place.

"I've been reading the reports," he said, smiling. "You do have a lot on your hands. Opening select sections of Hell's Cape as protected biospheres must be a sensitive endeavor. I kept promising you some experienced help, so I'm here finally delivering on that in person."

Jason waved to the rear compartment of the Otter. The hatch opened and two people climbed out in well-worn arctic gear. The woman tucked a long tail of curly black hair, shot through with a few strands of gray, back as she pulled up her parka's hood. She was helped out by a taller man, ruggedly built, whose age most people would have never guessed. Like their gear, they looked well worn together, an inseparable couple.

Jason introduced them. "My mother, Ashley Carter. And stepdad, Benjamin Brust."

Stella shook their hands, a surprised smile making her look even more beautiful. "It's great to meet you both. Come inside and we can get you all warm."

She led them all toward the Back Door station, the new entrance to the subterranean world below. As she turned way, Ben hung back and nudged Jason in the side with an elbow.

"Nice, mate," Ben said, his Aussie accent twanging a little richer, like it always did when teasing him. "Now I see why you wanted to come and introduce us in person. Found yourself a little sheila."

Both women glanced back at them.

Jason lowered his head, shaking it a bit.

Ben scooted up between the others and took both Ashley and Stella under his arms. "So the kid tells me you found an interesting cavern system under the ice."

"Do you know much about caves?" Stella asked.

"I've been known to putter around a bit."

His stepfather was actually an expert caver, with decades of experience, most of it right here on this continent.

"Well, I doubt you've seen anything like what we found down here," Stella said proudly.

"You'd be surprised how much we have seen," his mother said with a grin. "Someday we'll have to invite you back to *our* place."

Ben nodded. "Might be an adventure in there for all of us." He glanced back to Jason. "What do you say? Up for some fun?"

Jason hurried to keep up with them.

Why did I think this was such a good idea?

8:23 P.M., EDT
Roanoke, Virginia

Kendall Hess drove the rental car up the long tree-lined entryway to the private mental health facility. Rolling manicured lawns spread to garden parkways and small fountains. The building itself was divided into four wings, branching out like a cross in the center of these highly secured grounds.

The hospital wasn't on any directory and few knew of these forty acres that bordered the Blue Ridge Parkway outside of Roanoke, Virginia. It was for special cases, those of interest to national security. He had to reach out to contacts with BRAG, the FBI's Bioterrorism Risk Assessment Group, to facilitate getting a bed here.

He pulled through the final checkpoint, showed his identification, and parked. He had to leave a fingerprint at the front desk and was escorted by one of the nurses.

"How's he doing?" Kendall asked.

"The same. If you'd like to talk to his case clinician?"

"That won't be necessary."

The nurse—a soft-spoken, sober young woman dressed in blues and thick-soled shoes—glanced to him. "He does have a visitor."

He nodded.

That was good.

They crossed together down a long sterile hall painted in pastel colors that were said to be soothing. Finally they reached a door that required a special passkey. It led to a small clinical assessment space neighboring the patient's room. A one-way glass mirror separated the two spaces.

Kendall stepped to the viewing window. The neighboring room was paneled in rich woods, with a faux fireplace that flickered silk flames. Bookshelves lined the far wall, packed full.

He found it both sad and somehow reassuring that books still brought Cutter comfort, as if buried deep down under the assaulted cerebral cortex some memory persisted, some love of knowledge.

He saw that Ashuu sat in a corner, but she stared leadenly out the window.

Kendall had arranged for Cutter's family to be taken care of, to offer them lodging and a small stipend to remain nearby. Jori was going to a local Roanoke school, settling in well with the adaptability of the young. Cutter's wife was more worrisome. He suspected she would eventually return to the forests, maybe once Jori was in college. The child was bright, certainly his father's son.

Cutter lay on his back on the bed, his wrists in padded restraints, not that he was violent, but sometimes he harmed himself if not watched. He did take daily walks with the staff, and as he was in the presence of the books, he was also calmer when out in nature, some echo of his former self.

"They're getting him settled for the night," the nurse said. "The boy reads to him most every evening."

Kendall flicked on the intercom to listen as Jori sat on a bedside chair, the book propped on his thin knees, and read to his father.

The nurse nodded to the volume in hand. "His son told me his father used to read that book to him every night."

Kendall read the title and felt a twinge of guilt.

Rudyard Kipling's *The Jungle Book.*

Jori's voice was sweet, full of love for the words, for the memories they conjured.

> *"This is the hour of pride and power,*
> *Talon and tush and claw.*
> *O hear the call! Good Hunting, All*
> *That keep the Jungle Law!"*

11:48 P.M.
Takoma Park, Maryland

Gray sat on the porch swing, a cool beer balanced on the rail in front of him. The night was still hot, over ninety degrees, heavily humid. It put him in a sour mood—or maybe it was the long day visiting various assisted living facilities, narrowing his choices to those with memory care units.

A cool hand slipped into his fingers. With just the touch, the pressure inside him loosened. He squeezed her hand, thanking her.

Seichan sat next to him, freshly returned from Hong Kong. She had dumped her bags at his apartment and come straight here, roaring down the street on her motorcycle, arriving in time for dinner. She and his father got along handsomely.

Then again, who wouldn't?

Look at her.

Even in the darkness, she was a sculpture of grace and power, feral and tender, soft curve and hard muscle. Her eyes caught every bit of light. Her lips were as soft as silk. He lifted a hand and ran a finger down along her chin, tracing a trickle of sweat along the pulse of her throat.

God, how he had missed her.

Her voice dropped a full octave to a sultry darkness. "We should get you home."

His body ached at that invitation.

"Go on ahead," he said. "I'll make sure the night nurse has everything she needs, then I'll follow."

Seichan stirred, began to rise, but she must have sensed something and settled back to the slats of the swing. "What's wrong?"

He turned away, noticing a flicker of fireflies in the bushes beyond the porch rail. They came earlier every year, some said as a harbinger of the changing climate, a reminder of the great forces that truly controlled the world, making everything else seem insignificant and small.

He sighed, hating to admit that sometimes he was too small. "I can save the world countless times. Why can't I save him?" He shrugged heavily. "There's nothing I can do."

She found his hands and held them between her palms. "You're an ass, Gray."

"I never denied that," he said, discovering a small smile.

"There is always something you can do. You're already doing it. You can love him, remember for him, live for him, care for him, fight for him. You show that love with every hard decision you make . . . that's what you can do. It's not *nothing*."

He remained silent.

There was one other thing he could do—but for that, he needed a moment of privacy.

"I get it, Seichan." He shifted her hands back to her. "Go on. I'll be right behind you."

She leaned forward and kissed him on the cheek, then more deeply on the lips. "Don't leave me waiting."

Never.

As she headed down the steps toward the driveway, he entered the house and nodded to the night nurse on the sofa. "Going to go check on him before I go."

"I think he's already asleep," she said.

Good.

He climbed the stairs and crossed down the hall to his father's bedroom. The door was partly ajar, so he quietly entered and moved to his bedside.

From a pocket, he slipped out a vial and a syringe.

Days ago, he had made an inquiry with Dr. Kendall Hess about the counteragent to Cutter Elwes's threat. He had heard Hess believed the drug might help improve other neurological impairments. Gray made his case to Hess directly, and a sample was sent overnight to his address.

He filled the syringe now.

Once, what seemed like decades ago, he had been offered a similar choice, something that might help his father's Alzheimer's. He ended up pouring it down the drain, believing he had to learn to accept the inevitable, not to fight what couldn't be fought.

He lifted the syringe, pushing a bead to the tip of the needle.

Screw that.

Seichan's words echoed to him.

. . . fight for him . . .

He leaned over his father, jabbed the needle into his arm, and pushed the plunger home. He yanked the syringe back before his father's lids could flutter open. When he did wake, those eyes got wide upon seeing his son looming over him.

"Gray, what're you doing?"

Fighting for you . . .

He leaned down and kissed his father on the crown of his head.

"Just came up to say good night."

Epilogue Arboreal

The pack moves slowly through the jungle, lumbering in line, their numbers much smaller since starting this long trek. Echoes of fire, rock, and ruin follow them. They remember digging with their strong claws, discovering older tunnels that led them into this endless forest, freed at last. They remember blood and death. They remember betrayal and pain. They remember the blue spark and the sting of steel.

Their memories are long.

Their hatred even longer.

Author's Note to Readers: Truth or Fiction

Time to take out that scalpel and dissect this novel, separating truth from fiction. We are at the cusp of several critical changes in this world. While few doubt that the planet is undergoing its *sixth* mass extinction, it's the paths that we take from here—as a species, as a society—that split in many different directions. One of the goals of this book is to walk down several of those paths and see where they might lead. But how far down those paths are we already? Let's find out.

First, this novel tackles the real schism currently found in the environmental movement: between old-school conservationists and a new breed of ecologist, between preservationists and synthetic biologists, even between those who want to stop this pending extinction and those who welcome it. The following four books were integral to building this story and are a great resource for anyone interested in the subjects raised in this novel.

Regenesis: How Synthetic Biology Will Reinvent Nature and Ourselves by George M. Church and Ed Regis (New York: Basic Books, 2012).

The Sixth Extinction: An Unnatural History by Elizabeth Kolbert (New York: Henry Holt, 2014).

Apocalyptic Planet: Field Guide to the Future of the Earth by Craig Childs (New York: Vintage, 2013).

Countdown: Our Last, Best Hope for a Future on Earth? by Alan Weisman (New York: Back Bay Books, 2014).

But let's look at some of the specifics, starting with the

Science

Synthetic Biology

When it comes to creating artificial life, milestones are toppling like dominoes, even faster than I could write this novel. Here's a brief timeline that pertains to topics raised in this book (but one that barely scratches the surface):

2002: The first artificial virus is created in a lab.

2010: Craig Venter's group builds the first living synthetic cell.

2012: The engineering of XNA (xeno nucleic acid) proves successful.

2013: A fully functional chromosome is reconstructed from scratch.

May 2014: Scripps Institute adds new letters to our genetic alphabet.

XNA

Multiple labs have produced various strains of XNA. It has proven to be hardier, and yes, it can be used to theoretically replace the DNA in all living creatures. It's also believed to have once been a predominant form of life on this planet. So could a pocket of such life still be out there, hidden in some shadow biosphere? Only time will tell.

Facilitated Adaptations

The goal of Dr. Kendall's research—to discover ways to enhance species to better suit environmental changes—is actively being pursued in labs from a real-world perspective.

Even Cutter Elwes's creations were based on a clever installation project called "Designing for the Sixth Extinction" by Alexandra Daisy Ginsberg. She proposes that we should seek to release bioengineered creations into the wild (and has even gone so far as to patent some of her imaginative life-forms). Fascinating stuff. Her work is viewable on the Internet.

Evolution Machines

1. The **CRISPR-Cas9** technique described in this novel is real! It's already revolutionizing the world of genetic study and manipulation. With a little training, a novice could perform these advanced techniques. The precision of this control has been described as offering researchers the equivalent tool to editing individual letters of an encyclopedia— without making a spelling error.

2. **MAGE and CAGE** were invented by genetic engineers from Yale University, MIT, and Harvard University. They allow large-scale edits to a genome and hold great promise to revive extinct species.

De-Extinction

I describe in the novel how labs around the world are trying to revive extinct species. These include the woolly mammoth (from elephant DNA), the passenger pigeon (from ordinary pigeon DNA), and an extinct oxen known as an aurochs (from cattle DNA). But there are also many other methods beyond gene editing to restore these species, like somatic cell nuclear transfer.

And, yes, there is indeed a Russian named Sergey Zimov who is building "Pleistocene Park" in Siberia as a home for woolly mammoths.

Extremophiles

The search for new chemicals and compounds has turned the hunt for unusual organisms living in harsh environments into a biological gold rush. In turn, scientists have discovered life growing in many places that were once considered to be inhospitable to life: in boiling sea vents, deep under the ice, in toxic wastelands. Entire ecosystems have been discovered, leading to the term *shadow biospheres*.

Indestructible Viruses

I based the organism that Dr. Hess engineered on a real-world microorganism: a bacterium named *Deinococcus radiodurans*. This stubborn little bug can survive radiation levels fifteen times stronger than the famously resistant cockroach. It's also renowned for its ability to endure freezing temperatures, dehydration, burning heat, and the strongest acids. Even the vacuum of space won't kill it. *Guinness Book of World Records* declared it the toughest form of life. Let's hope someone out there doesn't start playing around in that bacterium's genetic toolbox.

Jumping Genes (Retrotransposons)

Again it's surprisingly true that geneticists now accept that a potent engine of evolution is "jumping genes." Not only can these traits be transmitted to offspring but also *between* species, in a process called horizontal gene transfer. Though it's hard to believe, a full quarter of cattle DNA has been proven to have come from a species of horned viper. So be careful of that next burger.

Biohacking/DIY Biology/Biopunks

No matter what you call it, garages, cellars, and community centers have become hotbeds for genetic experimentation and patenting of new life-forms. I mentioned in this novel about a Kickstarter program that seeks to produce a glowing weed. This technology has even become "plug and play" with the introduction of "biobricks," a genetic toolbox for playing God in your own backyard.

The three major fears about synthetic biology and biohacking are *bioterrorism, lab accidents,* and the *purposeful release of synthetic organisms.* So I decided to go for the Triple Crown and tackle all three in one thriller.

Magnetism and Microbial Life

Can magnetic fields kill bacteria, viruses, and fungi? At the right static or oscillating fields, YES. The FDA has performed an entire study on the subject, even identifying the field strengths necessary to kill specific species.

Panspermia

This is the theory that life on earth might have come from a seed of organic life delivered to the planet via a meteor strike. The meteor mentioned in this book that caused the massive Wilkes Crater in Antarctica is believed to have triggered the Permian mass extinction, which came within a hairsbreadth of ending all life. So I wondered: *If all those environmental niches were emptied out by this extinction, what if that same meteor brought something foreign to fertilize those newly emptied fields?*

Antarctic Life

The Russians are currently continuing to drill into Lake Vostok, a lake as big as any of the Great Lakes, yet isolated for millennia miles under the ice. What life might be found there? Early signs: There's plenty. But that southernmost continent is rife with odd biological details.

—In 1999, a virus was discovered on the ice that no animal or human is immune to.
—In 2014, a 1,500-year-old Antarctic moss was brought back to life. Likewise, in Siberia, a virus that had been frozen for 30,000 years was resurrected.
—The petrified remains of great forests have been found in multiple locations on that continent.

But so far, we've been literally barely scratching the surface. What's truly under that ice is yet to be discovered. It should be interesting because of . . .

Antarctic Geology

Only recently have we begun to understand how weird that continent's geology truly is. While the continent presents a frozen face, down deep it's a warm, wet marshland. There are hundreds of subglacial lakes, often with rivers flowing between them, some as large as the Thames. There are waterfalls that flow *up*. There are active volcanoes, some with lava flowing under miles of ice. Just this past year (early 2014) scientists discovered Antarctica has a trench that dwarfs our Grand Canyon. In all of that strange and otherworldly landscape, what might yet be undiscovered?

Hacking the Brain

In my novel, Cutter Elwes has discovered a novel way of altering human intelligence to his own end. Is that possible? If anything, it's likely conservative. The computer hackers of the eighties and nineties are becoming the biohackers of the new millennia. Even now researchers are studying viruses and bacteria that use chemical signals to control emotions and human thought. With the exponential rate of our ability to manipulate DNA— faster, cheaper, and with more control—anything will soon be possible.

DARPA's Biological Technologies Office

DARPA has already been working at the cutting edges of robotics, prosthetics, and artificial intelligence. But in 2014, this new office was specifically born to go all in on biotechnology, to "explore the increasingly dynamic intersection of biology and the physical sciences." Stay tuned!

In this novel, different researchers espoused various pathways around or through this sixth extinction. I've attended debates, read extensively, and pored through articles on the multiple sides of this complicated issue, but I thought I'd talk a little about the origin of some of these

Scientific Philosophies

Conservation/Preservation

This encompasses those environmentalists who seek to save species or bolster environments to support the endangered. This camp also includes those who seek to revive the extinct. In some circles, this is viewed as "old-school environmentalism."

Synthetic Biologists

Right or wrong, this is where the young, excited scientists seek to use genetic manipulation and the creation of synthetic life to reengineer the world. While there certainly is a measure of hubris and danger down this path, it also shows great promise.

New Ecologists

I came upon a fascinating interview of ecologist Craig Thomas in New Scientist, where he espouses a new philosophical way of looking at extinction: basically as an opportunity. That a great extinction could lead to new and exciting life-forms, new pathways for evolution, even creating a New Eden. It's a fascinating alternate way of looking at this Sixth Extinction.

Dark Mountain

It would be hard to do this movement justice in a small paragraph. So I encourage you to check out their website (http://dark-mountain.net), where you can read *Uncivilisation: The Dark Mountain Manifesto* by Dougald Hine and Paul Kingsnorth. Again it's a radical new way of viewing this great Sixth Extinction.

In the character of Cutter Elwes, I tried to create a person who espoused a bastardized version of the last three philosophies, while pitting him against Kendall Hess, who advocates for the first two. And in fact that very philosophical war is being waged in the scientific community right now.

And it wouldn't be a Sigma novel without a little (or a lot) of

History

Darwin and the Voyage of the *Beagle*

Charles Darwin did visit the Fuegian natives in the Tierra del Fuego region of South America. The people were skilled sailors, and it's not beyond the realm of possibilities that they had crude maps of their voyages in their possession. One other true detail is that Darwin did in fact *not* publish his famous treatise until twenty years after that fateful voyage. Which begs the historical question: *Why?*

Maps, Maps, and More Maps

Within these pages, you'll find examples of ancient maps that depict what seemingly appears to be the continent of Antarctica—but without ice. While these are real maps, centuries old, the debates about them continue today. But what we do know is that ancient people have been navigating the world's oceans for much longer than originally suspected. The nautical timeline for humankind keeps getting pushed farther and farther back into history. And with the destruction of the famous Library of Alexandria—that vast storehouse for all ancient knowledge—who knows what great truths vanished in those flames?

Germans in Antarctica

All of the historical details about the Nazi exploration and interest in Antarctica is based on facts, including the cryptic statements by Admiral Karl Dönitz during the Nuremberg trials and his oddly light prison sentence.

Americans in Antarctica

Operation Highjump, led by Admiral Byrd, was a real operation involving over 5,000 men. Yet it still remains shrouded in mystery. Byrd's snow cruiser is also an actual vehicle and was shipped to that continent, only to eventually vanish into history (or under the ice). And yes, the U.S. government did test atomic bombs down there.

British in Antarctica

The British Antarctic Survey has been going strong down on the southernmost continent almost longer than any other country, changing its name in the process as described in this book. And the Haley VI station is an active British research post (unless it slid into the sea like it did in the pages of this book). It does indeed look like a centipede wearing giant skis.

Most of the "tech" of this book was already covered in the Science section, but there are a couple of additional gadgets worth mentioning.

Technology

Captive Air Amphibious Transport (CAAT)

While these vehicles are still in the prototype stage, they have built scaled-down versions of this vehicle that are fully operational. In fact, I chose to base the smaller CAATs featured in this book upon those prototypes (and I had to greatly refrain myself from not calling those mini-CAATs . . . "Kittens").

Sonic Weapons

Long Range Acoustic Devices (LRADs) are employed across the world by police and military forces and operate basically as described in the book.

The more portable *directed stick radiators (DSRs)* are a patented design by American Technology Corporation. As far as I know they're not being actively produced, but they function pretty much as described in the story, including the ability to broadcast speech or to be used as a directional microphone for eavesdropping.

So if you're going into a dark cavern under Antarctica you might want to buy stock in that company.

Just a couple of words about

Locations

Tepui

These strange otherworldly plateaus stretch through Guyana, Venezuela, and Brazil. Many have never been walked by man, and the strange, isolated ecosystems up there are pristine and untouched. The mythologies described in this book are also accurate, as are those strange sinkholes, caverns, and tunnels. Sir Arthur Conan Doyle set his novel *The Lost World* atop one of these tepui, so I figured surely that's where Cutter Elwes would set up shop, far from prying eyes.

Mountain Warfare Training Center
I was able to visit this facility outside Bridgeport, California, and while most of the details are accurate, I did take a few liberties on minor issues (sorry, guys, I owe you some ribs from Bodie Mike's Barbecue). But the base does indeed have a V/STOL airfield used for training, including working with the tiltrotor Ospreys. And the "Son of Osprey," the Bell V-280 Valor featured in this book, is currently in development.

Mono Lake and Ghost Towns
Likewise, I visited Mono Lake several times and I hope I did the place and its people justice. Also if you're ever up there, do check out the local ghost towns. Just watch out for helicopters full of commandos.

One Last Historical Note

I hope you enjoyed this book. It's the *tenth* novel in the Sigma series, debuting on the *tenth* anniversary of the first (*Sandstorm*, 2004). Knowing that milestone was upon us, I thought I'd use this opportunity to tease a bit to the past. Like seeing the return of Ashley Carter and Ben Brust, those stalwart Antarctic explorers, who along with Jason, found themselves in much trouble in my very first novel, *Subterranean*. Additionally, in this new book, I also wanted to acknowledge what's to come, with some big changes hinted at in these same pages—because Sigma's greatest and boldest adventures are still on the horizon.

So I hope to see you out there!

Jim Rollins

PS: Bring sunscreen (and extra ammunition).